KAMIN-TOLAGH

a novel

Edwin Ahearn

Book III
Book IV

Kamin-Tolagh

The tug of history, often very ancient history, is felt throughout these works. A large amount of information about the past is disclosed in the narrative, but for the purposes of these extracts a reader needs to know that long before the land was Arbhal it was Owan, and the Owanil, a gifted, energetic, but often arrogant people conquered and then lost a vast empire on both sides of Arnan, the inland sea.

Books I and II begin shortly after the end of the Jinzal War and the investiture of the Rodlakh as Rabsahi. Kamin-Tolagh has won honor and recognition. He is now the trusted Captain of the Household. Yet, there are important confidences that are kept from him. He grows restless and yearns for adventure. The military expedition headed by Shumat, Captain of the Armies, and Kamin Tolagh set out to the Farther West on a mission to destroy the last of the jinzal. What he discovers changes the course of history

Book III and VI resume the tale when roughly three years have passed. Kamin-Tolagh has founded an empire amid the wild tribal lands of the Farther West. His rule restores the old ways of Preference. Though he is condemned as an outlaw, many families leave the Heartland to join with him and take up new estates. The old legends and new tales of riches spur Kamin-Tolagh to explore and conquer unknown lands.

Kamin-Tolagh

III

18.

Descending through foothills to flatter country Kamin-Tolagh, wanting word of events before proceeding to the Abu, left the main riding, and turned north taking Tau-Suaka with just five of him men. With a half-day's rough going he met the road he had first come by, midway between the Abu and its descent from Landegh.

In an encouraging sign of vigilance, within minutes he was being hailed by the plain-faced officer, Luzhan, leading a half-squadron of tribal troops.

He reported that all was quiet both on Landegh, and at the Abu, though he understood there had been unspecified trouble between two of the southward tribes, and an ambassador from "some other Hrin" had been disappointed to miss Kamin-Tolagh, but would return. Luzhan meant, other than the following of Iolfrant.

At the Great House, Lavsila, ostentatiously displaying a newly-arrived dispatch, gave perfunctory attention to the successes of the expedition, and was impatiently certain his news was more urgent than Kamin-Tolagh's desire to wash off the dust. He had, at least, seen to it that cool *raminat* and some fruits were ready.

"Even Iruvakh," he reminded, "has kept warning there was sure to be trouble, where differing customs, and traditions, and tribal laws come into conflict."

"What conflict?" The assessment had less to do with the mixed formations of tribal troops than with new conditions brought about by peace; men, a few unintimidated women, those with things to sell or trade, were moving far more freely in this safer Froghushei; the reed hats of the Hwenala were as common now among the eastern tribes as the well-made arrows of the Laughing Owl, dried fish of the Anga-jai, or the prized meal-root of the Ntara-golal (wrongly called `turnip' by Lavsila) among the Gudi-la or Man-mani.

"Kambanal — " proffering the much-brandished dispatch — "gives the full story. We had only rumor and gossip till now."

Kambanal had remained in Man-mani country, and wrote that what remained of the once-numerous Chon'la tribe was in arms, one of their young men, a trader in the wood-carvings of K'daab's People, having been mutilated by the Hwenala.

An act in accordance with Hwenala law: having taken one of their maidens against her will, the Chon'la man had been seized and brutally gelded.

"Against her will!" Lavsila spat contempt. "With these apes, that means, against the will of her father or her brothers. The girl was no doubt glad enough to share her bed with a man who did not stink like a swamp." The men of that coastal tribe were never far from the fetid smell of the mud with which, on ceremonial occasions, they daubed themselves.

"According to Iruvakh, you will see Kambanal writes, the girl will not now find a mate among her own people. The girl!" he mocked, "Neither will the man. She, if her brave protectors let her live, can be brought here to the Abu. If she saves a little money as a servant, she can still catch a husband. All the Chon-la man can do is grow fat, piping his indignation. Vermin."

Reasoning even the strongest sense of outrage was unlikely to send the few dozen Chon'la men clambering across the dividing hills for a direct attack on the Hwenala, Kambanal had merely kept a force at Larghai's Notch, reassembling half a squadron of Kargul' for the purpose, so as to avoid any chance, or even hint, of other tribes taking sides in the dispute; the Chon'la were under the protection of the powerful Laughing Owl. and any tribal force composed of various peoples would be in danger of splitting into factions.

His instincts were right; any general taking of sides in this could swiftly undo the empire; the *rabhsai* would hardly need a single squadron to complete its destruction. Kamin-Tolagh rubbed his temple, and felt the gritty corner of an eye.

It was early afternoon. More than the long journey itself, its plodding pace had left him very weary. "Serious," he decided. "Not yet worse than that. I shall ride for the Froghushei in the morning."

"Tomorrow?"

"I need a bed. And a woman."

But Lavsila was not questioning delay; on the contrary; "Then you will have time to see Dvasslo. The man is waiting outside." He spoke the name of his former drinking-companion with the disdain due a tradesman and now a spy: Dvasslo was paid a small wage for telling what he could learn of Hrin intentions when followers of Iolfrant came to the Abu, and Kamin-Tolagh had small doubt the man was also being paid by Iolfrant for similar information the other way.

"For what?"

"To show you some samples, he says, but I do not doubt he has Hrin matters to chew over."

He came in now with the obsequious cringe of a Harbor Way merchant, and did indeed have specimens to show, models for the Empire's first issue of coinage. Just before leaving for Kargul, Kamin-Tolagh had been drawn in profile by Kambanal, and Dvasslo had found Hrin of his own following to make the dies, which had now been used to produce first clay and then lead test-pieces for the two denominations desired. The reverse of each showed the star-pattern of the Siv'loi Banner, and had the word *KARGUSAI* with space for the year. Kamin-Tolagh had already decided his great oath-taking would take place a month later; in the absence of Kamin-Tarú there was little point to holding it on her birthday, and the new day, which would also be the date of issue for his coinage, coincided with the second anniversary of his rout of the Hwenala and adoption of the Siv'loi Banner, and would thus begin Year 3 of the Empire.

Lavsila, for once impressed, examined the smaller coin. "What will this be called?"

"Kambanal suggests, *tolakhi*." In gold, it would be equal in weight and value to the plakhi of Rodlakh's realm. Though it would scarcely see much circulation, the four-tolakhi piece was better. With greater space for detail, the portrait was recognizable; Kamin-Tolagh had insisted on a left-facing profile, so the scar along his jaw could be represented, and here there was room for his name (alone, with no title) to arch above the head.

"A handsome piece," Lavsila judged. "What will Rodlakh *Rabhsai* make of it, when he sees it?"

When Kamin-Tolagh asked Dvasslo about the Hrin ambassador who had been here in his absence, it reminded him of touching the horns of a snail, the swift, smooth drawing in of the sly face. "What would I speak with the man?" as if sulking. "He is of the *tveyusto-hrid-minyist*."

Lavsila rolled his eyes upward despairingly, and for once Kamin-Tolagh was in agreement; they were beyond words, these Hrin. Of anyone, Dvasslo, who could put a price on anything, ought to be least troubled by religious loyalties, and yet his peevishness here appeared genuine.

Lavsila said, "From the following of the *Hrithust* Nestos, I think?"

Dvasslo allowed that was so, and grudgingly added the ambassador, Navridn, was actually half-brother to Nestos.

"But Nestos was foster-brother to Iolfrant, not so?" His grasp of so much Hrin lore was tribute to his taste for conspiracy rather than a genuine breadth of intellect. "Who supported his claim to be *Hrithust* over his birth lands, when still thought to be an adherent of the *tveyusto-hrid* — ?"

"*Minyist*," Dvasslo, making a face. "For that reason, because Lord Iolfrant met the truth of *dveyust-ranga-hrindan* and he did not, Nestos hates him more."

Well, but it slowly emerged the clash of beliefs echoed a practical conflict; notwithstanding religious incompatibility, Dvasslo admitted the following of Nestos was "most like us," by which he seemed to mean that *onhritha* was Iolfrant's nearest rival in commerce, seamanship or absolute prosperity. The exclusion of Nestos had been in mind when Huolafidn originally proposed Kamin-Tolagh trade only with supporters of the *dveyust-ranga-hrindan*, "and this is why this Navridn comes here now."

That explained nothing. "But we declined any such agreement," Kamin-Tolagh objected. "Hrin other than Iolfrant's have been coming to Larghamit; some of them must have been from this Nestos."

Most, Dvasslo agreed, who were not of his following. "But now the *Hrithust* Nestos has heard of your alliance with our *Hrithust*. His ships' masters tell him about your *squadrons*, and how you are making many *squadrons* with tribes — "

Lavsila guessed the rest. "Nestos is afraid we will lend Iolfrant our troops, so he can make war on the other *hrithuod*, and impose the *dveyust* — impose your system everywhere."

"Or that you will train Iolfrant's men to fight in *squadrons*,"

"Iolfrant knows, and Nestos will be told, we take no side in the religious disputes of the Hrin." Still true, but there might be a use for those differences in helping maintain his position at Zelu Bablakhi, if Iolfrant hoped there was anything to be gained by staying friends — or equally if he feared Nestos would learn the secrets of warmaking from Kamin-Tolagh.

"Lord Iolfrant," remembering to earn his money, "is curious about what is said and settled at any meeting with Navridn."

"There will not be any secrets. Nothing in our agreement, Iolfrant's and mine, says he or I cannot have other friendships."

"Our *Hrithust* says the same. Huolafidn tells me he is making another journey to your Then'mala, and maybe all the way to Kadon Dinul. To buy more wheat, it is said."

"Dolvid would like nothing better," Lavsila, when the Hrin had left, promising to make minor changes asked for in the coins, and to oversee their making, as soon as Kamin-Tolagh released the gold, "than to buy others to carry on Rodlakh's warring for him."

"How can he do that?" Much more credible the other way about. "If being robbed of half their gold will not make Hrin fight, how can Dolvid do it from Kadon Dinul?"

"There is fighting other than swords and lances, Tam. They are devious, these Hrin — look at how Iolfrant came to be *Hrithust*. As well to let Iolfrant think you have an understanding with Nestos."

"We shall have an arrangement with Nestos." One, he hoped, that would make alternative shipping available to him; an absurd weakness that for swift reinforcement of his garrison at Zelu Bablakhi he was dependent on the men who most wanted him dislodged there; a sudden mysterious absence of Hrin vessels at Larghamit would be a danger-sign. One he could do little about as things stood.

Lavsila was still trying to defend his earlier theory: "Dolvid is very adept with unusual alliances — as you, better than anyone, should know, Tam."

"You are not to use that name," irritated at several points, "Not even in private." Tú's pet-name, Kamin-Tarú's, from her childhood.

"Oh?" Lavsila began to smile, saw he was in earnest, briefly considered protest, and ended in a sarcasm too veiled for indictment. "Very well, *Asai*."

The contingent of Tau-Suaka's mounted bows with which he he started south at dawn, more than should be needed, was intended to to overawe. Freighanai was up and in the saddle, but Kamin-Tolagh excused him this campaign; he had begun moving to a larger house, not only to accommodate his wife and children, but in affirmation of his captaincy. A number of the largest dwellings on the mound had not been assigned permanent tenants, against when the Empire had men and women of rank to fill them.

With these hardy troops and well-watered horses he dared cut across the wide eastward swing of the trail that took in the waterhole, picking up the established way again not far from where it divided, right fork beginning the ascent into the Notch. Weary and dusty as the sun was sinking, he met with the force Kambanal had placed there, and was greeted by the laconic Nizhadh, who told him he had evidently missed whatever excitement there was going to be.

At last word, survival of the mutilated Chon'la man, his condition not improved by the journey back to his original village, was still in doubt. Two days ago by twilight, about twenty vengeful men of his tribe, mainly young, had tried to creep past Nizhadh's watch. Fully armed, they had not put up any fight when enveloped by regular cavalry.

"Captain Kambanal," taking in stride elevation of a younger man he had outranked at year's turn, "said you would want this settled, *Asai*, with the smallest fuss. So we kept the young heroes overnight, and I walked them back to near their home country, and let them go, except for four that kept themselves hot to drink 'Wenala blood." He used his thumb to indicate. "They're still with us up at the camp, *Asai*, but their temper's no better. Makes you glad you don't know what their gabble means."

Hunghi, expert wielder of the whip was at Zelu Bablakhi, but another man, his pupil, almost as good, was with Tau-Suaka, and in the morning the four young Chon'la were tied up and given a restrained flogging which left weals but drew little blood. Leaving them in misery to make their way home, Kamin-Tolagh rode on, and at the Man-mani village met with Iruvakh. Pressed into protesting service, he was fuller than usual of warnings against arbitrary settlement of complex questions, but did not refuse to ride to the edge of Hwenala country.

There, adopting the familiar, sideways stance to disassociate himself from what he interpreted, he conveyed Kamin-Tolagh's warning to the Hwenala head-man that another such incident would lead to his deposing, but reluctance turned to open protest when Kamin-Tolagh had Tau-Suaka seize half a dozen hostages, at least one of whom would be executed if their Chon'la victim failed to recover.

Drawn aside from any hearer, trembling with varied emotions, Iruvakh spoke in a low, fierce tone. "It goes against every principle of justice to make laws for offenses already committed. You have made no stipulation for cases where a man offends the ways of a tribe not his — indeed, you reserved to head-men the right to give judgment according to their traditional laws and customs — "

"Always excepting customs that are abhorrent — " it was easy to maintain an unruffled calm; their agreement on the special definition of Iruvakh's standing, which, while he no doubt regarded it as impunity, actually conceded his powerlessness. "A similar practice of the Laughing Owl — "

"An unnecessary religious ritual most would call barbaric is not the same as the ordained penalty for breaking an established law." A cooling evening, not far from the *dao* valley where the Siv'loi Banner had been named; pale stars were beginning to appear overhead, though yellow light lingered at the horizon.

"You do the Hwenala head-man an injustice," Iruvakh concluded.

Kamin-Tolagh wheeled on him. "Understand, justice is not the question. We shall have justice where we can, but above that comes rule."

"What could contribute more to successful rule," Iruvakh, unintimidated, asked the luminous sky, "than acknowledged justice?"

"Fear," instantly. "In the Heartland, where fair law is understood, or your Irbat, there is time for the niceties and debates of Owani justice. Here, I am like a commander in the field, where any hesitation may be seen as weakness."

"The tribes, *Asai*, are not your armies."

"And disputes between tribes are not going to swallow up my armies. The Jai, the Anga-jai, the Laughing Owl with the Chon'la, the Ntara-golal, the Gudi-la," Kamin-Tolagh enumerated, "were not my conquests; they came to me for protection. If that means nothing but freedom to war among themselves, they will soon learn they are not as safe as they imagine. You can pass the word, no act to provoke conflict between tribe and tribe will be tolerated, and in any dispute between tribes, I am the only judge. The wild men they hid from — " he gestured to where Tau-Suaka's men, dismounted, were awaiting his further orders — "are no longer wild, but still to be feared. Anything I order, they will carry out, if it is to burn a village to the ground, or kill a head-man and all his clan."

"The greater reason to keep them under restraint."

"Restraint must be earned by restraint." This hardness was not first nature for him, but his willingness to threaten brutal measures, if necessary to carry them out could save him a great deal of wasted time and effort, perhaps in the end save lives as well.

For the first time, at the head-man's hut, Chamya greeted him with the welcome-cup ritual, taught him by Lavsila, in the common Heartland delusion it was an immemorial Owani custom, though Kamin-Tolagh, with all Owanil of real standing, was taught it had a Gabhani origin, and was adopted by Plakhat Gabh'Owan in tribute to Pir Kallikuk, his colleague in the Wars of Cleansing. Two-handed, he solemnly accepted the cup from Chamya, and expecting vapid Man-mani beer was pleasantly surprised to taste a pale and inoffensive wine.

"From the store of my stepfather," not explaining why it had remained a secret so long.

Each time Kamin-Tolagh saw the boy he had visibly grown, and would, after all, be tall among his own people. With his slender hips and a neck that, merely by existing, was long by Man-mani standards, a strain of Owani blood somewhere was easy to believe: not at all farfetched to imagine, for example, that one of his two grandmothers could have been of the admixture to be a *jinzai*-mother; such a woman mated to a Man-mani would produce normal human sons.

When Chamya spoke about tribal matters, marriages, deaths, minor disputes over property, placement of a new hut, Kamin-Tolagh was pleased by the boy's growing sense of responsibility, dismayed to watch the young enthusiast vanishing into this staid official; on an impulse he offered to teach him finer points of lance-work, and at once the old eagerness returned; "Like a *noble* of your country?" he asked in delight. For Kamin-Tolagh, to have an excuse for staying a few days was good; at the Abu, Fretasi, after only enough time to wash off the grime of her journey, had put on her responsibilities with her clean, fashionless clothes, and immediately begun asking awkward questions about record-keeping, wanting a count of the exact value of gold so far received, and details about disbursement of money and value of traded goods. Events and topics in their headlong sequence during the brief time since his return were conspiring to convince him running an empire could be a complex and laborious job.

Chamya was exactly right; with the rest of his armed company, like any *péfrapravádai* of Kargul — or the Household — he had been given the ordinary lance drill, and learnt use of the weapon in formation riding; Kamin-Tolagh's whim placed him with the highborn who studied the elegant, difficult and dangerous art of individual mounted combat. Not a mere survival, as with the Vrobani Chase, its lessons could be useful in real battle, but its discipline was concerned with style and manner far beyond any practical application, and was a cultured accomplishment to place alongside courtly correspondence or fluency with the Script of Shâl.

For Chamya and his young kinsman Sladra, needed as an adversary, they had to waive the traditional stipulation that a man learning the lance must ride his own mount; both used *pefral* borrowed from the cavalry, two of the smaller and lighter animals, great horses still.

For two mornings lessons were in the broad space of the Meeting Place, but quickly became too much of an entertainment for girls coming to draw water at the well (or pretending to), the girls in turn providing unwanted distraction for his two young pupils in an exercise where a lapse in concentration could be fatal. On the third day Kamin-Tolagh moved his classes to the level pasture between river and barracks. Mornings were cooler now, often with white mist rising to leave behind a heavy dew prized in this thirsty country; the afternoon sun blazed, but its heat now faltered slightly towards evening, day after day ending in rich displays of blood and flame, slowly purpling over Flamûrai.

It was gratifying how Chamya took to this sport, quickly mastering the first essential, that how well the left hand controlled the mount made everything else possible. He was quick to perceive, too, that for him horsemanship and cunning would have to compensate for his lack of weight and reach. The lance-points were snouted with a wicker guard like an elongated basket which laced on, but there were still falls and bruises, though no serious injuries. Each noon, the boy's mother with her unfathomable eyes observed their return from practice, and listened in grave silence, or with terse, emotionless interjections, to her son's animated accounts in their language.

If I were that Osré-dnë, Lavsila had said, *my dream would be the day when Noh-Sra-Lal-Hin rode off into the rising sun, and Chamya became head of the tribal confederation you have made.* Never, as Kamin-Tolagh had pointed out, and recent events had proved; without him, the tribes would soon be back to their old bickerings.

She would look for a way to borrow the magic of the Siv'loi Banner, but as with most of his conspiracies, Lavsila could not say how, nor why the other tribes would accept Man-mani leadership, after centuries of dislike.

Kambanal, dispatched after Kamin-Tolagh's arrival to make sure the Chon'la remained at home, returned with news the castrated man was out of danger, and stayed to take part in the lance-work, in which he had some experience. He was an exceptional horseman, but while admiring him as a squadron fighter, Kamin-Tolagh was disappointed at his lack of finesse or subtlety with the lance; riding against his otherwise most accomplished captain he had to hold himself back to make the bout last longer and provide the intended demonstration for the young pupils.

Beside the river, catching breath between rides, Kamin-Tolagh received word of fresh raiding in the south, but raiding with a difference, according to the hasty dispatch from Nizhadh. A filled granary of the Gudi-la had been set on fire, pigs and goats had been killed and left where they lay; at much the same time miles northward there had been an attempt to set fire to the *dao* valley, but Nizhadh with tribal troops had interrupted that exercise, and had inflicted a swift defeat on the small band of raiders. Again, Hill Froghul who had survived the Great Fire and subsequent campaign, but according to report there was also one Man-mani among the dead, and he, like his allies, looked well-fed. His weapon had been a sword of Dakbân steel.

Nizhadh, of all practical men, was not given to prattle, and would hardly have spared time for merely picturesque details, hurrying as he now was for the south, hoping Kamin-Tolagh or Kambanal would follow to fill the gap he was leaving. The nourished appearance of the dead fit together with the new wanton destructiveness of the attacks; in the past, Hill Froghul raids had been made by hungry men in search of supplies; they had set fires to distract defenders, not to destroy food they might carry off.

Given the dispatch to read, and reaching the same conclusions, Kambanal said, "If it is Hill Froghul together with the last of the Sranadatta clan, who is feeding them?"

"Or arming them. They retreated southward, into what is said to be high desert," Kamin-Tolagh pondered. "Beyond desert, the Hrin lands." Those, he believed, of Svedion, Iolfrant's sole ally among *hrithuod*.

The policy of the raiders was evidently to strike quickly at widely-separated points: he told Kambanal to cross eastward of the hills, taking regular cavalry with fifty mounted bows.

"On this side, Niburai can take a force south as far as the Hwenala country. The Man-mani must also stand to arms. I shall return to the Abu with a small escort."

Kambanal, as rarely, let perplexity show. "Is Niburai — ?" he half-commented, as near as he had come to questioning his lord's wisdom. The youthful Niburai was still struggling with his rise from file to squadron leader, his proudest boast that he had lent Kamin-Tolagh spare breeches on the morning after the Great Fire.

"For the most part, valley tribes can now defend themselves, and Nizhadh has it well in hand," with more confidence than he felt. Nevertheless, if, indirectly through his friend Svedion, Iolfrant was aiding and supplying these raiders, it could not be with any hope of overthrowing or mortally damaging Kamin-Tolagh's rule here; leaving aside the idea of simple revenge, guessed intent was to keep the dreaded *squadrons* occupied, unavailable to reinforce the distant garrison at Zelu Bablakhi. Recalling the story of Iolfrant's journey to Kadon Dinul, Kamin-Tolagh was chilled by the thought all this could be concerted with an assault by the *rabhsai*'s armies, crossing Landegh.

After a late start, riding as far as the Notch with Kambanal's company, forced to spend a night there, he grew steadily angrier on the thirsty ride back, deciding as he came closer to take captive all Hrin traders or hired workers at the Abu, ships' masters and their ships at Larghamit, so long as they belonged to either Iolfrant or Svedion, and hold them hostage against any attempt to expel him from the trading-station.

If, that was, the Abu remained in his hands, as it had five days ago when Freighanai had sent a routine report. Past the lone stand of substantial trees the Abu remained stubbornly invisible, and Kamin-Tolagh scanned the stony plain for some sign, the dust, perhaps, raised by an army on the march. At last, a few miles from home, he halted his company on the crown of a hillock, and, as before, sent a scouting-party ahead.

They returned in half an hour, having encountered a message-rider and his two-man escort setting out to find Kamin-Tolagh in the south. Freighanai's dispatch was in unexcited contrast to the turmoil left behind, the ferocity of his imaginings; the only real news was that the Hrin Navridn had returned, and

Dvasslo was warning that unless the forge soon had metal to work with, they could not have coinage ready by the stipulated date. The gold was in fact with Kamin-Tolagh, concealed in the loads of half a dozen pack-animals.

Lavsila said, "That would be a Hrin trick, all right, to equip and supply others to do their fighting for them."

Recalling he had said much the same about Dolvid, Kamin-Tolagh said, "Who would not, if he could? We would like nothing better than to have the rival *hrithuod* warring among themselves, to keep Iolfrant from any thought of seizing back Zelu Bablakhi for himself. Where is this Navridn?" he asked the hovering Freighanai.

Navridn's command of the ordinary language of Arbhal was fluent, but marred by a strong accent of vulgar Ninkufu, as picked up at dockside in Thenimala, and by the monotonous, rocking rhythm with which Hrin spoke their own language. He was young, short and slender with a slight, wispy beard; more Hrin might choose that way of disguising the receding chin, except their growth of beard, by contrast with the thick, black head-hair, varied between sparse and non-existent; Dvasslo, for example, evidently never shaved, and was lightly downed, like a peach. To go with the exceptional fecundity of his facial hair, Navridn had an intensity not previously observed among his people, as if keeping barely in check a vast anger, but after compliments his actual proposal was mild and reasonable; his *hrithust*, he said, desired only assurances the Empire of Kargusai was not ready to support the *Hrithust* Iolfrant in his policy to exclude other Hrin from seeking trade where it was to be found. A greed, he implied, only too common to those who guided their lives by the falsities of *dveyust-ranga-hrindan*.

With the immediate and specific in mind, Kamin-Tolagh offhandedly gave assent to the general principle, reiterating his desire to deal impartially with all who came in friendship, then startling the man by asking how many ships of his following were now at Larghamit.

The answer was three, homeward bound from a long westward voyage, and willing to do business with the cargoes they had acquired, mainly fruits, pepper, rare woods and some cloth. This offered hope for the need to reinforce the Zelu

Bablakhi garrison swiftly, and Navridn, though mystified, agreed he could, for a fee, place his cargoes in safe storage at Larghamit to be called for on his return, and take as many men and mounts as the ships would hold. When given a rough idea of the intended destination, however, he changed his mind; by treaty with Iolfrant, ships of his following did not make landfall on the westward shore of Flamûrai.

"This would mean war."

"But this," Lavsila objected, "is the very policy you came here to dispute."

"In new lands, yes. For Hrin, this is not the *ntveyusta* of any one *onhrith*. Elsewhere, the *utveyuodn* is settled by our oaths to each other; ships of Iolfrant do not go to our farther places."

Foolish, Kamin-Tolagh concluded, to ask for consistency where the rules were unknown. Having accepted hospitality, Navridn withdrew, quite content with a meeting at which nothing tangible had been accomplished; reinforcements would have to be sent overland.

"Unless Huolafidn has ships to take them," Lavsila absurdly suggested. "He arrived at the Abu past noon." To Kamin-Tolagh's incredulous stare, he shrugged. "If Iolfrant wishes to make war by proxy and still pretend friendship, you should take advantage of it."

This was a shadow-world where Lavsila was at home sooner than Kamin-Tolagh, who had wanted to make captives of Iolfrant's followers. Huolafidn's readiness to find room in his three vessels for sixty men going to Zelu Bablakhi, and to set out as soon as they could be aboard, should make nonsense of the whole idea Iolfrant was behind the renewed raiding, but Hrin logic was not his. He witnessed the two representatives of their rival *hrithuod* pass within a handspan near the crossways without acknowledging each other's existence, yet later heard when one of Navridn's vessels at Larghamit, beached too near the waterline, was picked up by the tide, Huolafidn's own ship put out to save it from being driven on rocks.

Morning brought Kargusai quietly to its most precarious: the sixty mounted archers under the last trusted officer he could send, the youthful but steady Luzhan, had ridden for Larghamit with Huolafidn; maintaining watch on Landegh together with the vestiges of communication and patrol left no reserves to deal with any further crisis, except for eighty or ninety tribal levies going through their drills, half-trained and poorly mounted.

On the subject of mounts, Dvasslo casually let drop the *Hristhust* Nestos was considered horse-breeder to the Hrin, one field, it seemed, where religious incompatibilities could be waived, since Iolfrant was said to obtain animals from his otherwise-estranged foster-brother. The Hrin mounts Kamin-Tolagh had seen at Zelu Bablakhi, the few they had brought for their use here, were workmanlike rather than inspiring, short-legged and broad in the beam, but sturdy and staying. Mares of their kind might be successfully bred with *pefral* stallions, perhaps, and Neliukh, the newly-arrived expert was in ribald agreement, "How those gals never dreamt of being filled, *Asai*."

Before a second and possibly less futile meeting with Navridn, he took on a difficult subject with Freighanai. They were in the one pleasing place of a Great House he loathed, a small back room overlooking the garden with its trickling rill and dark-leaved trees bowing over a tiny, dark pool. Fretasi, with a sheaf of parchment-scraps, was waiting, threatening to discuss financial questions, and he let her stay, seated at a small side-table.

"Are we keeping our forward scouts out on Landegh?" he asked unnecessarily; his orders would not be allowed to lapse.

Freighanai nodded. "They go as far as that first ridge, *Asai*; from there they'll see anything sizable moving ten miles away."

"If the Army of the West comes, we'll have no choice. We shall have to evacuate the Abu. It would become a trap for defenders."

"Then we would head south for tribal country, *Asai*?" An obvious inference, there being nowhere else to find food and water.

"I want all pack-animals and the spare mounts kept loaded with supplies, ready to leave at an hour's notice. Arrows, tools, everything useful we can carry with us. Necessities only."

Freghanai pondered this in silence, long-faced. At last, "Then we wouldn't be taking the women and children." Not a question; the sums were self-evident. Families would delay and encumber the retreat, and every animal was needed for the army's baggage; nor were hardships of survival with the tribes anything for women and children to share.

"Servants and workers will be left behind, too," deliberately reducing the emotion.   "We can win a war of waiting. The Army of the West cannot keep itself supplied indefinitely, hauling its needs across the breadth of Landegh, and we'll have mounted bowmen there to harry them." Conviction began to come as he reasoned on: "Shumat is a fine soldier, but he has not tried living off this sort of country. We would hold all the good tiles; we know the tribes, the lie of the land, places to set ambush, where the water is. We may end by extending him a truce for his evacuation of the Abu and his retreat across Landegh, in exchange for a pledge the *rabhsai* will honor."

"All takes time, though," obviously thinking of the families, of his family, left in enemy hands.

"Shumat would not permit women and children to be harmed."   Speaking, Kamin-Tolagh had a sudden vivid recollection of Dorrmas by the entrance to the so-called Hatchery, red to his elbows, face and hair spattered with blood. But a different case, and how it had happened, Shumat's remorse over imprecise orders, made any approach to a repetition the more improbable.

A father, particularly, of daughters, had other anxieties. "You have ridden with him," Kamin-Tolagh told Freighanai, who remained glum. "You saw, he keeps tight discipline. He would not permit any molesting of captives. Again, the *rabhsai* — " remembering when Kamin-Tarú was in Rodlakh's hands — "is altogether opposed to any use of hostages."

What would happen if Shumat's food ran short with an army to feed was another question; at best guess he would ask for a truce and expel dependents from the Abu to become Kamin-Tolagh's concern.

The man allowed a rueful half-smile. "We've learnt a few things, *Asai*, since we came to Kadon to help out Ban-Sila's Household."

Though scarcely true for himself, not entirely for Freighanai, Kamin-Tolagh saw what he meant. Young soldiers from back-country Kargul, coming north for the first time in that winter before the Jinzai War, at first refused to believe the new people they saw in the streets were not just a different kind of Owani, rather than the half-apes and unteachables of Other Race they had heard of all their lives. Though Kamin-Tolagh knew it to be false, he never discouraged the myth, common with the race-proud *péfrapravádal* of Kargul, that the celebrated achievements of Sebhal had been made feasible by an Army of the West driven by ruthless blood-lust of men hardly better than *jinzal*; those same men had become their brave and stalwart allies at Kamsilat, and now here he was, comforting Freighanai with the thought his wife and children would be in the hands of those same soldiers. Actually, he reflected, he would much sooner trust to the discipline of the mounted archers in the Army of the West than Tau-Suaka's lot, let loose in Drin Navuna or Kadon Dinul.

He noticed Fretasi, impassively following the conversation. "I have brought you here," contritely, "in perilous times."

She made a mouth. "I would be with the army," she said incontrovertibly. "I am of your *nimum*, not a dependent, and the horse is mine."

Shortly after, she was trying to make him see how, though money once disbursed was no longer his, ability of his empire to pay its way was affected when soldiers and their wives purchased goods from the Hrin, and he must, therefore, keep records of all such imports. The point remained obscure, but he did not doubt she was right.

Waiting was worst, in a silent world. With ways again unsafe for individual riders, he had instructed his officers in the south to hold their dispatches till there was real news, and the only regular reports that came were of unevent, west and east, Larghamit and the watch on Landegh. The first of his gold coins were struck and were splendid, but there would now be no great oathtaking; the present crisis might pass, but he could not foresee a time when he would dare bring all his trusted officers together here.

First news came from Kambanal in the south, and was welcome. Following Kamin-Tolagh's argument that the chief object of these new raids was destruction and the tying-down of troops, he had reasoned the most probable target east of the hills, the place where the greatest damage could be inflicted by fire, was the close-set, fenced village of K'daab's People. Sending only token contingents mainly to alert the Jai and Ntara-golal in the south, trusting the main Laughing Owl tribe to defend itself, he had gambled by concentrating his forces near that settlement, and won what he called a *substantial* victory at very small cost. There were many enemy dead, but he also had prisoners, among them an unmistakable Man-mani, who was expected to have information about any part played by "our southward allies" in feeding and equipping the well-armed raiders — Kambanal had no one with him to question the man in his own language. He wished to remain on guard in tribal country till certain the back of their enemy was broken, but would forward prisoners to the Abu as soon as an escort could be spared. Again, neither of the Man-mani Kamin-Tolagh most wanted, Nifra, father of Siv'loi, and Sra-Min-Talla-Tyu, last son of Sranadatta, had been found with the dead.

"Your Tau-Suaka," Lavsila decided, "will be helpful in questioning prisoners." Much the same thought had already occurred. With his whip, his wrist cocked for real business, Hunghi could flay a man to the bare bone.

At nightfall on that same day a message-rider from Larghamit delivered a dispatch from Yaënsilat, brought with Huolafidn's returning ship. There had indeed been an assault on the trading-station at Zelu Bablakhi, but not by its former sole possessors. A wild people from upriver, not the same as those who brought the gold, had come down, some on foot, others in a horde of small boats, actually no more than dug out logs, and assailed the station, shooting small, flightless arrows from tiny bows. One of Kamin-Tolagh's first orders there had been to extend the compound stockade so that, awash at high tide, it no longer left an open strip of shore when water was low, but the attackers, beaten off in their ragged attack by land, had been able to beach some of their boats within the enclosure, and there had been, Yaënsilat said, brisk fighting among the buildings. He had noticed Hrin vessels hovering offshore, and explained their inaction as cowardice, confirmed by behavior of the few Hrin at the station, assayers, traders and laborers, who barricaded themselves in the larger of the storehouses, and took no part in fighting.

It was clear the attackers were allied to or had been somehow encouraged by Iolfrant's Hrin, who had waited offshore to claim the prize. Unsuspecting Yaënsilat, however, wrote that with only Hrin defenders, or their former auxiliaries, the post would surely have been lost, but disciplined fighting and superior bowmanship had held the place with comparative ease. With a lessened body of enemy licking their wounds out of bow-range of the stockade, a fresh arrival of Hrin vessels had caused the others to vanish, and Huolafidn's trio of ships had landed the sixty reinforcements under Luzhan.

An arrival which must have convinced the enemy they had no chance of capturing the trading-post. Abruptly, they turned instead on the neighboring village, whose inhabitants had been making themselves inconspicuous. Yaënsilat's opinion was, the invaders actually expected his defenders to sit and watch a sack of the village, `and thank Hrafi it wasn't us,' as he sarcastically put it.

Instead, he put every man in the saddle, and sortied to rout the enemy. He doubted more than sixty or seventy of an estimated initial four hundred had survived to escape. At the time of writing, his primary concern was with the gratitude of the villagers, which was threatening to bury the trading-post under gifts of fruit and fish. Lavsila was right: the contradictions in the behavior of Iolfrant's followers could be explained only by a determination to keep up the appearance of friendship. "Born gamblers," Lavsila, witheringly. "The *dveyust-ranga-hrindan* must have gods who know how to lose the wager and keep their stake."

In both actions, Kambanal's and Yaënsilat's, losses had been relatively light, mainly confined to auxiliary troops, but three men of Kargul had been killed. No one of note, though Kamin-Tolagh knew all three, and for the first time there was now a widow living here on the mound at the Abu; he would pay her maintenance till she married again, as, being young, childless and pretty enough, she surely would.

Now news came that was not victory, a dispatch from Niburai to say Nizhadh was missing, having gone up into the hills, leading Gudi-la in pursuit of an enemy they had beaten off. Since the Great Fire it had become possible for men to cross the dividing hills; the most southerly way was winding, rocky, in places threatened by a return of brush, but with all its difficulties could save five or six days from the journey between the Gudi-la country and that of the Ntara-golal. Nizhadh's most recent report, enclosed with the one from Niburai, spoke of catching the enemy as they turned their attention to the eastward tribes. He was full of praise for the fighting qualities acquired by the Gudi-la, together with the Laughing Owl in the east much the most promising of tribal troops; an irony, then, that Gudi-la men returned without him, telling a tale of ambush.

Just what had happened would never be known; the Gudi-la levies maintained their officer, Nizhadh, had ordered their retreat, his absence from it not at first noticed. A second dispatch from Niburai, almost overtaking the one it superseded, had the end of the tale; Nizhadh was dead. His terribly mutilated body, not at first identified, had been found on the hill path. Most disfiguring wounds had been inflicted after a death most probably caused by an arrow through the throat.

The men who had fought with him through the Jinzai War had been indestructible, but Kamin-Tolagh's first recollection was of Nizhadh solicitously bringing him a heated stone, on the bone-chilling heights during the Zelu Bablakhi expedition. Without remedy for loss, his thoughts turned to revenge.

19.

For guide, the expedition had the Man-mani prisoner captured by Kambanal, Cho-matta, whose connection with the Sranadatta clan was a remote one. Allowed to witness the interrogation, by Tau-Suaka and Hunghi, of another captive, one of their own kind, who died in the process, Cho-matta had become eager to serve Noh-Sra-Lal-Hin. Through one of the Man-mani porters employed at the Abu, he told enough to make clear the *Hrithust* Iolfrant had indeed been behind the new outbreak of raiding.

Not directly; with Hrin, nothing was direct. The fugitives, a strange collection of remnant *Sranadattanil*, a few renegade Hwenala from the old bodyguard, and a core of Hill Froghul, survivors of the Great Fire, from time to time augmented by stragglers, all united only by hostility to the new ordering of the northern Froghushei, had been given refuge, not by Iolfrant, but by his lesser ally, Svedion, whose *onhritha* began on the farther side of the reputedly impassable high desert to the south. With their women and a small number of children, he had installed them in a hill village evidently emptied for the purpose. Oyestri, however, mentioned by Huolafidn as elder kin to Iolfrant, had supplied the rebel alliance with weapons, mounts and pack-animals, small amounts of gold with promise of greater to come. The proffered theory behind the raiding urged by Oyestri was that the valley tribes, seeing their new master was unable to protect them, would join in a general rebellion; while Iolfrant could not believe this, it amused Kamin-Tolagh to wonder how the raiders imagined spoils were to be divided. Would the remnant Man-mani help the Hill Froghul return to their old haunts, and to their former parasitical life of plundering the valley tribes? If it had not entailed his own defeat, success for the ramshackle coalition might have been more entertaining to witness than their failure.

His own no less assorted force could at least boast a common purpose, a final end to the threat of raids; not an invading army, it ought to be enough for the punitive counter-raid he intended. Knowing he might for the first time have the fighting strength of a civilized enemy to face, he reassembled two of the Kargul' squadrons as his hammer. Not wanting to take either Freighanai or Kambanal from defense of the Abu and the tribal country, he brought back from Zelu Bablakhi the experienced Yaënsilat, in some ways preferable to either; his uncomplaining endurance on the former campaign had set an example for younger men, or shamed them to silence, yet his willingness to offer opinion in place of grievance made common soldiers feel they did not lack a voice. He would act as *kímukan*, for the Kargul', as well as overall second-in-command, and with him had come some of the best mounted bows, to help make up the hundred Tau-Suaka led. Again for the first time, balance of his small army consisted of two tribal squadrons, mainly Gudi-la, with men of Kargul as officers down to file-leader level.

Iruvakh, as ever, had been passionately opposed to taking away able-bodied men of the tribes from a late planting availability of water had at last made possible. An exaggerated protest, possibly made with an eye on some future when there was extensive autumn planting, for which, this year, there was neither water nor seed. Of the famous winter wheat there was only enough to sow terraces benefitting from Lavsila's grudgingly-completed irrigation — where, according to Iruvakh, in widely-spaced rows, fresh green shoots could be used for grazing before year's turn, and would then lie dormant through the cooler weather. In the rainy season, ordinary wheat would be planted in the spaces between rows, and there would be early and late crops for harvesting. The manner, pure *Mankh'*, was too severe to suspect a fable, although to Kamin-Tolagh it sounded more sorcery than husbandry.

Climbing into scrawny woods beyond the Ntara-golal pastures, a contingent of Tau-Suaka's vigilant bowmen were in the van. In open country, they would also be used as flankers, but for now the force maintained column formation, soon coming into dense brush not touched by the Great Fire. Here, defined paths had sometimes to be cleared and widened with the use of curved knives, tedious, cursing work they were glad to leave behind when, by evening, they crossed the summit and began a faint descent, matted growth thinning, giving way to clumps of low bushes and trailing thorn whose knife-hard spikes were to be avoided by both man and mount. After brief rest they went on by light of an immense, pale-gold moon near the full, bright enough to cast their shadows on the bare ground.

After travelling well into morning with little change of terrain, they used some shade under leggy, emaciated trees to sleep away the heat of the day. By next evening, veering to the east, they were climbing again, skirting bulky mountains dark and menacing by moonlight. With a steepening ascent, they came past dawn to the rim of the true desert, flat tableland except for scattered bastions of rock like abandoned fortresses: the western Landegh, which men called featureless, was a wildly varied landscape compared to this emptiness. A ripple of low, dun ridges receded to the horizon, a world drained of color under a blank early sky.

From here, with the guidance of Cho-matta, they followed a faint trail, wandering from waterhole to waterhole; they could have made do with the water they carried, but their guide was uncertain of his directions, only sure this way led where they were going, and held to firm ground; there were wide stretches, he had been told, where sand was loose and shifting, and horses would soon be floundering to their hocks, and strange marshlands, where oily, foul-smelling water sweated to the surface and made treacherous bogs.

Again at midday they halted, finding a narrow cleft which provided some shade, though the day had not gone beyond warm, and night when it came was cold, stirred by eddying breezes. For three days they plodded on without event, except for their first casualty, a man who disturbed a harmless-looking snake sleeping in the shadow of a rock, and died from its bite after only three hours. Following a long westward swing to a startling green patch of growth about a restless natural well, the south-eastward course resumed, and they were approaching mountains, not so high as they were abrupt, rising as stone islands in a sea of dust. The better-defined trail rose hardly at all, but was soon threading a way through lesser peaks, a place where, if anywhere, an ambush might be expected. New terrain changed the order of march, a half-squadron of lances now preceding the bows, but nothing happened to challenge their cautious advance. The island crags were threshold to loftier mountains, and the next midday halt was in dappled shade of trees still hung with lifeless grey leaves, by the course of a bitter-tasting stream which raced down to lose itself in the flats far below.

A new start found them climbing steeply, and at midnight under the round moon they reached the summit, felt and smelled as much as seen, moist cool air on their faces, sense of a watered country with grass and trees. Their guide, generally abject and fearful, permitted himself a ration of self-congratulation; he had led them to a place he knew.

Witnessing the prolonged death of his fellow-prisoner, besides turning him into a believer in Noh-Sra-Lal-Hin, had reminded Cho-matta that during his time here he had learned the language spoken by the Hill Froghul; through one of Tau-Suaka's men he explained they had reached the borders of lands claimed by *Hrithust* Svedion. The village where he and his allies had been harbored was not a two-hour ride below. A substantial stand of fir-trees, nicely spaced with scarcely any underbrush over the packed cushion of fallen needles, was a good spot for another halt, Kamin-Tolagh himself stretching out gratefully on soft ground.

By morning light, the column having swung twice across the steep descending slope, site of the village was easily visible, a slight conical mound standing out from the opening of a wide valley, approach by a track trodden and worn into something near a road, winding down by wooded slopes, trees now leafless. Dubovai put the distance at five miles.

Though unchallenged, it was unlikely their incursion had been entirely unwatched, and had been afraid word of their arrival had preceded them, but nothing else was moving on the visible portion of the trail, and the village, clearly, was not abandoned; the thin ribbon of smoke from more than one cooking-fire could be seen, and an early line of washing flickering in shadow. Steep-roofed dwellings were close-set up to the crown of the low hill.

Checking the advance, Kamin-Tolagh came up beside Yaënsilat. "We can set fire on three sides, and burn the village to the ground."

The frank face creased deeper in Yaënsilat's perplexity. "You think we can clear the place without a fight, *Asai*?"

"We did not come to take prisoners. These are the men who defiled the body of Nizhadh."

"There would be women, *Asai*, children."

Was this a *péfrapravádai* of Kargul, rider in a force feared for its toughness and lack of pity? Kamin-Tolagh did not exult in sufferings of the innocent, but quite aside from revenge for Nizhadh, there were the hard demands of policy. "We shall see no end to these raids, to attacks on the tribes, their women and children, too, unless we show we have the will and the power to retaliate."

Yaënsilat cleared his throat, and let his deep-set eyes come up to meet Kamin-Tolagh's. "I am a soldier, *Asai*, nothing else, and I've never done less than my duty, fighting *jinzal* or men with weapons in their hands. This is well-known."

"A soldier's duty," levelly, "is to obey orders." Not conceivable the man actually meant to refuse. "The village is to be surrounded, and burnt to the ground."

The second's pause was like an hour, with too many within earshot. Tau-Suaka was dark and smoldering, other Kargul' officers tense; even Dubovai had suspended his mapmaking to watch the outcome.

"My duty has not included burning-alive women and children."

"My orders are clear, are they not?"

"Clear, *Asai*; your orders are always that." The old soldier had to wrench the next words from himself: "I can't be any part of this. I'm no mutineer; others must do what they must."

Unbelieving, Kamin-Tolagh had to conceal anger, but also avoid an appearance of pleading with the man. At odds, they were together on unfamiliar ground; he was unused to having his orders so much as questioned, but certain Yaënsilat in a long career had never disputed, much less refused, a direct command. Merely to justify his orders was too much concession, but Yaënsilat's popularity, the respect he was given, made it necessary to isolate what could become a dangerous infection.

"One hard lesson can, in the end, save many lives. If it is seen how tenderly we treat them, this *Hrithust* Iolfrant will never lack for hirelings to do his fighting for him; we can never have security." He turned to his squadron officers with a face of sardonic tolerance. "Some of us as we grow older, are crippled, not by stiff joints, but by squeamishness. There may come a day when my father is fit for nothing bloodier than fine-sewing."

The others laughed, well beyond any merit the joke possessed, which represented no one's opinion of Yaënsilat, but provided a welcome release of tension. From the corner of his eye Kamin-Tolagh saw Yaënsilat flush, rigid-jawed. Yet he was edgy, too; he had caused this crisis in pure reaction to what was abhorrent to him. That could be admired in a private man, but must be condemned in a soldier.

Still in his public voice, Kamin-Tolagh said, "More of us might find room for such softness, if we could forget Nizhadh, and how his body was mutilated in death." He remembered Yaënsilat, in the most hopeless days and nights of the Zelu Bablakhi expedition, sustaining Nizhadh's hard-pressed imperturbability.

"*Asai*," the old soldier began, "Nizhadh himself would not — "

"The captain," Kamin-Tolagh broke in, "is to command the rearguard for the supply-train — " where there was no apparent danger to the baggage, a duty usually given to the least warlike, often to sick or wounded men.

"Do not force me to arrest you," this quietly.

Worn face gave no clue. He must know Tau-Suaka would kill him on the spot if Kamin-Tolagh ordered it. The Kargul' officers, surely, would obey any order short of that.

At length, a weary nod. "I'll defend the pack-train, *Asai*."

"You are relieved of field command," not showing any emotion. Dubovai's promotion to squadron-leader had come earliest and made him technically senior officer here, but he lacked field experience since exchanging sword for mapping-pen; Niburai, who had managed to insert modest self-praise into his account of his actions following the disappearance of Nizhadh, would now have the chance to perform under his lord's eye.

"Bravery," in a voice for everyone to hear, "is needed in battle, but there can be another courage in carrying out a harsh but necessary policy, where the only danger is pity. We did not begin this war on villages, but we can end it here."

Seventy years ago in the War of the Widowed, under his great-uncle Tobhsila, the Cavalry of Kargul, slipping past forces commanded by Banak south of Kanzan Tâl, had used terror as a deliberate weapon, and were said to have burned twenty villages and one hundred farms, raped a thousand women, slaughtered three thousand of every age and sex in the Lower Paowan, before Banak could intervene. While the numbers were questionable, Kamin-Tolagh would not necessarily defend this episode, glossed-over in the public provincial history; by hardening popular resistance to Karguli dominance, it had only made final defeat more absolute. But it did go to show how very odd, by the remorseless traditions of Kargul, Yaënsilat's sudden scruples were. The readiness and even relish with which men of Kargul took part in the action the veteran officer declined, their lack of any distaste for the ferociousness of their Hill Froghul allies, were more in accord with the normal ways of this cavalry, perhaps of any soldiers let off the leash.

Setting the wood-built village afire was easy; a number of men carried stone, steel striker and fluffed tinder-cord, while for insurance against camp-sites where no fuel was available, several of the pack-horses, as water and other supplies were consumed, had been given bundles of dry brush to carry. The village stood a little aside from and above the main way, making it easy for regular cavalry, including the fire-setters, to pass by and circle the farther side without a general alarm being given; a woman who, testing the dryness of her overnight line of laundry, saw the soldiery, was killed before she could raise the village. Tau-Suaka's men invested the nearer and downwind side.

From the end of a long straight stretch of track, immediately before the looping descent which took it by the village, Kamin-Tolagh was able to see most of the action. After the first billowing puff of smoke, it took less than a minute for the fire to blaze up, and there was never a hope of extinguishing or even seriously slowing it, not if there had been hundreds to fight it, and limitless water. But clearly few able-bodied men were left here; most had already been killed raiding, and the cries of fear and pain that came were scattered. Those who tried to escape mostly emerged onto the track, where Kargul' lances or Hill Froghul bows quickly finished them, but when convinced there would be no large number of villagers to deal with, Tau-Suaka's riders began making it a game, laughing to harry a smoke-blinded or half-burnt woman or child to and fro, using their short swords to give gradually disabling wounds, killing only when there was no further sport to be had.

Down on the road a small knot of about six, men, women and older children, emerged together from smoke and flame, and among them Kamin-Tolagh at once thought he recognized Nifra, the father of Siv'loi, who died far too quickly, spitted by a cavalry lance as he turned to the sound of hoofs. When, with smoke from the burning village now rising in a thick column, age-warped houses blazing like tinder, Kamin-Tolagh rode down, it was not the man, but another Man-mani Cho-matta could identify. Some Man-mani bodies Kamin-Tolagh could give names to; first corpse he saw was of the woman, the much-widowed Myanachë, killed together with her infant son, presumably the child of Sra-Min-Talla-Tyu. That body, Myanachë's final husband, was not seen. With Nifra, he might have died in the fire, or quite possibly been killed in one of the unsuccessful raids, his remains not found, or left unidentified.

A mile down, the track met a defined and well-kept road coming in from the east, following a small river, where the men could wash away soot and caked blood. In the midst of slaughter Tau-Suaka's men had managed to rescue some stored food from the village, and the army feasted on plain cheese and tough-crusted bread, chunks of ham and sweet red apples, while the bloodshot pillar of smoke climbed into the still air, a sign for the whole long valley.

The eastward road, Cho-matta told, led over hills to peopled parts of Svedion's *onhritha*, seaward lands, his principal city a seaport. Southward, for a time remaining beside the river, the way passed through a gap, distantly visible from where they stood, the border with territories of the powerful neighboring *Hrithust*, Iolfrant. Tau-Suaka's man was contemptuous in translating the rest: there was a *great* valley where a *great* river ran, and there were rich farmlands and *great* cities.

Having done all he could to proclaim his presence, Kamin-Tolagh knew the proper course was immediate withdrawal, forces intact. Armed Hrin had yet to be seen, but it would be foolhardy to linger with his tiny army in the midst of a people that must number in the tens, hundreds of thousands. Yet to come so far without a glimpse, at least, of Iolfrant's domain was unthinkable. Leaving a small guard to keep concealed watch on the eastward road, he moved forward with the main body.

Soon they were passing through a village which straggled along both sides of the stream, houses more substantial than anything in the northern Froghushei; glazed windows, and two short, well-built bridges, one wooden, the other of cut stone, were further evidence of civilized skills. Hrin faces cautiously observed them, and one man, boldly standing outside his door, shouted what sounded like angry defiance, which Kamin-Tolagh quickly ordered dark-faced Tau-Suaka to ignore; there were no weapons to be seen. For the first time, he saw women of the Hrin, or a woman and a girl, short, drably clad in loose garments which covered them from neck to ankle. He could not tell if the bodies were as shapeless as their covering; faces were plain, but brows less prominent than with most of the men, and the typical receding chin of their people was not incompatible with feminine good looks. What would be considered beautiful among the Hrin was anyone's guess, but a place where gold was worked with such intricate delicacy could hardly be without feeling for a woman's grace.

Beyond the houses, the broad and well-kept road, leaving the riverbank, climbed lazily to a rounded swell, deeply grassed. Pointing out signs, farther up the slope, of former cultivation, Dubovai speculated Hrin numbers were in decline.

"Maybe," Kamin-Tolagh said. "But with gold to spend, and their mastery of the seas, they may be buying what they used to grow for themselves." As with most of what he said nowadays, this was greeted with grave respect.

The silvery line of the river still visible in its deepening cleft among overhanging trees, they came to where the road made a long, curving descent before mounting gradually to a shoulder above the water-gap, valley's end. There was the squared jut of some structure, a small fortress, or a stone barrier guarding the pass. More urgently, a mass of soldiery was deploying, rough-clad infantry, some bearing short bows, most with shields and a long-weapon, a pike with an added cutting edge near the end. Where the space was opened by a widening of the leftward slope, they were sorting themselves into three unequal divisions, rightmost and largest, numbering near three hundred, straddling the road and blocking the pass, most of the bowmen on the higher ground to the rear.

Behind them again, cavalry was streaming into view, men in what had to be ceremonial dress, high-crowned helms festooned with colored streamers, scarlet-and-gold tunics with short, very ample sleeves. The mounts were the broad, short-legged animals of the Hrin. Their main weapon was the same halberd the infantry carried, unwieldy for a mounted man, no match for the long, light lances of his force. The horse moved to the flanks and to fill the two lanes between masses of infantry; while they lacked the precise formations of highly-trained cavalry, they took up position without jostling or discussion, and kept their place quietly.

Each time Kamin-Tolagh finished a count, fresh horsemen appeared over the skyline; he was far outnumbered, with the opposite cavalry alone more than his entire army. Plainly they were not here to offer a welcoming address: so well-prepared a force could not have been assembled in the short hours since his assault on the village, which meant his advance must have been observed earlier. If, as he assumed, these were troops of the *Hrithust* Iolfrant, it seemed strange the village of their allies had not been either evacuated or warned, unless these forces had been dispatched to defend that place; if so they could now see the smoke that told them they had come too late.

Was this a fight he needed? His tribal squadrons were probably a match, man to man, for the Hrin, his mounted archers and the regular cavalry far superior; at odds of three or four to one he could win. Not without casualties, and he was in hostile country, where an adversary could replace his losses, while he could not. Another thought occurred: likely Iolfrant's ally, Svedion, whose lands these were, had also been forewarned, and the two *hrithuod* could be working together; victorious but weakened by victory, he could find any retreat blocked. A withdrawal now, smartly executed, could keep his forces whole, but turning tail, as it would be seen, could mortally wound prestige, and expose his position at Zelu Bablakhi as the bluff it was.

Nearer now, the Hrin cavalry with their flapping saddlecloths, rich tunics, which had protective fronts of varicolored leather, the ribbons on their high headgear, were more than ever a quaint ceremonial guard. Next to Kamin-Tolagh, Tau-Suaka gave a menacing, chuckle, and said there would be dead worth despoiling — *baring*, as he put it.

He was told to extend his contingent leftward, to hold the advantage of the slope: if the Hrin had come to fight they had already committed a tactical error by keeping their backs to the pass they defended, when they should have deployed to their own right, the upper ground, flanking any possible advance, and increasing the effectiveness of their bows.

Not to forget he was facing troops of a nominal ally. With all their trappings, the Hrin displayed no banner, and he did not know whether they would understand the signal for a parley, colors dipped sideways and the proper trumpet-call. Nor, though some of the most peacock-like of the riders appeared to be directing their men, could he identify an overall commander. If there was to be fighting without talk, he wished the small Hrin bows would begin with some ineffectual shooting, so he could reply, exploiting the range and accuracy of Tau-Suaka's archery; as quarters became closer that advantage lessened. Nevertheless, he would not open hostilities till certain the Hrin meant to fight; they might have forces as large or larger in reserve on the far side of the gap.

Pace of preparation was sedate enough for a ceremony. To the left of the road but inside the Hill Froghul archers he placed the squadron mainly of Gudi-la, giving its leadership to Niburai, while taking personal charge of the two regular squadrons. He missed Yaënsilat's calm strength, and would have wished to go over the dispositions with him, but he was in exile, thoughtful back with the baggage-train, and what was considered the weakest half-squadron, Laughing Owl with no other Karguli officer.

Now, at the rear of the opposite army, up near the pass, an animated discussion or dispute was going on, with much gesticulation, at a guess advocates of immediate attack pitted against those of defense; at the distance he could not tell if either Huolafidn or Iolfrant himself was a debater. From his position, Tau-Suaka was eyeing Kamin-Tolagh in baleful hope, almost audibly requesting a sign to begin; the bloodletting at the village had done nothing to slake his appetite.

Alert, Kamin-Tolagh's most inward thoughts were elsewhere. Here, days from any home base, his empire could founder, and he was considering how little time he'd had to enjoy what skill, daring, hard work and amazing luck had won. After each triumph there had come a fresh threat, an opportunity demanding urgent action, niggling demands on his attention. He had relished the days with Chamya teaching lances, but beyond any other desire wished Kamin-Tarú could have been here to share his good fortune, to marvel and to laugh: the acclaim of the Man-mani, the tremendous fire and its unexpected profit in the deadly loyalty of Tau-Suaka's men; his successful gamble with the search for Zelu Bablakhi, his likeness on gold coinage, all of it would attain its fullest glory, would take on the reality which eluded him, seen through her wondering eyes.

All at once the Hrin leaders resolved or agreed to break off their dispute, fanning out to ride to their various stations. A movement began, a large mass of infantry crossing diagonally to threaten his leftmost squadrons. Instantly, Kamin-Tolagh waved his men forward down the slope, so that the Hrin would have to bring out their horse to meet him.

Tau-Suaka's bows began, looping their shafts, as ordered, at the rearward ranks of the infantry, where the opposing archers were. At the charge, Kamin-Tolagh's men clashed with twice their number of Hrin cavalry, and drove it back in disarray; as expected, the unwieldy halberds were no match for the long lances or nimble swords of the *péfrapravádal*. The abrupt recoil of the foremost enemy horse turned their own reinforcements, but swung them right in the path of the tribal squadron supporting Kamin-Tolagh.

They failed. As soon as the front eight lost their forward drive, others behind checked their mounts, veering aside, and a fresh body of the high-helmed enemy, circling the rear of their infantry, completed the repulse. Cursing, his advance threatened with engulfment, Kamin-Tolagh saw Niburai, momentarily surrounded, fight his way clear, his great horse lunging madly.

Trying to signal Tau-Suaka he must advance from his flanking position, he knew the Hrin had victory in their grasp. Everything for him was moving with an unnatural slowness, and wistfully he saw he was only a squadron short of turning the battle. Stung by the Hill Froghul bows, the enemy center had shrunk back, so advance of the cavalry that had thrust back the tribal squadron and extended on his left had also opened a yawning gap.

His only reserves were odds and ends he had no means of organizing, preoccupied as he was with discouraging the Hrin from seeing their huge numerical advantage could by absolute weight crush his individually superior cavalry. Then, over his left shoulder, he saw old Yaënsilat, leading a company he must have cobbled together by sheer force of will in record time, checking and reversing the retreating Gudi-la, adding them to a near-squadron of Laughing Owl, bawling at the rearmost half-squadron of Kargul' behind Kamin-Tolagh to disengage and join him. Which, led by a reanimated Dubovai, they did.

Yaënsilat read the field perfectly, drove into the breach, and cut clean through Hrin cavalry crossing from the left. Ignoring infantry blocking the road, he wheeled right on the rear of the main Hrin cavalry, and threw it into panicked disarray. At the same time the momentarily victorious enemy horse at Kamin-Tolagh's left were struck by the arrows and then the short swords of Tau-Suaka's men, who had crossed directly in front of timid forces to fight a way to their embattled lord. The entire Hrin left turned to a rabble, their thoughts going instantly from victory to flight. Yaënsilat, too astute to pursue beaten men into a narrow pass where they could turn and make a stand, wheeled back, and was among retreating infantry. They had no thought of fight, throwing down weapons that encumbered their escape, but their sheer numbers impeded Yaënsilat, preventing him from turning his rout of the cavalry into a hunt; piecemeal the survivors broke free of the melée and joined the retreat, riding for shelter behind the cowed but largely intact infantry from their own right.

Kamin-Tolagh, finding his trumpeter, had the recall sounded. Tau-Suaka, chasing Hrin cavalry, angrily checked his horse, then swiftly unslung his bow to shoot a last shaft, which brought down one of the caparisoned enemy. Letting the men loose would have begun a great slaughter, but not without loss, and the Hrin, who could renew their armies, could better afford to lose a hundred than he ten. This field, clearly, was his.

As it stood, even on the losing side, losses were small relative to the numbers engaged. Shumat had told him the greatest part of the killings often occurred after the battle was decided; men who could no longer think of anything but saving their own lives were quickest to lose them.

He began an advance at the walk, while enemy infantry continued to quit the field, trickling back through the gap like slow-draining water. A grinning Yaënsilat wheeled a virtually intact force to come in line with Kamin-Tolagh, and gave a jaunty salute. "Your pardon, *Asai*, I couldn't see such a chance go a-begging."

"You did well." Coming closer, Kamin-Tolagh murmured, "Between us, we were not far from losing that fight."

"Oh, I don't know, *Asai* — " but he did know, he must.

"You understand, you have left me no choice. I cannot restore you to command. If you were to retire, you could keep your house at the Abu." *And your life*, he did not say; there was only one punishment for mutiny.

"Understood, *Asai*," with a somber little nod, but he was twenty years younger than the man who had refused to burn the village.

His charge had won the fight, but that was only one reason for relief and gratitude; everyone now would understand leniency, and it would not be attributed to softness; he was released from the necessity of executing a man universally respected and loved.

In the water-gap, a square, stone-built fort or blockhouse in poor repair marked, he assumed, the end of Svedion's lands or the beginning of Iolfrant's. Garrisoned with bows alone it could have held the pass a long time against forces larger than Kamin-Tolagh's and more able to afford casualties, and its abandoning was sign of how completely the Hrin had been demoralized by failure. Behind, directed by Niburai, tribal troops were collecting discarded weapons, many with notched edges and blunted points; strange that a race of accomplished goldsmiths produced such inferior steel, and stranger that they armed their own soldiery with poor blades while using Dakbân swords and knives in trade at Zelu Bablakhi.

A richer booty could be claimed from the fallen cavalry and their mounts; few of the men had been killed, but many had been unhorsed and made their escape on foot, and most saddles and harnesses had fittings of gold, some horses equipped with gold-embossed visors to match the vambraces their riders wore on the weapon-arm. The absurd helms, also, had precious metals and gems for ornament, and there were swords with hilts worth the price of a farm. No doubt some of the soldiery would manage to pocket smaller items, but the main booty was to be collected and divided in correct proportion, one-half first going to Kamin-Tolagh's treasury.

He would have liked a clue as to Hrin intentions, but most of the live and unwounded enemy still on the field were the rough-clad infantry, who seemed to speak no language but their own. They sat down on the ground in small circles, mainly bewildered, dispirited men, not worth guarding or treating as prisoners once disarmed. They had the rat-faced, big-eyed look of the ill-fed, and there were faces, arms, thighs crusted with scales and sores, scalps ravaged by ringworm. It came to him the

Hrin he had encountered hitherto, even the ordinary sailors of the ships' companies, were relatively well-off, and far greater numbers must belong to a servant, or say a slave class. They did not appear different in race from their masters; smaller stature and bonier faces were, rather, the signs of underfeeding.

"No wonder there is no fight in them," Dubovai reflected. "Their lords tell them, foreigners are coming to take what is ours — how can that mean anything, to a man who has nothing?"

With no answer, Kamin-Tolagh glanced at him sharply. A keen assessment from someone who, beyond always knowing which way was true north, had not previously displayed much intellectual capacity. One able to probe into the reasons behind obedience needed watching.

Mapping requirements ready, Dubovai rode beside Kamin-Tolagh past the pitted, decaying walls of the fort, where mortar had largely ceded to moss and tufts of spiky weed, and together they had a first astonished sight of Iolfrant's domains.

Far to the south were shadowy forms of dark hills; westward and closer, sharper, bonier heights, but all the rest was a vast green bowl, interrupted only by gentle swells in its long descent to where there must be a river, a great one, wandering through the spacious valley. Nearer, there were streams and tree-fringed ponds, imposing buildings of rich farmsteads, dark clusters of many villages. Orchard groves with their bare branches were a reminder of coming winter, but there were trees not shaped like cone-bearers that must keep their green leaves all year. Under the heavy limbs of an enormous oak that might mark the boundary, Kamin-Tolagh wished his empire could be made of such lands, fruitful and consoling.

Afternoon sun found a gap in dark bars of cloud, and a shaft of golden light striking near the darker crease of the distant river woke an answering flame.

"The city where Lord Iolfrant sits," Tau-Suaka translated flatly from Cho-matta. "Its name is Hyolenstr, and there are great — ah — great *halls*, roofed with gold." There was, the tale continued, a much greater city where the river came to the sea, but Kamin-Tolagh had already heard of that, and its name, Guodvestr, the place where Iolfrant's ships went and came from.

The city with roofs of gold! and Kamin-Tolagh with his handful had routed Iolfrant's army. He was flooded with the resolve to go on, cap defeat of the *Hrithust* with his deposing, and rule here in his place.

Sun and clouds shifted, and the spark of golden fire died. A mile away across pastureland, the retreat of the beaten army had been checked, and they had been reinforced; there was much movement on what were evidently excellent roads. He had defeated, obviously, only a fraction of the men available; what Dubovai said about the fighting-spirit of the ordinary Hrin was true so far, but even farm-laborers, poor apprentices, the workless might rally against invasion of their native soil — and one of Kamin-Tolagh's squadrons had broken in a charge. Then, too, someone, probably Dvasslo, had called Iolfrant's capital a sacred place, their *Mankh'* as well as their Inilun Barabhi, and an attempt to assail it might yet rouse from indifference the fervid believers in the *dveyust-ranga-hrindan*. Not now, he nearly said aloud; this prize would have to wait.

"We shall make our camp here." With Tau-Suaka's bows behind the blockhouse walls, the Hrin would not dare trying to dislodge him; if he could not go forward, he was not going to be seen to retreat.

In the morning, under a feather-light but persisting rain, he was ready to give the order to start for home, when a watcher on the upper platform of the fort called warning of a large mass of cavalry moving up from the south. Coming at the walk, they soon vanished behind a wooded hill, and Kamin-Tolagh made use of the minutes before they emerged in sight again, foregoing any depth to bring a bristling front of lances up level with the fort, and giving the bowmen there a point beyond which enemy would not be permitted to pass unchallenged.

His *pefrai* twitching its ears beneath the dripping boughs of the huge oak, he watched the Hrin emerge. Their battle-unit for cavalry was much larger than a squadron, somewhere about one hundred and twenty, and three such companies came slowly into view, then part of a fourth, while behind them was a further mass of horse in no observable order. By him, men of Kargul and tribal levies, knee-to-knee, lances levelled, shifted nervously in their saddles; *cavalry*, the standard manual held, *loses four-fifths of its effect when standing in defense.* Yet all rules could be departed from; in this narrow place, with deadly bows to blunt any assault, the Hrin could surely be withstood.

Still at a distance of a third of a mile, they halted, and after a pause a smaller group, about thirty, came on, headed by four of the most gaudily decorated. Soon, they stopped, probably unaware they were now within bow-range, and two in the front rank awkwardly unfurled a large, square banner of a heavy, brocaded fabric that hung limply in the moist air. Again, a smaller detachment resumed the advance, and sensing a parley, Kamin-Tolagh moved out in front of his lances so as to signal Tau-Suaka not to begin shooting. The banner, he now saw, hung on uprights between two riders, depicted a large golden eye on a field of intense blue. The dozen Hrin riders approached to forty paces before again halting, and Kamin-Tolagh, gesturing the bearer of the Siv'loi Banner to his side, joined also by Dubovai and Niburai, walked out till he had halved that distance.

With a flourish, he thrust the point of his lance into soft soil next to the road, and caused the colors to be dipped sidelong. A leader of the Hrin, who did not carry the halberd, replied by drawing his sword, and handing it to a man behind him. With two companions, sagging banner following, he rode forward.

His loose tunic was a gaudy swirl of red, gold and blue, face under the high helm that of an old man, cheeks shrunken and deeply scored, chin altogether vanished into the slack, drooping skin of the neck. Eyes, set amid multiple creases, were red-rimmed but piercing, and with the arid, resentful mouth gave him what struck Kamin-Tolagh as the appearance of intense evil. Yet, grotesquely, something reminded him of his mother: the face of an incurable schemer, watchful and shrewd.

"In the name of the *Hrithust*, Lord Iolfrant," proclaimed in excellent Owanilú, voice thin but clear, "I greet you, Kamin-Tolagh *Asai*. I am kinsman to Iolfrant, Oyestri of Hyolenstr."

"We have heard you named. I would have wished the *Hrithust* to be here, so I could ask him for what reason his men have assailed soldiers of a friend and ally, some of them the same who defended the place where we trade together for gold, Iolfrant and I, and where, but for our help, Iolfrant would be unable to return."

"Ah. My duty, since our *hrithust* could not be here, is to offer congratulations on your victory."

Which victory, Kamin-Tolagh wondered, *or both?* "Over your own armies? Is this a Hrin custom?"

A chilly smile came. "You have met, *Asai*, only a small fragment of the armies this *onhritha* can muster. You were, I regret, mistaken for an invader, coming with so many armed men to pay a visit of courtesy. If the *Hrithust* had only been here, the mistake would have been avoided, perhaps."

"An invader? Now, when I rode out to meet you, is the first time I or any of my men have set foot on lands claimed by your *hrithust*." Oyestri's interesting mission seemed to be to put Kamin-Tolagh in the wrong, without offering any further provocation. To an extent, terms of the debate were defined by his formal, astonishingly correct use of a language which put all strong feeling at a ceremonial distance.

"The *Hrithust* Svedion is an ally, with whom our Iolfrant is one in thought."

"Then your Iolfrant would be aware his ally has harbored and given assistance to my enemies, men who have robbed, murdered and destroyed among the tribes I protect. In pursuit of these, not only murderers but traitors, we came prepared for war. No Hrin was killed until we were forced to defend ourselves against those with whom we have no quarrel."

Oyestri considered this narrowly. "You are far from your home, *Asai*, to speak of defending yourselves."

"A man sometimes has to dig deep to destroy the roots of a weed. It is not for sport we make war so far from home."

"Then your object in coming here is accomplished," suggesting news of the burnt village had reached Oyestri.

"Not so," hitting on an inspired way to test how far he had intimidated the Hrin. "The chief of my enemies, the Man-mani, Sra-Min-Talla-Tyu, a traitor as well as a murderer, may still be alive. Until I have him captive, or see his body, my task is incomplete."

"And you have heard the man is here, in Hrin lands?"

"He could be nowhere else."

"If he were found?"

"There is no *if*."

"War," sententiously, "is fickle with her favors. Your *tveyusta* has been to gain one battle — "

"If by *tveyusta* — " he mispronounced the word, and did not care — "you mean I have better men, better mounts, better weapons and better tactics, yes. War has not been fickle with me; she jilts those who fail to satisfy her needs."

"But my *hrithust* has no reason or desire to quarrel with the Empire of Kargusai." Oyestri paused on that thought, and he was improvising now, outside any instructions received. "We might help you search for this man — " short of winking he could hardly have made plainer the hunt was going to succeed. "In the meantime, as a sign of his goodwill, to compensate you for any losses you have suffered, and in hopes our friendship may be restored and strengthened, the *Hrithust* Iolfrant asks that you accept these tokens of his esteem — " Twisting in the saddle, he gestured, and the cavalry straddling the road parted to allow passage to a yoked pair of pack-animals. Dismounted, assisted by the drivers, Oyestri made proprietary gestures to expand on the good heart of his *hrithust*, while laying out on the ground a small treasury of gifts; a set of six gold drinking-cups made with the customary Hrin skill, a weighty bolt of brocaded cloth, a gold-and-silver sheath holding a fine Dakbân sword, given a dazzling hilt set with emeralds, and finally two kidskin bags filled with small, flat bars of pure gold.

Thoughts stumbled over each other. This was a haul to make his expedition hugely profitable, to silence for a year at least Fretasi's warnings as to his empire's fiscal base. Yet its lavishness was at the same time an earnest of the immense wealth Iolfrant must possess, and a gauge of his fear — or his desire to buy time to prepare himself for war.

He wished he had Iruvakh here; the key to the Hrin was religious conflict Kamin-Tolagh did not understand. He could not remember details of the turncoat way Iolfrant had made himself *hrithust*, and the part played by this Oyestri was yet more shadowy. If, with his tiny army, he could overcome the entire military capacity of Iolfrant, if only demoralized men expecting defeat lay between him and the taking of Hyolenstr, it would still be nothing but a raid if he could not discover how to rule here; this was a people too numerous and too complicated to simply subdue, and what combination of factors would cause the other *hrithuod* to ally against him was a mystery; if Iolfrant, as no doubt he would, took to his ships and evaded capture, would he find refuge elsewhere in the Hrinani? and were they enough of a people to suspend religious squabbling to combine against the foreign usurper? Or could Kamin-Tolagh win the support of Nestos and the others by proclaiming he would impose the *tveyusto-hrid-minyist*? — if that could be done without provoking a general revolt. What he needed was a Chamya, a new *hrithust* here like his new head-man for the Man-mani, someone through whom he could rule, while leaving most of their traditions intact.

Failure would not be a mere setback; if by his actions he unified the Hrin against him, if they discovered they could fight — it had been hinted, with help from Rodlakh — then they could easily crush his unpopulous empire. Far better to take his profit, and let them think the threat had gone away; in a year or two he would have larger and better armies, and an improved knowledge of his enemy.

He nodded coolly to Oyestri. "I accept the gifts of the *Hrithust* Iolfrant, and I, too, hope our friendship may be renewed."

"He then asked for permission to bring wagons for carrying off the Hrin dead and wounded. I told him he could take back the unwounded men as well." He laughed. "He did not dare ask for their weapons. We left them there, stacked in a great pile, except we took some usable arrows."

"Do they have anything equivalent to our *ramidul*, any healing skills?" Lavsila asked. The full tale of the expedition had consumed time and wine here at the former Captain's house, and the mood now was warm and confiding, as it had not been for half a year or more.

Kamin-Tolagh described what he had seen of Hrin medicine, which used herbs and draughts as well as cleansing. Actually, he had taken greater interest in the wagons, which had large spoked wheels, tall as most Hrin, made of a tough, pale wood for which there was no word in the Owanilú. Where the smaller wheels of a wagon back home would be fitted with an iron tire, heated and shrunk to the wood, these had several windings of stout cloth, but treated with some unknown substance, soft and yet springy, and on the hard road the wagons rolled smoothly, extraordinarily quiet.

Lavsila, his interest in mechanical things wakened, began to ask absurdly detailed questions, points no one could observe, but Kambanal, who had drunk least, interrupted: "Did they produce the last of Sranadatta's brood?" Deeply angered by the death and mutilation of Nizhadh, he had been strong for retribution, and disappointed not to be part of the punitive expedition; the account of the massacre at the village he heard as a regrettable but at the same time satisfying necessity.

"They did." He shuddered slightly. Past noon on that damp day Oyestri had returned with a small band of followers, bringing not two but three Man-mani, Nifra, Sra-Min-Talla-tyu, and a third man, said to be of their kin.

"Did you not question them?" Lavsila asked.

Kamin-Tolagh smiled astringently, recalling all the faces, Oyestri's ingratiating but smug and malevolent, those of the three bound prisoners streaked with blood, mouths blurred with blood.

"They had been blinded, and their tongues cut out." According to Oyestri, for defiling the holiest of places, for which this was the established Hrin penalty.

"Then it was only by chance that this ordained punishment also prevented your discovering what friendship there had been between Iolfrant and your enemies, to what extent he was behind the raids."

Kambanal said, "I would not have thought any of the Hrin I have met would have the stomach for this." His youthful face was still wrinkled with distaste.

"Such things," Lavsila loftily declared, "are merely the other side of their cowardice."

There was an apt response, but he let it go. "You have not yet met Oyestri," he told Kambanal. "He offered us food, but I said we had plenty. There were farms for plundering on my way back. I can well believe he knows poisons." His skill with that craft may have helped Iolfrant to power.

"Hanging them was a mercy," in reply to Kambanal's question as to where the captives were now. "The oak was at hand." A holy tree, perhaps; Oyestri's expression had suggested the act was a sacrilege as great as the one invented to explain disabling of the Man-mani, but he still had not spoken. At the same time, Kamin-Tolagh had hanged the guide, Cho-Matta, who was of no further use; back with his tribe, or here at the Abu, he would surely have been murdered.

"Too much mercy, Man-mani will say," Lavsila commented. "They would have spent longer dying at the hands of their own. Young Chamya will not be pleased."

"Chamya is not your concern," coldly. Lavsila was right, of course; Chamya would have been wolfishly eager to oversee a painful end for the last of his stepfather's family. "The executions were of greater service in completing humiliation of the Hrin. The men had been under their protection." He had been far from certain, also, that the men could be kept alive on the journey back, or that he could endure the disgusting, strangled noises made by tongueless men. Tau-Suaka's men were becoming more proficient; some captives executed after last year's raids had been so long dying he had eventually ordered them used for archery practice, but this batch, with care in tying and positioning of the knots, were dead as sacks in minutes.

The proper end, Kambanal sentimentally said, of Siv'loi's tale, death of the father who had acquiesced in her murder, but to Kamin-Tolagh that small Man-mani incident was remote beyond any sensation, lost in time, large events, larger political considerations. Discussion of the future, how well and how long the frantically unreal alliance with Iolfrant would hold, was filled with unknowns. He could imagine Iolfrant making overtures to *hrithuod* of the other creed, trying to persuade them the new danger to the north was something they all shared, but whether the threat was enough to overcome their religious rivalry was not predictable. Lavsila boasted his friends at Kadon Dinul would be able to inform him about any military help Rodlakh gave the Hrin.

Another year from year's turn, and Kamin-Tolagh believed he could lead out a mixed army twelve hundred strong, still leaving the tribes better able to defend themselves than they now could. Till then, he could keep up the puppet-play of friendship as well as the Hrin, and maintain his foothold at Zelu Bablakhi.

Of happenings, none catastrophic, in his absence, one in its minor way was another watershed. Kambanal asked, "Has Freighanai spoken to you about the man Sedhsilai?"

"From Yaënsilat's old squadron," Kamin-Tolagh identified. "I know the man — he was our baker."

Lavsila interposed. "He wants to marry a girl of the tribes."

"Of the Jai," Kambanal, to negate any possibility of a *jinz'onoyu*.

"To *marry* her? Why?" A few men of Kargul had paired off with tribal women, as others preferred to go from one to another, but where, so far from home, were the advantages of marriage?

"You have said," Lavsila was quick with his explanation, "a married man with his wife here can have one of the small houses for quarters."

"But that is not the reason," Kambanal, hotly. "I have talked with the man, *Asai*; living-quarters may be a part of it, but he wants to acknowledge his children, and he wants to stay with this woman."

"Should such a mingling of bloods be permitted?" Lavsila asked. "Why would any true Owani — "

"Who would marry them?" Kamin-Tolagh interrupted. "He is not thinking of a tribal marriage?" Kambanal's assessment left no room for the idea of rites binding on the girl, which the man could ignore at his convenience.

More tentatively, Kambanal said it was believed by the soldiers that Iruvakh, if authorized by Kamin-Tolagh, could perform all rites of the *Atarlum*, funerals and calendar observances as well as marriage.

"Iruvakh," Kamin-Tolagh pointed out, "ceased to be *atarlai* years ago. He was not of the *Nôdhilum* — " the Order which, in the realm, normally solemnized a marriage in religious form. "The *Atarlum*, in any case, has no standing here. None."

Lavsila opened his mouth, and closed it. Nothing could upset his foolish conviction this enterprise was in some unexplained way the final hope of Old Owan.

"You could marry them, *Asai*. As Captain of troops in the field, you are also their magistrate. That is, if the law of the realm — "

Is still binding on us, Kamin-Tolagh completed in thought, as Kambanal halted, confused. And if not, what did any of it signify? of itself, Kargusai had no laws concerning marriage, property, inheritance, legitimacy of children, only a ruling class who, though they had renounced all allegiance except to him, persisted in their delusion the law was the law, unchanged. Such paths back to the realm were proving more obstinate than the stone road he broke in autumn.

20.

On almost the last day of the year Âna bore Rodlakh a second child, a daughter, Seluvoi. Again, Morú was midwife, and she remained at Kadon Dinul so forty days later she could at last fulfill her old promise, and help in delivering a child of Dolvid's own; Aëlu gave birth to a daughter they named Ayalis. Morú, always a battleground between plain practicality and melting sentiment, said many moist-eyed things about what friends the two new girls were bound to be, looking ahead to when they would attend each other's weddings; for the *rabhsai's* daughter she had already decided on the half-brother of Ayalis as a husband, till Dolvid reminded her once again, perhaps at last convinced her, that Sedukh's father was Sebhal, who would have been Seluvoi's great-uncle. On his present tyrannical showing, he did not add, Sedukh, a robust two, was not going to be much prize for any woman.

Morú, staying with Dolvid and Aëlu in their house to the newly fashionable south side of the lower Avenue was joined by her husband, Untimarr, in Kadon for a council meeting. With him came their younger daughter, Morulis.

Even before she was invited to a feast at the New Residence, Morulis, now past sixteen, had created a furor. Dolvid remembered her only as a small child, though Âna had spoken with wonder about the arresting prettiness of the shy girl she had met, three years ago. Nothing prepared him for what Morulis had turned into; her skin had kept its troubling, smoky bloom, and the restless eyes had a startling expanse of blue-white about huge dark-velvet irises. Small-boned and slender, she moved with a weightless natural grace.

Considering himself on the way to becoming the staid and elevated person his post required, Dolvid was wonderstruck as a boy, to the proud amusement of his old friend Untimarr, teasing amusement of Aëlu, according to whom Dolvid's shuffling, throat-clearing fluster was a sad disappointment to the girl, who for years had been hearing her father brag about his friend, that magnificent dignitary, the *Bôdhrai*, and had not expected another tongue-tied goggler.   That was mildly overstated, but it remained true when she had been under his roof for two weeks, he could not take his eyes from the girl at table with them, her flawless youth and vitality not lessening in astonishment; a relief to see she had a similar effect on Rodlakh, whose singleminded devotion to Âna was a byword; twice he lost his place in conversation with staring at Morulis.

Not many were proof against her. Sett, enchanted by the girl three years ago, was caught between delight and despair; she had become a young woman, but he in his latter forties was impotent to compete for her attention with the youths who swiftly gathered.   Shumat, since his long-ago marriage, had seldom seemed to notice what a woman looked like, but was equally mixed in his feelings. "You were wise," to Dolvid, "to begin your family late. Seeing Morulis, knowing she would be more likely to play at eyes with my son, makes me feel old." He was in fact just Dolvid's age, still short of forty, but his son Shudarr was fifteen and not much below his height. Like his friend Orbanak, the *rabhsai*'s younger brother, Shudarr had so far given less attention to girls than to swords, lances, horses, the lore of campaigning.

Old Faëdhal had never spared time for the opposite sex, but it should not have surprised to hear the old scholar join the chorus; he had always loved to surround himself with rare and lovely things, and he spoke about Morulis exactly as he would some precious work of craft, greeting her with an archaic courtliness that charmed and bewildered the girl.

One voice abstaining from the general anthem of wonder was Elamirr, Dolvid's assistant. He had known Morulis from infancy; their much-intermarried families were foremost of Burantal, and familiarity may have accounted for his offhand manner.   "I would not have expected her to grow up so handsome," grudging praise for one whose arrival at Kadon Dinul was threatening to displace acknowledged Heartland beauties, and had already almost eclipsed first public appearance of the *rabhsai*'s new daughter.

For the Families to grant such recognition to a girl of Mixed descent was both a tribute to her extraordinary beauty and a sign of changing times; the undeniable success of Âna as *rabhsayu* had helped prepare the way. By the time Untimarr and Morú, respective tasks accomplished, were ready to ride for home, Morulis was being taught finer points of fashionable riding by a good-looking Household officer, the son of Kizhunai, and had mastered the intricacies of courtly dance with the help of assorted Residence Quarter girls. Âna, perceiving how discontent Morulis was with the prospect of the narrow life at Burantal, asked the parents to let her offer the girl a position never before held by one of lower birth than daughter of a provincial overlord or of a royal captain — one which Âna had hitherto managed without, Dresser to the *Rabhsayu*. Untimarr could hardly refuse.

An honorary post, without real duties, and in the event it was Âna who would dress Morulis, curbing her untutored bent towards decorative frills, and guiding her to a soft simplicity for which Morulis was adornment enough. To school a girl of her upbringing in behavior appropriate to Kadon Dinul was, as Âna knew from her own experience, a far harder task. At home, among her father's people, she would hardly question the expectation of remaining unbedded till she found a husband, and so far that remained her assumption. Still, she was beginning to acquire flirtatious ways of the Residence Quarter, where virginity had no market value, and was an oddity rather than a virtue. Gently, Âna tried to make the girl see she could not belong simultaneously to both worlds.

"Even here at Kadon, there are women who keep to ways we learned were proper as children."

"Aren't they right ways, madam?" They were alone in Âna's dressing-room, where Morulis, bare-armed in her shift, had been trying to make her hair coil beside her cheek as Âna's did.

"That is beyond my wisdom," with a smile. "But I can say, among young men of Family, you will be called tease, or worse names, if your manner leads them to expect what your training tells you to withhold." A winding way to say it, but she could not be plainer without shocking the girl.

As, nevertheless, she had. "Are you telling me, madam, here I have to bed with a man because he asks me to?" On evidence, the question must already have come up. Disconcerted, flushed, the girl was so exquisite, Âna herself, with no idea of acting on it, not for the first time imagined it would be delicious to lie down naked with her, and exchange caresses. In this thought, there was more admiration than outright possessive desire; the same, she supposed, might be true for some of the men who, with a greater element of intent, longed after Morulis. *Dolvid*? she wondered, but detested the notion.

"I am not telling you to bed with a man, or to refuse a man — you will have to decide that for yourself — "

"Madam, I could never — "

"Yes, I said the same. You could never change — but if, after all, you do, remember, it will not be because Kadon Dinul is learning your ways."

Understandably, Morulis was more bewildered than before. Âna tried again. "I am telling you, you must be what your banner proclaims. Here at Kadon Dinul, too, there are promises expected to be kept."

"But in Burantal — "

"Not trothplight." She was starting to remind herself of some garrulous and opinionated old lady. "A woman can give undertakings with her eyes, with the turn of a shoulder, by agreeing to meet in a private place — you have to learn not to make such promises, or else to live up to them, you understand me?"

"I think so, madam."

"Our older ways are not comprehended, here, but they are usually respected," going went doggedly on. "You will be censured only if seen as inviting what you do not mean to grant. But if you do choose the Residence Quarter and its ways, do not forget, for many here an afternoon together on a bed is just an agreeable diversion, and does not mean a feathersweight more for the future than the same time spent riding together, or bowling at the arch."

"I don't — it could never be like that for me, madam."

Âna nodded agreement. "Yet it is tempting, sometimes, to dream about being — being another Kamin-Tarú."

"Kamin — ?"

"Kamin-Tarú, a lady of Kargul, who loves the sport for its own sake, and must have given great joy, to others, as well as to herself." A resigned mouth. "But that dream is a snare, for women brought up as I was, and as you were. We cannot keep the proper lightheartedness, and end up becoming attached to the wrong men."

"To bad men, madam? My mother — "

"Not bad men, no. If I proclaim I am looking for an hour's pleasure, and a man takes me at my word, he does not become evil for going on to other diversions, even if I misjudged my own desires. Often, a painful lesson, but he cannot be blamed. No, the wrong men we become attached to are the good men we cannot have, who have not said they would be ours." This, predictably, was so much *jinzalú* to Morulis, with incomprehension here compounded by disbelief of what she thought she did understand; not thinkable the *rabhsayu*, mother of the *rabhsai's* children, could be speaking from actual experience.

Odd how preparations, always half-hearted, for a strike across Landegh, a swift settling of the Kamin-Tolagh question, interrupted by overinflated panic at the sudden irruption of *jinzal* to the north of Kamsilat, had never really resumed; odder no one at Kadon Dinul had seriously tried to revive them. The subject inexplicably had gone off the boil, and Dolvid guessed they were all, in one way or another, relieved. Rodlakh, for his own stubborn reasons, remained opposed to outlawry for Kamin-Tolagh. Late last year, Tovakh, on his way north for the hunting, had proposed special convening of the Council to consider the case, and when Dolvid heard details of Kamin-Tolagh's second incursion into his home province, knew Tovakh would return to Kadon Dinul angrier than ever, not least for being unable to articulate what must be his bitterest complaint, his son's theft of blood-stock Kargul was not entitled to possess.
Elamirr's eagerness to espouse any measure designed to strike at hereditary privilege paradoxically made him Tovakh's ally, and he was bold enough to differ openly with Dolvid, who had practical, political reasons for the support he would in any case have given Rodlakh. As he tried to explain to Elamirr, it was not in the interests of Kadon Dinul to let Kamin-Tolagh's offenses as son, as Heir in Kargul, take precedence over his faithlessness as Captain of Household; this would be true if Kamin-Tolagh came from another province, but was vitally important in dealing with Kargul, which had all too often behaved like a separate realm, not subject to *Rabhsai's* Law.

Âna had proposed, and the *rabhsai* meant to promulgate, a guaranteed right of appeal, anywhere in the realm, to a royal magistrate in cases involving property rights, and there were to be created four new magistracies-at-large, without permanent seat, free to travel the entire realm to hear such appeals. Tovakh had the strongest reason for resisting this innovation; in the Kovilanu, once again easternmost region of Kargul, there had been a number of seizures favoring families of Owani blood, newly returned to ancestral lands. In seeking compensation, those they displaced could at present take their pleas only to provincial magistrates, allied, sometimes by blood, always by interest, to the dispossessors. Elamirr chose to be obtuse about connection between the two subjects, and Dolvid, not willing flatly to order him to drop his support for the outlawry patiently explained the magistrates-at-large would have, at need, backing of the General Cavalry, both to protect their persons and to see their decisions enforced, but infinitely preferable was if the sovereign power of *rabhsayum* were simply accepted fact — far less achievable with a province able to dictate to the *rabhsai* what was to be debated in Council. Elamirr was persuaded, and yet with him there was always detectable a lingering reservation, as if he half-believed Dolvid invented elaborate arguments to camouflage a covert partiality for his own race. An Owani such as Dolvid, with a commitment to justice, could never quite eradicate guilt over past (and lingering) unfairness, and yet he was not going to parade his credentials for Elamirr, something he felt no need for with Untimarr, or the Captain of Armies — or the *rabhsai*, nor his *rabhsayu*, not since they had attained understanding.

Though annoyed, Tovakh was turned back in his demand for a special convening of the Council, and had to be satisfied with giving growled notice he would bring up the outlawry again at the next regular meeting. In the meantime, by way of Hrin traders, came a puzzling, surely garbled account of Kamin-Tolagh's incursion into the lands of the *Hrithust* Iolfrant, which, while it sounded like an act of war, had apparently ended in a lavish exchange of gifts and compliments. The bearer of the tale was of a different following, and giving a third hand account; the only real certainty was that Kamin-Tolagh, as forecast, was turning his attention to the rich southward lands. Any defensive cooperation with the Hrin, however, remained as elusive as they were; from the *Hrithust* Iolfrant down, Dolvid could obtain agreement on the wisdom of alliance, but concrete proposals for training of his armies, the loan of young officers, were courteously received, and made nothing happen.

The nightmare was a conquest by Kargusai of a part, at least, of this gifted but strange and divided people, Kamin-

Tolagh's captaincy on land given wings by Hrin seamanship. But to share these worries with Shumat risked his annoyance, as if Dolvid was accusing him of inadequate forethought. The truth was, Shumat longed for action, and was surer than ever he had not been meant for administrative duties. In the Northeast, he'd had to maintain an army and its auxiliaries at strength, and often enough act as a chief magistrate for the entire region, but he was also never far from field service, taking personal command when there was a threat to the port or its lines of communication; since returning to Kadon Dinul from the West he'd had no reason to own a lance, and kept his sword sharpened, as he said himself, only to prevent rust. A recurrent paradox of a professional army, Dolvid told him, not very consolingly; those whose special aptitude for war brought them distinction were elevated to where they seldom if ever fought; not even high birth had saved Saidhan from the duller consequences of his youthful heroism.

Kept in the Colony by fragile health, Saidhan had met only one of his great-grandchildren, and seen his final grandchild, Sedukh. only as a small baby. When warmer days made the Arnan crossing reasonable, Dolvid and Aëlu journeyed to Kamsilat, so at a sturdy two-and-a-half Sedukh saw for the first time with wondering eyes the great forest of Kamsilat, in the Colony he would someday inherit.

Saidhan came to quayside to welcome his guests; he still sat erect, but, in concession to advancing age, on an ordinary saddle-horse, no longer a *pefrai*. He was jocose and expansive on the short ride, and with something near defiance walked without assistance up the steps of the Great House, where Doleni waited, dividing herself between gracious words for visitors and tense concern for her husband. At dinner, Saidhan spoke with great force and cogency about past years, and affairs in general, but lost the thread in specific discussion about recent events. These lapses were as distressing to Aëlu, who had spent years under this roof with Saidhan's kindness, as for Dolvid, whose happy personal recollections interwove with his sense of Saidhan as a warrior whose feats would remain a part of history.

But for him there were other anxieties, about the state of the Colony and the Army of the West, a force which for sixty years had owed its excellence to the efforts of Saidhan and his late son. Wanildhai, its present captain, was an outstanding commander in the field, but no maker of policy, and he, too, was aging. Over a year ago, Dolvid had spoken about the effect of losses in the war, and the cycle of retirement, and now he was afraid cheap victory over a dozen *jinzal*, together with relative quiet on Landegh, were engendering both complacency and a decline in standards. Ironic to contemplate they owed much of that calm, the rarity of tribal raiders, to the same fact that made vigilance so necessary, Kamin-Tolagh's conquests in the Farther West. Shumat, he decided, must visit the Frontier to make a professional assessment; Doleni was a lioness, pouncing on the smallest inadvertent suggestion her husband's powers were failing, and the same touching but unnerving loyalty was encountered when Dolvid tried to ascertain from an officer or a magistrate any details about the Colony's true condition.

He failed, too, in a sustained attempt to bring change to the paper mills on South Shore across the Navu Estuary. Export of paper had long been a mainstay of Colony trade, but during his exile Dolvid had seen the results of a new process, using bleached raw flax and scrap linen, which produced, with much less milling, a paper superior in every way to the wood-pulp method, stronger, whiter, more uniform in thinness. From the small mill in southern Paowan, he had brought samples to show the Kamsilat papermakers, hoping to persuade them they were going to lose their business unless they could match this better paper, which reduced production time would also make cheaper. Impressed, envious, they gave the chill courtesy of a polite hearing, convinced it would be lunacy to begin importing the needed raw materials, here where the supply of scrap wood was inexhaustible.

Apart from renewing of friendships, the sole accomplishment of the visit had to do with trees. To advance his plans, with Konir, for establishment of new forests east of Arnan — as also Aëlu's more modest intention of restoring and enhancing the sadly dilapidated Gardens of Kamzhinu — he obtained promise of large numbers of various seedlings to be shipped across to Owan Sai, roots bagged in moist humus. Some thousands of trees would eventually be needed, and Dolvid's offer to pay workers out of his own pocket was courteously but firmly turned aside by Saidhan.

At the end of their twelve-day stay, Dolvid could not shake off the notion he could be seeing Saidhan for the last time.

The old campaigner may have shared the feeling; he did not come down to quayside, but said farewell in the main hall of the Great House, hugging his grandson and then, with unwonted fervor, his former daughter-in-law. Despite malformed fingers, his grip, when he took Dolvid's hand, was still strong. "We have lived through brave times, been touched by remarkable lords and ladies, have we not, Master?"   His eyes glittered, thoughts perhaps with long-dead Laluvoi.

After a calm Arnan crossing, the storm broke at Kadon Dinul. Dolvid was greeted at the Bronze Residence by Arvat, who, despite their long acquaintance, nowadays tended to belong in Elamirr's camp. He scarcely waited for conventional news about his former employer, Saidhan, before giving account of the incident which came to be known as the Battle of the Arcades.

Bathrâd, a town just over a dayride east and south of Kadon Dinul was celebrated for the nearby dye-works, the drying lines on a clear day a vivid splash of colors visible for miles, and for an extensive covered market, the Arcades, where foodstuffs, furnishings, useful goods and frivolous trifles of every description could be bought or bartered for.   For travellers, virtually a mandatory stopping-place, and for the well-off a favorite amusement, an overnight visit from Kadon Dinul, a day's excursion from the easterly Arbhu Hills.

On a day warm enough for a foretaste of midsummer, men from armed followings of two large landowners came to Bathrâd. Though often with money to spend, those men were not welcome, making a habit of walking four abreast in the streets and between stalls of the market, sometimes shouldering townspeople roughly aside, full of loud talk and threatening laughter. Especially near evening, they were carefully avoided by women except those for hire, who sought them out; traders without muscular assistants for safety closed shop early.

On this occasion, men of the two followings quarrelled — over a pair of gauntlets, according to Arvat's account, though there were other versions. With tempers short, the disagreement soon came to blows and then to weapons; each side was reinforced, and it swiftly became a pitched battle, in which five armed retainers were killed, and many others wounded. Worse, a stallkeeper, after being accidentally stabbed, was trampled to death, and a dozen other bystanders injured, some with bones broken. The damage to property, which must be extensive, had not yet been fully assessed. "The *rabhsai*," Arvat concluded, "is furious."

Riding at once to the New Residence, Dolvid found Rodlakh closeted with Elamirr in the Private Audience Chamber, a scribe in attendance. Again, courtesies were perfunctory, and the *rabhsai* was indeed angry as Dolvid had known him. A proclamation was already drafted ordering the disbanding of all private armed followings in excess of twenty men.

This number was plainly impractical for some of the large landowners, who had a legitimate need for personal bodyguards, and had to control poaching and theft over large acreage. Many big holdings included what were in effect small hamlets, where various crimes had to be prevented, while the General Cavalry did not have the resources to offer escort for every shipment of high-value goods, as Shumat's concern with banditry demonstrated. Nonetheless, in Rodlakh's mood, tact would be needed, while Elamirr was obviously running with the bit between his teeth.

Dolvid said, "Has Fornival looked this over?" As law-consultant, his advice would be needed.

"Not yet. I was just about to send for him." Obviously untrue, and as he summoned and dispatched a servant, Dolvid was caught between amusement, and regret the *rabhsai*, after all, was human too, willing to lie about a careless oversight.

"Shumat? Has he been alerted?"

"I am not sure he is at Kadon. There will be time for that," compressing his lips testily.

"I think, *Deghi*, he should be in on this from the first. To enforce this, or any similar measure, troops are going to be needed."

"Troops?" Elamirr enquired. "You think there are landowners, Master, brave enough to defy a royal proclamation?""

Dolvid half-smiled. "I think a law would hardly be made unless someone, somewhere, was expected to defy it." To Rodlakh he observed the General Cavalry was spread thin as was, and Shumat would need time to assemble a good-sized force. After a grim nod from the *rabhsai*, another servant was sent to find out if Shumat was available.

A pause in the headlong rush had been attained, but looking at impatient faces, Dolvid was tempted simply to travel with the current, so great was the passion for sweeping remedies. Reasonable objections were only going to be fuel for Rodlakh's fury. With some intuition for Dolvid's feelings, indeed, he began answering objections not yet made.

"We have spoken often enough about the need to curb these bands of bullies. Bathrâd, or something like it, was bound to happen, with so many untrained men under arms. Time, past time, for strong action."

"But it seems to me — " reading over what was written down — "A date has to be decided. We cannot just say *forthwith*, as here. Fifteen days ought to be enough."

"Too long, some might say, Master," Elamirr said, and there was a sidelong glance for the *rabhsai*. Sarcely imaginable his apprentice would have the presumption to speak with Rodlakh about his, Dolvid's, supposed tendency to coddle the Families.

"We are the ones who need time. Shumat is going to have to collect at least ten squadrons, just when he is parcelling out his best for dealing with highway security — ten good squadrons, with a reliable officer. General Cavalry, not Household; this is not going to be seen as a private war of *rabhsai* against Families."

"Ten squadrons?" Rodlakh exclaimed. "*Ten*?"

"*Deghi*, we have to give an immediate demonstration of our resolve, by moving against one of those with a large armed following — Zhival, I would say; his men were half of the Bathrâd affair. We have to proceed with a force so overwhelming there can be no thought of resistance, and be ready to arrest Zhival himself, if he fails to comply."

Uncomplicated anger at last became shadowed with thought; Zhival, influential in his own right as a major landowner and grower of wheat, was also related by marriage to Vinilat, *Nim'* of Dramal, hence to the remainder of the Great Families.

The law-learned Fornival arrived, lean-jawed, somewhat stiff of manner, serious, though with an unexpected touch of bone-dry humor kept in an inside pocket. He was at the moment short of breath, and movements of his tongue behind closed lips suggested he had been interrupted at table. Bending over the draft document, he was soon shaking his head.

"What?" Rodlakh demanded.

Straightening, Fornival brushed unseen crumbs from his front. "This, *Deghi*, if you will pardon me, cannot be a simple proclamation. As law of the realm, it would certainly need consideration in Council."

"In Council!" Elamirr, with a riper contempt than was judicious.

Fornival studied the younger man. "The right of landowners to maintain armed followings, with certain restrictions only, as to weapons and body-armor, was affirmed by the Council of Thirteen in the reign of Dromladh — year Four Dromladh, if I am not mistaken. At that time, Kadon Dinul's desire was to encourage the practice, armies of the realm being inadequate to deal with the widespread banditry there was."

A law made in Council could only be unmade there. Elamirr gestured impatiently. "Why quibble? The realm has the forces to make law, and the Council can approve it at its next meeting."

Fornival was scandalized, Rodlakh astonished, but suddenly Dolvid was the angry one.

"Up to, and including, the reign of Kanavakh the Bloody," turning icily on Elamirr, "the powers of *rabhsayum*, though defined in the Treaty of the Wind Caves, were in practice more closely akin to those of ancient rulers, whose passing whims were law. When Army, Great Families and the *Atarlum* combined to depose Kanavakh, the realm having endured enough from his cruelties, they obliged his son Plakhval to subscribe his name to an agreement, before he could succeed. That agreement, the basis of an effective Council, was reaffirmed by each of the Gabh'Owan rulers, till the line became extinct, and after them, by Great Banak, when he took Sword."

"As by each of his successors," Rodlakh interposed.

"Exactly," Fornival agreed, but Rodlakh waved Dolvid to go on.

"None of us necessarily supposes the Council of Thirteen to be best possible body for making law. But if there is to be a change, it is the stated wish of the *rabhsai* to rule with the concurrence of more, not fewer voices." His tone was becoming gentler, as he summed up the lesson: "To override established law, no matter how worthy the objective, is to provide a precedent for future excesses."

Elamirr, who had been startled by Dolvid's force, faltered. "I meant only, where a measure is so obviously for the good of the realm — "

"If *rabhsayum* is not law," Rodlakh, but glumly, "it is nothing."

Dolvid, meanwhile, had picked up the draft. "With appropriate modifications in language," he said to Fornival, "how would this do as a provincial proclamation?"

He considered. "So long as it is clear there is no abrogation of the legal right to maintain such forces."

"We shall reaffirm it."

"What is this?" Rodlakh demanded.

"Of these private armies, most, by far, are here in the Paowan."

Fornival had reached his decision. "Yes. As a provincial proclamation, it will just about do — provided the regulation is seen as desirable by Orbanak *Asai*."

This was one of his mild jokes. Until Rodlakh's eldest son reached sixteen, Orbanak remained titular surrogate-Heir, and therefore, by tradition, *Nim'* of the Paowan, but he had taken no active part — or interest — in administration of the Heartland province.

"That is the way, then," Rodlakh said.

Having covered so much tricky ground, Dolvid came to where the bitterest arguments were going to be. "But twenty is obviously too few." Though both Elamirr and Rodlakh had their mouths open for retorts, he pressed on. "Many armed retainers spend part of their time doing farm work; the landowners will merely disguise their armies as laborers."

"No they will not," hotly, but Rodlakh quickly changed to grudging debate. "Or, if they do, it would be true no matter what number we set."

"A number that is reasonable can prevent a law openly derided. Besides, if complied with, a law reducing followings to a maximum of twenty would mean letting loose on the realm eleven to twelve hundred men, well armed but without employment — including survivors of the famous Special Forces Bolan raised to bully farmers." He did not mind it being seen he was proud of having these figures at his fingertips; following the earlier, tentative discussion of this same topic, he had worked hard to obtain close estimates of the strength each of the private armies could boast.

"Obviously, we cannot imprison or forcibly restrain a thousand men with no crimes committed, and most of them are not readily going to get other work — we have farm workers of greater experience unemployed as it is. It is no gain, to break up private armies so as to create larger and better-skilled bands of robbers."

"What is your figure, then?" Rodlakh asked.

"One hundred — " ignoring Elamirr's protesting noise, to add, "But the proclamation must make it unlawful for more than twenty armed men to ride together in a company."

A kind of calculating pause, Elamirr waiting to take his lead from the *rabhsai*, whose willingness to listen, a quality always admired, was gaining ascendancy over the urgency of outrage. "A law with some chance of being enforced is preferable by far; flouted laws are worse than none. But if, after Bathrâd, I tell them they can have one hundred bullies apiece — "

"That figure would unemploy some two hundred-odd." Of them, Dolvid thought, he could immediately draft almost half into the tree-planting scheme, which would begin in a remote tract of the province, far from large towns or busy roads, and with little temptation for them to desert and turn outlaw.

There came a strange interlude of dickering, like being at the Arcades, bargaining for a length of dyed cloth. Elamirr advanced reluctantly from twenty to twenty-five, Dolvid yielded to eighty, and Rodlakh at last settled on sixty as a feasible compromise. Newly-unemployed would then probably total slightly over three hundred, and Aëlu's restoration of the Gardens of Kamzhinu might be the beneficiary.

Elamirr said, "Captain Shumat, then, must begin quietly collecting the forces he may need."

"Quietly?" Dolvid said. "He is going to do it as noisily as he can, so every magnate of the province sees we mean business. When this proclamation is read," he told Rodlakh, "we shall hear other noises from the Residence Quarter — the Old Blood has again been singled out, and so forth."

"I know — " Rodlakh suddenly laughed. "We can call it Dolvid's Law, let them blame one of their own."

"That is no novelty." Relief the bond with Rodlakh had held was bringing him near tears. "*Rabhsai*, I am already the guild-smasher; can't Orbanak take the blame this time?"

Fornival's head came up. "These troops," drily. "To maintain this as a purely provincial matter, there must be a formal request for troops from Orbanak *Asai* as overlord of the

Paowan, which you, *Deghi*, must grant in writing." The Paowan had no provincial cavalry.

Shumat had just come in, tucking gauntlets under his arm, riding boots muddy. "Troops for what?"

Two days before effective date of the proclamation, when defiant noises were rumbling to a climax, Arvat arrived at the Bronze Residence with definite word the private armies were going to amalgamate and march on Kadon Dinul. Certain Shumat would have forces so placed as to make this suicidal demonstration unthinkable, Dolvid merely smiled, and in the end there was surprisingly little trouble from the magnates. Zhival, waking to two hundred first-class cavalry camped on his lands, gave in at once, reducing his forces to the prescribed number, and offering to help identify those responsible for starting the trouble at Bathrâd. With his help, fourteen were convicted, and exiled to the Island.

Other landowners quickly followed Zhival in disbanding their armies. No more than a handful were added to the workless at Kadon Dinul, some of the men, as forecast, becoming farm-hands without changing masters, while Shumat took the better soldiers to fill gaps in General Cavalry squadrons. With Konir, Dolvid recruited sixty for tree-planting, forbade them to carry weapons of any kind, and dressed them in new tunics at his own expense, green, but a paler shade than the robes of the *Edhrodilum*. They were set to work at once at his wife's project, clearing the Gardens of Kamzhinu and preparing them for replantings, and were jocularly named Aëlu's Frogs.

It was Âna who insisted the Bathrâd affair was not over while the question of compensation remained. She did not oppose a grant to the victims of money from the privy purse, but was adamant those who employed the rioters should pay for the damage they had caused.

"There is, or formerly was, such a law," Dolvid recollected, but when he consulted with Fornival learned the measure dated from a time when most servants were virtually the property of their employers; Fornival gave an opinion that as things were the law was applicable only to indentured craft apprentices.

Still Âna did not let it drop, making the point liability for compensation would give employers a stake in keeping their servants honest and sober, and preventing expensive incidents. She gave formal notice she would introduce a proposal in Council.

Midsummer, next meeting of the Council, this year's Great Pledging at Nîvu Din, Laënakh's seat, were still weeks away, but foreseeing a battle over Âna's law, Dolvid began his campaign early. The *Atarlum* vote was pivotal, and a timely concession was wafted in the direction of the Patriarch by persuading Rodlakh to withdraw from dispute over a piece of land claimed by both *Mankh'* and *rabhsayum*; it was a scrubby patch west of the Tan Lughsai road, hardly worth the time and breath already expended in debate over title. The provincial overlords were another question, and while he'd had success in the past dividing Daënakh of Ân, hence his brother, Laënakh of Nîv, from Tovakh and his habitual ally, Vinilat of Dramal, he was afraid he would use up all his influence opposing the outlawry of Kamin-Tolagh, if Tovakh was unchanged in his determination to introduce it.

Trying, with his covert informant, to get an indication of the present mood at Inilun Barabhi, he received instead news which would not become general till midsummer, not a happening to shake the realm, but Rodlakh would be interested.

"Kamin-Tarú is betrothed." It was a fine spring afternoon, as he sat with Âna and Rodlakh in the sun-filled Chamber of the Great Window.

"Betrothed to whom?" Rodlakh, a shade too sharply; Âna's eyes slid aside, and she made a little mouth. Apart from her, Kamin-Tarú was the only woman her husband had bedded, and had been first.

"The man is Taërinat." Âna's turn to be puzzled.

"Of Ninkufu," Rodlakh filled in. "Or at least his mother is; he is nephew on that side to Laënakh of Nîv. I have ridden with him."

"Then he would be Daënakh's nephew, too."

"No, not so," Dolvid corrected. "He is nephew in blood to Laënakh's wife, Tonilu; on his father's side, pure Island; his father, Yoraënai, has vineyards, and supplies grapes to the Patriarch's winemakers. Taërinat studied with the *Edhrodilum*, and is considered an authority on vines. That is the ostensible reason he was invited to Kargul; there has been concern over declining yields in Peframi Gorge."

"Ostensible?" Âna, instantly.

"Well, clearly Petakoi would choose an Island husband for Kamin-Tarú, one with close *Mankh'* connections. I am told she spent time riding with Taërinat, when she was banished to the Island last year."

"But her mother could not force Kamin-Tarú to take a man she did not want." Rodlakh's protest was again a little strong for Âna's taste. "I have heard nothing against the man, but he must be older by a dozen years." Suddenly conscious of his wife's cool gaze, he worked hard to achieve detachment. "He was pleasant enough when I knew him, not accomplished, though he plays a sound, careful game of *zhabhu*. No shortage of money in the family, though that would mean nothing in this case."

But the main point was, if Kamin-Tolagh were to be outlawed, and therefore banned from the succession, Taërinat, considering Kamin-Tarú's lack of interest in policies or governance, would be, effectively, Heir in Kargul.

Âna, dubiously, "But Kamin-Tarú is, what? past twenty, now — "

"Twenty-two in autumn."

"As the *rabhsai* says, she cannot be made to marry. She may be in love with the man."

"That, Madam — " picking up her faintly mocking formality — "is always possible, but she has hardly known him long enough. When you consider her ways — "

"Understood." Rodlakh looked to be in the dark, here, but Âna did take Dolvid's point; against expectation, Kamin-Tarú just might choose a husband for that reason, but with her experience would hardly do so on the basis of one or two satisfactory beddings.

"Then you think this is Petakoi's newest strategy?" Rodlakh said. "For what, beyond Taërinat's Island connections?"

"Kamin-Tolagh once told me his mother would betroth his sister to a *jinzai*, if it suited her purpose." Two years ago, he would have shared the joke; Kamin-Tolagh had said it on hearing

Petakoi had asked if Rodlakh might marry Kamin-Tarú. Hard now to tell whether the *rabhsai* might not take offense.

At home, Aëlu said, "Poor Tú. A dull man, or his letters are — he wrote to me, once or twice, with some questions about beekeeping, and never used one word where five would do. Perhaps there is more to him; he is said to be good-tempered. She must have given up hoping for her brother's return. He will be angry, won't he? when he hears." By contrast with many women, Aëlu liked Kamin-Tarú, and had been unmoved by Kamin-Tolagh's charm.

"He will be angry," still unsatisfied. The whole affair had an odd flavor, but perhaps he, with Rodlakh, found a married Kamin-Tarú outside imagining.

21.

Kamin-Tarú's high laugh was restrained by an attempt at self-reproach; Taërinat had been kind to her, devoted in his way, she did not dislike him, nor wish him any harm. Though he had numbed her with a boredom she labored to conceal, she supposed there were some who found him entertaining; he was vigorously, industriously boring on a bed, but most women would not know that, and settle gratefully for his persistence; with wine-growing, honeybees, and Early Island literature, he had broader interests than most of his class, was an accomplished rider, a passable dancer, tall, considered handsome, not without a self-deprecating charm.

The last three points had been indispensable; with her mother suspicious about all she did, Taërinat had to be plausible as a prospective husband. In the event, she was deceived with astonishing ease; Petakoi was charmed by Taërinat, and his Island connections were her blind-spot; if he was very nearly everything Petakoi would have wanted, why should Kamin-Tarú not be ready to marry him?

Preoccupied with the questionable loyalty of his soldiery, Tovakh did not need any fooling; he would never have pretended to understand what made a woman want a particular man, and was glad to take his wife's word the match was suitable, even if Taërinat was not exactly of the Great Families.

As pure comedy, the plan had deserved success. Late last year, after Kamin-Tarú had been unable to keep the tryst at his hunting-lodge, her brother had reached her with a long letter, describing the meeting with their mother, of which she had heard only Petakoi's entirely different account, and recommending she acquiesce quite soon in Petakoi's wish to see her betrothed. By these means, he explained, if it meant going as far as marriage, she would be able to remove herself from Inilun Barabhi and the vigilance of their parents. A man, Kamin-Tolagh suggested, whose home was in Ninkufu was preferable. There, it would be relatively simple to come and fetch her, and with all the highborn Owanil who made their home in that southern enclave, one who was fascinated by her, and the chance of marrying into the ruling house of Kargul, should not be too hard to find.

The letter had taken a month to reach Kamin-Tarú, excellent time considering its tortuous route: by two different vessels, with a brief pause at a Hrin port unknown to Kamin-Tolagh, it had reached Thenimala, and from there gone north and then east to the apple-growing country of Ninkufu, where an uncle to the war-damaged officer, Pivrekhan made and sold cyder. Under a new cover in the uncle's hand, it had come to Pivrekhan at Inilun, and to Kamin-Tarú by way of his sometime bed-friend, her personal maid, Antiyu.

Setting out by the same route reversed, her swift reply told Kamin-Tolagh the suitor he prescribed was already found; on the Island she had endured rather than welcomed the overtures of Taërinat, had ridden, dined, and, a few times, bedded with him, and been willing, as with many predecessors, to decline his proposals casually. Till now, when she learned the true value of his family's wide estates in western Ninkufu.

Visibly from the Man-mani village, Iruvakh's winter wheat had been living up to his improbable forecast and sprouting a second time when Kamin-Tolagh heard from his sister. She was confident Taërinat would renew his quest for her hand. The betrothal, as was a near-tradition, would be made public at midsummer, and in the weeks before that announcement she would find refuge from the erratic weather of a spring in Inilun Barabhi, staying with Taërinat at a lodge on his mother's dowry-lands. The place could not be better; while the coasts of the Ninkufu peninsula were often rocky or cliffbound, there, a half-day west of Thenimala, low green hills shelved to a broad white shore, where one of the curious Hrin vessels could easily be beached, with small chance of detection by any patrol. Particularly when Kamin-Tarú would have her escort commanded by Pivrekhan, overlooked because of his disability in Tovakh's steady weeding-out of squadron officers who had shared glory with Kamin-Tolagh in the Jinzai War. Spread thin as presumably reliable commanders were, Tovakh would happily spare one unfit for full duty.

When this message came, time was already growing short, but Kamin-Tolagh had had the foresight to pay a Hrin vessel with its crew to remain at Larghamit. Since last year's ransom, Iolfrant had strained to keep up cordial relations, but this ship was one from the following of *Hrithust* Nestos, whose anxiety to gain favor with the Empire of Kargusai was certainly not diminished by the humiliation of Iolfrant.

On a cool, breezy morning he was reunited with his sister, their mounts coming together on the coarse, tufted grass of a knoll by the sea. As they parted from their kiss he felt a quick sensation near panic; Kamin-Tarú was a stranger, a beautiful woman he had never met. Leaning, she looped her hands again behind his neck. "Tam. Oh, Tam."

It was Tú. She was more womanly in ways he could not reliably define, face leaner with a firmer outline, but when she tried to chide herself for making fun of Taërinat, the glints of childlike glee in her eyes were just as he remembered, and so was the laugh, far higher than her speaking voice.

From the seaward side, Tau-Suaka and a file of his men, proud in their new tunics with blue-and-silver facings, were watchful and impassive, and Kamin-Tolagh called to the leader, "This is my sister, our lady Kamin-Tarú, and all oaths sworn to me are equally hers to hold; her life is precious to me beyond my own." Tau-Suaka squared his shoulders, and gave the salute he had learnt with the Army of the West.

On recognizing her brother, Tú had raced ahead of the main riding, and now the rest of the escort came up, led by Pivrekhan, riding awkwardly beside Antiyu, Kamin-Tarú's maid. Both would embark with Kamin-Tarú. The man's devotion could hardly be refused, though Kamin-Tolagh had no idea what to do with him; he had never evinced a temperament for high command, and no longer had the body for hard service, but was bringing with him at least five men of the escort who had declared their intention of joining Kamin-Tolagh in the West. Behind was a plodding train of four pack-ponies, loaded with bags and bundles; Tú's announced plans, a long stay here with Taërinat, and then straight to Nîvu Din for the Great Pledging, had given her an excuse for bringing many favorite clothes and other belongings. "Most are still baled as I brought them from

Inilun. Poor Taërinat — " she stifled a new giggle. "He just stood with his mouth open as the men carried out the bundles. What could he do, once he understood Pivrekhan's men were under my orders? which would not have been his."

"He said nothing?"

"Nothing I can think of."

Pivrekhan remembered better. "*Asai*, I thought it best to assure him we were not robbers, we were taking nothing that was his. He said, `Nothing, except my life.'"

Kamin-Tarú bit her lower lip, and Kamin-Tolagh believed his desire for her was like nothing else in his life; he had habitually thought of his pleasures with other women as perishable imitations of love with Kamin-Tarú, and saw now that was wrong, *other women* was wrong; she was not, like *women*, to be reduced to a list of desirable traits; she was himself, present in every part of him.

"I told him there had not been any change; this was the plan from the first, I would never have been his wife. I meant to tell him, he was not losing anything he had ever really possessed." She was distressed his bitterness had only been increased, but to achieve this reunion she would have done much worse than make a fool of Taërinat. "I truly hope he finds a wife to his liking," but she could not prevent another giggle. She was sometimes passingly ashamed of things she did, but never for an instant wished to be anyone but who she was.

It was here now, and she was very glad, but in the dream of being with her brother she had not dwelt on details of daily life; already, before she embarked for the West, she was being assailed by unfamiliarity, busy, taciturn ship's crew, her brother's unamused relish for the abject devotion of Tau-Suaka and his following, not a personal guard she would have chosen, coarse and callous men. Kamin-Tolagh, to be just, had warned her his empire was only at the beginning of any polished life, and it had not seemed to matter, if they could be together. It did not, and they would be. Dismounted, they linked hands to board the waiting vessel.

The Abu, approached from the west, had become an odd sight; a city wall was rising, with the start of towers and a gateway, but a wall with no city behind it. The work, Kamin-Tolagh explained, had been begun by the half-skilled, but was now in the hands of Hrin masons, paid with gold taken from the Hrin. An obvious improvement to defensibility, but one the *jinzai*-breeders, in all their generations here, had never attempted.

As at Larghamit, he was disappointed by her silence: that she was here beside him was still a joy, and yet he was being denied a pleasure he had anticipated from the start. He had been certain his accomplishments would fill her with wonder, but tales of stunningly successful campaigns were for her a baffling journey through unimaginable landscapes; she was momentarily impressed by the gold, but otherwise could not understand what it was to ride on into unmapped country, food dwindling, kept moving forward only by a belief in self. What appeared chiefly to strike her was the emptiness; she asked about cities and all he could tell her was the sun reflecting from golden roofs of a rumored Hyolenstr, while at Larghamit and here at the Abu the rebuilding he had begun, improvements made, would be visible only to those who had been here from the beginning.

"The *jinzal*, are they all gone?"

"One is born, from time to time," lightly. "Any *jinzai* son is killed in infancy." He would tell her more, but not about the son he had fathered (her short-lived nephew), nor the end of Imyë. Someday, perhaps, not now. Not the first detail omitted from his tales, and that, too, was part of his faint dissatisfaction, though nothing he could blame on Tú. With his latest successful campaign, he said only the Hrin had delivered, besides their rich gifts, the last of his Man-mani enemies, nothing about the earlier annihilation of the village. He remembered her favorite old tale, where, in their young days, she had most loved to imagine them as hero and heroine, fabled history from the dim past, the years of Hruval, long before the First Empire began. Hruval's younger brother and chief captain, Yubhsilai, having captured a great Owani chieftain of the Aëni Confederacy, was sought out by the man's daughter, Noirúlu, who offered herself as hostage in exchange for her father's safety. Yubhsilai, moved by her nobility and beauty, gave them both their lives, and afterwards made Noirúlu his wife.

For the first time, Kamin-Tolagh saw the influence of such stories on his sister's actions at the time of the Jinzai War; she had put her life successively in the hands of two men who, incredibly, still guided their actions by such chivalrous principles

— or who wanted it to appear so. In the event, nothing had happened to alter her impractical view of war and governance conducted in the generous and forgiving gestures of romance; in time she would understand the severity, the intimidation real-life rule sometimes required; at the moment, if he told her about the burnt village, he was quite sure she would side with the decent, wrongheaded Yaënsilat.

Kamin-Tarú, abruptly, "What became of the men the Hrin blinded?"

He told her, and for the first time ever was justifying his actions to her; "They had brought death and destruction to my domains more times than I can count. When I first overthrew Sranadatta, I should have let the Man-mani deal with the clan; it would have been bloody, but in the end would have saved property and lives." Including Nizhadh's, not to be replaced.

She nodded succinctly. "They earned their death. It would be interesting to see a man hanged."

With the long double journey he had again been absent almost a month. Freighanai and Lavsila, who had advance word from Larghamit of his return, were waiting at the Great House; both knew Kamin-Tarú at least by sight, and Lavsila gave a brief, formal welcome in the Old Tongue. Kamin-Tolagh had sent Kambanal to assure the defense of Zelu Bablakhi, but Iruvakh, unusually, was waiting here, and his greeting, though ornate, was preoccupied; he was holding in his two hands a vast, shiny red-and-yellow striped gourd, of a long-necked shape some might find obscene, instantly amusing to Kamin-Tarú.

A curious introduction to disturbing tidings from a new quarter. On the far side of Flamûrai, Iruvakh said, lands westward of where the trace of the old imperial road snaked south for Gronu Kizh'klaëdhiyu, there had been a devastating irruption of nomadic bands, brutal and pitiless marauders, laying waste to large areas, plundering livestock, killing men, taking women and children to be their slaves, bringing terror to all tribes of the region.

Iruvakh was quietly proud of how he had acquired his details: happening to be here at the Abu, he had been summoned by Freighanai to try making sense of three brought from Larghamit by a patrol, meanly-dressed and unkempt men, whose language was unintelligible; all that could be at first ascertained was that they were seeking a leader or chieftain, called *Mnashra-Lakhínë*.

"Naturally," Iruvakh preened himself, "I recognized this as a version of the Man-mani *Noh-Sra-Lal-Hin*, and with that for a clue, found that with slight adjustments of pronunciation, these men were able to understand some of the most everyday Man-mani words, such as *foot*, *hand*, *man*, *sun*, and so forth." Giving, he did not fail to digress, fresh support to the tradition as to westward Man-mani origins.

Not the reputedly cognate Man-mani but a woman of the wholly unrelated Hwenala, a servant here, gave most help in understanding the speech of these visitors; the coastal tribe had evidently had dealings in the past with fishermen from across Flamûrai. Though with difficulty she had been able to understand and make herself understood; through her, in a mixture of her own language and the *Hwanió*, Iruvakh learned about devastation in the Kufshei, and that these men, representing a confederation of related but often rival tribes, had come to beg help from the new chieftain-of-chieftains here, whose invariable success in warfare was spoken all the way to the setting sun. Help, they clarified, for which they were prepared to pay: the ceremonial, functionally useless gourd, mistakenly presented to Iruvakh when he first arrived, was intended for Mnashra-Lakhíně, and its giving was, Iruvakh gathered, not only a token of high honor, but a solemn pledge.

Disappointed not to meet their hoped savior, but anxious, as leading warriors, to return to where the fighting was, the trio had left gourd and their plea in Iruvakh's hands, and departed west. They would return, so they had said, at the end of another moon, if still alive, but they had also trusted Iruvakh and the unseen Mnashra-Lakhíně so far as to give detailed instructions for reaching the upland fastness they had chosen for a place of last retreat.

"I thought to strengthen the garrison at Larghamit, *Asai*," Freighanai put in. "Luzhan's down there now, with a full squadron of lances and two dozen of the mounted bows, not to say a hundred-odd tribal levies — they can finish their training there just as well as here."

"Luzhan?" One of Yaënsilat's officers.

"He's got, as you know, *Asai*, a way with tribal lads. Who should I have sent, then, *Asai*?"

"You did well." Freighanai's question once again pointed out the shortage of senior men who could be trusted to make decisions; the death of Nizhadh had cost two of the best, him, and Yaënsilat. For the hundredth time Kamin-Tolagh sought and failed to invent a formula by which Yaënsilat could be reinstated, without unacceptable cost to imperial authority.

Lavsila, with the annoying smile that proclaimed a higher understanding, "What are the odds our great friend Iolfrant is behind this new unrest?"

The thought had already passed through Kamin-Tolagh's mind, a natural assumption. Iolfrant had certainly, if not quite admittedly, sponsored the destructive raiding in the Froghushei, and probably collaborated in the attack on the trading station; his habit of finding others to do his fighting was established, and these new wars were an immediate threat to the sole overland lifeline to Zelu Bablakhi, his only access independent of Hrin.

Yet there were limits, surely, to the *Hrithust's* influence with distant tribes, and to what rewards he could offer. "We make Iolfrant greater than he is, if we blame him for every squabble near our borders."

Iruvakh agreed. "Other visitors to Zhôl's Mound, men from the Farthest West, but north of these troubles, say there has been a great drought for the past three years in all those lands. That would make for unrest; one tribe displaces another, which then assails the next, like balls in bowling at the arch."

"Rodlakh should be grateful for what we are doing. If we were not here, the Army of the West would have more to keep it busy."

"Very true," Lavsila said. "But do not expect gratitude from that lineage."

"A pledge of what?" Kamin-Tarú smirked as she reached to fondle the narrowing neck of the potent gourd.

Iruvakh hedged a little; he could not be certain. As he understood it, presentation of this emblem was a sign of submission; the tribes in question, better called enlarged clans, recognized they came from a single stock, and in times of common danger would agree on the ablest warrior-chieftain, and present the gourd to say they would obey his commands as *Ashra-shâki'i*, chieftain of all chieftains.

"But after," Lavsila said, "when the danger passes, what? They go back to their own little wars?"

"It would seem."

"And now they wish to submit to my rule?"

"As I understand it."

A difficult question. Iruvakh was eager, presumably at prospect of bringing his skills as a grower to moister lands where improved methods would bring instant benefits, and that aspect deserved consideration; reliable pasturage and a few hundred head of beef cattle could enhance self-sufficiency for the Empire, a point where Fretasi, with her concern about paying for imports, was in full accord with Iruvakh. The military advantage of advancing his border so much nearer to Zelu Bablakhi was obvious. But according to Iruvakh again, with the concurrence this time of the map-maker, Dubovai, Kufshei between the head of Flamûrai and Gronu Kizh'klaëdhiyu, taking in enough territory to protect the southward road, and everything between the road and the shores of the Gulf, was more than equal to the inhabited area of Kamin-Tolagh's present domains, its overall population unguessed. Also unknown, strength and fighting capacities of the enemies against whom these confederated tribes were asking for help; his experiences this side of Flamûrai, even against a relatively disciplined people like the Hrin, led him to doubt there was anything in the Farthest West to withstand the concerted action of well-trained soldiery. But the proposition was not unlimited; sufficient preponderance of numbers could win any fight, the nearness of defeat by Iolfrant's forces only emphasized the point, and a single lost battle might begin a process in which his empire crumbled as rapidly as it had formed.

"We cannot protect them. We may be able to help them defend themselves, if they have any backbone to be stiffened." He had hoped for a tranquil period, so he could show his sister where all this began, the Man-mani country, before worst of the summer heat arrived.

The season was already late enough to make danger of an attack across Landegh less likely; his best course, he quickly decided, was to put together the strongest possible force, including most of the men Luzhan had at Larghamit, and simply ride down to Gronu Kizh'klaëdhiyu, neither avoiding any trouble, nor turning aside to find it. In this way he could perhaps gauge the strength of any enemy, without making an advance commitment.

"You," Iruvakh, "must come with me, as bearer of this gross gourd, which I do not mean to accept without knowing more."

Iruvakh might have refused, if he had not espoused this expansion of Kamin-Tolagh's sway; as was he made a face of resignation.

Not Kamin-Tarú, who was openly wistful about being left alone so soon. He wanted to tell her this was the price of their power to be together free from any censure, but was shamed by the force of that word, *alone*; for a woman of Kamin-Tarú's breeding, the Abu, the Empire, would be lonely in his absence. Apart from Antiyu, her maid, the austere Fretasi, the polished but irritating Lavsila, there was no one she could be imagined spending time with; for a woman with no interest in practical things, this was a bleak place. Yet it could not be entirely selfish, bringing her here, when she had been so eager to come. On the voyage, though they had touched constantly, there had been no privacy; it would be better, she would be better, when, alone together, they could confirm absolute mutual devotion.

22.

Days were still hot for the ride to Man-mani country, but Kamin-Tarú, released from too much idleness at the Abu, did not complain. In inadequate shade, waiting for the sun to dip westward, Kamin-Tolagh heard her impressions of those she had spent time with in his absence. Kambanal, brought back from the trading-station, delighted her with his unsoldierly graces and complete devotion to the cause of the Empire, so that she was already worried about where the young man would find a suitable wife.

"Lavsila," drily, "assures me many of the best young men and women of the Heartland will choose to come here, as we become an established realm — those who dislike life under Rodlakh."

"What is wrong with Rodlakh's rule? He has not filled the Residence with uncouth illiterates, as Petakoi said he would."

Her approval of Lavsila, if conditional, was a shock; she had met him at Kadon Dinul and dismissed him as negligible, but at an interval of three years saw improvements not perceptible to those who had been in constant contact with the man's unchanging skepticism about everything but the inborn superiority of the Owani race, his tedious addiction to theories of conspiracy. He had always been handsome, Kamin-Tarú reminded, but he was bronzed now, and appeared broader in the shoulders, to match the expansion in the subject-matter of his discourse, from design of precious little water-gardens to construction of twenty-mile aqueducts in hard and sunburnt country. His jokes, she said, were better now, and he was genuinely amusing explaining the improbable absurdities of various tribal customs.

"When I was at Kadon, Lavsila, so I was told by Ghuradh, the son of Khelagh, once expected to marry his sister — you know, Khalú, Bolan's wife, who was Dolvid's before."

"Very likely — " at last hearing a plausible explanation for Lavsila's extreme hostility to the *Bôdhrai*. He did know Khalú, a strikingly beautiful woman, who, at a feast after the Jinzai War, had made clear she would willingly make room in her bed for one of its heroes. Tempted, but aware of her history, guessing she was seeking her next husband, Kamin-Tolagh had preferred his garland of younger sporting-partners.

"She was once first jewel of the Residence Quarter, I hear they have a new one now, Morulis." The name, obviously not Owani, Kamin-Tarú spoke in three scornful syllables, *Mó-Rú-Lîs*. "Mixed blood is all the fashion now at Kadon, as you might expect. They say she is Burantal to the life, dark as a chimney-sweep, but she is learning the Old Tongue from the *rabhsayu*. Farm-girl teaching carpenter's daughter, that should be good to hear."

"Âna, actually, speaks the Owanilú fluently, with a good accent." His sister's scorn, sounding like the echo of something heard, was not quite consistent with her defense of Rodlakh's *rabhsayum*.

Kamin-Tarú hardly cared; the subject had reminded her she wanted to see the personal maid, Antiyu, as wife to Pivrekhan.

"Has Pivrekhan asked her to be his wife?"

"She is pretty," combatively. "He encouraged her to come here. He should consider himself fortunate to get such a bride, as he now is."

Kamin-Tolagh said nothing: Tú, he perceived, might despise Petakoi, but could not leave her entirely behind.

"I don't want to lose Antiyu, but no Owaniyu can be a servant here. She can train girls of the tribes to serve me. Kambanal says I should hear the full story of this Siv'loi from you."

Tact, Kamin-Tolagh perceived, could be added to the inventory of Kambanal's burgeoning virtues; his version of the tale took seriously the legend of Noh-Sra-Lal-Hin's deathless love for the girl. That Kamin-Tolagh and his sister could be lovers was not, of course, openly acknowledged.

"Kambanal was the one who named the banner," with a laugh. "The legend was his from the start. It did no harm, and went down well with both the tribe and the army." In brief, he told her how he had come to be Noh-Sra-Lal-Hin, and to preside over expulsion of Sranadatta and his whole clan.

"I wish I had been with you from the start," wistfully. Knowing his ways, she accepted his characterisation of the pretty Siv'loi as a transient pleasure accidentally immortalized, but was still unreasonably irked, he saw, that even as expedient fiction, a name other than hers should be linked to his in the founding of empire.

Where ways divided, start of the climb into Larghai's Notch and of the road to the eastward tribes, a permanent cavalry station now stood by the stream, severely practical barracks and stables, tribal mud-daubing methods adapted to a style nearer that of the realm. Here they parted from Iruvakh, who had been with Kamin-Tolagh in the Kufshei, and was now going to work among the Laughing Owl. In the morning, Kamin-Tarú asked, "Iruvakh — is he *anib'anuli*?" She confessed she had taken him for a man of the tribes at their first encounter, and been agreeably startled by the cultured and elaborate speech, in which he had called her arrival *more welcome than is a spring rain in these parched lands*. Yet she had detected no warmth to match this graciousness; not that he seemed insincere, but he spoke as he might to a tree, not expecting to evoke any response; she had seldom encountered a man so unaware she was female.

Since then, she had been puzzled, additionally, by his lack of conventional deference: on the ride there had been a mild dispute about excusing men from military training for the harvest, and rather than the brusque dismissal she would have expected, her brother gave a mollifying answer, promising drills would be over and men released within ten days.

"He might not be anything. If so, he has his choice here, a thousand boys of the tribes. Many not yet men sometimes bed with a man, and here neither would be called *anib'anuli*. Do you dislike him?"

"I do not know him." Having himself omitted mentioning his belief Iruvakh had once had the young Chamya for bedfriend, and left out the larger disclosure of the man's past with the *Mankh'*, Kamin-Tolagh readily recognized a lack of frankness; clearly she did not like Iruvakh. Evasions were a new and troubling trade between him and his sister.

It was otherwise with Chamya, who presented himself at the Visitors' Hut not a half-hour after their arrival in the village, to ask courteously whether they would not prefer to be with him at the head-man's dwelling. Just as he had at their first meeting, Kamin-Tolagh saw his sister take in at a glance the lean muscling, and make a new estimate of his age; at fifteen, Chamya was now tall for his people, but at the same age Kamin-Tarú had been taller than most full-grown men of the Man-mani. Chamya, beginning with his customary self-assurance in giving news of the tribe, became increasingly conscious Kamin-Tarú was a woman, and had to struggle against an unprecedented shyness.

"He does not know what to make of you," Kamin-Tolagh told her later. "Except for his mother, he has never met a woman a man need respect, and Osré-dnë is unique to the Man-mani — she has no parallel anywhere among the valley tribes. You will see when you meet her. But a young woman of standing is altogether new to him."

"Strange to hear the Owanilú spoken so well by one not born to it."

He explained how the Old Tongue came to be understood among the Man-mani, in turn giving him the language for his armies, the *Hwanió*.

"Was that what Iruvakh meant, when he said there would be a thousand additional men to learn speech?"

"Granted his love of round numbers, and of making each new hill to climb into a mountain — if the tribes of the Kufshei keep their bargain."

It was partly to distance himself from a tangled knot of new questions that Kamin-Tolagh had kept his promise to Kamin-Tarú, making this journey at a time when his absence from the Abu was less than ideally prudent, immediately after returning from the Kufshei.

At head of a force stronger than when he invaded the Hrin lands, he had taken the ancient road, for long stretches scarcely better than a faint memory, past the head of the Gulf, and southward to Gronu Kizh'klaëdhiyu, and three days into Kufshei fought a pitched battle with an uncounted horde of bushy-haired, fierce, but poorly-armed men out of the Farthest West, killing, capturing or putting them all to flight at small loss to himself, though as fighters this new enemy, properly armed, could have been a near-match, man to man, for Tau-Suaka's Hill Froghul, before they learned the cooperative arts of civilized soldiering.

Leaving most of his company at the pass, he had started back with only his bodyguard. With Iruvakh for guide and gourd-bearer, Dubovai to map the route, and a man able to interpret, he had made his way to the upland refuge described by the men who had visited the Abu. There, in tortuous negotiation, he reached what passed for agreement with notables of what were said to be the eight main tribal groupings, whereby, in exchange for his assistance, they acknowledged his authority, and promised each to send him one hundred warriors for military training, bringing as many mounts as could be found. Some ponies had been captured in Kamin-Tolagh's battle, but he was going to be desperately short of both mounts and weapons; lances could be manufactured easily enough, but he lacked steel and skilled smiths for the making of first-class blades.

At least half the new levies he would train for fighting on foot, and arm with bows as their principal weapon; any of Tau-Suaka's men could select, trim and true wood for a bow as other men could pick out a ripe apple, and women of the Laughing Owl had a particular aptitude for arrow-making, now binding on steel beaks instead of merely charring the points. Some of the earliest levies from the tribes of Froghushei, Man-mani and Gudi-la, were well-drilled enough to begin the training of these new formations.

Beyond these details there was the dominant question, whether he had acted wisely. He had accepted the gourd, and apparently undertaken responsibility for maintaining order over a vast swathe of lowland, hillside and forest, dotted with what must be two or three hundred villages and tiny hamlets, for some months at least using his present forces, already spread thin over places he had to defend. Kambanal was enthusiastic about an overland lifeline to Zelu Bablakhi; like any true *péfrapravádai* of Kargul, he loathed trusting to ships, and would have even if they had not been those of their strongest potential enemy. But there was no way to tell whether the marauding force Kamin-Tolagh had routed was representative of the fighting-qualities of others they might encounter, and whether the post he would try to maintain at Gronu Kizh'klaëdhiyu was strong enough to defend itself, so many days from any possible help. With this new garrison, as with Zelu Bablakhi, he had to strike a balance between effectiveness and the numbers he could afford to lose, if, as was not nearly improbable enough, he was sending them to an obscure and distant death.

He did not know how he could have declined. Of all assets of the Empire, Iruvakh's crops, the gold of Zelu Bablakhi, the discipline of Kargul and ferocity of the Hill Froghul, nothing was as essential as his invincible reputation. It had gone by mysterious means into lands he might never see; perhaps there were races by the Western Ocean who spoke in awe of the new warmaster who had arisen far to the east. One of the most ruffianly of the chieftains at the conference had reverentially grasped a corner of the Siv'loi Banner, and chanted words which, translated for and retranslated by Iruvakh, came out as 'Our homes, or villages, will be safe, wrapped in this *Âsh-mantu.*' An *âsh-mantu,* as Iruvakh understood, was any animal, plant or thing holding power; some clans believed themselves under the protection of wolves or the thorn, while villages often gave the name of a former warrior to a nearby standing stone, holding that it, or he, kept watch by night as well as day; they would say flattering words when they passed near it, and give it choice morsels from their meat-feasts, gratefully consumed, in lands scoured by crows, vultures and carrion-dogs.

The recent ineffectuality of their *âsh-mantu'u,* then, had led them to seek another, this with the lance of Mnashra-Lakhínë, Noh-Sra-Lal-Hin, beneath it. Well, but to be maintained, such a reputation had to be risked on new challenges; for Kamin-Tolagh there was no standing still; he knew intuitively that what he had achieved by bluff, audacity and seized opportunity would be doomed at the moment he stopped going forward. This new and undesired expansion could equally be his ruin, but ruin was not to be escaped by doing other than what had brought him so far.

"Will you have to fight the Hrin?"

"In the end. We may one day be living in those lands, which are greener and less arid than these."

"They do not look much like fighters. Are their women less ugly than the men?"

"I have had no dealings with the women; they play small part in the outside life of the Hrin."

His reply was cursory, while noting delightedly his sister kept her old intuitive powers, answering questions not asked. The Hrin were not much like fighters, and unless conquest and Karguli training could uncover a hidden spirit, he would continue to need the harsher northern Froghushei as a source for his armies. "I shall build us a house here."

"Why here?"

"Here, where I shall always be Noh-Sra-Lal-Hin — in the place where that name was first given." More and more huts near the crown of the hill, convenient to the well, were standing empty, as the village continued to trickle down to riverside. "Good stone here, and with Marsilakh to show what is needed, Hrin masons know how to cut and join it — or we shall bring men of the Guild from Kadon Dinul." At evening, with Tau-Suaka and four of his men for guard, conscious of being watched at a respectful distance by the villagers, he walked with her up the incline to show where he meant.

Chamya had spoken about moving the raised platform and canopy of Meeting Place down to the farther bank of the river. "We can turn this open space into our gardens — " trying to make his sister share what he could see growing on this scoured level.

"Gardens," she said despondently, but he showed her where the gully behind the village could be bridged at its narrowest by one of Lavsila's aqueducts, and a reliable source of water found in the hills above. "We shall have trees, grass, a waterfall... Here — " he gestured, "our house shall have a wide terrace, where we can dine, and watch the sun set over Flamûrai." Clasping her hand, he pointed out the distant gleam of the Gulf, and nearer, the small mound where Siv'loi was buried under the round, white stone.

"Will they call this house your memorial to Siv'loi?" She was standing exactly in the spot where the hacked and huddled body of the girl had lain.

"Siv'loi will become a name, a vague legend, if it is not so already. Here, as nowhere else, they will see it as only proper for Noh-Sra-Lal-Hin to take a sister-wife. What other blood is worthy of his?" He put a hand to her waist, and drew her closer, not dwelling on the counter-truth his thought entailed: bedding with Tú, mingling bodies with her, had lost none of that rightness which made nonsense of law and custom and conventional moral outrage, but at the Abu he had not been able to recapture the outward ease of when first they had become bed-friends, she then not yet fourteen, all alternating clarities, child and woman, nothing of the muddled in-between. So much of what he did here in the West had its eye on effect; he could scarcely take a drink of water without considering how it should be done by an emperor, confident in his power: impossible for him not to consider how Kargul' of the Abu — the Owanil, to include Lavsila and Iruvakh — would regard their congress, and how, if at all, it would affect loyalties, his ability to enforce his wishes.

Uncertainty had caused him to instruct Tú that at the Abu their public behavior would be of brother and sister; the first night in the house by the cliffs, after she yawned and left the table, he had sat drinking wine with Lavsila and Iruvakh another hour, though yearning to be with her.

"Fiunuvoi became wife of Hrâmi —" she made a pious gesture appropriate to the Owani tale of creation, the Time Before Time, "and they had the same Father."

Her hand, side by side with his on the pillow, was paler, more finely made, yet plainly from the same workshop, just as her matured body, leaner and firmer now, still smoothly desirable, was a woman's counterpart to his. By yellow rushlight as she half-dozed, he marvelled at the design of hands, and ran his fingertips up over her wrist and forearm to the soft bend where veins showed milky blue. She was not his, she was him, his completion, and everything with her was fulfillment, no searching or striving; other beddings labored to assert what could not be so, but theirs richly affirmed what was, as simply as blossom, leaves and fruit came to a peach-tree.

They had remained at the Visitors' Hut, and in the morning young women brought food; Osré-dnë herself came down the hill bringing wedges of the sweet, perfumed melon she miraculously could produce ice-cold in hottest weather, and with her customary appearance of private irony supervise the serving of breakfast.

An occasion for a great deal of watching; Kamin-Tarú's attention was equally divided between impassive Osré-Dnë and the three bashful, honey-skinned girls, who, even beyond Chamya, were thrown into confusion by their first encounter with a highborn lady, and had to be jogged back into their duties by a menacing word from Osré-dnë. They were fascinated by Kamin-Tarú's glowing hair, as by her morning-gown, a loose and airy robe of pale-green shuzi. Any wistfulness in their wonder could hardly be called covetous, since they could surely not imagine themselves possessing any of Kamin-Tarú's life.

After, she asked, "This Osré-dnë, can she see the future, like a *raf'yalu*? Or the well-woman of the Lunu Tezh' you met?"

Without troubling to give credit to Iruvakh, he explained the Man-mani were not a Froghuli people, and did not have well-women; until the fall of Sranadatta all the tribe's women had the standing of cattle, which made the respect given Osré-dnë so much more remarkable. "She is said to do some foretelling, though I have never heard any of her prophecies."

"She has a seer's face."

In the past he had indulged his sister's fascination with such nonsense, but now he wanted her to begin sharing in the pragmatic realities of rule. "She is an impressive figure, true. It makes her more useful."

"Choosing playthings for your bed?" You did not mention Man-mani girls had eyes. Or shoulders."

Still desiring more of his sister, he had experienced that same reminder; though he had not wanted a girl of the Man-mani since Imyë, the birth of her *jinzai* child, they remained prettiest of all tribal girls. Strange to him that while telling Tú quite truthfully how little there had been beyond transient amusement in other beddings, he could continue to feel attracted to that very inconsequence: having nothing to do with the depth of feeling between him and Kamin-Tarú, there was no reason for one to interdict the other.

He saw what had happened: his pursuit of variety and delight in its renewing adventure might have begun as consolation for that first loss of Kamin-Tarú, but eight years apart from her had let it become a thing in itself, a favorite diversion, and no more in competition with his love than any other game would be: if he had been passionate, some men were, about *zhabhu*, or bowling at the arch, he would not have expected reunion with his sister to make him give up those recreations.

Nor, to judge by Tú's interest in the Man-mani girls, was this an appetite to divide them; he could imagine her huge-eyed curiosity delighting in shared sport with a girl of their choice.

He was assailed, not by the sensual, but the sentimental force of his imagining, as if the presence of his sister could transform any greed into tribute, into a sign of his limitless affection for her. Voice clogging, he said, "They do not need to be taught how to please, or be pleased, these girls. If you would enjoy it — " but she anticipated his thought.

"Now we are together at last, with no one to say we can't be, I do not need any games — would you be pleased by that?"

"Not if you were not." Put aside, not really dismissed; he could forgo a gratification for her sake, but not pretend the desire was gone; here was a troubling flaw in the perfect accord they had believed a certainty. She, equally, he knew, loved him enough to allow him his pleasure, but their enriching unity was marred once either of them so much as thought in terms of what he or she would *give up* for the other.

"Will you still take women for your sport?"

"I may have to, now and again." Even in civilized Kargul, where he was only a mortal prince, devotion of his personal squadron had been deepened by his exploits with women, which, rather than envying, his men somehow claimed a share in. "For the sake of my standing."

"Life is hard," with arch mockery, "for men who think of nothing but their duty. What about my standing?"

"You are outside and above such questions. Everything I become, you are."

"If I paid her," back with Osré-dnë, "do you think she would tell me our future?"

"You must not show money," having no wish to be forced to punish the woman for the insult to his sister such an offer would undoubtedly bring. "What would you want to hear about our future?"

"Whether you will come to rule both here and in Kargul, as you should."

He leaned to kiss her, but while the thought had the epic texture of their childhood dreams, those games had never made her so disconsolate. She was unhappy over their father's determination to see him declared an outlaw in Council; a glimpse of how miserable she must have been, practically a captive in an enemy camp, forced to listen in silence to tirades against feats she would have wished to exult over.

"He, or Petakoi, can now add me to the list of outlaws." Habitually, she used the name now, though she still referred to Tovakh as `our father.'

"The Council met well over a month ago. We should have word by now — Lavsila's endless cousins have their uses."

"Do you see the letters he receives?"

"At times. He reads me what I need to know. I have no time to sift through a mountain of gossip to gain a pinch of gold."

"Or what he writes?"

"Only when he writes for me, to the *rabhsai*, or the *Bôdhrai*. If he wanted to carry on a secret correspondence," Kamin-Tolagh explained, Tú's face remaining dubious, "I could prevent it only by giving myself more trouble than ever Lavsila could cause. He cannot betray me, because I do not trust him."

"What is his use?"

"I thought you liked him."

"He makes amusing talk."

"That is his use. He is a hanger-on. If the Empire should fall, and we were all led away in chains, he would find a way to become a hanger-on with *rabhsayum*, or with the Hrin, or designing water-gardens in the Kufshei. In the meantime, he is winning the Heartland over to my cause, and means to make my name a rallying-cry."

"For what?"

"For all Lavsilas of the realm, admirers of yesterday."

But the unhearing Lavsila had his revenge. From him, on the third day at the Man-mani village, a dispatch came to inform Kamin-Tolagh a tattered horde of young tribesmen out of Kufshei was gathering by Larghamit, bringing a selection of livestock, pack-animals and even a few women. Evidently the promised contingents sent for training, their boisterousness and mounting numbers were causing nervousness in Kamin-Tolagh's garrison there, as with Hrin traders, who had to pass through part of the new encampment to make devotions at their shrines on the mound. Though there had been some jostling of contingents from rival tribes, the overall mood was far from hostile, and they complied with an emphatic sign-language request from Luzhan to allow unimpeded access to Zhôl's Mound. Freighanai was now on his way there, but clearly, at least to Lavsila, Kamin-Tolagh's presence was required to bring order.

Kamin-Tolagh had hoped for a week at least; the message reached him as he was setting out with Kamin-Tarú to spend half a day on the shore of the Gulf. "Next time," ruefully, "we shall have longer."

End of the Third Part

Kamin-Tolagh

IV

24.

Lavsila returned from the window. "It should be raining," petulant himself, irritating Kamin-Tolagh more. Of course it should be raining, it should have rained, but had hardly done so throughout the northern Froghushei. Maddeningly, from everywhere he did not rule, news was of ample or excessive water; Lavsila's informants told him the Heartland was having one of its mild, moist winters, while far to the south in the *onhritha* of Iolfrant, their great river, called a name like *Hflen*, had overflowed its banks; low-lying outskirts of the *hrithust*'s capital, Hyolenstr, had been emptied of people.

From yet farther away, the uttermost West, rumor came of the breaking of their long drought, which might well have done as much as the skill and vigor of Kamin-Tolagh's forces in pacifying those new adjuncts to Empire, where tribal leaders remained in an ambiguous state, neither fully allegiant, nor permitted to go back on their presentation of the gourd. The men they sent to be trained as soldiers took an oath of allegiance to Kamin-Tolagh, but did so in their imperfectly-mastered *Hwanió*, and no one could say whether they considered themselves fully bound by it; Kamin-Tolagh was naggingly aware it might have to come to the test, and would probably entail some executions, and exactions against a clan-chieftain or two.

The uncertainties, at their root, were his; if the Kufshei remained safe for his troops to ride through, if the tribes there provided him with men for his armies above what were needed for defense of their lands, he would be content to have them remain what in the days of the First Empire were known as "protected" lands. But those nominally sovereign domains at the fringes of the Empire proper were also called tributary, and in exchange for their safety from western invaders, the tribes of the Kufshei were going to have to provide some food.

There, too, the weather was the key; Iruvakh, who had scarcely begun any attempt to teach growing-practices west of the Gulf, was already warning rainfall was again below normal, and crops would be in trouble. This was to have been the year of excess wheat to sell the Hrin, and now Iruvakh was suggesting, on the contrary, the Hrin traders might have to be used as intermediaries for buying grain from Rodlakh's realm, not this year, perhaps, but a year from now, unless prospects improved.

"We unquestionably have increased mouths to feed," he lectured. "In every tribal village, there are far more children than before." Not that so many more were conceived, but formerly, at his most cautious estimate, seven out of ten children born to the valley tribes had failed to attain a first birthday. The end of Hill Froghul' raids had made starvation less likely, but as many newborn, and their mothers, were being kept from death by the introduction of habits anyone of the realm would take for granted, mostly to do with the use of soap and water, and disposal of various wastes so as not to encourage rats, crawling insects, or flies, "fever's couriers," as Iruvakh called them quoting, he said, ga-Kamanasalladh VI, the great Healing Patriarch of the Return.

Now Iruvakh assumed he was going to lay out his gold to rescue those who could not feed themselves; "an investment," he called it, pointing out that today's boy-children were the armies of fifteen years hence, but where was his guarantee this would not become a continuing process, the Empire a drain on, instead of a means to wealth? As he said himself, there were no improved growing-methods to compensate for a lack of water.

As a comment, generosity had already brought unanticipated discontent: about year's turn, one of the best of all tribal soldiers, Ku-Roäm, a man good enough to serve as half-squadron with his own Laughing Owl formation, had dared to convey, through Luzhan, a complaint against the training of men from the distant Kufshei. Not, as was first assumed, that he was afraid they might become a powerful enemy, but because they might be used for future campaigns, in place of his own men.

After the punitive expedition into the Hrinani, where Ku-Roäm's half-squadron had been part of the charge led by

Yaënsilat in the critical battle, Kamin-Tolagh had allowed successful tribal troops a share in the value of the booty. A pittance, one-tenth the portion allotted an ordinary trooper of Kargul, but enough to make them important when they returned to their villages, where any money was a mark of distinction. The Gudi-la squadron which had failed in the battle had not been rewarded; for a time Kamin-Tolagh had considered lining them up and executing every sixth man, a punishment for cowardice from the First Empire, but which had persisted into the early reign of Plakhsila *Kímukoi*, only two centuries ago. In the end, he had disbanded the squadron in their home country, and had the men stripped and flogged; at Lavsila's suggestion the whips were wielded by men of their own tribe, under armed supervision. The men were then permitted to seek reinstatement, but distributed among levies of other tribes.

As Iruvakh warned and Kamin-Tolagh wanted, an account of that affair spread rapidly throughout the valleys, but made less impression than word of the treasure won by the Laughing Owl: Ku-Roäm's protest came from the widespread conviction any campaign outside the Froghushei was bound to end in a division of spoils. The man, too valuable to punish for his presumption, had eventually said he understood the people of Kufshei had to learn how to defend their lands, but deep-set, doubting eyes continued to envisage heaps of captured gold being claimed by these undeserving newcomers to Kamin-Tolagh's service.

"I enjoy this weather," Kamin-Tarú said. "Pleasant for riding." The past ten days had been much alike, if anything cooler than in a normal rainy season, random, darting breezes, white cloud, half-hours of attenuated sun, frequent touches of moisture too wraithlike to be called rain.

"The Colony is undergoing drought," Lavsila, consolingly. "The *rabhsayu*'s brother is going to have to open up his hoard. Food stolen from the Heartland, going to feed the mongrel army."

"A very good mongrel army," Kamin-Tolagh said lightly, and, "Stolen?"

"The *rabhsai* forces sale at low market price, and has goods to sell low at a time when otherwise prices would be rising — he charges himself nothing for storage. What else is it but stealing, to cheat successful growers out of their profit?"

Kamin-Tarú asked, "Couldn't Rodlakh make a profit, when prices go up?"

"Cheap food, *Asayu*, gives him his hold on the rabble, and without that the House Arbhai-Navu would be looking for new lodgings in a week. As it is," turning back to Kamin-Tolagh, "his new laws have cost him whatever goodwill he had with better elements of his realm. The *Bôdhrai* imagines he can placate the Great Families by promising to name Bradhinal of Ân for Captain of the West, but how often can that be made to work? Of course, they will never do it."

"He is said to be a good soldier."

"Rodlakh would not dare put him in command at the Frontier. He's seen Cavalry of Kargul go over to you, *Asai*, and Bradhinal is, what, your cousin twice removed?"

"Cousin will do."

"Your forces, in alliance with the Army of the West? What could stand up to that? This *rabhsayum* cannot take the risk — Rodlakh's no fool."

"A ruler," Kamin-Tolagh baited, "who persists with measures so unpopular, with rebellion as near as you say would have to be a very large fool."

"Oh, I do not say he is not sotted with the notion of avenging the downtrodden for all the well-known wrongs they have suffered at our hands. That has always been his *bôdhrai*'s dream, and with a Mixed *rabhsayu* — but there's no rebellion near, not yet. Give it time, *Asai*. Already, the best people are saying among themselves, for choice, the captain who fought his way into Kamsilat to win the Jinzai War would be better for the realm than the one who shut himself up there."

"Shumat, you mean?" But Kamin-Tolagh found himself not immune to this blatant flattery.

"Oh, yes, Shumat, with his highborn wife, who never wore shoes before he married her. If the realm looks for a change, it will be to blood with some lineage."

"Petakoi has said," Kamin-Tarú offered, "if blood alone could settle the question, our ruler would be Finú."

"The Lady Finú," Lavsila gravely conceded, "is well-descended, on both sides."

Kamin-Tarú gave her silvering laugh. "One morning, she told me to bring her breakfast, and wanted to know how long I had been in service. She had been at Inilun Barabhi half a year, and seen me every day."

Visibly, Lavsila's mind went to thoughts of Kamin-Tolagh ruling the realm from behind a docile, captive Finú, nominally restored to her rightful place. That idea, if new to him, had been worn threadbare by Petakoi, only with Tovakh as the intended puppet-master — in this case, it seemed, not as another of her decoys, but a genuine reserve plan if for any reason her *jinzal* armies had failed to march. Both the harmlessly silly Finú, and her dangerous, half-mad sister had become nearly permanent parts of the household at Inilun Barabhi, but with the death of Radaghi's husband, an officer of the Karguli cavalry, the sisters had gone back to their estates near Thenimala in Ninkufu. They were still there at the time of Kamin-Tarú's sojourn, virtual neighbors to her disappointed trothplight, Taërinat.

"All the Great Families are well aware how unfit to rule both sisters are, and that either could be brought forward only as a figurehead." Kamin-Tolagh wondered why he was discussing this as if it could ever be real; Lavsila's preoccupations were constantly trying to tug his thoughts back to the old realm, back to the discarded past.

"But as long as the man behind that figurehead is an Owani, one of their own — "

Kamin-Tolagh could not disguise derision. "I would assume anyone who attempted to replace the present ruling house would have to overcome Shumat to do it." For him, the idea was additionally bizarre; he had seen some of the best-trained of his tribal troops fail to beat the inept Hrin; painful to imagine them against Army of the West or Household squadrons.

"Time is on your side, *Asai* — " as ever suavely sliding away from an untenable position. "The future belongs to one who can capture the hearts of the young. I am told more and more of the young Heartlanders are talking about coming to join you in your shameful outlawry — what a blow to Rodlakh's prestige, when the best blood of the realm chooses your service over his!"

"Who has told them they will be welcome here? Will they bring rain?" Increased population was not Kamin-Tolagh's most urgent need, nor did he see how it fit in with this dream of nurturing support for him at Kadon Dinul, if all his adherents came here.

Lavsila was genuinely bewildered. "We have talked about this, more than once, down to the particular houses we would make available — "

"It would be good to have fashionable company, Tam," Tú was wistful, and though the thought came from her boredom when he had to be absent, she was right in a wider sense; time had come for the Abu to become something better than a military outpost: a way must be found to plant, like Iruvakh's winter wheat, seed for the life of a real city, with gentler pastimes than weapons drill.

Meanwhile, as always with Lavsila, there were schemes within schemes, and he took this opportunity to renew his quest for a house here, one commensurate with an official rank of some kind.

On first hearing Kamin-Tolagh's plans for a new residence in Man-mani country, he had begun talking about one of his own on the ridge north of Zhôl's Mound by Larghamit, a house large enough for a family, he said, though what family was not clear. His wish was to be made Warden of the Port, responsible for order there, and for collecting import fees, of which he proposed to retain one-sixth for himself. Refusal had not cost Kamin-Tolagh five minutes of thought; with Hrin vessels constantly coming and going, various visitors to the sacred mound, increased traffic by land to west of the Gulf, and men of the Kufshei being trained nearby, Larghamit had become a crossroads of Empire, yet with only a handful of inhabitants other than the garrison, obviously best left as a military command; why pay Lavsila to get in the way of swift decisions by competent officers?

Undaunted, he had returned to an earlier theme, the need for a civil official, perhaps a magistrate, here at Abu Ninusai. This, too, would mean his occupying his own house; the one he wanted most was Kamin-Tolagh's favorite, too, against the eastward cliffs, with its wine cave, and unfailing supply of cold water, but Lavsila was willing to accept another of the larger houses, near the crossways. Kamin-Tolagh was tempted to ask whether, if he had to choose, he would want magistracy without the house, or, his likelier option, house without the magistracy.

Now he urged there were questions of rank and precedence it would be best to settle in advance of any new arrivals. Kamin-Tolagh agreed with the thesis, but his choices would not have been Lavsila's; any aristocracy here would begin with soldiers, with Kambanal and Freighanai. Law was and would remain the will of Kamin-Tolagh.

Lavsila's mistaken assumptions began farther back, in his recurrent attempt to identify the Empire with an absurd cause. "If your Heartlanders are looking for all they most admire in Old Owan, they had better go to Inilun Barabhi, and follow my mother. She has yet to learn she cannot bring back her imaginary past. I would not if I could."

Unexpectedly, Lavsila gestured to oblivion what had seemed his one sincere and constant belief. "People need a war-cry they can understand. This is a way they recognize, to express their anger and disgust with the *rabhsai* they have, the hope they would wish to invest in your leadership, *Asai*, and your enterprise here in the West."

Again, transparent flattery, yet there was a curious gratification, just as when he learnt from tribes of the Kufshei that his feats of war were praised in lands where he had never been. That, however, was an undemanding fame founded on innocent admiration of prowess, whereas when it came to the Heartland, he could not see why any there would become his adherents, speak his name as a talisman, unless they believed he represented or would in some way advance their interests.

"I have no desire," speaking plainly as to a child, "to interfere in the affairs, or laws, or governance of Rodlakh's realm."

"Understood, *Asai*." Yet still with the audible equivalent of a knowing wink, as if they were speaking in cypher, each aware what the other really meant.

"Not for any reason. And in particular, I have no interest in ancient privileges of the Owani people. Here in my domains, privilege goes with faithful service — "

"As it ought, *Asai*," soothingly.

" — and there's no reason why a Tau-Suaka or a Chamya is any less than an Owani of rank."

"Granted — " but here reservation was plainer, his sister startled, and Kamin-Tolagh could admit going farther than he meant in another unwanted direction; he also had no interest in an abstract idea of equality, as urged by the realm's firebrand reformers.

"Here, we have work and war to occupy us; we have no use for theories about races and ruling, and particularly about how other realms choose to govern themselves."

Lavsila nodded agreement.

"Unless Rodlakh is foolish enough to attack us here, when next we have dealings with his realm, it will be as a neighbor too important to ignore. A friendly neighbor. We shall have our rivalries, but friendship will begin with an undertaking by each ruler, admitting the right of the other to rule in his own way."

There would be great difficulties on both sides in living up to such a pledge, if the same treaty meant men and women passing freely between the shores of Arnan and the Farther West. Many men of Kargul, he supposed, would stubbornly regard him as Heir there, and on the other side, he could easily imagine those of Rodlakh's realm who made a career out of discovering injustice voicing objections about his treatment of the tribes. In the end the ties of blood could mean negotiating their way to a single sovereignty — not Lavsila's dream-domain in which Kamin-Tolagh replaced Rodlakh, but perhaps an approach to autonomy for Kargusai as part of a larger realm. Deferred, not dismissed, was the passing thought he would find a way to unite his New Kargul with the old province, and rule over both as a lord equal to the original *nimul* of the First Empire, who administered, under the Shâls, vast, populous tracts of territory, princes far greater than present provincial overlords.

To aspire to such a standing might be a war away, one in which his objective would be an attainable one, not to humble Rodlakh, a possibility existing only in Lavsila's wishful dreams, but to inflict on his armies such losses as to make compromise increasingly attractive.

These were not public thoughts: his men of Kargul, if it came to war against the realm of their origins, would surely fight better in the belief it was for survival, and beyond that, victory; he was not going to inspire them to heroism with the aim of achieving a standstill and a favorable negotiating position.

Lavsila was still with his schemes: "Inevitably, *Asai*, such rivalries, no matter how friendly, become — " but Kamin-Tolagh cut him off.

"I shall no longer be addressed as *Asai*. That is a form of address belonging to a realm which no longer recognizes me. I do not concede the authority of Rodlakh or his Council to affect my standing, but equally no longer acknowledge the realm which gave me that rank. Henceforth I shall be addressed only as *Lord*, and my sister as *Lady*."

Kamin-Tarú laughed with young delight, as at a new game, but Lavsila labored at a thoughtful frown, trying hard for a reasoned objection to an innovation he loathed on instinct. *Lord*, not a word of Owani origin, but deriving direct from the title the Gabhanil had used exclusively of and in addressing one of their High Captains.

They, and their Owani chronicler, Dolvid in his version of *The Song of Tales*, made a great deal of how those supreme commanders had been chosen by acclamation of the assembled clans, as if that gave them a special virtue over the natural choice made by inherited blood, creating a true man of the people. Well, but there was no doubt that to speak the word, *Lord*, created a larger disparity between speaker and the one addressed than did the familiar Owani *Asai*, a difference Lavsila perceived and hated, but excellent for Kamin-Tolagh's purposes, distancing him from his followers, as it distanced his rule from any other.

25.

Faëdhal, Master of Tongues, was in his eighties, no great age for an Owani; his mind was as keen as ever, but over the past couple of years he had suffered a number of minor accidents and ailments, and a wet winter added to his miseries. Hearing he was again confined with a stiff and swollen knee, Dolvid went to see him at his small house just outside the city proper. Ushered in by the latest in a long series of young men to keep house for the old scholar, negotiating as always with care in the narrow straits between delicate and precious furnishings with which the house was crammed, sideboards and emaciated tables with their costly cargoes of fine glass and carved wood, Dolvid was greeted effusively by Faëdhal, who insisted on hauling himself up from the depths of his chair to stand unsteadily. His stoop was more pronounced, but his handclasp was firm.

After they had disposed of small news about common friends, Dolvid sounded him out about the stubborn opposition to the compensation law, still muttering on after eight months with no case requiring its application. With his kinships, Faëdhal always had access to Residence Quarter gossip at its most unguarded.

"I have heard talk, too much talk. This law of the *rabhsayu*'s strikes me, if I may say so, as eminently fair and long overdue — so I say to anyone who slanders it, if one may speak of slandering a law. One hears it called `not equity, but revenge' — a stupid phrase of no real meaning, but as you once put it, *Bôdhrai*, self-interest takes its war-cries where it finds them — very apt."

"You do not know who might be the author of that particular war-cry? I am not contemplating any action, but am curious about where it began."

"Ah. Any axe, as the proverb goes, can boast the windfelled tree. The one thing worse, to my mind, than a foolish catchword, is how those who parrot it do so as if originating it, as a dog swaggers to proclaim how clever he is to invent fetching. As I recall, I first heard it in the mouth of Master Khelagh."

"As I from his son." Despite interception of one courier last year, Lavsila was evidently still finding covert ways to communicate with his Heartland kin.

"Ghuradh," despondently. "He will soon be fat as his father, and is scarcely less pompous. I heard he has a tale — well, no man of standing should circulate such bad coinage to give it currency beyond its merit. Marshfire, as I have not hesitated to say."

Uncoaxed, he would have left it there, but the tale, as it emerged, possessed a grotesque consistency. Ever since last autumn, at the same time as he had been petitioning at the Bronze Residence for repeal of Âna's law, Ghuradh had been passing along the rumor the *rabhsai*, chiefly under the baleful influence of Dolvid and the *rabhsayu*'s brother, would divest major landowners of large parts of their holdings, so they could be divided up among the undeserving many, acts for which disbanding of the private armies had been the necessary prelude.

"It was noted that immediately prior to the proclamation concerning armed followings, you had crossed Arnan to confer with Saidhan *Asai*, obviously to be assured of support from the Army of the West, which, having few officers of Owani blood, could be relied on to implement the confiscations — indeed, the common soldiers of the West would be its chief beneficiaries."

"That will be hard to maintain, now the Army of the West is to get its new commander." Wanildhai's bashful request to be allowed to postpone his retirement, for the unexpectedly sentimental reason that he wanted to complete fifty years of military service, and, on the same day, forty-four with the Army of the West (*"Fifty years,"* Shumat had wickedly said, *"since his first trumpet-call from the saddle of a* pefrai," Wanildhai's loud flatulence being next thing to a legend), had willingly been granted, but now Bradhinal of Ân, still evincing an attractive modesty about his worthiness to command where Sebhal had, would sail for the Colony next month. Confirmation in Council was assured, with Bradhinal's father and uncle to join with the *rabhsai*'s bloc of votes.

"For those who have need to believe nonsense," severely, "and there are such, men and women both, I cannot say why — all evidence against their thesis is made into greater proof; it will be said Bradhinal's appointment is to divert suspicion. The latest elaboration is, whole boatloads of saplings have begun arriving from the Colony at Owan Sai, where they are transferred to river-barges, ready for use as boundary-markers when the great estates are carved up."

"Quantities of seedlings are being brought to Owan Sai — " newly amazed at how any innovation could be given a sinister turn. "But not for that purpose." He began explaining the forest-planting scheme, but Faëdhal was not much interested, having rested his rejection of the rumor entirely on his knowledge of Dolvid.

That faith was a comfort, but scarcely enough to prevent stirring of a terribly familiar sensation, that of being isolated, drifting alone between those like Elamirr, who suspected him of secret partiality for the Families, and those same Families, who held he was plotting to destroy them.

Dismissing self-pity, he concentrated on possible origins of this tale, well beyond Ghuradh's wit to invent. Once, all that was far-fetched and devious would inevitably have a connection to Petakoi, but no longer, and in any case she had no interest in Heartland affairs. Lavsila, once again? Necessary, here, to fight against two opposed tendencies; while Lavsila's capacity for making mischief should not be underestimated, Dolvid was not going to attribute ubiquitous and irresistible malevolence to that not-very-formidable source.

"Something else: the ones who repeat these fantastic stories at most only half-believe their own words — like children, telling tales of demons in the dark, for the pleasure of scaring themselves. When Ghuradh came to see me last year, had he really credited all this nonsense, there would have been no object to his visit, nor in what he had to say to me. But it makes no difference when ugly rumors come untrue. If those who dislike me said I enjoy eating babies for breakfast, my proving the lie would not embarrass them, or change their feelings. They would just say, well, he is the kind of man who *would* eat babies for breakfast. You see, when all the seedlings are planted, no one will say, oh, then we must have been mistaken."

"Just so," Faëdhal agreed. "How distasteful untruth perversely persists — this is surely a point that must have a place somewhere in your histories?"

My histories! he groaned noiselessly, envying Faëdhal that scholarly detachment he had once had himself.

Yet not everything was grinding futility. The first magistrate-at-large continued hearing cases in the Kovilanu; Tovakh had greeted his arrival with threats, and the assertion that, as provincial overlord and therefore chief magistrate in Kargul, he had the right to set aside any of the decisions reached. Fornival, when consulted, unexpectedly ventured the legal point was ambiguous; Tovakh could lawfully overrule his *provincial* magistrates, though not normally a royal one, but it might be maintained in deciding property disputes entirely within Kargul, the magistrate-at-large was functioning as a superimposed provincial official; naturally, Fornival said, there was "no absolute precedent to guide us."

It was not certain Fornival recognized that in questions of who had the power, the precedents he had at his fingertips, no less written law, were eventually a history of disputes settled by swords: *rabhsayum* had the right to limit Patriarchal power not in abstract justice, but because Plakhat Gabh'Owan had the larger army and wider support when the Treaty of the Wind Caves was negotiated, and after that because Rodlakh could bully the *Mankh'* with threat of exposing their part in the breeding of *jinzal*, and so dictate terms for the Second Treaty. Here, too, presence in the Kovilanu of an entire regiment of General Cavalry, with ample reinforcements under Shumat himself held in readiness just across the Kôbh, together with the present weakness of his own cavalry, may have influenced Tovakh not to exercise his claimed power of reversal, and once the new magistrate's first decision had been safely executed, Fornival rubbed his hands together, dimpled smugly, and spoke arcanely of an *exemplary waiver* which Dolvid took to mean that Tovakh, by failing to object first time, forfeited the right to object ever.

Next month, with the congenial company of Âna's brother, Konir, Dolvid would journey up the Paowan to the country beyond the Angle, to oversee beginnings of a new forest. But before that time came, Kadon Dinul was shaken by news to eclipse all fatuous rumor.

Saying they could no longer be part of a realm whose aim was to deprive them of property and standing, a dozen or so men and women of Family, mainly young, announced they would join Kamin-Tolagh in the Farther West. Followed by a handful of servants and two wagonloads of their belongings, they set out southward, with the intention of finding at Thenimala a ship or ships of the Hrin that would take them. Much the most prominent, and, though barely thirty, the oldest, was Khalú Khelaghilayu, Dolvid's former and Bolan's present wife. Together with this report, Dolvid received an urgent summons to attend the *rabhsai*.

To match, it might be, Rodlakh's mood, the meeting was set in the always daunting expanse of the Oak-Wall Chamber. Elamirr had arrived unbidden, and the presence of Âna, in a light summer gown, was welcome relief to general gloom.

"Such a fashionable riding, *Deghi*," Elamirr had a fierce urgency, "is not going to make much speed. They could be overtaken and brought back." Word had come they had passed through Kred Bakali.

Rodlakh's frown deepened. "Brought back? This realm is not a prison. Anyone who wants to leave can do so."

"I have sent fast-messengers after them," Dolvid said. "Not to arrest them. I thought they should be clear about their legal standing. By serving a declared outlaw, which is their stated intention, they renounce their allegiance, and forfeit protection of *rabhsai*'s law."

"Why are they going?" Âna was genuinely baffled.

Elamirr's mouth shaped scornfully, but Dolvid spoke first. "Adventure. Some on the rumor of gold. Boredom, mainly."

Rodlakh complained, "This statement they have published — there are copies everywhere; the realm meant to strip them of rank and property, there is no justice to be had in the *rabhsayum* of Rodlakh — have we hammered the Families so hard? I thought we were evenhanded, but now this comes, on top of all the petitions against the compensation law, empty rumors of rebellion — " the last with a sour glance for Elamirr.

"The Families cannot complain of unfairness," Dolvid said. "Most of those leaving us are third sons and younger daughters, without much standing or property to lose. They are going, not in sudden despair, but with the consent, probably at the invitation, of Kamin-Tolagh, while this farewell message is nothing but mischief-making, with, I suspect, Lavsila's hand in it." None of the defectors was famed for literary accomplishments, but Lavsila had always been something of a phrasemaker, and could have been originator for that recurrent *not equity, but revenge.*

For Rodlakh this news only replaced one unhappiness with another. "How does Kamin-Tolagh, a declared criminal, dare to interfere in affairs of this realm? Perhaps we do have to prevent these Heartland puppies from going to strengthen our enemy."

Âna was swift. "What then? What will you do with them? Put them to death? Send them to the Island to salt eels? There is nothing they could be convicted of — you said, this realm is no prison."

As often Dolvid wanted to hug her. "It would put *rabhsayum* in an unfavorable light, *Deghi.* I can hear them called the Heartland Martyrs, if they were only brought back — to wait for another opportunity to slip away." No more diplomatic way to tell Rodlakh not to behave like a fool.

After lip-gnawing thought, Rodlakh said, "But I want it generally understood Kamin-Tolagh was instigator of this." He was deeply troubled by that parting declaration of the voluntary exiles.

Elamirr suggested, "A proclamation — "

"No, no," Âna, as if in pain. "That would do far greater harm than this childish farewell — for the *rabhsai* to be heard complaining how the wicked Kamin-Tolagh has seduced his subjects?" She earned, here, an unpleasant covert glance from Elamirr.

"We have less formal and less public ways of letting truth come out," Dolvid concurred. "But the best answer is to continue to treat the Families fairly, within the law."

Rodlakh was still despondent. He had begun his reign, after hard victory, in unlimited hope for a realm where ancient enmities would vanish. Great personal popularity, a new and benevolent Patriarch, the chastened docility of the Families and of Kargul, whose Heir was his friend — everything had gone to strengthen his optimism. But Rodlakh, in his own assessment, was comfortable only with clear-cut questions of good and evil, and the compromises, haggling half-steps and veiled intentions by which rule was maintained were always distasteful to him. This defection, then, was all the heavier blow to his self-esteem for having no one simple cause; no matter how much he accused the blandishments of Kamin-Tolagh and Lavsila, the idiocy of the Heartlanders, there was ample blame left over for himself.

In the silence, Âna asked Dolvid, "Why Khalú?"

A half-smile. "When we were all much younger, she was courted by Lavsila, and I suppose he asked her to join him there in the West."

"From what I have heard of Khalú's nature, I can guess she has another match in mind. She probably does not know about Kamin-Tarú."

From out of his pool of darkness, Rodlakh protested, "The whole realm is still talking about her broken trothplight and departure."

"I mean," Âna patiently amended, "Khalú could not know what, besides sister, Kamin-Tarú has been to her brother. Poor Khalú."

Dolvid said, "What makes you think she wants Kamin-Tolagh?" He did not disagree with the conclusion, but was surprised at how quickly Âna had reached it.

"Lavsila, originally, would have been her father's choice of husbands for her?"

"Their lands adjoin," Dolvid agreed.

"And you told me she refused a proposal from Tholat, then the Heir — "

"Evaded it, before it could be made — " a quick glance at Rodlakh but he showed no sign of offence; he could hardly remember much about Tholat, eldest of his brothers, dead now a dozen years. He was, however, mildly perplexed at Âna's familiarity with an intimate history he knew nothing about.

"To marry, instead," Âna resumed, "a man in favor at court, but seen as mortal enemy of her kin and class — "

"Dolvid here," Rodlakh, glad to be back on familiar ground.

"Whom she divorced, when he fell from favor with Ban-Sila, to marry Bolan, who was about to become Captain-General, but whose blood is not unmixed Owani." Âna reached her point. "In all Khalú's matings there is both ambition for herself, and rebellion against her kin. And here is Kamin-Tolagh, outlaw, and, by his own reckoning, an emperor. Poor Khalú," she said again.

And poor Bolan, Dolvid thought but did not say. As Âna had obviously judged, he no longer had any strong feelings about Khalú, though he hoped she would come to no harm. Elamirr said, "Some would say the realm is well rid of such subjects."

"If it is rid of them." Dolvid doubted many comforts or luxuries were available where Kamin-Tolagh ruled, and could not believe the young Heartlanders had permanently turned their backs on the lands of their pampered upbringing. Or on their kin.

"They will not be welcomed back," Rodlakh said, "if they change their minds in a year or two. I am with Elamirr — let Kamin-Tolagh have the joy of idlers and malcontents."

"Lavsila, clearly, is not done with this realm. His secret message last summer was nothing — he has nothing to offer, and what he did tell us could not be trusted; he just wants a lifeline to Kadon Dinul."

"To Rodlakh's *rabhsayum*," Âna amended. "Meanwhile, if your guess is right, doing his best to cause trouble for us."

"How can this be prevented?" Rodlakh at last hit on a purpose for this meeting. A crux indeed, or the emblem of one; fantastic to suppose they could continue to behave as if Kamin-Tolagh's conquests did not exist, or would cease to if ignored, increasingly mad now they would be indissoluably linked by blood to the heart of Rodlakh's realm.

In its narrower sense, the question brought Elamirr back to life; he was in favor of boarding and searching every Hrin vessel docking at Thenimala, meanwhile punishing with confiscatory fines, if not Island exile, all those who received messages from the West, measures he urged could be carried out under existing law, if stretched a little.

"What law?" Âna appeared ready to send for Fornival.

"*Asayu*, the giving or offering of assistance to a known criminal."

Rodlakh frowned. "Well?" he asked Dolvid, poised to pounce.

"The law, I believe, concerns those who knowingly assist a criminal *in the commission of his crime*, or aid him to escape justice. But, *Rabhsai*, what are we stopping? A dozen green fools of the Heartland have gone off after publishing a foolish utterance; to treat this as a serious sign of general disaffection gives it exactly the importance they would wish to command. I had hoped to make use of Dhunival to intercept some of Lavsila's messages, but after our encounter, he vanished, as I ought to have anticipated." Had anticipated without admitting it; in his heart he had wished the man, given an admonitory fright, would simply go away. The whole business of spying and prying filled him with repugnance.   "As for an attempt to prevent all communication between the realm and the Farther West, the means, as Elamirr outlines them, are obviously unacceptable. Ransacking Hrin vessels will make enemies of a friendly people, and drive them into Kamin-Tolagh's camp. Hrin vessels draw little water, and do not have to dock first at Thenimala; they could be beached anywhere on the Ninkufu coasts — we would have to search travellers, restrict trade and travel, hire informers... Does all this remind you of the final year of Ban-Sila's *rabhsayum*?"

"Some of the bullies Bolan hired could be found again." Âna was acerbic.

Rodlakh, made pensive by the reference to his brother's ugly reign, said, "Then there is no way we can stop these insults?"

"I can think of two ways," Dolvid said. "One, obviously, is to capture or kill Kamin-Tolagh, and that means war."

"Not a popular war," Rodlakh, bitterly. "When half the realm wants to see Kamin-Tolagh as part-hero, part-clown, Odi Kukkuk and Okseti Jester in one."

"Growing less popular as losses mounted, with the taxes to pay for it." In his heart, Dolvid was uncertain they could ever succeed in such a war, conducted at great and barren distance from home, but it would be impolitic to say so in Rodlakh's present mood.

"The other way?" Âna asked. Rather, she prompted; she already had the answer.

"Peace."

"We are at peace, aren't we?" Rodlakh's tone had a taut menace, as if warning Dolvid not to go on.

"We are at nothing; we cannot be at peace with what we do not recognize. Kamin-Tolagh has broken oaths and betrayed high office, suborned the loyalty of his father's soldiers, raided your realm — all crimes for which he cannot be punished — "

"Can he not," Rodlakh, darkly.

" — or not without a difficult war, which might cost hundreds if not thousands of lives, most of the dying, as always, done by men who have no stake in the issues. As you say, a considerable part of the realm sees Kamin-Tolagh as dashing and adventurous. His admirers are not all of the Old Blood," to forestall a contemptuous comment from Elamirr.

"You say, we are powerless."

"*Rabhsai*, there is one weapon you can always command." Dolvid wondered how he had come to need this ceremonious style with a man he once shared stolen cheese with, and within this same Residence. "Magnanimity. Lavsila and his cronies would be disarmed if you extended recognition, even a treaty of friendship, to Kamin-Tolagh's growing domains."

"You have changed, Dolvid," sadly. "Once, you would have said, justice is indivisible, and to be pursued, regardless of cost."

"In those days, I enjoyed the irresponsibility of being no one, and risking only my own life. I was in no position to condemn young men to die for the sake of things they do not understand." Impossible to share his vision of a death-struggle between Rodlakh and Kamin-Tolagh, coming closer.

"At least my *rabhsayum* has been dedicated to justice. If I reach out a hand to Kamin-Tolagh, it will be seen as softness, not generosity."

"If you do not, chances are his oathbreaking will be forgotten, and in time he will come to appear the injured party. As a friendly rival, with ties of blood to this realm — "

"Enough," harshly. Never before forbidden to speak on any subject, Dolvid saw the *rabhsai* was trembling with anger.

He, too, was exasperated. "Then let us talk about our readiness for war. Shumat's depleted squadrons have to be brought up to strength, and we shall need added forces to guard all coasts and borders, to keep watch on all those who show sympathy with Kamin-Tolagh. If, sooner or later, there has to be a war, let it be sooner, before Kamin-Tolagh is so strong the cost in lives will be tens of thousands. If we are not going to make war, let us make a proper peace, and save all this suspicion and unhappiness and wasted posturing."

It was the only time he and Rodlakh had really quarrelled, acrimonious, not softened by Elamirr's presence or Âna's attempts at mediation. The height of anger and depths of discourse were achieved when Rodlakh, accusing Dolvid of lacking all principle, compared his ethics to those of Petakoi. Even Âna's shocked protest failed to bring a retraction, and Dolvid responded he would rather be without principles than bind his hands with moral precepts he had no means to enforce.

For leavetaking, a frigid calm was restored. Dolvid, as he rode down the Avenue, was recalling Âna's warning when

Kamin-Tolagh's outlawry was in dispute. True; for Rodlakh, anything hinting at expediency had to be supplied with loftier motives.

He had announced his planned sojourn in the northeastern Paowan well in advance, but knew it was unwise to leave, as he did, two days later, without another meeting with the *rabhsai*. His companion, Konir, despite — or because of — the kinship with Âna, kept clear of disputes at the Residence not directly affecting his work; Kamin-Tolagh, the Heartland defectors, new laws, old quarrels were not mentioned during the dozen days they spent together, differing amicably on the best way to start seedlings, the best sites for each kind.

Calmed by long days among submissive infant oaks and beeches, he came back on an evening with foretastes of early summer in the bland air. Selfishly, because marriage could not for long be center of his life, he was as always deeply glad of Aëlu's serenity to welcome him home. She had taken note of trouble, but did not ask for an account, and he resolved he would see the *rabhsai* only when summoned.

Next day at the Bronze Residence he discovered the realm had not fallen apart in his absence. Those going to the West, by no sort of coincidence, had found a couple of Hrin vessels waiting at Thenimala, with room enough for them all, including their servants and belongings, but one young man, a nephew of Fornival's, had changed his mind on the gangplank, and was on his way back; Dolvid resolved to talk with him to see if he knew anything about Lavsila's part in the defection.

Reading documents, dictating others, working with his scribes and with the *bôdhloikil* who came, giving Elamirr whatever needed the *rabhsai*'s signature, he made do with word-of-mouth reports about the New Residence, where the atmosphere was said to be tense.

On the fourth morning a brief note came from Faëdhal, asking him to be at his house that afternoon. Puzzled by the unprecedented request, worried it signalled a worsening of his ailments, Dolvid rode there alone through a light rain. Outside, he was saluted by the leader of a file of Household cavalry waiting there in the saddle; perplexity growing he was admitted by the smooth-faced housekeeper, who silently withdrew to the interior of the house, leaving him among the glass ornaments, alone with the *rabhsayu*.

Âna was in a simple robe the color of late cornstalks, dark hair caught up in a blue band. "I have not much time. Like the *Bôdhrai*, when an old friend is said to be ill, I can visit, but not often, and not for long.

"Faëdhal is much better — " as Dolvid, bewildered, made one step in the direction of the bedroom. "He was generous enough to help me arrange this private meeting."

Clear at last, he was appalled at her imprudence, though few men were as safe with a secret as Faëdhal.

"You and Rodlakh," coming swiftly and seriously to the point, "must be friends. Because of his position, that means you must be his friend, no matter what."

Dolvid smiled without warmth. "It is difficult," stiffly, "to force friendship on one of his rank. Final say is his."

"Don't. Do not pretend humility. There is nothing he would not do to have your good opinion, short of abdication. Perhaps not short of that."

"Good or not, he can choose which of my opinions he wants to hear."

"He has seen fit," she interposed swiftly, "to brush aside your advice in the Kamin-Tolagh affair — advice, pardon me, which could have been offered more tactfully."

"Tact! Rodlakh and I once shared a leaking boat we could neither steer nor stop. He trusted me to win his Residence for him."

"And just as you fought for, he is *rabhsai*. He cherishes recollections of those great times — why else is he so bitterly wounded by the treachery of Kamin-Tolagh?"

"Very well," on his dignity, while certain he would reconcile with Rodlakh. "But such feelings cannot dictate what is wise policy. Where welfare of the realm is concerned, I have no feelings of my own; If I urged peace with Kamin-Tolagh, it was not because I approve of what he has done."

"Well." She smiled ruefully. "In your urging, you implied the *rabhsai* was irresponsible enough to send men to die without a second thought, which you know to be untrue: you yourself told me after Kamsilat he wept for the dead when everyone else was cheering victory. You might also have found a more tactful word than *posturing* to describe his attitude." Her old vehemence abruptly broke out. "No feelings of your own? You have been back at Kadon Dinul three days, and have not sought audience with your *rabhsai*, after a fortnight away. Is it for the welfare of the realm you are sulking at the Bronze Residence?"

"Sulking?" But Âna seized his wrist and drew herself close.

"I can stand it only as long as you can," voice in her throat. "Not a second longer. You are needed."

In his own throat, a swelling had to be fought back before he could speak. Enormously conscious of risk, he rapidly kissed in turn each of her eyelids, and drew back. "Someday soon we're going to have to make up our minds."

"To what?"

"That we made our choices, four years ago."

For smallest division of a second, her eyes showed a signal other than assent; anger, perhaps, reproach, a mad urge to rebel, gone too quickly to label. "I know," gaze unwavering. "When there is time."

26.

"They will want land," Lavsila had said, preparing to leave for his vigil at Larghamit. "Growing land."

Having had from Hrin traders advance word of the Heartlanders' embarkation in Thenimala, he began haunting the port so as to be there to greet the Heartlanders, several of them his kin by blood, marriage, or both. Plainly he intended to be a person of consequence among them, the man in the know, the old hand, the voice with Kamin-Tolagh's ear.

His forecast, Kamin-Tolagh understood, did not mean those pampered hands were prepared to plow and sow, hoe and harvest; what the Heartlanders would want was to be landlords and oversee tenant farms. As Fretasi speculated, that must be how past empires had worked, with a warrior-king seizing lands, in extreme cases killing or driving away the original occupants, or else simply replacing the ruler or ruling clans — in effect, what he had done with the Man-mani. Or one of the old empire-makers might turn landowners into his tenants; whichever was the case, having accumulated greater territory than he could personally oversee, he would have to divide it up among new landlords of his creation, an aristocracy.

In the Age of the Shâls, not only Empire but the realm at its center, except for the still extensive but proportionally minor holdings of the *Atarlum*, belonged absolutely to the ruler, *nimúrai*; though the term freehold was in use, the condition, as it was now known, did not exist. Royal domain being perpetual, even provincial overlords could never be more than holders, in practice, of hereditary leases. Since the Return, although the idea of descending tenancy continued to be used for assessment and collection of taxes, *rabhsai* was only the largest among many true freeholders, but here in the new Empire there was no rival power to prevent Kamin-Tolagh from claiming, as ancient rulers had, absolute ownership of all the lands his armies could seize and keep subdued, and then auctioning off the right to exploit them, for growing crops, cutting timber, quarrying and mining. Rodlakh's *rabhsayum* sold or leased rights to various imports and monopoly goods; Fretasi was coolly respectful of the hallowed glories of dominion, but was quite certain, in her austere way, that profit came first. As she said, there could be no peace, honor, security, or justice, no rule, unless the overlord could maintain the largest and best-trained armies equipped with the best weapons, all of which cost money.

"Who will bid on the lands the Laughing Owl farm?" he had baited Lavsila. "Or the woodlands of the Gudi-la?"

"Not those lands. You will have to conquer the Hrin."

Fretasi's hard-headed reasoning suggested he should regard the coming of the Heartlanders as a potential source of wealth, a second Zelu Bablakhi; if so he was going to have to keep irritation in check; he disliked them at sight, riding untidily into the Abu. It was midmorning, they having paused overnight in the usual half-way resting-point on the Larghamit road, resuming at first light and so escaping the worst heat of the day. A small escort was with them, but otherwise the careless, chattering company might have been riding in the meadows by Shufloi Kadonu, rather than a harsh West, where cavalry swords were a precarious hedge against surrounding savagery.

Till the various vacant houses found their tenants, the Heartlanders were to be accommodated at the Residence and another of the nearby mansions. When they assembled that first evening in the main hall to be introduced to Kamin-Tolagh and his sister, the first face he saw was a familiar one, and smiling invitingly; Ondhayu, one of the last pair of girls to share his bed in his brief tenure at Kadon Dinul. Still small, no longer a girl, she had passed twenty without entirely losing her sporting eye, but while he read, as she intended, her willingness for a renewal, she was here as companion and near-trothplight to some degree of cousin, Pranúdhanai, younger son of Prômsilakh, a leading Heartland grower of wheat, feed and fruits. Tall, large-toothed, with a confident manner, and the loud voice of a horse-trader, he went at once to the subject of *dao* spice, about which he was well-informed, suggesting intelligent, full-time management could increase yield and virtually eliminate pilfering. "I would be prepared, *Asai*, to bid for exclusive right to oversee production and sale of the *dao*."

Though much of the income earned was necessarily in the form of bartered goods, the popularity of the spice only increased, and all that could be grown was sold. Almost, Kamin-Tolagh asked what the young man would expect to pay for such a lucrative monopoly, but recognized it as a brink, after which there was the sheer descent into dickering, another thing an emperor did not do. Whether in correspondence, or rapidly since the ships docked at Larghamit, Pranúdhanai's knowledge of *dao* and its production could have come only from Lavsila.

He, garlanded with unction, was at the farther end of the hall, stooped over to speak intimately with his kinswoman, the small and slender Khalú, still astonishingly lovely, though showing sooty signs of fatigue about her usually luminous eyes. She, above all, was the one Kamin-Tarú was discreetly assessing, noting, her brother knew from experience, the subtlest indications of fashion in such details as where a cloak-fastener was worn.

Inspired, Kamin-Tolagh told Pranúdhanai, "All such questions will be discussed, not with me, but with Lavsila, who is to be imperial agent for these transactions." The young man showed a faint surprise, as Lavsila undoubtedly would, though he surely would not decline the post. While retaining final right of approval, Kamin-Tolagh would allow him a small commission on deals he made; the regard of a true Heartlander for other Heartlanders was superseded only by loyalty to his own profit, and these newcomers would find their ally swiftly transformed into a potent adversary.

"Uh — " Pranúdhanai's wordless interjections were even louder than his speech. "I understood, *Asai* — "

Kamin-Tolagh brushed aside further talk. "Lavsila will also instruct you on the proper way to address me."

They learned swiftly, warned by abrupt withdrawal of Kamin-Tolagh from that first meeting; by the time of the feast next evening *Asai* had been banished in favor of the more abject *Lord*.

A strange and elusive event; bewildered Heartlanders trying to identify or create familiar forms in a place much less like home than they had imagined, some, probably, already wondering why they had come, others determined to preserve

Residence Quarter imperturbability, Residence Quarter courtesies, reminding Kamin-Tolagh of raiders routed in the new territories west of Flamûrai, men who clung by fierce habit to their light shields woven from a sort of tough dried fronds, perfectly useless against the steel-tipped arrows of Tau-Suaka's Hill Froghul.

Absence of any of the servants who had followed their riding, men and women of Other Race, was another reversion, one to be watched; these blood-proud young newcomers were going to be disappointed if they hoped the Empire would permit them the high-handedness the realm now denied; enforced service would have no sanction in Kamin-Tolagh's law, and any who wanted to leave their masters and strike out on their own would be allowed to do so — protected, in fact, against seizure or retribution. He had no special interest in the wellbeing of Others, but could not afford little dark pools of resentment starting to seethe here at the Abu, an infection that could become an epidemic, once spread to the tribes.

Khalú's appearance in a close-fitting white gown, entirely without sleeves, was startling for women of the Abu, to whom it looked almost tribal, but the Residence Quarter Heartlanders had already made their asessment of the officers' wives, and effectively dismissed them. Ondhayu, in whose full-lipped mouth *Lord* sounded less an honorific than a teasing challenge, informed Kamin-Tarú the incomparable Morulis — notwithstanding her breeding, the reigning maker of fashion — loved to display her slender, perfect arms, and had made sleevelessness all the style at Kadon Dinul.

To offset their disregard of their own lesser compatriots, the newcomers were fascinated with the Hrin of every degree, not excluding Dvasslo, who was smirkingly present.

By now accepted as part of the life of the Abu, his vulgarity had grown to match his confidence, and he normally found his drinking-companions among least-educated of the soldiery. But he remained on cordial terms with everyone, and must have at least one acquaintance with each tribe of the Froghushei; he had the knack of finding friends wherever there was money to be made, and was becoming, if not wealthy, comfortably prosperous, "one fourthing at a time," as Fretasi said; the man's profit came largely from numberless small transactions; tooth-twigs acquired from the Gudi-la sold at two tobhai a dozen, the excellent sewing thread of his own people (though not of his region), nothing was too minor for Dvasslo to consider.

While he had declined any payment for his help at the forge, saying the purification of metals and their forging were religious matters for any true follower of the *dveyust-ranga-hrindan*, clearly he expected his generosity to be kept in mind. But he had been shrewd enough to forestall complaint by being first to suggest he begin paying rental on the storehouse he had turned into his shop and trading-post, and he surrendered without complaint the transactional tax initiated by Fretasi — so readily, indeed, that it must surely be under-assessed.

Without ever travelling in northern Froghushei, Dvasslo contrived to unearth all each tribe possessed that could conceivably have a price put on it; he had somehow discovered excellent dancers among the Ntara-golal, and the half-dozen who came, perhaps because of their tribe's intermittent contact with the Hrin over the centuries, readily adapted their dance to the rhythms of musicians also brought in by Dvasslo on very short notice, men and one plain woman of his home *onhritha*, performers on instruments that looked much stranger than they sounded, pipes and plucked strings.

But his former master, Huolafidn, was also in attendance, courteous, reasonable, unreadable as ever, and while he had arrived virtually arm-in-arm with another shipowner from the following of Iolfrant's friendly neighbor, Svedion, the two of them, like Dvasslo, were newly willing to associate with Navridn. Religious differences were supposed to be insuperable — and yet here were three adherents of the *dveyust-ranga-hrindan* on smiling terms with one whose close kin and *hrithust*, Nestos, was an adherent of the infamous *tveyusto-hrid-minyist*, confirming Iruvakh's recent perception rival *hrithuod*, notwithstanding religious antagonisms, were inclined to cooperation as never before.

Before, he meant, Kamin-Tolagh's brief invasion. The outcome of that expedition, what was seen generally as Iolfrant's craven buying off of Kamin-Tolagh, had endorsed the low regard in which men of Kargul already held the fighting potential, the resolution, they would have said the manhood, of the Hrin, which in turn was what lay behind Lavsila's airy recommendation they should be conquered, presumably on a day when there was no other pressing business.

Iruvakh's view had rather vaguely ascribed the new tolerance in part to the conciliating personality of Hridveyuth, the holy man of the Hrin, contrary to his earlier assertion Hridveyuth's teachings were incompatible with the *dveyust-ranga-hrindan*. Yet when Kamin-Tolagh, as if in casual curiosity, brought up the subject, urbane Iolfrant and volatile-seeming Navridn made what was practically a joint statement, admitting they had differences of detail with the Hridveyuth, but nothing but praise for how he had rekindled the faith of the common people, everywhere in Hrin lands. "In this," the learned Huolafidn added, "he has been not unlike your Zhôl."

"Not," hastening to eradicate any conceivable offense, "Not, Lord, that we would compare this living man to your well-loved god, whom all revere. But it is said the honored name of Zhôl is sounded now in every corner of your realm, as never before."

"My realm? I have no realm but this."

"The realm of your beginnings, Lord," Huolafidn blandished. "Our *Hrithust*, who journeyed as far as the city, Kanzan Tâl, before winter, was told gatherings for Zhôl's Day were the largest ever seen."

Kamin-Tolagh was at a loss, but the loud-voiced Heartlander, Pranúdhanai came, unwitting, to his rescue, not shy of joining the discussion by way of an overheard remark. "It has been a genuine joy for us, Lord, who have always been proud to call ourselves Children of Yoëlladhu, to see this spread of faith to others not born with our advantages."

He meant, of course, those not of pure Owani descent, a welcome at complete variance with Lavsila's contemptuous dismissal of these changes. If the *Mankh'* continued to recruit adherents among the very people it had once sought to exclude, the tide would become irreversible, no matter what Patriarchs succeeded Dozhusai, and any who still trumpeted the necessary dominance of the Owani race, would have lost their best ally and only doctrinal weapon.

Not without a struggle; to Kamin-Tolagh, the strongest parallel between Zhôl and the Hrin's Hridveyuth was that their popularity called for the same unctuous approval with the same disdain not far beneath the surface; Pranúdhanai and the Hrin leaders understood each other very well. It amused Kamin-Tolagh to think of the self-styled Children of Yoëlladhu, like

Lavsila, like his mother, landed with and unable to disown all those brothers and sisters they had never wanted, or wished for only as minions, but religious affairs of Rodlakh's realm were no longer his urgent concern.

Those of the Hrin, however, might be his key to survival, and it brought him onto familiar ground, recognizing one place where the Hrin ruling classes could ignore differing beliefs: in the unspoken expectation religion would keep the common people in their place.

Main food had been served and eaten, and now there was circulation among the three long tables, a search for order, watched impassively by the bodyguard under Tau-Suaka, who appeared to think assassins could lurk among the Heartlanders. Who, in turn, were plainly made uneasy by the unblinking vigilance of men who, despite the decorated uniform tunics of which they were so proud, retained their look of untamed ferocity.

Kambanal, quickly recognized as influential, was at the center of one knot of new arrivals, while another group was being instructed by Dubovai, trying to convey the extent of the Empire, its position relative to the realm and surrounding lands; his gestures were not much different from some unlettered countryman giving vague and useless directions, although he was the one man alive who always knew exactly where he was and how he got there. Lavsila stood nearby, nodding and smiling as if he had invented a toy named Dubovai, now displayed for the first time.

Another small group, entirely of women, was focused on Ondhayu, who was explaining a newly popular method of fortune-telling, brought to Kadon Dinul by a woman of the Northeast, said to have come to Narn from some distant land. As far as Kamin-Tolagh could overhear, it had to do with correspondences between birthdays and spins of a kind of top with significant markings at the rim; Kamin-Tarú, as always with these matters, was fascinated, but he could never sustain interest in any method of allegedly peering into the future.

Khalú took the opportunity to approach him, with a compliment on the surprising quality of food and wines; the fowl were from the country of the Anga-jai, while the beef had been purchased from the Hrin, in the form of cattle, slaughtered at the moment of coming ashore at Larghamit; though they lost flesh on the sea-voyage they were spared the parched journey to the Abu.

Virtually anything, he told her, was available here to those with money to pay for it. Smiling she asked, "Have you ever had Bérovan almonds — " and then, after a long pause, lightly, a mere flick of her pink tongue, " — Lord?"

"Who has not?" The name was misleading; Bérovan was a hamlet not far from Dônshei, in central Dramal, miles more northerly than almonds could be grown; the place where the nuts were transformed into a prized sweetmeat.

"Anyone poor," she answered him; the almonds, if delicious, were staggeringly costly. "The two related families that make them buy exclusively from one grower, in western Ninkufu, the only one, so they say, to give them almonds plump enough. They use pear-wood for the smoking, and have standing agreements with orchards in Nîv, to buy old trees as they are replaced. Their honey must be Island, and the little pots the almonds are sold in — " glazed earthenware, with a matching cap — "are imported through Narn — all this, for the sake of a pleasing nibble. Still, they would never find buyers in that bare country; our kinsman Zhival is sole wholesale purchaser, and brings them to where they can be sold. As my father says, nothing is too much expense or too much trouble, if a profit can be made at the end."

Notwithstanding improbable subject, she was plainly flirting. Unexpectedly, no matter how aware he was of her purpose, nor how little his concern with ordinary commerce, Kamin-Tolagh was stirred by her account, a strange sort of romance to illustrate the idea and function of empire, honeyed almonds as emblem of the compound transactions enabled by the spread of peace and order; what fascinated him was how such a complex process could ever have started: obviously, the makers in Bérovan were not becoming hugely wealthy, and could have made a living in other ways — selling fifty times as many ordinary smoked almonds, for example.

These thoughts could not be discussed with Khalú, whose elegantly provocative dress, whose effortless assumption of superiority — whose history of matings with the influential and celebrated — made her something of a Bérovan almond herself. But the subject, he perceived, was of no particular interest for her; all the more remarkable that she had seen others fascinated by the story, and brought it here to impress him, learnt like a child's lesson.

She was less inclined even than Ondhayu to accord him the deference he had prescribed, but she had spent most of her life on familiar terms with the *rabhsayum*, as Khelagh's daughter, wife first to Dolvid, then to the now-discredited Captain-General. To whom she was still married; with deliberately harsh effect Kamin-Tolagh asked, "How was Bolan when you left him?"

"I have not seen him in over half a year, Lord," very coolly. "My brother is to declare my divorce — or has done so, now Halving has come and gone. We did not expect Bolan to contest this."

That answered the easier side of the peculiar sum. A few paces away, Kamin-Tarú was rapt over the wonders of prophecy, and in her absorption had forgotten her promise to maintain an aloof distance from their guests. Observing her, lips slightly parted, eyes with the trusting wonder of a five-year-old, Kamin-Tolagh could not be annoyed, but was only flooded with tender regard — and that was what made Khalú's advances so odd. At the Abu, apart from an occasional unthinking caress by Kamin-Tarú, he and his sister still maintained the proprieties, but he doubted anyone was really deceived; Lavsila exulted that the tale of how Kamin-Tarú had fooled her trothplight and decoyed her mother had scandalized and delighted the entire realm, and with allowance for exaggeration it would have seemed in all the world no one but a small child could be unaware they were lovers.

Ondhayu was not the same; her eye was a challenge to pure sport; she was reminding him she knew how to give pleasure (better, undoubtedly, after four added years of practice). She was offering an interlude, no doubt with the approval, perhaps at the urging, of Pranúdhanai, in hopes it would result in preferential treatment for them as a couple. But Khalú, obviously, was not trying to obtain special favors for her pairing with Lavsila, whom she must suppose already high in Kamin-Tolagh's regard, and with whose attentions she had been noticeably offhand. She was out to capture Kamin-Tolagh for herself, and that implied either an almost insane confidence in her ability to compete with Kamin-Tarú, or an equally implausible obliviousness.

The multiple irritations were unreasonable but real, worse for being unnecessary. In absolute fact, there was no power to prevent him having the whole gaggle of Heartlanders seized by Tau-Suaka's men, conducted to the middle of Landegh and told to make the best of it; he owed them nothing, and could not be controlled by public opinion; some of the Kargul' families, he was certain, would applaud.

But not Kamin-Tarú. His temper did not improve when, coming for breakfast, he found his sister already at the table, using a sharp-pointed knife to pick at stitching in the shoulders of her favorite robe, apricot-colored glazed linen.

"You could get a woman to do that for you."

"It would take too long to explain."

"Antiyu would understand." The girl was to stay on as mistress of Kamin-Tarú's household, despite betrothal to Pivrekhan, who was hardly racing headlong to a marriage that, before his disabling injuries, would have been beneath him. Kamin-Tarú did not reply, and observing the gown was going to lose its sleeves, her brother guessed Antiyu might understand too well.

"Khalú's arms," his sister declared, "have no shape to them."

"I shall bed with her. Once."

"Once," Kamin-Tarú echoed. "Unless she pleases you enough for twice. You said you had no interest in any Heartland women."

He helped himself to fruit. "This is a policy question, and may save a great deal of trouble. Lavsila will have her, but not till she has learned all she can expect from me."

Tú gave a typical fluid fidget of her shoulders. "I might want to try one of the newcomers, for the sake of my policy — Pranúdhanai, or that Harbor Way boy. He is very pretty."

"You can't," without much emphasis; he knew his sister's mood, half-teasing retribution which normally achieved its object simply by being spoken. "You could never manage it without some servant or bodyguard knowing. My standing would be affected."

"What about my standing when you have Khalú on her back?"

"As with the Other Races, women here are admired for their *chastity* — " he heavily stressed the word, which had no true equivalent in the Owanilú.

"Are we rulers? To rule over savages, who treat women as their goods, we have to adopt their ways?"

This called for a strong denial, but any leader, as he tried to point out, unless ready and able to kill a challenger, had to be worthy in ways his followers could understand; birth, wisdom, cunning, prowess — details varied from place to place, but throughout the tribes, as far as he could tell, chieftains, war-captains, male deities, were expected to have many women, from the Man-mani headman with his traditional four wives to the hero-god of the Gudi-la, whose forty young girls went as signs of his power, with the great herd of milch cattle and abject array of defeated enemies. Whereas women, on the contrary —

"Who," contemptuously, "could admire the *chastity* of one among forty, waiting for her turn to come again?"

"Nevertheless, with Tau-Suaka's men, for instance, and most of the tribes, if you were to bed with one of the Heartlanders, it would be seen as weakness in me if I did not kill him, and at least beat you."

"This is nonsense."

"Rule is: what could be more nonsense than men by the hundred who will ride where they may be killed, because I say so?"

"You are their lord." For her, it was simple.

"I am their lord, not by law and custom, but by force and nonsense; my rule, our rule will end when I cease to be admirable to them." Not for the first time he felt deep envy for the web of tradition and institution which helped a *rabhsai* maintain power; the wholly despised Ban-Sila had been unseated only by a chance murder, and Rodlakh, once proclaimed, did not have to keep proving his right to rule.

Kamin-Tarú was pondering. "It is unfair," at last, not meaning his struggle.

"I grant you. Lavsila would tell you, this is the world without Owani enlightenment." Yet contrary to what the Others affected to believe, the Owanil did not seek fairness by pretending there was no difference between men and women, having long ago grown beyond that absurdity: there was no reason to censure a woman who, as she had, enjoyed many men, but neither was it especially admired: Tú was enchanting, but aware any woman not actively repellent could have as many partners as she had time for, merely by proclaiming herself available, while a man, no matter how handsome or powerful, still had work to do — and must have a noteworthy and reliable weapon to wield.

"Unless you would like to beat me. Would you enjoy that? I could have a pretty whip made, to keep at bedside."

This was peacemaking, but she was still aggrieved. "When we take some of the Heartlanders down to see the tribal country, a way could be found for you to bed a man with no one the wiser, if that would give you pleasure. But he will have to be discreet; if he ever swaggers over you, Tau-Suaka will see to it his next boast is made in a higher-pitched voice."

She tried and failed to hold back a giggle, and threw a slack ball of picked threads in his face. "I do not want to bed with anyone but you."

"Than what are we debating?"

There was a pause, while she folded under raw edges she had made, to see how her gown would look unsleeved. "I thought you did not want any more women."

"I told you, this is policy. I was not pleased last night."

"To me, you seemed flattered, at times. If I were a man, I would choose Ondhayu over Khalú. She looks the better ride."

He waved that away. "They want to turn the Abu into a new Residence Quarter. I do not say life here won't be better for a little polite society, but first, they must learn, they have no standing here, except what I decree."

"And so you let Khalú share your bed."

"Once. Once. She is bound to be a leader among them, because of whose daughter she is and who she has married. They will see I can discard her, with no claim on me, and it may help teach them to be humble."

"She is scarcely as high as a child," using a flat hand to measure off shortness. "No taller than the *rabhsayu*. Was that Siv'loi of yours also half-grown?"

"I can't remember," mystified by the turns his sister's mind could take.

"Liar," but he judged she was happy enough with a theory that left her as uniquely tall.

"Khalú is said to be a good horsewoman. As the Heartland judges." This had derision under it, born of Tú's confidence, not misplaced, that in this skill she had no equal among women.

All the same, Khalú was vain as Kamin-Tarú, vainer, with a self-absorption complete enough, he reflected, to have survived marriage to two of the most famous men of her time; fascinating how skilled she was at making her compliments reflect back lustre on herself, so that his setting of the Great Fire was a parallel for the bold measures she had taken to rid her estates of foxes, years ago.   Remarking his officers were obviously ready to die for him, she managed to suggest his rare faculty for inspiring trust could be fully appreciated only by one who, like her, shared it; all this could easily have engendered, had he permitted it, a strange feeling of competition, striving for an achievement she could neither share nor match, but that was contrary to his plan.   He resisted, on the same grounds, the temptation to ask further, discomfiting questions about Bolan, the rumored decline, for example, in his health, or to mention birth of a daughter to Dolvid, though that must surely annoy her.

For the sake of his standing he was now in reluctant permanent occupancy of the large, official Residence, but had brought Khalú to the place he preferred and Lavsila coveted, the former house of Kemunai, by the cliffs, though its stock of wines was now much depleted, still most skillfully made of all the buildings of the Abu, and coolest in the heat of summer.

When it came to bedding, Khalú enhanced her nakedness with a shift of white shuzi, but her skin was scarcely less smooth, and she gave a pretty imitation of gradual submission leading to frenzy.   She panted out she had never been pleasured so, but he had been with too many women not to know what was real, and when she set about prolonging and heightening his enjoyment, all he had learnt in his fabled thousand beds was not enough to make her transports sincere.   He wondered passingly why she bothered to pretend, and instantly answered himself; she was here to please, if she could to create in him the illusion of dependence, and many men, she must have discovered, were prouder of effects than of the most steadfast causes — not out of any real regard for the woman's enjoyment, but because to bring about ecstasy, and extravagances of gratitude, was an achievement.   Somewhere, however, Khalú must have experienced what she could now imitate so well.   Almost well enough to deceive herself, as if she needed very much to believe in the sport for its own sake, and so be spared confronting the colder but more pitiable ambition that brought her here. She was going to end by hating him, but if her joy had been genuine she might have had some consolation for defeat.

He allowed her to fall asleep in his bed, but in the morning was up before she wakened, and when she did was blind and deaf to her invitations.

"Breakfast will be brought you. Dawdle all you want."

"Will you not have breakfast with me?"

"I must be gone."

"Then I shall see you later." Not quite a question.

He shook his head. "I shall be working. Tomorrow, I leave for the south."

"Where your tribes are? I am eager to see that." Sitting up in bed, small, slightly clad, hair in disarray, she looked half her true age.

"Your kinsman, Lavsila, can accompany you. I shall be with my sister."

She blinked a little at his brusqueness, but was slow to understand what nothing in experience prepared her for. "I, naturally, had thought you and I — "

"You were mistaken."

"I believed — " she crossed arms to caress her own shoulders — "I was pleasing to you."

"So you have been," briskly. "Hardly less than the best of my girls from the tribes, and that is high praise."

But for one of her standing and pretensions, an insult, impossible to be other than calculated. Khalú flushed, and anger flickered like summer lightning over her mouth and in the mobile eyes; he could find unexpected admiration for the swiftness with which she saw remonstrance was useless, imposing calm, though hands made agitated little pluckings at the bedcovers. "Those girls cannot know how fortunate they are," she said with a contrived smile. "I am grateful you made time to teach me. One sees that tribes and lands are not the only empire where you are unquestioned lord."

"I like to keep my edge well-honed."

"It would be good to be your whetstone as often as need arises," briefly veiling her eyes to point the slight pun. The submissiveness here implied would have been a monumental concession on her part, if she had kept out the irony, which left no doubt about underlying arrogance, certain she could never be reduced to weekwifedom.

"I have no lack of fresh diversion. You Heartlanders are going to have to make your own amusements."

"Yet a man, my lord, such as you, needs a woman at his side worthier of his standing than a girl from the tribes. Of his proper blood, let us say."

"I have my sister," maintaining his air of half-elsewhere good temper. In her face he could read the answer to the puzzle of this doomed attempt; she had not been unaware, but having heard tales of him with Kamin-Tarú had decided not to believe them.

Though disconcerted, even now she was not finally convinced, but tried to stammer out clarification of her offer, which Kamin-Tolagh broke into, boorishly inattentive. "This house is also a favorite of your kinsman."

"Lavsila?" dully. She seized on the other half: "A good house, most unusual."

"Lavsila most assuredly thinks you came here to be his companion."

She rolled her eyes prettily. "Oh, this has been going on for half my lifetime; he talked about me as his fated bride when I was only sixteen. Ever since I was a girl " she said, and the feigned wonder in her voice set his teeth on edge, the clumsy pretence of modesty, "Men have been deciding I am necessary to their lives, I cannot say why. It is nothing I do."

"When you join together Lavsila can have his wish; this house will be my bride-gift to you." A pity to give up the place, but the gesture was irresistible; Lavsila would always suspect Khalú had earned the reward overnight, not he in years of what he would call and truly believe was faithful service.

Lavsila took on the familiar pose of being privy to special information. "Not all the Heartlanders who came here are Family. Some, or one, at least, is Craft." The distinction, practically lost on Kamin-Tolagh, who found the claims of both groups equally ridiculous, was of enormous importance to Lavsila, although he at once began to modify his judgment in the particular case of Valubran, the youth Kamin-Tarú had called pretty. "He has double half-masterships, in enamelling, his father's craft, and goldsmithing, his grandfather's. But his father is very near the Families; *his* father was related to Rhunsilakh, *Bôdhrai* to Lambarr — his son, indeed, manages the New Residence for Rodlakh *Rabhsai*, so the family remains prominent, despite — or as one should say with this *rabhsayum*, helped by — Rhunilat's inexplicable marriage to a Mixed girl, daughter of the notorious Arvus — "

"Valubran," Kamin-Tolagh prompted threateningly.

Lavsila, with minimal elaboration, spoke of the boy's reputation for skill, and said he had agreed to work for Tavrotosai, either renting a share of the existing forge, or if that was not feasible, having a new one constructed. He would be making jewelry. "He has worked with both his grandfathers; his mother's father is Vulakh, who has the shop in Harbor Way — the best of the jewelers, the place against the city wall by the end of — "

"I know Vulakh's shop," Kamin-Tolagh said. "But there is little demand here or in the south for work of that quality, and what there is the Hrin can satisfy."

"No, no. That is not Tavrotosai's idea. You see, Vulakh's wife, Valubran's grandmother, was daughter of Karabadh, who was outside the Guild, and made trinket jewelry, rings, necklaces, bracelets, a dozen at a time. He was quite celebrated in Banak's reign, and never pretended his stock was anything but pretty trash. Less well known — " in his element, Lavsila at last came proudly to his reserved information: "Karabadh, while young, changed his name from Rholivan, so no one would remember his father was Rholivai."

"*Rholivai*? As in *rholivaïn* — ?" to Kamin-Tolagh, as to most others, not a person, but a word of the Owanilú, the name of just such a cheap imitation gold as Karabadh must have used in his trinketry.

Yes, Lavsila confirmed, but invented by and named after Valubran's great-great-grandfather, and he, unfortunately, had tried to pass off the metal as gold, eventually, in the reign of Plakhat III, doing some coining, for which he had been convicted and exiled to the Island; he had been considered lucky to escape execution. "Less riskily used," Lavsila summed up, "the recipe for Rholivai's metal has remained in the family; Valubran knows the alloy, and its proportions."

"We shall have to be wary of any gold that comes from a forge Davsslo shares with this boy."

"Oh, I thought it best not to introduce Valubran to our Hrin friends, not even Dvasslo. They would far sooner admit to having a murderer in the family — a defiler of graves would be nearer."

"Khalú," abruptly, "is an accomplished woman."

"One I have long admired," blandly. "Notwithstanding her penchant for ill-advised marriages."

"You could do worse in a wife. If you do decide to marry, you may take Kemunai's house for your own; Khalú found it pleasing."

Cutting short bewildered gratitude, Kamin-Tolagh entrusted Lavsila with his most important job, one suited to his temperament. "I have to pick a quarrel with *Hrithust* Iolfrant, with his following, and his alone." A waking dream, the picture frequently came back to him, the golden roofs of Iolfrant's Hyolenstr gleaming in the sun — but that gold might be less in itself than as emblem of all the wealth there was to be had from the intervening lands, the great fecund bowl of Iolfrant's domain.

"It should be easy enough to provoke an incident at Zelu Bablakhi — or here at Larghamit."

"We do not want a rift which leaves Hrin free to choose sides; as we see, they are nearer an alliance than ever before. You must find a way to discredit him in the eyes of the other *hrithuod*, so that at worst, when we make war, they will stand aside."

"Then you are thinking of conquest?" He was thinking of estates for his cousins and cronies.

"Of bringing Iolfrant to heel. He is too soft to hold all he has."

By end of this year, if starvation was avoided, including levies from newer lands west of Flamûrai, he would easily be able to lead out a force of a thousand and a half trained tribal soldiery, without leaving their homelands unguarded. Such current information as the Heartlanders could give did not suggest Kadon Dinul was preparing forces for an early attack on the Empire.

Lavsila contrived to be sly and baffled at once. "A religious question, with those people, Lord. A practice the *dveyust-ranga-hrindan* would permit, but the other would condemn. I am going to have to learn how these superstitions work."

"Consult with Iruvakh if you must, but do not discuss what I plan."   Conceivably he would decline to supply information for such a purpose.

"If he can spare me five minutes," sardonically. Iruvakh, with his endless lore about quaint customs of the tribes, had become, willingly, a favorite of the newcomers. He had arrived late to the welcome-feast, not in the tattered clothes he wore among the tribes, nor the plain approximation to the robe of an *atarlai*, but in actual suitings, hardly worn though of an old-fashioned cut; the original Iruvakh, son to the Hereditary Warden of Irbat, had briefly come out of hiding.

"Is it true," Kamin-Tarú, idly, "you have been different since I came here?"   Under a blinding white haze, she sat on a flat rock, dangling her feet in somnolent water, and he felt a familiar ache of desire, insatiable, no matter how often or variously he possessed her body. A quarter-mile out, a skein of fat, blunt-beaked sea-birds rocked complacently on the oil-like swell.

"How different? Who says so?"

"Some," she evaded diplomatically, "say you have lost your thirst for conquest."

"Some Heartlander, who has not lost his hunger for profit." He wished they had never come. Lavsila kept reminding him how much the defection had enhanced his prestige at Kadon Dinul, but prestige was not much of a meal, not at the price he paid in exasperation; these idlers wanted to be handed estates as secure, pleasant and productive as those of the Paowan. "What do we need them for?"

"Company." Afraid she had offended him, she covered his hand with both hers. "Oh, when I am with you, it doesn't matter if all the world is empty, you are all the world. But you are gone so much."

"Not by choice. The Empire requires it. Someday, not long, when we are safe — "

She leaned to him with an affectionate little cry. Moved, he could not stop brooding on her quoted remark: no Heartlander had been here to know how he was before Kamin-Tarú's arrival, so, while his sister might have heard it from Khalú or one of the others, the idea could have only one source.

"One day, Lavsila is going to find himself between two men he has promised opposite things, and each will have a sword in his hand."

He wished he could make his sister understand how her coming here had changed, not him, but what was real. It would require too many well-considered words: here in the sapping summer glare of tribal country all thought shimmered away into inconsequence.

27.

While they had discussed every aspect of the realm, its laws and governance, Elamirr seldom spoke about his personal life, and had long outgrown asking advice: a double surprise when one morning he greeted Dolvid with, "You have known women, *Bôdhrai*?"

Dolvid made an ambiguous noise, but his manner was not forbidding.

"Why must women be how they are?"

"Which woman?" mildly, but Elamirr was launched.

"They want us as heroes, but then make us their fools. They can't be pleased; they drive us mad for a game, then weep at our anger. Why must they be like that?"

This, Dolvid thought, was very odd. He guessed who was cause of this outburst, but if Elamirr had been tricked or disappointed by — well, Arvat, for instance — he would wonder why Arvat was so, not why men were. "I have known women as different as Petakoi is from the *rabhsayu*, or Kamin-Tarú from Falis, your aunt. You cannot speak of *women* as being any one thing."

"Aye, Master," Arvat, just coming into the Old Audience Chamber. "But when all is said, they're women, just the same." This, much better than Dolvid's complicated thoughts, was what Elamirr was looking for, and led the young men into a ritual as predictable as the Lesser Responses at the *Mankh'*, concerning excesses and shortcomings of an entire sex. Between them, Dolvid calculated, the pair had known about three women well, not counting mothers and sisters — which Dolvid very much counted in the case of Arvat, having wished ten thousand times he had one-tenth the good sense of his sister, Tellis.

Morulis, unnamed cause behind these rites, was scalding if not actually breaking half the hearts of the Heartland. Elamirr, brought up, as the girl was, in a more austere tradition, could not teach himself that to take her riding or bring her to a feast did not bind her to him; she could dance next day with another escort, come to the evening gathering with a third, and his torment was only heightened seeing most of the others were youths of Family, with their effortless command of graces he lacked. From his own half-ripened beginnings, too many years ago, Dolvid could remember how gloom came to spoil whatever chances he'd had in competition with rivals who, not caring as he did, readily surpassed him in all good-humored, superficial attentions a girl would require — and Elamirr at his best had a reputation for glumness.

As he glowered on, discovering no way either to imprison or renounce Morulis, he became subject to erratic moods, fits of ferocious energy alternating with hours of listlessness. Notwithstanding their differences, Dolvid had not before had reason to complain about Elamirr's attentiveness, but for this time he was no longer reliable, failing to complete necessary tasks, making elementary errors in procedure, once mislaying an important document. Dolvid had from time to time thought of using a valid excuse to be rid of Elamirr with his discordant views, but now had not the callousness to make use of the young man's unhappiness, and stayed silent, not placing blame when Rodlakh became sarcastic over the need to have an entire official letter redone.

Fortunately, it was a curiously muted period for the realm's conflicts; Dolvid and Rodlakh had put aside their quarrel, at the cost of not discussing Kamin-Tolagh, while the defection of the Heartlanders seemed to have provided a release of some sort for the feelings of their kin, and bitter opposition to Âna's compensation law grumbled away to silence, a dying summer storm. As had, also, the threats of Tovakh against the magistrate-at-large in the Kovilanu.

Kargul, however, was behind a new subject for disagreement between Dolvid and Elamirr. The Patriarch, Dozhusai, returning from His annual Island sojourn, asked for audience with the *rabhsai*. Dolvid and Elamirr attended, while the Patriarch brought only His mask-faced secretary-scribe.

This year, as His predecessor had often, He had entertained Petakoi at the Summer Palace in Drin b'Afon, joined by Tovakh when Vinilat's indisposition had cancelled his normal autumn hunting in Dramal. In table talk, the serious problem of the succession in Kargul had been discussed. This was curious in several ways, and Dolvid thought Petakoi must have her eye on some large prize, to consult a Patriarch she must continue to regard as Rodlakh's creation, a usurper.

"A question," Dozhusai said in His high voice, "which had been troubling me, as it should, legitimacy and ordered continuity being keystones of a peaceful realm. Petakoi *Asayu* touched on a proposal to adopt her nephew, Pedh-Sivai, into the House baKargul. It is generally allowed he is a splendid young man, of good Island stock. Before an irrevocable decision, however, they agreed we should put the matter to the *rabhsai*."

"Tovakh and Petakoi, I am sure, were pleased to employ so eminent an ambassador," Rodlakh, for the sake of saying something. He made his face judicious, but was plainly nonplussed. Though in courtesy they would keep the *rabhsai* informed, who Tovakh and Petakoi decided to adopt into their House was surely their business, and only if they had chosen a known criminal or dissolute would the Council consider refusing to ratify the change of succession. Tovakh's father, indeed, nephew to the then-*nim'*, had been adopted as Heir after the death of Tobhsila.

"Just so," *g'Asalladh'* nodded when Dolvid cautiously conveyed this thought. "After loss of Tobhsila made adoption a grievous but absolute necessity."

Abruptly Dolvid saw that habit had him, with the *rabhsai*, asking the wrong question; for once what Petakoi had in mind was not the point, but what the Patriarch was up to.

Gradually revealed; Tovakh had remained passionately condemnatory on the subject of his offspring, Petakoi equally adamant, but Dozhusai persisted in hoping for Kamin-Tolagh's reconciliation, not only with his parents, but with his realm and his *rabhsai*. He, *g'Asalladh'*, proposed dispatching to the Farther West envoys of the *Mankh'* to explore such a settlement.

"By the untold mercy of Aëlovoi, it may yet be he can be brought back to the wisdom of Maëdhi."

Dolvid, whose eyes were on Dozhusai's broad and candid face, sensed the stiffening of Rodlakh's body, and moved quickly to say, "His Enlightenment displays His usual generosity in offering to mediate such a difficult case." Poor policy to allow the *rabhsai* to reject the proposal out of hand.

As he certainly would have, if Dolvid had not prevented it, by apologizing to the Patriarch: "You must understand, *g'Asalladh'*, this is a complex matter, where questions of law, public opinion, and the dignity of *rabhsayum* all need to be discussed." This wrung from Rodlakh the grudging commitment to give it his consideration, and on the promise of an early answer, the Patriarch, having raised one or two minor points about observation of the Halving, stood to depart.

"It cannot be tolerated that such *aën'modha* as may have come to Us in interpreting the Way should be denied to any Child of Yoëlladhu who desires it."   His mildness was misleading; while He had remained on amiable terms with *rabhsayum*, and had given way on many points, Dozhusai was far from spineless, and could display unexpected firmness where the acknowledged prerogatives of the *Mankh'* came into the question.

When He had gone, Dolvid cautioned Rodlakh, "If Petakoi is true to form, all the Great Houses on this side of Arnan will hear about this offer of Dozhusai's, if they have not already."

"It does not matter," bleakly.

"BaKargul has duped the Patriarch — " Elamirr seemed equally to deplore and enjoy the thought.   "This proposal to adopt the nephew must have been a bluff all along, and Dozhusai prides Himself He has softened Tovakh's feelings towards his son. Ha!"

Dolvid was less confident; this was too near his prediction. Petakoi, with her firm faith in the particular purity of Island families like her own was genuinely promoting adoption of her nephew, an Heir without any blood of the House she had married into.

"It makes no difference," Rodlakh said.

"If what I heard was what *g'Asalladh'* meant to be heard," Dolvid said, "I think it does matter, *Deghi*.   It is a delicate business."

Elamirr protested. "I thought, *Deghi*, this talk of considering His offer was only courtesy. Kamin-Tolagh is an outlaw."

"I am not going to let the *Mankh'* send its envoys, no matter what."

Carefully factual, Dolvid reminded that while the *rabhsai* could decline to be associated with the proposed negotiations, he could not forbid the Patriarch to send *atarlal* anywhere they were needed.   That right was specifically guaranteed in the Second Treaty, imposed by Rodlakh himself, signed by him, this clause explicitly reaffirmed after the well-publicized meeting in 2943. To attempt such a ban would in any event be nothing but an empty gesture; the realm, as the *rabhsai* had declared, was no prison, and if it were, would be a very poor one, with more ways out than a summerhouse; *atarlal* could not be prevented from going to any port or any place near the frontiers, or be confined there when they did. In this light, Dozhusai's parting remark had been indirect but courteous notice of an act for which He required no permission.

Aware of Rodlakh's growing agitation, Dolvid acutely missed the judicious presence of Âna, who was in the middle of her third and by far most difficult pregnancy, and tired easily.

"I do not agree," Rodlakh, tautly controlled. "Fear of my displeasure, the threat some privilege might be withdrawn — you yourself have made use of such pressures in the past."

Dolvid shook his head. "Dozhusai may be hoping for a reconciliation in the House baKargul, but that is at the margins of His policy. Clearly, He hopes to bring the Farther West into a domain He holds greater than any realm — He cannot be blamed for that, and is not going to be dissuaded by a threat to boycott *raminat*, or new restrictions on the *margul*; He is a mild man, but this is center of His life."

"Not the center of ours," Elamirr said. "I do not see how this is so different from the threats of Tovakh baKargul against the new magistrate; confronted by the power of the *rabhsai*, he had to sheathe his claws."

"Opinion is the difference — " incredulous that it needed saying, as if nothing had changed in Rodlakh's reign, and they were discussing the *Atarlum* that disdained and tried to repress the Other Races: during His visit Dozhusai had mentioned proudly but without undue emphasis the next batch of *Mankh'* pupils to take their Lesser Oaths on their way to be *atarlal* would include three who called themselves Mixed — first such since Banak's heavyhanded and unfortunate attempt to force the issue, sixty years ago. "You are aware, *Rabhsai*, I have had more reason than most to dislike all the *Mankh'* once stood for, but if it were still that same home of exclusion and privilege, people not themselves devout would be offended by a *rabhsayum* seen as denying religion to those who desire it, as at times of birth and marriage and death. How much more so, under a Patriarch who is cheered in the streets by people of every race?"

"Is it possible your past causes you to overestimate its importance? No one is trying to interfere with faith as such. Do people really care whether others are chanted over by these pious shufflers of the *Mankh'*?"

"I do not believe it, *Deghi*," Elamirr said, while Dolvid smothered an inward wince: this was exactly the attitude that could wreck the hopes of this *rabhsayum*. "The really important point, as I see it," the young man expanded, "is that the *rabhsai* be shown as standing firm."

"Dozhusai values harmony as much as He does the observances of His faith." Rodlakh's words were reasonable and cogent, but his manner was edgy and impatient. No doubt anxiety over Âna's condition distracted him.

Dolvid shook his head again. "It would very quickly be out of His hands. The few who have tried to rally feeling against you would be handed a weapon they would not need instructing how to use; if it becomes generally known we have used coercion to keep believers with Kamin-Tolagh from proper observance of their religion, many who till now have seen them as we do, renegades, will think they have been wronged."

"Let them — " Elamirr began, but Rodlakh held up a hand.

"Then you would actually advise me to permit this? I have no choice but to allow an outlaw to form an alliance with the *Mankh'*, in that place?" He meant, where *jinzal* had been bred.

"That is not what I advised."

"You say it cannot be stopped."

"Not by forbidding it."

"Well, what then?" exasperatedly. "Yes and no, both at once? Is that our reply to the Patriarch?"

"*Deghi*," carefully. "This brings us to a subject I am forbidden to mention."

"Forbidden?" Rodlakh unexpectedly grinned. "Who in a lifetime successfully forbade you to speak your mind?"

"This move of Dozhusai's, then," with a deep, steadying inhalation, "forces the play. Where Kamin-Tolagh is would not matter, if *atarlal* of the *Mankh'* could visit there escorted by the Army of the West. If Tovakh has sanctioned today's embassy by the Patriarch, then his son's outlawry is no obstacle; we can escape damage by being first to offer reconciliation."

"I have told you, this cannot be." Smile vanishing, Rodlakh's mouth set in a stubborn line.

"The offer must be made publicly," laboring on, "so if refused, there can be no mistake who is to blame."

"Anyone with sense," coldly, "already knows where blame lies. I am not going to insult the loyal by rewarding treachery."

"Aye, surely, *Deghi*," at the same time miming deferential regrets to Dolvid. "To obtain a pardon, it is the criminal who should beg for it, not — "

"And primroses should grow on nettles, but do not." This was the sort of posturing that for uncounted years had obstructed the kind of realm Rodlakh said he was striving for; easy to remember the father, Lambarr, normally as amenable as Dozhusai, near the end of his reign obstinately refusing to moderate the language of a proclamation that in one phrase — also a slight to religious susceptibilities — threatened to cancel a half-century's work of conciliation. "It is not for Kamin-Tolagh's sake we should take this step."

"I have said no. Do you, of all people, suddenly hold we can have justice where we pander to privilege — that we can rule fairly without ever displeasing the *Mankh*?"

"The *Mankh'* is not the question, *Rabhsai*. As long as their interests differ, we can modify the privileges of any one faction — we could break the Guild exclusions because they had little support among the Families; we dismantled the private armies without threatening the provincial cavalries, the challenge to Kargul of our magistrate-at-large meant nothing to Heartlanders. What is perceived as an assault on religion unites them all, Island, Families, the Great Families — "

With, he did not add, sympathy in quarters where once it would have been unthinkable; this Patriarch was no conscious politician, but would know intuitively He had only to speak of exiles deprived of the Thought of Zhôl, and decent people of every race would deplore the *rabhsai*'s action — while for old believers, there was a figurehead leader waiting at the door. Elamirr, with a different perspective, supplied the omission. "Those who do not respect the realm's justice can join their kin with Kamin-Tolagh in the dustlands. The realm would be better for it."

Dolvid closed his eyes, summoning calm. In seven centuries of Island exile, the Owanil had never ceased to call this home; how could anybody think they would forget the shores of Arnan in a few years on the far side of Landegh? Kamin-Tolagh was going to return, that was certain; the question was whether he would come as friend or would-be usurper. "I myself," despairingly, "would willingly go to the West to see if an accommodation can be worked out."

"Curse your obstinacy, I have said, no. Not now, not ever. The subject is closed."

A few days later, Elamirr expressed surprise when Dolvid dictated a formal reply to *g'Asalladh'*, stating the *rabhsai* did not at present wish envoys of the *Mankh'* to propound with Kamin-Tolagh conditions for his reinstatement, maintaining the letter of the Treaty by omitting to mention the question of His sending *atarlal* on His own account — as if the Patriarch would have chosen for His negotiator a file-leader from the *Adanum*, or perhaps his pack-pony.

"You opposed this decision, Master."

"We are the *rabhsai*'s men," astonished it needed to be said. Aside from that, Dolvid did not say, it might be done a lot worse by someone else.

Rodlakh, given the letter for signature, smiled and handed it back, saying it was no longer needed: during Halving he'd had an informal meeting with Dozhusai, and conveyed his feelings adequately. Exactly what had been said remained unknown to Dolvid; the Patriarch, of course, though He may have nodded mildly, would not consider Himself bound by a royal dictate which overstepped the Treaty.

The year ripened, and when at last there was chance for a private word with Âna, she was recovering from premature birth of a third child, another son, who had lived only days and never been named. Not as worn as he had feared, she joined in Dolvid's concern over Rodlakh's highhandedness, but admitted if she had been well she would have devoted her energies to discouraging a less momentous decision: betrothal of Morulis to Elamirr, which would shortly be announced. They intended to marry at Zhôl's Day.

Âna shook her head. "He will want a Burantal wife, here at Kadon Dinul. I have been a woman penned in that sheepfold;

he is going to find it hard leading her back there, after her years of grazing free."

"Why?" echoing the entire Residence Quarter. "Why, when she can have any man she wants by bending a finger?"

A wry mouth. "Something familiar, I would guess, among everything that is exciting but strange. He is spoken of as the coming man." Âna forced a smile. "The *rabhsai* thinks it will do very well."

Nothing happened, but that was no comfort; not now but two or three years in the future the consequences of Rodlakh's inflexibility would begin to tell. Summer was like a dream, where voices and the report of events came from places he could not reach. He worked, gave advice, and remained impotent to affect the slow, silent gathering of the storm.

The realm remained misleadingly tranquil; weather was mild, furor over new laws muted, banditry on the roads much reduced by Shumat's vigorous campaign. Unprecedented acreage was in cultivation, while an ambitious drainage scheme of Konir's in the flat country south of Shemugrân had helped, for a time, in reducing unemployment.

Shumat was the definition of loyalty, and preferred to stay aloof from politics, yet even he, alone with Dolvid at the Bronze Residence on a warm summer day, expressed doubts about the growing influence of Elamirr, his prominence in a circle whose opinions were too loudly worn. "There are those, not only soldiers, who find it worrisome."

"He has been my pupil. If he has failings, I must be as much to blame as anyone."

"I don't think we care who's to blame. The question is, where is this leading us? Some baby idiots with noses my shape think there's nothing too bad for the ones with noses shaped like yours, and they've found their champion. He's got less judgment than my *pefrai*."

Dolvid was embarrassed; he, too, had loyalties, and not to a very old friend could he confess Elamirr would have been curbed and perhaps dispensed with long since, if Rodlakh had not adopted him.

"Be that as it may," reaching for his outshirt. "I have to look for a wedding-gift. How long since you last browsed the shops in Harbor Way?"

Without answering, Shumat reached for the heavy bronze token hung from the chain about Dolvid's neck, Rodlakh's Beech-Tree emblem embossed. "If your present is for Elamirr," weighing the medallion, "I can tell you what he would like best."

As they emerged by the side steps into sunlight, Elamirr himself rode up. "News," he called out, dismounting, throwing reins to a guard. "Bolan is dead."

The story was brief. Bolan had been found in his bed, evidently suffocated, though there was nothing to suggest anyone had come near him. Suicide was impossible, murder unlikely.

"A strange end," lightly. "But after his wife divorced him and went west, who had a reason to kill him? He was of no consequence."

Shumat let his eyes meet those of Dolvid, who said, "Had he died ten, even eight years ago, he would have been given a hero's funeral." Here, beside the Old Bronze Residence, as a boy of fifteen, Dolvid had first met Bolan, a fresh, absurdly ambitious junior officer of the Household, determined to make his name.

"As is," Shumat, soberly, "but for you and me, there will be few mourners."

"Or are we mourning our own younger selves?"

Elamirr looked on, baffled.

28.

Arrival of the *Atarlum* came as an insidious challenge to Kamin-Tolagh's absolute authority, for him an irritating exercise in diplomacy. The visit had begun with an unintentional, perhaps unnoticed, rescue: the *Mankh'* party, attempting a crossing of Landegh in this most improbable season, had used up its water, and would still have been a day-and-a-half from hope of any more, assuming either men or mounts could have kept going so long. Spotted by Kamin-Tolagh's forward scouts at their easternmost lookout, the travellers were shortly intercepted by a mixed tribal force under command of Nuvakh, a countrified junior officer from Western Kargul, by upbringing too deferential to robes of the *Atarlum* ever to tell at-Sholidu, leader of the group, how near he had come to disaster.

Apart from another *atarlai*, the remaining six men of at-Sholidu's tiny command, without exception tall, strong, well-armed and tightly-disciplined, though drably dressed, were said to be ordinary servants and handlers for the animals.

At midday, forewarned by a scrawled message from Nuvakh, Kamin-Tolagh, outside the Residence, gave the visitors a greeting less than welcoming, and in consideration of their obvious fatigue, perfunctory; he assigned them to a nearby building, and set an evening hour for another meeting — an interval which gave him time, as transpired, to be progressively exasperated by realization he was effectively alone in seeing the embassy as an unwanted intrusion.

Sequel, clearly, to the coming of the Heartlanders. Lavsila, to judge by his smirk, had expected it, and regarded the event as some sort of victory, but whether he had given the *Atarlum* a direct invitation, or merely failed to discourage the visit, it soon became impossible to accuse him with something seen generally as a benefit. Yet at first, when Kamin-Tolagh said the *Mankh'* had nothing the Empire needed, Lavsila used a typical trick to make himself a mere bystander, saying, "There are people, I believe, here at the Abu, Lord, who would not agree, now the *Mankh'*, so to speak, has come to them."

"I do not ask them to agree or disagree. There is one ruler here. If they wished to crawl to the *Atarlum*, they should have stayed at Kadon Dinul. I may yet turn them out on Landegh, and let this at-Sholidu show them the way home, if they can survive the journey."

That was for the Heartland contingent, whom he would never mind offending. But to his disgust, it was quickly apparent Freighanai, even the impassive Fretasi, were delighted to see functionaries of their cradle-religion once again, and his sister, while making no comment, was surely with them.

Even so, he might have maintained his arbitrary stance, if the other *atarlai* with the officious at-Sholidu had also been of the Patriarch's personal suite, but *g'Asalladh'*, maybe with an unsuspected shrewdness, had sent at-Vadhival, a *ramidu*. Tall and slender, conspicuous in light blue robe of his Healing Order, he was generally observed when he rode in, and barely allowed to rest from the hot, grimy exhaustions of a summer journey on Landegh before being besieged by soldiers of Kargul and their wives, concerned, mostly, with various afflictions or suspect symptoms in their children, though there was also discussion of remedies for the outbreak of crab-lice among one squadron that had spent time west of Flamûrai.

Coldly, Kamin-Tolagh was struck by fresh recognition even here, days away from established laws and precedents, councils and treaties, jostlings of rival interests, no rule was absolute. His will was the only force that commanded Empire, but he needed arms and bodies to enforce that will; Tau-Suaka's company would always obey without question, but was not enough to move tribes, make war on the Hrin. To lead armies, he still needed the trained soldiery of Kargul, who followed him because he was their lord, and because he knew how to win fights, but might lose enthusiasm if he was seen as depriving them of their religion, wives and children of the benefits brought by the *Ramadilum*, and perhaps, later, the *Manadilum* — although in no case, he made up his mind, would they be permitted to come here and teach history and lore of a realm left behind. Neither his subjects nor the Patriarch's were going to perceive any lessening of his power; if compelled by opinion to admit the *Atarlum* into his empire, he could yet make clear he was granting a favor.

Rather than large hall with its chair of state, he received them informally, seated at table in the small dining-hall, together with his sister, all eagerness at the prospect of novelty, an intolerably complacent Lavsila, young Kambanal, quiet and attentive, and equally watchful Tau-Suaka with a selection of his best men distributed around the walls. Iruvakh, by rare chance at the Abu, for his experimental plantings near the southern cliffs, had been summoned, but had not yet arrived.

To any son of the *Mankh'* less overawed than Nuvakh, at-Sholidu would have remained formidable, a square-framed man of moderate height but infinite confidence, thick-necked, holding the ground with a strong grip, alert stance proclaiming readiness for instant action. Though clad in dark blue robe with the beeswing whorls that made him a member of the Patriarch's personal retinue, at first sight he put Kamin-Tolagh in mind of a wrestler, such as were seen at Pledgings, offering to take on all comers. But his dry bark of a voice, his terse and decided utterances, were reminiscent of a certain kind of old-fashioned soldier — for example, the irritating, long-departed Talfoyan, with his passionless self-assurance.

Yet he began in ostensible respect, with a full-deference. "*Asai*, I bring cordial personal greetings from *g'Asalladh'*. It is His regret that not before now has He been able to give His attention to these domains." By his name he must be from the south of Kamanta, but he had no trace of clotted Island accent, considered not so much regional as rural and uncouth, despised by better-educated Islanders, such as Kamin-Tolagh's mother.

"You have come a long, hard road to bring good wishes," Kamin-Tolagh said, not hiding skepticism.

"We, not I personally, but the *Atarlum*, have *returned* by that long hard road, a road that was, as you must recall, made under our instruction."

A heavy-handed reminder this place had belonged to the *Mankh'* for centuries before the coming of Kamin-Tolagh, who felt stirrings of an anger hotter than the chafing annoyance of this meeting. "Does *g'Asalladh'* mean to assert sovereignty here, then?"

"*Asai* — "

"Inform the *atarlai*," Kamin-Tolagh rapped, turning to Lavsila, "how, properly, I am to be addressed."

As hoped, an awkward moment for Lavsila, who briefly gnawed a lower lip, before, predictably, finding a way to soften the demand. "Our Lord Kamin-Tolagh has renounced claim on any title within your realm, *at'ai*, hence any designation in the Old Tongue; as ruler here, he is to be addressed only as *Lord*."

"Lord," at-Sholidu repeated, and, with an arid attempt at ingratiation, "This, actually, accords precisely with instructions of *G'Asalladh'*, who emphasized you were to be addressed, Lord, as effective ruler over these lands — "

"*Effective* ruler?"

"As you are aware, Lord, under terms of the Second Treaty, *g'Asalladh'* retains right — "

"The Empire of Kargusai," Kamin-Tolagh interrupted "is not a party to any treaty, with the *Mankh'* or with any other power of your realm. Here, *g'Asalladh'* has no rights. Unless he intends to seize them."

Lavsila was stricken, while at-Sholidu, his arrogance parading as humility, spread his upraised palms in innocent disavowal. Kambanal looked up, earnestly troubled, a face filled with desire for reasoned discussion, but he did not speak, and Kamin-Tarú, lips parted, turned to her brother in reproach. "Some people," with that apparent inconsequence which, as so often, went right to the heart of the problem, "must desire rites for their marriages."

Two readily came to mind, her Antiyu, and Lavsila here, each with a less-eager partner; Pivrekhan clearly believed a maid, even personal maid of an empress, was no wife for his crippled dignity, while Khalú, by her own account having evaded marriage with Lavsila for half her life, had gone on pretending uncertainty whether her divorce from Bolan had taken effect, till word came of his strange death.

At-Sholidu said, "For just that reason, Lord, and no other, *g'Asalladh'*, of His *aën'modha*, has dispatched this mission, His distress Children of Yoëlladhu lacked due ceremony for forms of their lives — not to say their deaths. Lacked also — " this with a gesture to his companion — "benefits of our healing, and other skills."

Here, before Kamin-Tolagh could respond, Iruvakh came in, dressed shabbily, as he had been for tending his plants; that there was any other possibility would not have occurred to anyone before his isolated evening of somewhat rusted splendor at the Heartlanders' welcome-feast. Just inside the door, without having made proper obeisance to Kamin-Tolagh, he said, "At-Vadhival!"

The taller *atarlai* turned to show surprise, but no pleasure. On Iruvakh's side, pure exclamation rather than a greeting; plainly, the two men had little use for each other.

Lavsila asked, "You know this *ramidu*?"

"Lord," Iruvakh said, belatedly acknowledging Kamin-Tolagh, but as always with a hint of satire in his use of the honorific. "At-Vadhival knows this place well; he was here — was it three years?"

"More than four," the *ramidu* allowed.

"You were of the *jinzai*-breeders?" Kamin-Tolagh said, and to at-Sholidu, "Our understanding was, the present Patriarch rid His house of all those who served His predecessor in that abominable enterprise." He supposed continued presence of Iruvakh was a surprise to the visitors; Dozhusai would hardly have sent one of the former residents with any idea of his being recognized. His dispatch of a *ramidu* no longer seemed as artful as it had; no doubt at-Vadhival had acted as guide for the party.

As was, it served to put at-Sholidu on the defensive; with the help of the man. he explained he had been spared in the purge following accession of ga-Dozhusai-Arbhali, since, as Iruvakh grudgingly agreed, he'd had nothing to do with breeding, training, or leading *jinzal* armies, but merely ministered to those who had, as to the entourage of the so-called True *Rabhsai*. Iruvakh, notwithstanding renunciation of the *Mankh'*, had given more direct assistance to the breeders with his work among the Man-mani, but not knowing Iruvakh's present standing in the Empire, at-Sholidu, if the thought occurred, did not dare enunciate it, and Kamin-Tolagh was content to watch him try hopelessly to regain his initial assurance.

Yet for all the strategy, demands on behalf of *g'Asalladh'* were very modest, by His assessment practically non-existent, since He was said to claim only the right to continue sending His *atarlal*. Suspiciously modest, and to Kamin-Tolagh it began to be strange there was no written message from *g'Asalladh'*, as if He feared providing evidence of this overture. Though nothing had been mentioned about the *rabhsai*'s possible reactions, at-Sholidu labored to dispel any idea Rodlakh had been consulted, insisting they had come there in complete secrecy.

A statement made plausible by his complaint they had not meant to cross Landegh at high summer, but had been several unplanned weeks on the journey. Beginning with an attempt to come here by "the old way," landing at Peframi as a pilgrimage to the tomb of *Kirova-Kindhri* in western Kargul, forced to return when, having slipped across the border and wasted three days on the ancient mountain way, they had come to a place where the road was broken, and been unable to find a way past.

Kamin-Tolagh said nothing, but felt an obscure anger, as if his decision to destroy that connection to the realm was being criticized. From that came the thought the Patriarch was trying to position Himself to mediate between the Empire and Rodlakh's realm. Once in mind, nothing could seem likelier, or require greater caution; *g'Asalladh'* could certainly gain prestige and power from a role as peacemaker, and Kamin-Tolagh had no wish either to be cornered into a disadvantageous settlement, or be seen as highhandedly rejecting what others might call reasonable terms.

After going back to the Island, the expedition had set out again, using another way often taken in the past according to the *atarlai*, crossing by ship to a forsaken spot on the westward shore of Arnan, nominally within the Lunu Tezh' Protectorate, but uninhabited, practically unvisited. From that landing, a meandering trail, often barely-discernible, led generally westward through wild and barren country above the headwaters of the Grân, south of the high hills dividing Lunu Tezh' from the settled and better-guarded Colony, lands Kamin-Tolagh had traversed from south to north in the Jinzai War, and so to the ill-defined border between Protectorate and the waste of Landegh, where the trail picked up the *jinzai* road two or three days beyond Drin Navuna.

"Whatever the unwisdom of attempting Landegh at this season, Lord, having set out while it was still spring, I was unwilling to wait for autumn. As *g'Asalladh'* has said, for those deprived of our assistance, too many seasons have already gone by."

Their assistance! but there was no direct mention of how it was to be paid for, nor who would maintain authority over their activities — not till after at-Sholidu's proposal, made as offhandedly as he could manage, that "for the sake of convenience," it would be best to function, for now, under established terms of the Second Treaty, only with Kamin-Tolagh's prerogatives, "where applicable," replacing those of *rabhsayum*.

Obviously, a prepared position, so the Patriarch, after all, had anticipated need for negotiation, but Kamin-Tolagh could have happily choked Lavsila, who was smiling and nodding at everything the *atarlai* said. Yet many provisions of the Treaty could have nothing to do with Kamin-Tolagh; he derived no benefit from a Patriarchal promise to limit the size of His bodyguard, so the *rabhsai*'s reciprocal guarantee of safety for *atarlal* wherever they went would be, for Kamin-Tolagh a gratuitous service. "I cannot *guarantee* safety for a well-armed double-squadron of my own, here in these lands, which could and should have been set in order a thousand years ago, if your *Mankh'* had been able to see beyond the one thing it desired, mothers for *jinzal*. Besides — " Kamin-Tolagh waved off any response — "there is page after page of the Second Treaty dealing with institutions which have never existed in the Empire of Kargusai; the *manal*, the *margul*, *nôd'yanul* — "

"Is that to say, Lord, they never can exist here?" at-Sholidu managed to ask. Surprisingly, at-Sholidu himself, before joining the Patriarch's personal staff, had been with the *Nôdhilum*, considered most genial, least doctrine-bound of the four orders, famed chiefly for running the *margul*, wayside hostelries of the realm, though its members also performed death and funeral rites. "If, for example, there was a great discovery of gold or precious gems, and ten thousand men and women left the shores of Arnan to come here — "

"They will not find a welcome waiting," Kamin-Tolagh said, though the idea excited Lavsila, who was longing to ask about the extent of disaffection in the realm as seen through the eyes of the *Atarlum*. Questions Kamin-Tolagh was quite certain this *atarlai* would not answer; at minimum, his instructions from *g'Asalladh'* must include a warning to stay clear of controversy between realm and empire. Yet if the Patriarch indeed saw Himself as eventual conciliator, He must have begun by ascertaining Rodlakh's conditions.

"The *rabhsai*," Kamin-Tolagh ventured casually, "What might the *rabhsai* think of this embassy? If he knew of it?"

"Under the Treaty, the *rabhsai*, as *g'Asalladh'* states it, has no power to prevent our coming here."

"Under the Treaty, men of the *Adanum Plakh'* are restricted to duties directly bearing on safety of the Patriarch's Person. Oh, considering all the possible dangers of Landegh,

Dozhusai can hardly be faulted for giving you men of the *Adanum Plakh'* for company — "

For an instant, at-Sholidu seemed ready to deny Kamin-Tolagh's identification of his muscular escort. Then, "His Enlightenment's concern for the safety of His servants needs no defense."

"Then why such secrecy?"

"Lord, I am not in the Mind of *g'Asalladh'* —" once more the man's humility bordered on insolence. "As we all must, I obey."

"As you all must," Kamin-Tolagh clarified.

"As I said, Lord. His Enlightenment, however, has made no secret of His distress at the division between you, Lord, and Rodlakh *Rabhsai*, or that within the House baKargul. Which," he added quickly, before Kamin-Tolagh could express indifference, "has approached *g'Asalladh'* with reference to the altered succession."

Here, Kamin-Tolagh sensed rather than saw a general cringe among his advisers, as if in expectation of an outburst. Annoyed by the *atarlai*'s presumption, he would not let it be thought he cared who would be *nim'* in Kargul after his father, and made a mild, dismissive gesture. "*G'Asalladh'*'s distress is to be regretted, but these are affairs of another realm."

At-Sholidu cleared his throat.

"*At'ai*," Kamin-Tarú said respectfully. "You and your following must be hungry." She was at the brink of an invitation, and Kamin-Tolagh forestalled her, with, "Food will be sent to where you are quartered. We shall not detain you now."

Lavsila's turn. "My table — "

"Will have to wait," Kamin-Tolagh interrupted. "We have matters to discuss. Of our own," he told the visitors, noting his sister's shock. Why? Functionaries of the *Atarlum* were no holier than other men, just more devious; with him, she had observed them from earliest childhood, blandly offering opinions of the *Mankh'* on everything except religion, plotting with Petakoi, apparently for the advancement of Kargul, but to what darker purpose Kamin-Tarú was now aware.

At-Sholidu, clearly, had not been prepared for dismissal, but quickly covered anger with frozen irony. "Then we have your leave, Lord?"

When the delegation had left, Lavsila, reminded he was an official of Empire, not a fashionable host of the Heartland said, unrebuked, "But you cannot prevent *atarlal* from coming here." As Kamin-Tolagh turned on him with slow menace, he amended it: "I mean, Lord, only that this, clearly, is a thing most here at the Abu would desire."

"What most here would like is not necessarily what is good for the Empire, which I alone decide."

Kambanal, much less offensively, simply pondering facts, offered, "Even as a practical question, unless we are going to turn them away at our gates, it would be difficult to prevent, if they are willing to brave the Landegh crossing."

"No, the *rabhsai* could prevent it for us. *Atarlal* would never attempt the journey unescorted; Rodlakh's treaty may oblige him to let them go anywhere, but he does not have to give passage across the Lunu Tezh' to soldiers of the *Adanum*."

"If he knew about it," Kambanal said.

"Word about the trail they use could come to him. One of the Hrin traders, when he visits Thenimala, could be in possession of an interesting rumor." A tempting thought for its own sake; Rodlakh would be given the embarrassing problem of stopping the escort without appearing to violate the Second Treaty, in a realm where, according to all reports, this reformed *Mankh'* could count on widespread sympathy.

Lavsila remained exasperatingly blind to any reason why the Empire could want to reject the Patriarch's overtures; his normal habit of seeking duplicity in the most straightforward transactions failed him here, just where all Kamin-Tolagh's experience suggested it would be most justified. To Lavsila, he said, "If the *rabhsai* failed to interfere, that, too, would give us useful information; it would mean he is in this venture with the Patriarch."

"That I cannot accept."

"You yourself have called Dozhusai Rodlakh's puppet."

He had, but now Lavsila chose to believe this visit proved *g"Asalladh'*, in all His apparent compliance, had been bowing only to the necessity of His time.

"And wishes to come here, where He can act with greater independence?"

"Lord," Kambanal ventured, "Would the *Atarlum* be taking belief out among the tribes?" He was perhaps thinking of religion as a way of unifying different peoples, newly irritating

Kamin-Tolagh, who saw the advantage of a shared single faith, but wanted his authority to be all the tribes held in common. The start of a wrangle between Lavsila, who truly supposed the *Atarlum* had come here precisely because they still desired a place where *Children of Yoëlladhu* could mean only those of pure Owani descent, and Iruvakh, who maintained that had never been the view of most at the *Mankh'*.

This required a laborious reminder; except for the final years the *jinzai*-breeding scheme was carried on without the consent or knowledge of Kamanasalladh, the Patriarch of that time, under direction of *Menadhi*, Head of the Teaching Order; when he succeeded to the Patriarchate was when Iruvakh had quit the *Atarlum*. "Though he never took them so far," Iruvakh instructed an incredulous Lavsila, "the policies of ga-Kamanasalladh, who came from my Order, the *Edhrodilum*, were nearer those of the present Patriarch. In those days there were some here, among men hand-picked by *Menadhi*, mark you, whose private opinion was we should be instructing the tribes, not merely in husbandry and healing, but religion. To say so out loud would have been folly, but I was not the only one to hold that *Children of Yoëlladhu* must include all men — all women, too — or else have no meaning."

"But you," Kamin-Tolagh waved Lavsila's protest to silence, "never instructed the tribes in religious matters."

"Oh, but I did, Lord," with a near-smirk. "In all religious matters. I never tried to *persuade* them, but the Laughing Owl, Man-mani, even the Hrin, have heard teachings of the *Mankh'*, as I understand them, just as they have learnt a little about each other's beliefs, as we have about theirs. The One Way became for me only one among many ways."

Now Kamin-Tarú stole Lavsila's protest: "But there has to be one truth."

"Lady — " Iruvakh's patience could as easily be an insult. "Those who can continue to think so are, I am sure, the happier for it." The echo of regret, Kamin-Tolagh guessed, must be for Iruvakh's own younger self, son to an hereditary provincial official, sent to the *Mankh'* to acquire learning and polish, who had in effect renounced his high inheritance for the drab life of an *atarlai*, it could only be out of a genuine contagion of faith.

The hint of solution to the arrival of the *Atarlum* was hovering. "Would you wish to rejoin the *Mankh'*," he asked Iruvakh, "now there is a Patriarch whose *aën'modha* you can approve? — " a monumental heresy, making even the undemonstrative Kambanal wince.

Iruvakh gave an unsmiling chuckle. "Lord, Greater Oaths are not renounced and resumed at will; there is no welcome waiting for me at the *Mankh'*."

Perhaps, but it was negotiable, everything was negotiable where powers contended, and Kamin-Tolagh's plan was to make Iruvakh not merely the *atarlai* he had been, but the Patriarch's deputy here, *Filiarch*, as Kambanal soon supplied, determining and directing activities of the *Atarlum* within the Empire, but under Kamin-Tolagh's control. That was not exactly how he presented it to the man; observing unwilling interest, Kamin-Tolagh played on old rancors, telling him if other members of his old Growing Order came here to work, it could be under his direction, helping to carry out schemes once ignored or dismissed as impractical. The gleam in Iruvakh's eyes was unmistakably covetous, but his reservations were not so easily overcome.

"The powers of *g'Asalladh'* have been limited by treaty, Lord, never divided. He cannot agree to any delegation of His authority, particularly to one whose convictions are, at best, suspect."

Guessing Iruvakh was putting up the objections of *g'Asalladh'* as an easy way to avoid confronting his own, Kamin-Tolagh nevertheless debated the point, observing that no Patriarch had ever before sought to extend into what was, despite the race of its ruling class, a foreign realm. In any event, the notion the powers of the *Mankh'*, under the Treaty, were outside all modification was a fable; in Kamin-Tolagh's recent lifetime, even the formidable Owan-Alladh XX, with a *rabhsai* under His tutelage, had been aware how limited His influence was in, say, Lower Paowan, compared with the awe He commanded at Inilun Barabhi, or in Lavsila's Residence Quarter. "Here, we have a far weaker Patriarch, desiring to extend His sway into new territories. He will be willing to make concessions, supposing once inside the door, He can find a way gradually to consolidate His power."

"If the tribes become believers — " Kamin-Tarú started, once again going simply to the heart of her brother's concern, the question of divided loyalty.

"No reason why they should," Lavsila, flatly. "If *g'Asalladh'* wished for followers not of our kind, He could send his *atarlal* wherever they are to be found; there are tribes on tribes days to the northward, some easier to reach than this place. He has come to you, Lord, to us, because we are true Children of Yoëlladhu, sole race to whom the Promise was made."

Iruvakh made an impatient noise, but Kamin-Tolagh, not because he agreed in principle, thought for his own reasons he might have to embrace this exclusionary view. Kambanal, usually keenly attuned to lofty language, was so preoccupied he completely ignored Lavsila's flight. "There is no one, Lord, without some creed," he said. "Care would have to be taken not to offend religious feelings of others — of the Hrin, as well as those of the Empire."

"No one is forced to follow what the *Mankh'* teaches," Kamin-Tarú said.

Iruvakh nodded vigorously. "Precisely, Lady. If the Tale of Zhôl, as I understand, has found many new adherents within the realm, it is because they choose to embrace words that move them; I do not see that either *g'Asalladh'* or the *rabhsai* has used any coercion."

Lavsila, meanwhile, on his covert quest precisely to find means of provoking war by offending the religious sensibilities of at least part of the Hrin, exchanged a dark glance with Kamin-Tolagh, before asking, "Have we heard how many *atarlal g'Asalladh'* would envisage sending here?"

With that, debate showed signs of dissolving into useless conjecture, Kambanal wondering whether *g'Asalladh'* would sign a declaration formally renouncing all claim to what had once been the Lunu Jinzalladhiyu, Iruvakh observing the obvious title for a proposed Filiarch, *g'Asati*, could not be used, since the term, Blessed Son, already applied to Zhôl.

Inconsequential in itself, the remark meant Iruvakh, for whatever reasons of his own, was seriously contemplating acceptance of the post; Kamin-Tolagh tried to steer a cunning course between encouraging him to dream his powers would be real, and giving advance warning no actual independence of action would be tolerated. Hard, as ever, to either bribe or intimidate a man whose needs were mysterious, apparently immune to threat.

A clue was in how he had put on best clothes to help greet the arrival of the Heartlanders, but though Iruvakh had seemed to desire their acceptance, he had not won much beyond that — a degree of deference, possibly, from those impressed by his birth, but no popularity. In the Heartland, one of his descent who had chosen the *Mankh'* would be regarded as odd, and here his attachment to the tribes, his way of giving solemn respect to absurd and inexplicable superstitions, only increased his outlandishness — and made it unlikely he could ever win widespread sympathy in any dispute with Kamin-Tolagh over the proper place of the *Atarlum* in life of the Empire.

Nothing was settled when Kamin-Tolagh met again with at-Sholidu, Iruvakh having commented only that he would wait to hear what the Patriarch's envoy had to say to the proposal. What he did say was as near as he dared a rejection out of hand; he had never heard of a like arrangement, had no authority to discuss it, would, if Kamin-Tolagh intended an actual proposal, submit it to the Wisdom of *g'Asalladh'*, but could scarcely imagine it would meet with favor.

"Then, *at'ai*, I cannot say what your welcome will be, when you return. Or if you return; there would be little object in your coming back without agreement to my terms."

The coarse features went rigid as stone. Aligning of thumbs, brief lowering of at-Sholidu's eyelids, and Kamin-Tolagh knew the man was making use of a *Mankh'* trick for keeping anger subdued. "Lord," measuring his breaths. "It would be a pity if this question ended by depriving your subjects of what they desire and deserve."

This had distant threat in it, but Kamin-Tolagh remained equable. "*G'Asalladh'*, then, in His wisdom will surely know what to do."

Suspecting at-Sholidu had meant to remain some time, or at least to leave his companion, the *ramidu*, as emblem of Patriarchal tenure, Kamin-Tolagh made plain he was dismissing the delegation. He could make a ruling on permanent quartering for *atarlal* when and if a representative of the *Mankh'* brought back a satisfactory reply.

Urgent news came to justify and reaffirm his brusqueness, and the Patriarch's man was waved away as if forgotten. A new threat west of Flamûrai, where a mixed double-squadron was menaced, if not yet actually assailed, by a force estimated at over a thousand poorly-armed but confident invaders from the southwest, camped between them and the small garrison at Gronu Kizh'klaëdhiyu, making concerted action difficult. With Freighanai needed for northern Froghushei, Kambanal left at once leading lances and bows, intending to form another squadron from newly-trained tribal levies near Larghamit. The patchwork composition of these contingents was another reason against permitting the *Atarlum* to interfere with tribal beliefs: at present, as if reflecting Iruvakh's exaggerated open-mindedness or Kamin-Tolagh's boredom with religious questions, men of different tribes with wildly varied tales of world's beginning and nature of the gods could ride knee to knee and camp side by side, but a zealot of the *Mankh'* with *Mankh'* convictions about the One Way could start an inf=ection of intolerance capable of wrecking the quiet harmony of relative indifference.

Fresh news from west of the Gulf was slow in coming, but Kamin-Tolagh was not unduly anxious; in open battle disciplined formations could prevail against odds of six and even ten to one, and at any moment he had larger forces under arms than ever before, proficiency of the tribal troops steadily improving. But his was a bigger vessel, with more places to spring sudden leaks, and abrupt need for reinforcements anywhere still entailed a complete reshuffling of resources, to keep reliable officers and a stiffening of genuine cavalry at the points of greatest danger, east and west of the hills in tribal country this side of Flamûrai, Zelu Bablakhi, the eternal watch on Landegh, Larghamit, the Abu itself. Genuinely preoccupied, he did make time to inform at-Sholidu his riding would be accompanied by a squadron escort, to go a full day farther east than his patrols normally did.

At-Sholidu said coldly, "A number of your subjects, Lord, have asked when our return can be expected."

"That, *at'ai*, is your choice, or your Master's." Again, Kamin-Tolagh ignored implied threat of disaffection, and almost added that it depended, partly, on how soon they left; with Zhôl's Day past, they were waiting now only for the slightest sign of moderating weather, but the worst sustained heat of the year held everything in a glassy immobility.

"In the realm, you are perceived as last champion of your race, in a world gone mad with mongrelism. " Lavsila's thought, with due allowance for the self-seeking source, had some cogency; it needed more than breaking a road to be divorced from history; Kamin-Tolagh could consolidate his rule, conquer the Hrin, attain an independent prosperity, but still the only *Kamintolaghi* he cared about would be written by the shores of Arnan, and an acceptable settlement with Rodlakh required sympathizers within that realm. Though the cavalry of Kargul might still be his for the asking, support, obviously, would not be forthcoming from his family, and yet his baKarguli heritage would mainly count against him in Rodlakh's immediate circle; there was after all something to Lavsila's frequent contention he must cultivate a following where dissatisfaction with the present *rabhsai* went deepest, the landowners, guilds, unmixed Owanil of the Heartland, watching ancient privileges of race dwindle away. Or so they held, but in the extravagant comments of his contingent of Heartlanders he could detect a message other than the one they wished to convey, an implacably hostile *rabhsai*, egged on by envious advisers, the renegade Owani, Dolvid, worse than any Mixed. No doubt Rodlakh had begun to loosen the exclusionary grip of the Owanil on wealth, but equally certain he had acted with caution, careful to maintain an appearance of fairness, justice long delayed. Maybe, as his detractors here proclaimed, Rodlakh's eventual goal was to break the influence of the Families and shatter the Guilds, but if so he obviously knew it could not be done in a week or a month, that now and for years to come they remained a power to be placated — and therefore, for Kamin-Tolagh, an ally worth having.

What he was doing here, what, for other reasons, he had already done to keep the *Atarlum* from going freely among the tribes, would be read in the distant Residence Quarter as confirmation of his Owani partiality, and that they were mistaken could not matter; he would never be in a position where they could demand recompense for their support.

Or — and the thought came to him as a dagger-thrust — Lavsila must dream Kamin-Tolagh, carried on the tide of some lurking popular movement, could magically displace Rodlakh and the House Arbhai-Navu, come to be master of two realms, new and old, most powerful ruler since the Age of the Shâls. Preposterous, but when he let thought drift outside reason into enjoyment of impossibilities, much like voluptuous details of the imagined bedding of a woman (such as Aëlu) he knew he would never have, he could not see what difference it made; the Families might help him in the foolish expectation he would revive Preference, but once *rabhsai*, what could they do when he disappointed them? He would, for example, make every effort to keep Shumat as principal captain of the realm, and could imagine no case where race would take precedence over competency; it would be only prudent to retain Tau-Suaka and his men for personal guard.

But his supporters would never admit disappointment; once established, his reputation as a champion of Owani privilege would not be overturned if he were to follow present policies exactly; when Rodlakh appointed a Mixed magistrate, the Families called it another marker along the road to oblivion, whereas Kamin-Tolagh as *rabhsai* could do the same with a meaningful covert nod, and they would all agree he was shrewd, from time to time, to throw a meaningless bone to the mongrel mob.

"The West is where true Children of Yoëlladhu have always looked for succor," Lavsila said, unerringly choosing words he would slur. They had just opened a third bottle of pale Peframi wine, soothingly cool, from the depleted store that had belonged to Kemunai of the *Adanum Plakh'*. At table, Kamin-Tarú, head on folded arms, was dozing next to Lavsila, whose house this now was; Khalú was sleeping somewhere, and Kamin-Tolagh did not know whether they considered themselves man and wife, though certain they would not dare defy him and ask one of the two *atarlal* to solemnize their marriage, prohibited till his relationship with the *Mankh'* was clarified.

They were half-celebrating news that had come at last from Kambanal, uncertain whether or not he had defeated an enemy, though clearly the danger was diminished; he had fought and easily routed a rabble of young barbarians attempting to blockade the southward way, but without pause had been peaceably approached by others of the same people, seeking, so they said, nothing but friendship. As often before, there was a bemusing effect to the swift sequence, the bland manner with which these tribes could dismiss yesterday's aggression, as if it had never occurred. Kambanal, however, had not let pass the opportunity to make peace, having been first, a year ago, to give definition to Kamin-Tolagh's feelings; if odd by civilized standards, where wars were declared, fought and ended by negotiations, or by total destruction for one side or the other, these brief tests of strength followed by wide-eyed blandishment, conveniently relieved the Empire from need to pursue struggles to a conclusion against adversaries with nothing worth taking.

"I mean," Lavsila amended. "The Empire is in itself a great achievement, and will be greater, when the Hrin are conquered, which not even Larghai could do."

"But — " Kamin-Tolagh, displeased with himself for not being immune to this blatant flattery.

"A bridge," airily, with a looping gesture. "Magnificent alone, but a bridge, also, to your rightful place at Kadon Dinul; many would see it as such. Why I have maintained my contact with the influential of the Heartland."

"As with this officious *Mankh'*," bitingly.

A pause, and Lavsila, as if suddenly recalling, said, "Young Valubran, you know — "

"At the forge, yes." Beyond his work, the little Kamin-Tolagh knew of the youth he disliked; at the Heartlanders' welcome-feast Valubran had been ingratiating in a servile way, but the lurking half-smile of a would-be wit, and the tilted set of his head suggested a high opinion of his own abilities or attractions.

" He scandalized the *atarlai*, Sholidu. He told him, here at the Abu, you stand for Raëdhi Himself, and Zhôl is yet to come."

Kamin-Tolagh, after a moment of frowning unfocus, felt the coming of ice-cold rage. Curious, not that Lavsila would relate such a scrap of gossip, but that he assumed a jocular manner for a remark he must find offensive. Working at the forge, Valubran spoke with a variety of people, and must have been repeating something he had picked up, but its gross blasphemy was not the reason for Kamin-Tolagh's anger; Zhôl was conceived in a union between Aëlovoi and Raëdh, and the impious enjoyed pointing out that in at least one venerable invocation Aëlovoi was called `Sister of Raëdhi.' As often happened, the less-than-learned young metalsmith had perhaps confused the incident with the more consistent tale of Hrâmi and Fiunuvoi, but in either case the allusion was to incest.

Kamin-Tarú had rolled her couched her head a little to the side, and was regarding her brother with one watchful eye.

"I shall have to prescribe a cure," Kamin-Tolagh said, all dulling effect of wine subdued, "for such misplaced wit."

Lavsila was just enough short of drunk to say nothing, waiting for a better clue as to how this was to be played.

"If, for the sake of my independence, I have been less than welcoming to envoys of *g'Asalladh'*, it is not to give license to disrespect and blasphemy." The youth was going to pay for his impertinence, but to punish him for his real offense would admit more than Kamin-Tolagh cared to: it might be feasible to have his revenge and at the same time appear as defender of religious sensibilities, whose sole quarrel with the *Mankh'* was a political one. "Before at-Sholidu departs, I shall make Valubran apologize. After a whipping from Hunghi, he should be contrite enough."

Kamin-Tarú raised her head an inch or two, and with blurry pleasure mumbled words of which only `smooth young back` were distinct, surprising Kamin-Tolagh. A fondness for flogging was not unknown, especially in Kargul, sometimes as giver, recipient, or both, quite commonly as spectator; the subject was reputedly given many loving pages in the *Epranda*, the ancient, often-suppressed manual of necromancy, odd lore, and the delights of pain, but he had not been aware his sister shared that taste. Lavsila, meanwhile was trying, in his impaired state, to reach an acceptable way of expressing strong disapproval.

"The boy is of no birth. But, Lord, to have an Owani publicly flogged, and by, well... "

"By one of my personal bodyguard?"

"The Owanil must have the respect of — must be given respect; they alone have skills to administer — " a very hard word for him — "to administer an empire. Who else understands courts and justice, and making of boundaries and, and treaties? Maps," he added vaguely.

"The Hrin may have better maps than ours, though we never see them. But Dubovai will be respected, and others who make themselves useful. We shall treat no whole race with the respect due its best, nor with the contempt earned by its worst."

Lavsila abruptly but unsteadily stood, pointing an admonitory finger. "Besides, Valubran — " he began, but had gained his feet not for the sake of emphasis, but out of urgent need to relieve himself. Without continuing his thought, he went off, steering successively at clutchable landmarks. Kamin-Tolagh recalled the man's warnings had all gone the other way when the excessive beating and half-starving of servants had been forbidden.

The inadequate light dimmed further, as the rushlight guttered, drowning in its oil. "If nothing else," Kamin-Tolagh, with a sour smile, "it will be good if *g'Asalladh'* will sell us some *ôdul*."

Kamin-Tarú said earnestly, "But you can't make an empire of only tribes. We need games, fashion, gossip."

"There are the Hrin."

"They have no men," with unexpected bite. "Real men do not need to hide their women from the world."

Kamin-Tolagh reached for her hand. "We shall keep the Owanil, but on my terms, not theirs. If I am to be their last hope, they must learn to obey me."

"The flogging of Valubran," with a slight sigh, "should be worth seeing." In the darkness outside, the wavering of their rushlight was mirrored by the whiter flicker of distant lightning. For the hundredth time, Kamin-Tolagh had rebuked Lavsila's assumptions about race, yet was disgusted to find that vision of a *rightful place* waiting at Kadon Dinul remained with him from disjointed talk, a place which, by Lavsila's assessment, depended on his reputation as a friend of the Owanil.

After weeks of fierce heat, the weather boiled over; hammering bursts of rain came, so violent it seemed a marvel walls and houses could remain standing and undamaged. The lower part of the Abu, the old *jinzai* drill grounds, was for two days under water, and as was later learned, floods, destructive torrents and earthslides came to many places; huts in the newer Man-mani village, next to the river, were washed away, and part of the road through Larghai's Notch was blocked by a giant gush of mud from the hillside above. For once in agreement, Lavsila and Iruvakh, each from his own perspective, deplored the wasted water, Lavsila that he had not been given men to dig the reservoirs he wanted, Iruvakh with an additional lament for all the good growing soil scoured away, to end, he said, in Flamûrai.

Skies soon cleared with a drying wind from the north, and a chilly night told Kamin-Tolagh the *Mankh'* delegation would soon be gone. In early morning he sent Tau-Suaka with a couple of men to arrest Valubran at the forge, and bring him for swift trial, like a soldier on campaign. In the realm, since the time of Plakhsila *Kímukoi*, the accuser was required to bring evidence for his charge, but military justice, at least in the field, retained former rules, by which the accused had to prove innocence.

He was not seen at his best, scared, bewildered, unclear exactly what the charge was. Dressed for the forge in a thin shirt, once away from his furnace he seemed to be shivering equally with cold and fright, retaining not much of the somewhat girlish good looks, said to come from his mother, a locally notorious Harbor Way flirt (according to Lavsila's account) some twenty-five years ago.

Sentenced to a dozen lashes, guessing they would be laid on by the notorious Hunghi, Valubran became a shade Kamin-Tolagh had never seen before in a living person, not white, but wan grey with a tinge of green. Knees buckling, he was led away between two Hill Froghul, and now all that remained was to implicate the *Mankh'* in the punishment.

Yet at-Sholidu, loading his pack-ponies, departure set for late morning, expecting the promised escort, was anything but pleased to be informed by Kamin-Tolagh there was to be a ceremonial leavetaking at the parade-ground outside the gate.

The purpose of his embassy still in mind, he could hardly slip away unnoticed. Mounted, flanked by his leading officers, Kamin-Tolagh had not less than two-thirds of all Owanil of the Abu as spectators, while servants and workers from the tribes peered discreetly over the main wall.

As pointedly as he dared, the *atarlai* said his party wished to reach first camping-place before nightfall.

"An easy ride," Kamin-Tolagh assured, "and a plain road. We cannot let you leave knowing we have done nothing to make amends for the insult given you by a subject of this empire."

"Insult, Lord?" genuinely puzzled. "To my knowledge, every member of this riding has been treated with nothing but courtesy." Ignoring the offense for which Valubran was being punished, that was still a considerable overstatement, though within the bounds of diplomatic fiction.

"My counsellor, Lavsila — " who either was once again sleeping late, or else wanted no part in these proceedings — "informs me the youth Valubran uttered, in your presence, the grossest of blasphemies, which must be considered offensive. If, as we all hope — " he had gradually raised his voice, so that now most of his officers and enough Heartlanders could hear him plainly — "this visit of yours is to be the beginning of enduring friendship between Empire and *Mankh'*, we cannot have this ugly incident lying between us."

"Nor need it," at-Sholidu, promptly. "Nor does it. The youth was, as I see, Lord, mainly thoughtless. If there had been guidance from the *Mankh'* over these past years, no doubt such carelessness of speech would be unknown."

Not bad, Kamin-Tolagh silently conceded, but motioned with a finger to Tau-Suaka, who gave a wag of his head. At once, young Valubran was led out between guards. Blood had not returned to his face since sentencing, and he was sleepwalking; behind him came Hunghi with his permanent expression of calculated cruelty, though carrying, as instructed, a length of stirrup-leather, not his celebrated triple-thonged whip, potentially deadly.

A murmur went among assembled residents of the Abu, Heartlanders as always carefully aloof from soldiers' families. At Kamin-Tolagh's sign, Pivrekhan hobbled forward; normally a quiet-spoken, even shy young man, he had in reserve a parade-ground voice of remarkable carry, one power to survive his terrible wounding. As Valubran, shirt stripped away, was brought to an unwilling embrace of the weathered, deeply-creviced flagpole, Pivrekhan, at Kamin-Tolagh's prompting, proclaimed the youth's crime as "blasphemy, giving offence to our honored guests of the *Atarlum*."

Notably, of the Heartlanders, Tavrotosai, who had sponsored Valubran at the forge, did nothing but blink and bite briefly at his lower lip; Pranúdhanai, considered a leader, was no more demonstrative, while beside him his betrothed, Ondhayu, showed an interest not unlike Kamin-Tarú's, eyes dark, small, pink tip of tongue visible between her full lips. Public floggings, so long as offenders were young and healthy, might provide an inexpensive form of popular entertainment.

"Lord," at-Sholidu in an urgent murmur, aware of the attempt to get the *Mankh'* blamed for this severity, "If I may claim privilege of a guest, let me ask that this boy's crime be forgiven. He is at an age where, as we can all remember, indiscretions are only to be expected." What was supposed to be a winning smile of shared reminiscence went with this, a mood for which at-Sholidu had no gift, grating harshly with his normal aridity. His quick glances, side to side, suggested he would like a way to disassociate himself and his calling from the whole proceeding.

At the same time, Lavsila, on the scene at last, used a complicated dance-figure of his horse to draw Kamin-Tolagh a little in the opposite direction so as to stammer out, at last, a cogent argument against the whipping of Valubran. The boy, he urged, with a little persuasion and the promise of reward, might be an indispensable ally in helping Kamin-Tolagh pick his quarrel with the *Hrithust* Iolfrant. He had so far been resistant to the idea of using the family recipe for false gold, *rholivaïn*, for that purpose. Ever since conviction of its originator, his descendants had each in turn sworn an oath to sell the alloy, if ever, only honestly; in his rapid near-whisper Lavsila ventured the opinion Valubran was ripe for a change of heart.

Kamin-Tolagh had no objection to exploiting the situation in any way that occurred; hardly anyone could have overheard at-Sholidu's plea, so it could not be thought he had influenced Kamin-Tolagh to leniency. At the same time, the Heartlanders had to be given part of the show they had come for, with the demonstration of his absolute power for which he had brought them. Neither would he give Lavsila so cheap a victory. He nodded to Tau-Suaka, who spoke a word to his kinsman. A heavy thwack, and a broad stripe of red was painted across Valubran's bared back, while a noise, somewhere between sigh and low, percussive groan, came from the watchers.

Hunghi drew the leather back. "Wait," Kamin-Tolagh commanded, and trotted to the base of the flagpole, throwing his reins to one of the Hill Froghul as he dismounted. The side of Valubran's face was pressed against the rough spar as if for comfort; he had bitten blood from his agonized lower lip, but his eyes were empty and unfocused. Mainly, and contemptibly, this was fear of Hunghi's reputation; many young boys, Kamin-Tolagh not excluded, had survived a dozen with the stirrup-leather, to ride and wrestle next day.

"Valubran — " Kamin-Tolagh had to speak the name twice more to secure enough of the youth's lapsed attention. "You wish to escape further pain? You can."

After a long, disbelieving, or possibly uncomprehending pause, "How, Lord?"

"Lavsila has mentioned a plan to you."

This, unimaginably remote from present concerns, was too difficult for Valubran. "To do with use of your *rholivaïn*," Kamin-Tolagh prompted.

"Lord, I have never made or sold any *rholivaïn*." Valubran, so much as possible, cringed further, as if in expectation of added punishment.

Kamin-Tolagh put a hand on the youth's fettered forearm in reassurance, although in fact filled with disgust for this cowardice, and aware time was short before anger overcame his concern for policy. The onlookers, too, were restive.

Still in an undertone, he said, "I don't care about that. My question is, if I remit your punishment, will you give me your promise to do what Lavsila asks of you, and to maintain absolute secrecy?"

A simple proposition. Hunghi, feet still straddled, watched with dark-eyed indifference, like a bricklayer interrupted by a discussion between architect and builder.

At length realizing he might escape more pain, Valubran let his eyes meet Kamin-Tolagh's. "Lavsila's plan, Lord?"

"He has said what he wants from you." This, of course, was largely assumption.

"He has, Lord, but in my family — " Now enough calmed to read Kamin-Tolagh's limited patience, Valubran hastily abandoned that line. "Yes, Lord, anything he wishes. I promise."

"You have had a small taste of what might be the reward for breaking your word. No one here can or will help you, if you anger me."

"Lord."

"And will you now — " Kamin-Tolagh changed to his public voice, "come with me to the *atarlai* and ask his gracious pardon?" With care, it could be made to seem Kamin-Tolagh's impulse to clemency had overruled the implacable *Mankh'*.

An instructive morning, he decided, with everyone, not excepting Lavsila, to some degree puzzled, Heartlanders uneasy with disappointment and apprehension, at-Sholidu exasperated but maintaining a rasping courtesy right up to his departure. After his reprieve, Valubran had instantly acquired, and showed every sign of maintaining, an abject, cringing gratitude, which. while it set Kamin-Tolagh's teeth unpleasantly on edge, was probably useful.

Though they were likely to return, departure of the *Mankh'* delegation meant relief from the feeling of oppression they had brought. After a nap in luxuriously cool afternoon, he was waiting now for Lavsila, who would explain details of how they would trap Iolfrant's follower, Huolafidn. Entailing, he had been warned, payment of a large sum to the trader Dvasslo, which, purely for the sake of propriety, Lavsila would handle.

Kamin-Tarú, still drowsy, came and sat beside him at the table, and took his arm affectionately. "I wish the Marionettes of Burantal could visit us here."

He gave her a quick look, but there was no sign of any satirical intent.

29.

Unstill snow on the *Mankh'* road was dry as sand or sawdust, frayed and fretted by the wind in long, rippled spears, or rising suddenly in a cloudy spiral. From this window of the Bronze Residence Dolvid had watched weather for more than a few seasons, and he was all at once reminded of the day a dozen years ago, when the grim news had come about the Tan Lughsai fire, the death of Lambarr.

That, however, had been late, a year when winter had come twice, bringing its worst after a false pass at spring; this year it had come too soon, and Dolvid could not remember such bitter cold so early; still short of Fire Days, ice had spread almost the width of the Paowan Estuary, and Arnan itself was frozen, in places a mile out from its eastward shores, all ports virtually closed. Throughout the Six Provinces, troops, both General and provincial cavalries, labored incessantly to keep roads open, thwarted by heavy snows and driving winds; all journeys were dangerous, the Colony completely cut off from the capital.

It was this sensation of being stranded on an inaccessible island that had brought back memory of the Tan Lughsai Disaster, and yet they had suffered from scarcity of news before winter ever descended. In Kargul, his spy, Mansi, for the past year and over, had feared she was under suspicion of complicity, not less than foreknowledge, in the flight of Kamin-Tarú, particularly since Mansi's daughter had accompanied the fugitive, and after supplying that excuse had ceased to write her reports for Dolvid. Disappearance of the trader Dhunival, since his fright over carrying possibly seditious letters, was now complete; his warehouse at Thenimala was said to be boarded up, and if alive, best guess was he too had gone to join Kamin-Tolagh. If he had stayed, Dolvid consoled himself, there could be no messages to intercept; the long road south must be impassable in a dozen places.

Arvat, shoulders hunched against the chill, came to inform Dolvid he had visitors, waiting in the Old Audience Hall, where a hot fire was laid. One was Dolvid's good friend Konir, Âna's brother, and the other, Arvat's brother-in-law, Rhunilat, responsible for day-to-day functioning of the New Residence, and seldom seen here. Both were bright-cheeked and red-nosed from the scything wind, but otherwise the contrast between the two was almost laughable: Konir greeted Dolvid with a nod and a roll of his eyes, before reseating himself, completely at home, while the tall, long-necked Rhunilat, beginning visibly to thicken about the middle, stiffly waited to be waved to a chair, and then sat primly upright. He cleared his throat, and observed the cold showed no sign of relenting.

"How is Tellis?" Possibly some small talk would put Rhunilat at ease. In girlhood, his wife had been Dolvid's pupil, and one he had come near leaving his first wife for.

"Well, I thank you, *Bôdhrai*," he replied, adding tentatively, with a small laugh, "She is writing a book."

"History?"

"No, no, *Bôdhrai*," hastily, to reassure Dolvid his wife would not presume to compete on the master's home ground. "A romance. Or, well, something like a romance — " proud but baffled. "A tale, certainly, of her own invention. She is keeping a copyist employed."

For the several hundredth time. Dolvid wished he could have the coolly intelligent Tellis here, in place of her erratic brother, Arvat, who now reappeared with a pot of hot spiced *raminat* and cups for all. Konir, no less reluctant than Rhunilat to come to the object of this rare visit, wondered about survival, in such bitter weather, for the saplings he and Dolvid had planted in eastern Paowan.

At last, with drinks poured and Arvat tactfully sent away, Konir edged nearer a subject. "Rhunilat has come here at my suggestion, to bring you some Residence Quarter gossip."

"The *bôdh'loiki* is always a welcome visitor," with a slight bow for Rhunilat, who remained reluctant to take his cue.

"My thanks, *Bôdhrai*," returning deference with interest. "Um, as you are aware, the Residence Quarter never lacks for tales. The jest has it, the closer one lives to the Residence, the less one knows for certain, and the more one guesses, about what the *rabhsai* may be doing. Or thinking." The nervous laugh came again, and Dolvid thought a jest might be more succinctly phrased.

"No doubt," inching closer to a point, "you have heard the, um, rumor that in the Farther West, the outlawed Kamin-Tolagh has received *atarlal* of the *Mankh*?"

"That goes beyond rumor, I think —" trying not to revisit the grim satisfaction of gloomy prophecy fulfilled. "I see no reason to doubt the story."

"Some are saying this went against the wishes of Rodlakh *Rabhsai*, as he expressed them to *g'Asalladh'* Himself — " this, at last, came out in a precipitate rush.

"Some?" keeping his voice neutral.

"Well, Ghuradh, as an example. As you are aware, *Bôdhrai*, I am in attendance at the New Residence every day. Where Ghuradh claims to get his information, I cannot say, but he had the temerity to tell me there had been a meeting, last summer sometime, where the *rabhsai*, these are his words, forbade, *forbade* sending of *atarlal* to Kamin-Tolagh's, that is to say, the lands Kamin-Tolagh claims as his. I denied it, naturally, *Bôdhrai*, though it is a tale that does not need denying; legally or in common sense, such a demand is unthinkable. Under the Second Treaty — "

"Isn't it wonderful — " turning to Konir cheerfully, though his feelings on this business were not improved by having to lie about it. "When you arrived today, I had just been thinking how, with the roads blocked, we starve for news. We have not yet

found weather, it appears, to keep marshfire from spreading."
Konir dutifully chuckled, but his eyes too had a rueful
expression; probably he had heard enough from his sister to
know this gossip was true.

Dolvid could not flatly deny the tale, nor would that have
been useful. "As you say, it is beyond believing. No *rabhsai*
could afford to interfere like that, in a question of religion."
Here, he was completely sincere.

"But," Rhunilat complained, "it does not die. Only last
night, one of Ladh-Sivai's cousins mentioned it again, and, as
you can imagine, with their kinsman in the West with Kamin-
Tolagh — well. I was wondering, *Bôdhrai*, if this persistent
rumor might not merit a formal denial from, ah, from the highest
level? You will appreciate how damaging it is to have alleged
the *rabhsai* would try to impede any Child of Yoëlladhu from
making his or her proper devotions."

"Indeed," blandly. "And since, in fact, such an attempt
would be bound to fail, the *rabhsai* would be seen as malicious
and at the same time impotent."

"We — my thought was — " Pink-faced, overcoming a
stammer, Rhunilat was stoking up to say something important.
"*Bôdhrai*, our real love and respect for Rodlakh *Deghi* should not
blind us to the fact there are people — not many, but not a mere
handful, either, who do not altogether condemn Kamin-Tolagh.
I myself have no use for such sentiments, but this sort of rumor,
ah — "

Dolvid assisted him: " — helps his admirers portray
Kamin-Tolagh as less a criminal and more the exiled champion
of besieged ancient rights." He guessed sympathy for Kamin-
Tolagh must be growing, to bring Rhunilat here in this weather.

"Exactly. And now comes — " looking for assistance to
Konir.

Who was ready. "The other side of the coin. You have
heard your Elamirr has a scheme?"

"The kin-purge?" making a long-suffering face. "He has
mentioned this to me, rather tentatively." Not to be taken

seriously; Elamirr had proposed *for the safety of the realm* there should be a decree barring from positions of authority or trust all those related to the Heartlanders who had joined Kamin-Tolagh, and any who did so in future. "I did not give it deep consideration. I did tell him it was nonsense; you do not judge a person's loyalty by that of a cousin or a niece." Once again, Dolvid tried to lighten the mood. "He may have thought I was defending my own position — if a former wife and her cousin count as kin."

With Rhunilat, Konir was not happy. "He casts a wide net when naming relatives. You did not forbid him to speak about it?"

"At the Bronze Residence, we encourage free exchange of ideas. Besides, unworthy things often gain value by being forbidden, as in the story of *The Gem of Desire* in the *Tale of Songs*."

"We are not children here," Konir said, glancing once at Rhunilat. "Curse it, *Bôdhrai*, let us not pretend: what he has been careful not to mention is race. Elamirr, you will be delighted to hear, has been looking for somebody to bring forward his measure in earnest. Me he has not dared approach — I am the right race, but the wrong kin — but he has visited all other *bôdh'loikil* who could never be affected by his decree."

Malvus at the Mint, easily guessed, Sontarr at the Treasury, Sett in charge of trade — all with Mixed blood.

Rhunilat sniffed. "According to my wife, *Bôdhrai*, to these meetings Elamirr brought Arvat, who asserted his father would have endorsed this plan."

"He would not." Dolvid had enjoyed many lively debates with Arvus, a man passionately opposed to all the *Mankh'* stood for, yet always a good friend. "He had much too much sense."

"So my wife told her brother, and not gently. She was, is, very angry with him."

She would be, and not only because her husband was related to some of the so-called Exiles — as were Faëdhal, Master of Tongues, and Kizhunai, Captain-Counsellor for

Armies, Fornival, *Bôdh'loiki* for Law. There were, besides, magistrates, tax-assessors, senior officers of Household and General Cavalry, and most by far were completely loyal to the *rabhsai*.

"I am gratified to learn," Rhunilat offered, "all those Elamirr did approach dismissed his idea in short order. Nevertheless, *Bôdhrai*, for there to be such a proposal, in this realm, in the *rabhsayum* which has dedicated itself to healing —"

"Yes — " seeing readily why this had been paired with the former question, and perhaps why he had been visited by two high officials, of different bloods, but of the same mind on both issues, an emblematic display of unity outside of race. At the time of the furor over Âna's Compensation Law, he had been angered to hear some of the Families parroting the catch-phrase, `Not equity, but revenge — ' and here was Elamirr's brain-child, effectively a way to exclude from office, considering the web of kinship and intermarriage, all those of unmixed Owani descent; exactly the former slogan of the malcontents, `Preference turned on its head.' That it stood no chance at all of being adopted was neither here nor there; already it had fueled smouldering suspicions.

"As I say," thinking it through out loud, "any official action would only dignify this nonsense more than it deserves. In talk, you could call it the overzealousness of young *rabhsayanil*, never remotely countenanced by the *rabhsai*. Arvat I shall reprimand today, and Elamirr when he returns — when he can return." To celebrate the sixtieth birthday of Untimarr, his wife's father, Elamirr had taken Morulis to Burantal, and might well be trapped there by snow.

Konir said, "Shumat insists the Burantal road will be kept open."

"Then Elamirr will shortly be reprimanded, and told to desist from this folly."

"By the *rabhsai*?" Konir asked.

"No, I'll do the knuckle-rapping, no need to bother Rodlakh with it.   The question of his supposed illegal instructions to the Patriarch I do mean to raise with him; there must be an explanation for what can only be a misunderstanding. I can readily imagine he expressed *annoyance* the so-called Exiles were to remain in good standing with the *Mankh'*. That is a long way from attempting to forbid it."

Rhunilat, relieved, satisfied civil war was not imminent, soon left, to direct, he said, closing off of unused suites at the Residence while the extreme cold persisted. Konir lingered, saying he had questions about food-supplies to discuss.

"Elamirr," he suggested, when alone with Dolvid, "may resent the skill of the Families in flattering his wife." Just eighteen, Morulis, despite wearing sash, showed no sign of becoming a typical wife of Burantal, and at feasts, where she was always a center of attention, the sour face of her watching husband had become a standing joke.

"You, too, have achieved new fame, along with our forest-to-be."

"The song? I have heard it." The city inaccurately remembered that at the time a spring ago when Heartlanders had emigrated to the West, Dolvid had been away in the Angle country, setting out saplings. The invention had spawned a satire, to a traditional tune, in which disaster was piled upon disaster, each verse ending with the refrain, `*But the* Bôdhrai *was off, planting his trees.*'

"A kind of flattery. Back when Rhunilat's father was *Bôdhrai*, nobody cared where he was, so I've heard."

He went on to outline a selection of his own troubles, with all ports closed, and roads only intermittently open. With the good harvests of the past three years, he'd had the foresight to warehouse considerable grain and smoked meat, not only at Kadon Dinul, but in other main cities. Most urgent problem was fuel, where the same conditions that increased demand complicated supply. Nothing could come across Arnan, and while there was firewood cut and ready in the Forest of Nîv, the road south of Kanzan Tâl had been impassable for days.

"Peat, too, in southern Paowan. But that also has to come by way of Kanzan Tâl."

"You say the Burantal Road is open? The marshlands of Shemugrân must be frozen solid. Carts could not go that way, but unless the snow is too deep, packhorses could bring back loads of peat."

"They can drag skids behind them, too," brightening.

"Untimarr, in Burantal, can help put together a string of pack-animals."

"Very good," he stood, eager to be started. "My thanks."

"'*The* Bôdhrai *was off, planting his trees,*'" Dolvid quoted corrosively. "If there had been someone doing that twenty-five years ago, the Heartland would have more firesides to sing by today."

Konir, grinning broadly, was about to leave, and did a creditable imitation of being struck by an afterthought. "Just the same, the *rabhsai* is going to have to be told about Elamirr's madness — if not by you, by Âna. It has gone beyond a question of youthful misjudgment; all Kadon Dinul knows he's had influence in the past."

"Still, he is my assistant. Or receives his salary for that."

"Yes, but Rodlakh would intervene, wouldn't he, if you wanted to dismiss Elamirr? Then he must be the one to curb him — this is not just insubordination. This poison can recruit supporters for the one in the West faster than all the lies your Lavsila can think up."

"You are right. But the other is more troublesome."

He meant, because true, and Konir did not want to comment, only making a face before actually taking his leave.

Having asked for a wholly private meeting, Dolvid had no need to bring up Elamirr's proposal; from one of several imaginable sources the *rabhsai* had heard, and was impatient to discuss it. They had their talk in a small, snug ante-chamber to the Personal Suite, where comfortable chairs were set in front of a hot sea-stone fire.

"Why did you not tell me about this?"

"I meant to, at this meeting. When I first heard about it, I judged it was too silly to bother you with."

A hard look. "Not, I hope, because you ever dreamed I would support such foolishness."

"If you had, I would have resigned my post."

A faint dismissive wave. "For that matter, I would have forced my own abdication: *Rabhsai* is arguably a position of trust, and through Laluvoi I must be related to several of those who joined Kamin-Tolagh. But then I am to Kamin-Tolagh himself."

This hint of humor instantly evaporated, and Rodlakh was angry. He brought a fist down on the arm of his chair. "I will not have this. Here at the Residence, we have tried to set an example for the whole realm, showing how men and women of ability can rise, and can bring together their talents for the common good, whether they call themselves Owani, Gabhani, Mixed. or anything else. Elamirr! I don't understand. You have been more than generous with your time and your teaching — he has been made welcome among the Families, where his choice of wives is much admired."

"And a little envied."

"A little!" Uncharacteristically, Rodlakh smirked, and with another swift change of mood, confided, "The *rabhsayu*, this between us, does not want to hear me praising Morulis, but I cannot make myself blind, can I? Those eyes, eh? And the breasts, perfect — at Halving, she wore that thin white gown, and the breeze pressed it against her body — " He shuddered pleasurably.

"But you did not say that to Âna?"

"She has not been altogether herself, lately — distracted. It may be time for another child."

Dealing with complicated feelings of his own, Dolvid winced privately to think how Âna would spit fire, hearing childbearing prescribed as a remedy for any woman's unhappiness, and more pointedly, hers.

"How is Aëlu?" It followed logically enough; the time was coming near when her third and Dolvid's second child would be delivered; as before, she was radiant and unperturbed. Next, the *rabhsai* asked after Sedukh, just past his fifth birthday, with the muscled arms and legs of an eight-year-old; otherwise he seemed to Dolvid no worse, assuredly no better, than any other boy of his age. The purpose of this meeting was in danger of dissolving in a general discussion of the five children they had between them fathered or fostered, troubling Dolvid with memory of Rodlakh's amiable, ineffectual father, Lambarr *Rabhsai*, who would let family take precedence over the most pressing affairs of state.

"With the Elamirr business," he said.   "I would recommend against a public repudiation of the kin-purge. Let it remain too silly for comment."

"But Elamirr, the author, Elamirr is going to hear about my displeasure. It is inexplicable, after all I have done to put those divisions in the past."

Now. "Word is also abroad," he made himself say. "You tried to prevent the sending of *atarlal* to the West."

"And now they are there," grimly. "We have to consider what can be done."

"*Rabhsai*," persisting. "The Families are gossiping — "

"Those who object do not have much love for me or my House."

Where had it gone, the old ease, when they could simply talk, as two men? Dolvid tried a last time to make Rodlakh see this was not just another trumped-up excuse for making trouble, but a genuine grievance. "In deploring this attempt, the Families will have support from the Craft Families, and many ordinary

men and women, some who have never called themselves
Children of Yoëlladhu — who, quite possibly, used to distrust all
the *Mankh'* stood for."

"I am still their *rabhsai*."

On the brink of reminding him the oath at his accession
had included a promise to honor and protect the beliefs of his
subjects, Dolvid drew back. The gulf between them felt
unbridgeable; a minute ago Rodlakh had been about to ask how
they could retaliate against *g'Asalladh'* for his stubbornness in
sending *atarlal* to the West.

"If you have a fault — " noting his hesitation — "it is an
excessive love of being proved right. You opposed me on this
point, that is why you are making so much of it."

"No, it is because this is the most dangerous
miscalculation of your entire reign. Nothing can be worse than
a policy that creates justified resentment, at the same time as it
is seen to be ineffectual."

"Would it be better," he flared, "to be seen as a weakling,
coddling renegades, giving in to everything they demand?"

"*Rabhsai*, religion has never been yours to grant or
withhold. The best course is to admit there was a mistake, and
permit *atarlal* free passage through the Colony, which is their
right, under the Treaty."

"We remade the Treaty."

"And reaffirmed the central provision."

"Do you forget what we said? We had won against *jinzal*
by the weight of a hair, and we came as near to abolishing the
Atarlum altogether, having the *Mankh'* torn down, stone by
stone."

"And in the end agreed we could not, not if we wanted
peace in a realm where the *Mankh'* will always be, for many, the
home of truth. So we resolved to change the *Atarlum*, prevent its
excesses, make it answerable to the realm — "

"And once again they are journeying into the West, to the
very place where they bred *jinzal*, and you tell me I can do
nothing to prevent that."

"There is nothing you can do; the Patriarch informed you of His intentions only in courtesy. This very right you reaffirmed as His in the meeting of 2943, not an abstract right for Him, but a practical guarantee. If, in clear breach of Treaty, we keep them from going to the Frontier, there are a hundred ways for them to reach the Farther West in secret, and we shall have the worst of both worlds; here in the Heartland it will be as bad as if we had seized *atarlal* and kept them in chains. You are going to risk tearing your realm in two, for the sake of inconveniencing the *Mankh'*?"

"We hold high tile — " one of Rodlakh's rare attempts at cynical manipulation. "The realm at large still has not heard who trained and led the *jinzal* armies."

Dolvid had not overlooked the point. He shook his head. "Exposure is no threat against the present Patriarch. Dozhusai would say, not wrongly, *jinzal* were the work of evil men within the *Atarlum*, which His Patriarchate has long purged. If He had not been so successful, there would be less danger in trying to bully the *Mankh'*." Together with representatives from the *Manadilum* nominated by Dozhusai, Dolvid was very near agreement on a long-standing dream, a plan for reopening the *manal*, not the old bastions of Owani privilege and exclusion, but as realmwide schools, where, in ordinary language, letters and simple reckoning would be taught to any boy or girl, religious instruction limited to the Tale of Zhôl. Paradoxically, the vigor Dozhusai had brought to His pursuit of compromise, His acceptance of the *rabhsai*'s authority and the limits on His own, His determination to make the Growers and Healers available to everyone, irrespective of race or belief, had made Him into a force risky to ignore; whenever they returned from their travels, men such as Konir and Shumat, neither of them exactly bred in the old *Mankh'* tradition, invariably remarked on the new popularity of the *atarlal* in remote places, with ordinary people unlikely to know anything about the Descent of Yoëlladhu.

A calculating *rabhsai* might have tried to identify himself with this religious resurgence; even when most exasperated with

Rodlakh, Dolvid admired his refusal to bid for cheap popularity by appearing, suddenly, as leading champion of the Cult of Zhôl. Yet there was a great deal of habitable territory between an insincere piety and what could only be seen as wrongheaded hostility to a changed *Atarlum*. In a confiding moment, the Patriarch had lamented His inability to expunge entirely the reactionary party at the *Mankh'*, and this dispute could only strengthen their case against His conciliatory policies.

"Dozhusai has made concessions, but no Patriarch can compromise on the right to send His *atarlal* where they are needed and asked for; that is the pass where He will stand and fight, and can count on plenty of allies; law, tradition, public opinion."

"And the *rabhsai*?" bitterly. "Who is on my side? If I let the *atarlal* go freely into the West, and twenty years from now a new *jinzai* army is ravaging the Colony, who will take responsibility for that? Very fine to be so sure, but it is I who pay for errors of judgment, I and the realm."

"*Jinzal* are not an issue." They had been through this so often, Dolvid had no patience left, but his immense effort to control anger was if anything too successful, the taut calm in his voice sounding a great deal like contempt. "It would be sixty years at the least before they could be bred in numbers to be a danger; if the *Mankh'* had wanted to breed them it would have sent its people in secrecy, without informing us, and if Kamin-Tolagh desired a *jinzai* army, he could have begun it without help from the *Atarlum*, but every reliable witness reports he has taken great precautions against the birth of *jinzal*, and killed the few that have been born. However, *Rabhsai*, if we want to be absolutely secure, against not only *jinzal*, but all dangers that could be bred in secret in the Farther West, our remedy is simple. The West is a danger, not because it is so distant, but because we turn our backs. If, notwithstanding all his crimes and failings, you could reach an accommodation with Kamin-Tolagh — "

"I am the *rabhsai*!" he shouted, all at once on his feet, knuckles white, as was his face, which had been flushed. Filled with failure, Dolvid did not want to meet his glaring eyes.

"You shall not presume so on our friendship." The voice stayed harsh, though he was trying to justify to himself his unwonted fierceness.

"*Deghi*," miserably. "If I were arguing for my own benefit, you could call it presumption. I would much rather be somewhere quiet, studying texts and writing history."

"Nevertheless," still angry, still explaining anger. "I will not be harangued like an apprentice."

Dolvid reached for the satchel he used for documents. "Then I have your leave, *Deghi*?"

"Till you find suitable forms of address."

He made half-deference, but just as he imagined the decision to go had calmed him, he was overtaken by a fresh wave of choking annoyance. All absurd; this was immensely important, and nothing was decided; he could not be sure Rodlakh would not renew efforts to dictate to the *Mankh'*, and nothing came more helpful than the unspoken sarcasm, *I shall return when I have learned to say what you want to hear.* He let his eyes meet Rodlakh's without faltering, then turned away.

Instantly, Rodlakh said, thick-voiced, "Dolvid — "

"*Rabhsai*?" turning back.

"If there is news of importance, or a document for me to sign, do not send Elamirr. You bring it. I do not want to see Elamirr. I do not say he should be dismissed — if you think so, I shall not object, but I would rather he is not completely disgraced — for Morulis's sake, not his."

"Elamirr has his usefulness," lightly. "When he can restrain that appetite for plots."

The attempt failed. Rodlakh nodded as if only half-hearing, and picked up the sheaf of pages Dolvid had brought him today.

After Fire Days, winter gnawing on, Dolvid took independent action to kill the persistent and much too accurate rumors. Having given written notice of his intentions, and received no response, he took advantage of a slight moderation in the cold to summon all the *bôdh'loikil* to the Old Bronze Residence, and address them, saying there had indeed been a meeting between the *rabhsai* and the Patriarch, at which the subject of *atarlal* going to the West had come up. At that time, Dolvid related, *g'Asalladh'* had generously offered to mediate between *rabhsayum* and Kamin-Tolagh; Rodlakh's reply, that with Kamin-Tolagh's outlawry formally proclaimed, peacemaking must begin with his suing the Council for relief, had been misinterpreted, though not by the Patriarch, as trying to forbid all dealings between the *Mankh'* and Kamin-Tolagh's claimed domains. Such an attempt, he observed, quite apart from its violation of letter and spirit of the Second Treaty, was altogether alien to the nature of a *rabhsai* whose tolerance for all varieties of belief and opinion was well-known.

A few fairly easy questions came, but on the whole his fiction satisfied the gathering. Rodlakh, who had evidently thought better of pursuing the point with *g'Asalladh'*, made no objection, while the Patriarch, if He heard of it, was wise enough to let the revision pass without comment.

One familiar face was absent from that gathering, Faëdhal, who was ill. His many minor ailments were gaining ground, and the cold was no help. Dolvid went to see him, at the same time to be sure he was being kept warm and well-fed by his devoted housekeeper. The old scholar had a bed made up in his main room, where a peat fire was burning, and was dozing over some parchment pages when Dolvid arrived. He was excessively grateful Dolvid had spared time from his large concerns, but a little embarrassed to be seen at less than his best.

Typically, though more testily than in younger years, he complained about copyists' errors in the manuscript he was working with. "I am losing all patience with these small annoyances — " and then came his thunderbolt: "Time, I think, and past time, for me to retire. I shall offer my resignation to the *rabhsai.*"

Inconceivable; Faëdhal was part of Dolvid's entire life at Kadon Dinul; he had first met him in childhood, and the man was inseparable from the calling. Unchangeable, learned, at times pedantic, always great-hearted, without him the Residence would be a foreign land.

He reminded him, "You have the rank of *bôdh'loiki.* Properly, your resignation should be addressed to me, as *Bôdhrai.*"

"Yes, certainly, that is understood," but he was flustered; Dolvid was not normally a stickler for forms. "Everything, you may be sure, will be done correctly."

"But then I shall reject it. Yours was always intended as a lifetime appointment. The new crop of children," Dolvid cajoled, "will quite soon need your tutoring."

"Ah, Dolvidhai," eyes paler than ever, suddenly swimming with tears. "You are asking, if I may venture, too much. If we count the somewhat unsystematic assistance I gave to Great Banak, I have taught three generations of that House. You cannot wish me to stay till I make a fool of myself, till I become poor old Faëdhal who used to be such a respected master."

"You will never be less than honored," he assured him. "We would, however, be prepared to consider application for an indefinite leave of absence — paid leave, so long as it is understood you will be available from time to time for consultation on questions of usage and translation. Here at your own house, I mean. My dear master, you know you cannot live out of harness altogether."

"Well, I, naturally — " he was overcome, and Dolvid's throat was choked with emotion.

"In the meantime, till you are ready to return to daily service, I think we should ask Tellis if she can find time to start the royal children in language."

Eyebrows rose. Tellis had been, long ago, such a good student, and become so valued an assistant when the *Song of*

Tales was being prepared, it had not occurred to Dolvid he was recommending the Old Tongue be taught by a Mixed, daughter of a Deniant — and one of a sex Faëdhal continued to see as unapt for learning.

Although he had decidedly excepted Tellis, with Laluvoi and now Âna, from his general strictures. After the moment of shock, his face cleared. "Excellent. Their own children have, let it be noted, unusually fine command of the Owanilú, and a good accent — the elder two, that is." Third child and second son was only five. "Between us," Faëdhal added slyly, "I suspect she may have given pointers to her husband, too. He makes far fewer mistakes than he used to."

Rhunilat, a man entirely of the Families, as Faëdhal was. A pity Tellis had not been here to receive this ultimate accolade.

When, shortly after, Aëlu gave birth to the son they had both wanted, they gave, with the tearful assent of Faëdhal, the name Faëvid to the boy, so linking the old scholar with his long-departed friend, Vidukh, Dolvid's father.

The weather had relented a little, ice on Arnan beginning to crack. Owan Sai remained closed to shipping, but the southerly ports were freed, Zelkova and Inilun Barabhi in Kargul, and then from Nambalus in the Lower Paowan came news which eclipsed any other; at Kamsilat, Saidhan was dead.

The closing thud of a vast volume of history; Saidhan's military career had spanned seventy years, when he carried a lance for the last time at the age of eighty-seven in the Jinzai War, and that was sixty-four years after the feat that made him famous; as Aëlu said, "Now the War of the Widowed really belongs to the past."

Yet, with Dolvid, she mourned him personally; fourteen years his daughter-in-law, she did not forget his unfailing consideration, no less at the time when the news of his son's death was fresh.

With mention of that loss, it came suddenly to Dolvid he was foster-father, Aëlu mother to the new titular *Nim'* of the Colony, Sedukh. In view of the boy's age, Rodlakh was newly glad they had sent Bradhinal of Ân to lead the Army of the West.

"To keep the Colony in trust for Sedukh," Rodlakh pondered, "there will have to be a *Moradhilum*, I suppose, with Doleni as, um, *Maëdhrayu*."

"*Moradhiyu*," Dolvid supplied; a little-used word, it had kept its distinct feminine form.

Âna warned, "Doleni is seventy-seven.   Other arrangements may be needed before Sedukh can rule at Kamsilat."

With difficulty and delay, the provincial overlords gathered at Kadon Dinul for Saidhan's funeral; Vinilat was snowbound in Dônshei for three days, and Ân was represented by its Heir, Bradhinal, there being no hope of getting word to Sebira in time for Daënakh to attempt the long, cold journey from the north.

Tovakh, unabashed, again seized the opportunity to bring up the question of outlawry for Kamin-Tarú, which would clear the ground for Petakoi's Island nephew, Pedh-Sivai, to be implanted as Heir in Kargul. In one sense, Dolvid was gratified by the attempt, an indication contrary to Rodlakh's fears: arrival of the *atarlal* in the Farther West had not been part of a secret understanding between Kamin-Tolagh and his parents; Tovakh's continued anger was plainly not feigned.

Equally pleasing was Rodlakh's renewed refusal to allow the new outlawry to be discussed in Council; Âna was tartly amused, but if nostalgic regard for Kamin-Tarú could prevent succession in Kargul from passing to a plump and pompous young man with all the Islander's passion for past glories of Old Owan, it would not be the first good cause to prosper for frivolous reasons.

Council dispersed, Doleni, who had kept her composure intact through all ordeals of death and obsequy, officially and brusquely informed the *rabhsai* she was not available to serve as *Moradhiyu* for the Colony. Sixty years ago, she had come to Kadon Dinul from the South, to become Saidhan's bride, and go with him when he was made Captain of the West. At this late date she admitted candidly that apart from her husband, she had detested practically everything about life at Kamsilat: wood was a miserable material for building, and the trees clustered too thick about the Great House; visits from other families of note to ride with or plan dinners for had been a great deal too rare, and the sea-journey to Kadon Dinul in search of some society had always made her sick. Less polished than the home of her origin, Thenimala in Ninkufu, Kamsilat also lacked its lovely climate; henceforth, Doleni pronounced incontrovertibly, she would divide her year between summers here at Kadon Dinul and winters in the South, with intermediate stops at some of the provincial seats. Useless to try changing her mind.

Dolvid was puzzling over the gap Doleni's defection created when, at their next regular meeting, Rodlakh, with a thoughtful air, asked, "Would you, will you go to Kamsilat? As *Maëdhrai*?"

"I?" bewildered. The suggestion was obviously serious, and surely a dizzying honor, for one whose family was altogether obscure. If, instead, he first felt a chill, it came not from the offer, but the circumstances. Only a short while ago, such an idea would have been brought up for discussion, among Rodlakh, Âna, Dolvid himself, certainly, perhaps Shumat; the question would have been, not *will you go?* but *would this be good to think about?* Here, he was alone with Rodlakh, who had apparently consulted no one — not Âna; she would have immediately sought Dolvid's views. If the kin-purge had not put Elamirr in eclipse, Dolvid would have suspected he had initiated this, with the object of taking his place as chief advisor.

As he yet might, if Dolvid was the width of Arnan away from Kadon Dinul. Elamirr's hand-picked supporters at the

Bronze Residence already approached a separate establishment. "*Rabhsai*, I think I am more useful here."

He laughed. "I do not mean to be deprived of your counsel. When my grandfather sent his friend Saidhan to the West, it was not to be rid of him. Kamsilat is only three days away, when our weather is sane, and I would expect you to return often. It is not as if you have not chosen and trained able men among the *bôdh'loikil* and elsewhere. Later on... "

That was left unfinished, and to invent an ending was not easy; the world could change out of recognition in all the years before Sedukh was ready to rule in the Colony.

As morning mist lifting to admit the rising sun, Dolvid felt suddenly like singing. The *rabhsai*, never mind for what complicated reasons, was offering him freedom from the daily burden of troubles and annoyances; only three days! but distance would inevitably rob crisis of its urgency; at Kamsilat he would have time of his own again, to spend with Aëlu and the children, to resume his histories. He would miss the intoxication of being next to the wellspring of power, at the heart of large events, but that was also a wine going brackish, now he had to spend time devising strategies for urging his views, instead of the old, open honesty.

Still, not right. "This, *Rabhsai*, ought to be offered instead to Aëlu, mother to the rightful *Nim'*."

Rodlakh's frown was puzzled. "She is, true, adored there in the West. But Aëlu has not shown much taste for matters of state. You would not expect to be parted from her?"

"No, *Deghi*. If this is your wish, Aëlu and I will go to Kamsilat together. But titular authority should be hers, considering there will be times when I need to be here at Kadon, perhaps for a month or more. I do not need a title, other than *Bôdhrai*." This, too, embraced strategy; as Protector, Dolvid would have occupied the *nim*'s seat at meetings of the Council, leaving the *Bôdhrai*'s place enticingly empty, whereas Aëlu beside him as acting *nimu*, made, with Âna and Shumat, a powerful alliance.

"It is a long way from my wish. But who else, with the remotest claim, could I trust to rule at Kamsilat?"

Informed she was to be named to *moradhilum*, Aëlu did not need to be told it had been offered first to him, but he found her question odd — odd, that was, in being first in her mind: "What does Âna think about this?"

"Âna? We have not discussed it." He was perpetually uncertain how things stood between the two women; they were in no sense friends, nor was there the least apparent hostility; they behaved with a sort of remote mutual cordiality.

She had the ghost of a smile. "I would expect her to be against your leaving. She was distressed, it is plain, when you fell out with the *rabhsai*. She is going to feel you're abandoning her — leaving her without an ally against the advocates of extreme views."

"She will have allies," relieved to discover they were talking about policies. "Shumat, with most if not all of the *bôdh'loikil*, and her brother is strong as well as capable. Whatever comes, I can be back here inside a week; there are not many crises that can't wait that long."

"Shall we maintain the house here?"

"We can afford to." Each of them had been named in Saidhan's will, Aëlu additionally for extensive lands to be held in trust for Sedukh, and there would be the *nim*'s share of Colony revenues. Never able to spend his salary, Dolvid was abruptly wealthy.

"I have not forgotten when the prospect of ten acres, six years in the future, was a fortune." Aëlu shook her head. "But I do not think we should cross Arnan with Faëvid so little, not while that cough lasts.

"No, no — " reassuring with a quick touch of her hand. "He is strong as a *pefrai*, but they have not made ships to keep out cold breezes; we need more than a hint of spring. Also, before you can go, you have a lot of writing to do."

"Writing?"

"Policy. Some happenings might not wait a week. What if the Families, with all their armed retainers, were to march on the New Residence? That was a rumor, once."

"They will not."

"No, but you have exact plans for it."

"Oh, plans exist for all sorts of unreal contingencies." In a manner he made airily dismissive, he explained how the object would be to postpone open conflict for as long as could be, closing the city gates after sending dispatches summoning all nearby garrisons of General Cavalry, then using Household to intimidate the uprising, and offering an absolutely unconditional amnesty to the leaders, so long as their forces dispersed before nightfall. "The objective, just as with the business of the *atarlal* going to the West, is to maintain the safety of the realm, without creating martyrs."

"You don't have to justify your avoidance of bloodshed to me, but would this be what Dorrmas would do? Or Elamirr would advocate?"

"Shumat and I have discussed this kind of situation, many times — " but Aëlu's point was well-taken; Shumat, as commander, had taken responsibility for the Lunu Jinzalladhiyu massacre, but his sole fault had been failure to anticipate the hotheadedness of Dorrmas, now in charge of the Household.

Rodlakh, with his dilute patrilinear Gabhani line in the ascendant, had characterized Aëlu as a woman uninterested in policy. If there was a strain of truth in that, choice, not capacity, was the reason; astutely, she urged for all these cases, however improbable, where delicate handling was needed, procedures should be written out, and kept ready for use — plans given authority of the *rabhsai*'s signature.

Dolvid groaned at the labor it would involve, and the continuing uncertainty of his relationship with Rodlakh. "Well, as he, with considerable force, has reminded me, he is *rabhsai*.

When he has heard enough of my gloomy advice, he can find a new *Bôdhrai*."

"He'll never do that."

When she heard Dolvid was going to leave Kadon Dinul, Âna was not just displeased, she was furious, an anger he had not seen in her since the days of their earliest acquaintance. She found him alone one evening, working at the New Residence library, and with no preliminary accused him of betraying Rodlakh.

"By acceding to his wishes?" — with the feeling of fending off a physical attack.

"*Acceding*? I told him this was the worst day's work he had done as *rabhsai*, but you! I counted on you to refuse him outright."

"How would I do that? In the end, he has to be aware of his own needs."

If anything, she became angrier. "Don't talk to me as if you were some boy-trooper of the cavalry, *yes, sir, ride over a cliff, sir? whatever you say, sir.* You are the most powerful man in the realm; all you had to do was say, rather than go to the Colony, you would resign your post, and he would have found someone else to judge chicken-stealing cases at Kamsilat, and make sure the Army of the West buttons its tunics."

"I cannot live by constant threat."

"Who would credit such virtue?" she taunted, and the quarrel was joined in earnest. Unlikely to be intruded on here, for five acrimonious minutes they exchanged insults untrue or unmeant and mostly both, and yet from the furnace some adamantine facts managed to emerge undistorted. Rodlakh, he saw, no matter what Âna said about betrayal, was determined, approaching six years of reign, to emerge from tutelage, to become, at least for a proving time, his own *Bôdhrai*. While she, clearly, far beyond the guesses of Aëlu, had endured great pain over the differences between her husband and Dolvid, risking

Rodlakh's bad temper to take Dolvid's side in the dispute over his attempt to dictate to the Patriarch, and acquiring a loathing for Elamirr such as the old Âna used to express only for the most arrogant of the Old Blood. And yet, in some inexplicable way, Dolvid was to blame when her life with Rodlakh was made unendurable by these clashes.

Voided of venom, they fell into a sullen silence. Dolvid felt his misery was incurable, and then Âna said, "When he told me you were going to Kamsilat, I could not continue to argue with him. I was afraid I would start to cry, and even he would guess why." Unwarned, her gentleness had returned.

She was weeping now, and struggling for control. "Is this discreet? How is it we are left alone?" Though not many at the Residence made much use of the library, access was permitted to a number of poets, students and would-be writers of history, most very young, among whom Dolvid was regarded as a sort of ancient monument.

He explained; he had chosen this time as the one day when the more extensive Bronze Residence library was opened to outside scholars; he was assembling a list of books he wanted copied for Kamsilat.

"Books," he added, not daring to close the space between them, "are not what I'm going to miss most." She met his gaze blurrily.

Just one week later he was at the same task in the same place; it had become evident not all the books he wanted could be copied in time for his departure, some would have to be sent after him in batches. Already there had been brilliant days, with heaped snow, sparkling like shattered rainbows, visibly shrinking; Aëlu was satisfied with Faëvid's condition, and some of their personal effects had already trundled down to Owan Sai for shipping across Arnan.

Evening was coming to an unusually hushed Residence. Rodlakh, in Konir's company, was travelling up the Paowan to inspect reported flooding the far side of Dônshei Bridge, and perhaps go on for a look at the infant forest begun last year. Dolvid, alone at the copyists' table, sat poring over a badly-organized catalogue of early rolls.

He heard the inner door open and close, and Âna was alone at head of the short stair down from the entrance. She was smiling, very simply dressed in a rough brown robe, loosely girdled with bundled strands of black and scarlet leather. The dark hair was no more than brushed out, and in the soft light of the *ôdul* she was very young, younger than the keen-faced girl, then slow to smile, he had first met six years ago, almost to the day.

Her progress down the steps was a studied saunter. "I was hoping you would be here."

He had stood, but she came to seat herself on a copyist's stool, and to take one of his hands in both of hers. The grasp was a light one, but he could feel a tremulous tension; an unlooked-for late visitor to the library would find enough here to start gossip.

"Oh, Dolvid," and after an immense pause, "What are we going to do?"

"We? We, the realm, Rodlakh's *rabhsayum*?"

"Yes, if you wish," without enthusiasm. Three, four times now, her eyes had ventured to meet and then evade his, and a word came to his mind so unlike her he would not at first accept it: shy. Âna was acting shyly, and interpreting that, he was able to read what any other man, any wordless creature, would know by instinct. His blood began to surge, and he knew her fingertips felt the change in him. With a quick, familiar flick of her head she shook hair away from her face, and let her eyes challenge his, proud of her instant happiness.

But this, protested the cautious *Bôdhrai*, his eternal shadow, was stupid, unnecessary as dangerous. The two of them spent great parts of their separate lives in patient counterplots to save the realm from its dangers and follies, and could negate it all for the sake of pleasures anyone could live without. Here, the prudent argument was beyond disputing, yet that desiccated voice was immediately drowned in certainty he would bed with Âna. Equally, he was sure she was not acting on a momentary impulse, that she too had listened to all reasons against it, and pushed them aside.

"It may be," she murmured, as he moved to embrace her, "we'll never have another chance together — never," with peculiarly focussing emphasis, so he glimpsed the rest of his life as a dimming succession of varied scenes, none of them including his body next to hers. Not that his departure for the Colony would be a final farewell, but he felt it would in its fashion confirm the pairings they had chosen, over five years ago, so future meetings would hold no illusion of remedy. But in her voice there was a hint of panic, also, as if she was afraid his habitual good sense was going to rob them of this present consolation.

In a tone advertising his alliance with unreason, he asked, "Where, then?" She would not have begun this without that answer.

There was a suite at the Residence for use of each provincial overlord. None of Vinilat's family or household was at Kadon Dinul, and the empty Dramali Wing was unguarded, easily reached from the library entrance; as interlopers they slipped along the short corridor and up a few steps.

Again, at last, Dolvid was naked next to a naked Âna, all the more miraculous for being completely natural, rain laying the dust of a long drought, or sunrise dispelling gloom of an endless-seeming night. Only, with fierceness and joy, there was a lingering melancholy. "We have not done enough of this," she whispered, after a second renewal.

And there was a great deal yet to be said. She asked, and instantly withdrew, a question touching as absurd, whether she gave him greater pleasure than Aëlu did. She was illogically pleased to hear now a son had come, they intended no further children; women of Owani descent unmixed often conceived and bore children well into their fifties.

"Rodlakh wants more — a family like his father's. I think he would wish to bind the realm together by supplying husbands and wives for all the provincial Great Families. I am not going to bear him a child each year-and-a-half, as I have — especially now, with your going." She was very decided. "It keeps me away from the realm's business too much." He could not justify or explain the pain there was in this; hardly news he had no say in what she did with her body. Nights outside time were conducive to forgetfulness.

"What I really would want — " tenderly, caressing him, but he would not permit that, kissing her to silence before she could say she wished her children had been his. Quiescent for a moment, she rolled over with a cry of despair.

"How am I going to endure it without you? When there is some dreary conference to go to, I console myself by thinking *Dolvid will be there*. How can I look down towards the Bronze Residence, knowing I shan't see you riding up the Avenue?"

"When you do see me," lamely, "we shall have work to do." Nothing he had ever done could make him responsible for this inconsolability, and he was appalled to feel pride as well as sympathy.

Abruptly, she asked how long it would be before all his books were copied, and was pleased at the answer, months at the least. If she needed to communicate privately with Dolvid, a batch of books would include one he had not ordered copied, and there would be a letter from her, fastened inside the back cover. She would not, she promised, take the risk for sake of sending endearments, but only for matters of policy, where she believed the *rabhsai* was being poorly advised, or some important fact withheld from Dolvid.

"You, too, might want me to look into a question, or follow some course I am too stupid to see — you must find a way to reach me privately."

"I shall," he agreed, if distractedly, and with a low laugh she captured his wandering hand.

"Will Kamin-Tolagh return?"

"I think he will," sadly. "I see a force driving Rodlakh and Kamin-Tolagh to a test."

"Then we should make war on him now?"

"No — " thinking, what curious lovers' talk this is. "Last year, the autumn before last, we might have had a quick triumph. Now, we must keep watch."

"He is said to be getting stronger."

"I don't doubt that; he has been breeding mounts that are half-*pefral*, and his tribal levies must be improving. But if it comes to war, it will be the defender who has the advantage, and the attacker, him or us, who has to supply his armies over great, dry distances. If we went to the Farther West, we would need as many troops to protect our supplies as to fight the main war, but the same would be true for Kamin-Tolagh, invading the realm, unless — "

A thought he did not want to finish, but she picked it up: "Unless he can count on help from within the realm."

"But he can't, so long as we do not follow policies to make him a present of it. The Old Blood, those who mourned Ban-Sila, but would have acclaimed the coming of their absurd True *Rabhsai*, the ones who allied themselves with Kargul when we came to take the Residence for Rodlakh — even those have found life without Preference is far from intolerable; with general prosperity and peace, there is not much clamor for Kamin-Tolagh to come and lead them from bondage. I can think of only two ways to make allies for him, and they have both been floating in the air; what they see as an attack on their religion, or what they call Preference turned inside-out, excluding them from office because of their race.

"With all the friends he could recruit," he supplemented, "Kamin-Tolagh can't win. But it would make a much costlier struggle, and it is hard to see how it could ever entirely end."

She was watching him from a childlike position, chin tucked to her shoulder. "Have you said all this to Rodlakh?"

"It is all written in a document on policy, which I may or may not give him."

"Do. He is going to remember his reliance on you, when you are — *away*." The last word had to be guessed, lost in a sudden sob.

They said nothing for a time, and Dolvid knew he had to go soon.

Âna conjectured, "If only we could tell the tribes that obey Kamin-Tolagh they would be better off under *Rabhsai*'s Law, as their cousins in the Lunu Tezh', or the Colony. With the Heartlanders above them, they will never be better than slaves."

"If you could tell them, they would not believe it. They might not understand what had been said. Words that can only confuse are sometimes better left unsaid."

"No," she said.

In muted light of a single *ôdu*-globe on the farthest wall, a long silence of steady gazes was filled for Dolvid with flickering recollections of other times, and a surge of sentiment. As he had expected never to, decided not to, he began to tell Âna exactly how long he had loved her, the slightly shorter time he had known it.

"There was a time," she confessed, "when I nearly hated you, for not saying so, when it would have changed everything. Now, you wind all through my life, and wrap around my life, and all I feel is gratitude. We have to hold this, keep it, what we are here. Our feelings."

"We shall," knowing it could not be so.

The dull, squelching grass of the Residence grounds still showed dwindling patches of snow; the afternoon cool but bright. "I remember you dislike ceremony," Rodlakh said, "but Rhunilat tells me all the *bôdh'loikil* have asked to ride down to

Owan Sai tomorrow. Two squadrons of Household will come to your house in the morning for escort."

"Two *squadrons*?" a grimace. "I did not anticipate such determination to make sure we really leave."

The answering laugh was cursory. "Orbanak has asked to be one of the officers." The *rabhsai*'s brother was nearly eighteen, and Rodlakh was very proud of his keenness with lance and sword.

"I am flattered, *Rabhsai*. He would want to say farewell to his friend, too." Being Household, it must have been difficult for Orbanak to keep up the friendship with Shudarr, Shumat's son, since he had become a file-leader in the General Cavalry, attached to the Kred Bakali contingent. After tomorrow, they would have the width of Arnan between them; Dolvid had offered on impulse, and Shumat readily concurred, that the lad might profit from service in the West. Privately, Dolvid, who liked Shudarr, had also wanted to get the youth away from his father's over-critical eye; in endorsing the transfer Shumat had added his hope the Army of the West would achieve what nothing else had, make a man of Shudarr. To Dolvid's mind, at seventeen, something other than sober maturity was to be expected, but if he had said so, Shumat would have told him again about all the backbreaking, demeaning, earnestly responsible tasks he had undertaken before he was twelve, forgetting Dolvid had been with him a decade after on the Narn Campaign, where distinguished service had not been incompatible with interludes of boisterous horseplay. Besides, Dolvid silently demanded, wasn't that why we labored? in hopes our sons would have lives less drudging than ours? But Shudarr was the uncharacteristic myopia of a supremely gifted soldier and otherwise generous man, and it could only be hoped distance would improve the father's vision.

Seeing he was expected to make a general comment on his sendoff, Dolvid said he was honored beyond his merits, although he would rather have made a quiet and unescorted way to the waiting vessel. Rodlakh halted their walk, and regarded him with thoughtful intensity. "There has been a loss of frankness between us, I cannot say why. But you must realize you are going to Kamsilat because there is no one I can trust one-half as much. Strength is needed there — and a great deal of hard work, I am afraid."

He'd had a long private session with his grandmother, earlier in the week, and learned for the first time Saidhan had been able to do very little in the final year-and-a-half of his life, inaction concealed by a conspiracy between the old man's pride and Doleni's loyalty. A number of official posts vacated by death or retirement were unfilled, and there was a mountain of back cases awaiting judgments.

"You are needed more there, but I shall miss you at my side."

"As you have said, the *bôdh'loikil* are very able. And the only *Bôdhrayu* you need is always beside you."

A nod. "Âna is going to miss you, too."

This, notwithstanding tomorrow's rituals, was their personal farewell, and Dolvid was uncomfortably caught between sentiment and sourness. He was sure to be back at Kadon in a few weeks; he was parting, rather, from habit, from five years of almost daily attendance. On this Rodlakh, who, having shouted him to silence a short while ago, wondered there had been a loss of candor; who sent him to the West because he could be trusted, but did not omit a fretful warning against dealings with Kamin-Tolagh. Who had not yet admitted he had been wrong in trying to impose his views on the Patriarch, yet let stand without comment Dolvid's ingenious and completely misleading reinterpretation of the incident. Did all friends become in time beloved exasperations?

30.

Where, as bleakly described by Iruvakh, training armies of *jinzal* had once clashed in mock battle that left many dead, or wounded beyond any use except meat for others, the frisk of newborn half-*pefrai* foals was for Kamin-Tolagh a sign of hope. He had purchased saddle-horses from the Hrin, and wrung from the last-defeated tribal coalition west of Flamûrai a tribute of small, hardy beasts, but armies needed mounts such as these colts would be, strong, big-boned, trainable, fierce in battle, while fillies, remated with the stolen stud, would produce offspring so much nearer full-blooded *pefral*. Like every horsebreeder Kamin-Tolagh had met, Neliukh, half-brother to the lamented Nizhadh, relieved a general lugubriousness with flashes of grim ribaldry, but even he was grudgingly optimistic about progress here, so long as feed and water could be found.

Water! News that came of late-winter floods in the Paowan was galling, when once again throughout the West spring rains were reluctant to arrive, scant when they came.

"According to Iruvakh," Lavsila said, "the eastern tribes, the Laughing Owl and those, proclaim there are to be eleven dry years."

"Eleven?" Without war, the Empire could scarcely hope to survive two.

"Meaning merely *many*, above what can readily be counted." A sound rather than adroit horseman where going was rough, he lifted first one hand, then the other, to convey the tribe's limit of ordinary enumeration.

They were riding with a strong company of Tau-Suaka's men to Larghamit, where several Hrin vessels were in port.

Conquests and submissions west of Flamûrai had advanced the claimed frontier of Empire to Gronu Kizh'klaëdhiyu, so the Hrin could no longer evade a landing tax by beaching their craft a little beyond the old port. Many that came brought what they had to sell to the Abu, and surrounds of the store run by Dvasslo became a little market, where goods were bought as well as sold, but others with rarer or more costly things to trade, and especially when a number of craft arrived together, set up shop on the Larghamit foreshore, and when word came to the Abu, the Heartlanders and soldiers' families, hungry for amusement, would make an excursion of it, particularly when the visitors included one of the better-known dealers in jewelry, like Huolafidn, or those celebrated for fine fabrics, glazed pottery, some of the choicer fruits. Yesterday, hearing Huolafidn was back, a dozen or so of the most fashionable had made the ride, among them Khalú and Kamin-Tarú, with whom, apparently, envy on one side, contempt on the other, was no barrier to behaving as friends.

With summer yet to come, the journey to Larghamit could be made as a continuous ride, without need to shelter from midday heat, but that also meant enduring uninterrupted recital of all Lavsila had learnt about religious beliefs of the Hrin as they affected the goldsmith's craft — or it would be truer to say, of Hrin priestcraft as it extended to metalworking. "With them, stoking the fire is religion. If they fail with a piece of craft, it is because devotions were not properly made, and the forge must be repurified.   Such alloys as they permit are in fixed proportions, each with its sacred meaning; there are those that can be blended only at full moon or dark of moon, and to depart from holy proportions is blasphemy."

"You must write a treatise for the *Mankh'* library." He would have been satisfied with an assurance Lavsila had learned enough for their purposes, without enduring a recapitulation.

"Hear me out, Lord. As you may know, with even the costliest jewelry, gold is often admixed somewhat with other metals, to make it harder, or more brilliant, or easier to work.

Huolafidn is, by common consent, greatest living goldsmith, as he is also a leading priest."

"His prices reflect his piety," sardonically; for his sister Kamin-Tolagh he had purchased a brooch of Huolafidn's, depicting with breathtaking immediacy a great panther or leopard caught in graceful mid-leap, stupefyingly expensive. As in Kamin-Tolagh's childhood, when they were a distant, mysterious people, the craft of the Hrin was celebrated chiefly for its mastery of intricate detail, fine filigree and delicate layering, but their best smiths on occasion produced pieces of austere simplicity, such as the pair of plain gold candlesticks Kamin-Tolagh had also acquired, and which were to play a part in the discrediting of Huolafidn.

"But it is held by some of those Hrin, who do not follow the *dveyust-ranga-hrindan* that Huolafidn's kinsman, his *Hrithust*, forsook the *tveyusto-hrid-minyist* of his upbringing, precisely because his adopted creed permits certain alloys which are an abomination to the other. This Dvasslo told me; he envies Huolafidn's reputation."

"But Dvasslo was in Huolafidn's company; he follows the *dveyust-ranga-hrindan* himself. Are we wise to trust him?"

"Dvasslo," complacently, "is now entirely of Dvasslo's following, and I can tell you where he will come down in any question between belief and profit. He is too deep in now to recover a conscience."

Breasting the last rise as the sun dipped to dazzle them, they came on a scene livelier than Larghamit had known, most likely, in all the centuries since the First Empire receded from these shores. Broad waste of beach and dune between the lapping shallows of the Gulf and remnants of the old wharves was studded with booths and makeshift stalls, and visiting Heartlanders had set up overnight tents, playing at the rough life with the help of a multiude of servants. Nearer the water a couple of newly-slaughtered lambs were being flayed and butchered, and another Hrin trader had unloaded a giant mound of oranges; a dealer in brocades appeared to be doing a brisk business, and Kamin-Tolagh could envision the grim set of Fretasi's mouth over all the gold that was being drained from his domains.

The ruined town was being gradually transformed by presence of a permanent garrison; the east-west axis had been cleared and mended, and standing walls incorporated in construction of new dwellings; the massive old building near the center had been put in better repair. On the low ridge beyond the town, notwithstanding denial of his bid to be made Warden of the Port, Lavsila had laid out the house he wished to build, after making a number of test digs to find water; two wells had succeeded, and he was constructing a windvane pump to increase the flow.

With a gesture he indicated the conical hill, Kafai Zhaëli. "According to Iruvakh, Lord," voice carefully withdrawn from any personal opinion, "*G'Asalladh'*, if and when he learns of the shrine to you, will insist on its removal. No Child of Yoëlladhu, he says, can accept the worship due Raëdh."

"Insist?" irritably. "Let *g'Asalladh'* come here in Person, and see to the dismantling, if the Hrin permit it. Iruvakh knows there is no tribute paid here to any Child of Yoëlladhu; the shrine is to Noh-Sra-Lal-Hin and his Siv'loi. No business of mine in any event; the site is not within my domains." With the main *Hrithuod* of the Hrin, he had agreed hill and the path to it would remain extraterritorial, with access guaranteed for all who had holy places there; as they spoke, smoke was rising from some ritual, and the celebrants were from a tribe of the distant north.

"Iruvakh has instructed us on the importance to the Hrin of these places. They have fought wars among themselves over the defiling of shrines."

"So he told us," Lavsila agreed, and was visibly working on ways to make that information useful.

His sister's innocent wish for the Burantal Marionettes was often in his mind during the arrest, denunciation and staged discrediting of Huolafidn.   Detained at quayside by forces powerful enough to overawe his ship's company, he was permitted to bring part of his crew to the Abu, where Kamin-Tolagh presided over a formal hearing in the main hall of the official residence.   At his urging, a number of other Hrin merchants were present, most from the following of his *hrithust*'s chief rival, Nestos, though there were two belonging to Svedion, Iolfrant's ally and fellow-adherent of the *dveyust-ranga-hrindan*. Actual proceedings were conducted by Lavsila, with a dangerous smoothness almost able to convince Kamin-Tolagh he had been sold false gold.

When first charged with having passed off a base-metal candlestick, Huolafidn protested, exhorted and mocked, mainly in his own language, for fully ten minutes, dividing his demands for true witness to his well-known probity and devotion between his countrymen and, as it seemed, a number of observing gods. Kamin-Tolagh, silently gesturing to Lavsila to let this diatribe run its course, could not tell how well, apart from Huolafidn's immediate company, it went down with other Hrin; they were warily watchful, and even an adherent of the *tveyusto-hrid-minyist*, while gratified at discomfiture of a rival, might wonder what this incident meant for all Hrin who dealt with Kargusai.

Crux of the hearing was getting Huolafidn to admit the candlestick was his work, which, in the end, he could scarcely fail to do; the one he was handed was perfectly genuine. Huolafidn spent a long time turning the piece over, weighing it in his hands, doing his best to look for his tiny secret marks without betraying their existence, and at last admitted the candlestick appeared to be his, only there was a small scrape on the base, which had not been there when he offered it for sale. To this, Lavsila readily agreed; a tiny quantity of metal had been taken for assay.

He had intended to offer it to other onlookers for examination, but there was no need, as Huolafidn thrust it into the hands of the nearest, demanding he attest to the craftsmanship, the true *utveyuth* which it evidenced. A nodding of heads in recognition and acknowledgement of its excellence, though a pair of followers of Nestos, one the opinionated Navridn, made in their own language, with gesticulation, what were apparently demurrers to the religious claim.

Last to handle the piece was Dvasslo, and Lavsila now drew attention to where two men carried in a small table, and set out three glazed dishes. He held up a small vial in a distinctive teardrop shape, and again there was a general murmur of recognition; a solvent familiar to all the Hrin. This vial, indeed, had been obtained at Zelu Bablakhi, from Iolfrant's man responsible for approving the gold brought there in trade.

Lavsila now displayed a mint-new four-tolakhi piece, and dropped it into the first dish. Carefully, he poured a few drops from the vial, and, as expected, nothing happened; it might as well have been water. Into the next dish he put a large bronze nail, and this time the liquid seethed and smoked.

He took the candlestick from Dvasslo — to be accurate, took *a* candlestick from Dvasslo; Kamin-Tolagh, doing his best to watch for it, had not seen the substitution, though it must have been made. This time, Lavsila first poured a little of the clear liquid into the third dish. He held up the candlestick, and used a small knife to make a second small scrape across the one already on the base. A tiny flake of metal dropped into the dish. The liquid fumed and boiled.

As a hubbub rose, he confirmed the test by allowing a drop of the solvent to dribble onto the actual candlestick. The result was the same, it smoked, and a dark stain appeared.

As the Hrin crowded closer, Huolafidn showed puzzlement rather than shock: he knew he had been tricked, but could not understand how it had been worked. Lavsila permitted spectators to examine, even to handle the stained candlestick, but when one man of Svedion's following held it too long, took it back, saying it was needed as evidence of Huolafidn's guilt.

It would, in fact, bear all but most minute examination, having been made from the original by Valubran, working mainly at night at the forge, in a process which involved a quantity of beeswax. Through Dvasslo's help, it even had Huolafidn's secret markings in barely-accessible places. The finished weight, less than half the genuine piece, had been unsatisfactory, but Valubran had bored out beneath the socket for the candle, and inserted a core of lead; a very practised hand, with the original available, could have detected an oddity in the balance, but no one would be given opportunity for that comparison. It continued to amuse Lavsila that for Valubran's deceptive alloy one rather rare ingredient had been supplied by Huolafidn himself, zinc, a white metal used by the Hrin for coating chains and other tackle aboard their seagoing vessels, to retard rusting in salt water.

Over protests of Huolafidn, Kamin-Tolagh gave his judgment. The Hrin, he was told, had savage penalties for counterfeiting; anciently, the Owani punishment had been for the smith to have his hands chopped off and burnt at his forge. "We of Kargusai have our own remedies," he continued, turning to where the menacing Hunghi stood, holding his triple-thonged whip. Fear, for the first time, crossed Huolafidn's face, as he reflected, no doubt, how far he was from effective help, how little sympathy he could count on from his own people.

Having displayed threat, he turned to a lordly clemency: while clear there had been a fraud, he was not entirely satisfied Huolafidn had not been duped in some way by one of his company, who might have substituted the counterfeit candlestick for a genuine one. Nevertheless, until there was an acceptable explanation, he was henceforth banning Huolafidn, together with all followers of *Hrithust* Iolfrant, from any dealings with the Empire of Kargusai.

"Where is the genuine candlestick now?" It was evening, and Kamin-Tolagh was alone with Lavsila.

"At the forge. A pity to destroy it, but we cannot be sure Dvasslo will always keep quiet about his part in this. The gold is his reward, after Valubran melts the piece down." The Hrin merchant, publicly renouncing allegiance to Huolafidn, hence to Iolfrant, had been excepted from Kamin-Tolagh's ban.

Lavsila went on to suggest to have had Huolafidn flogged would have made Kamin-Tolagh's anger more plausible, and been a greater provocation to Iolfrant. "Although," he added with a smirk, "In his heart, Iolfrant may enjoy Huolafidn's disgrace; the swift change of heart which allowed him to become *hrithust* has often been unfavorably compared, I am told, to the pedigree, through many generations, of Huolafidn's devotion to the *dveyust-ranga-hrindan*."

Kamin-Tolagh shook his head. "A flogging would only have won him sympathy. As is, Iolfrant cannot accept my decision." The intolerable aspect would be end of the enforced partnership in the trading-station at Zelu Bablakhi, Iolfrant's only known source of gold. At this moment, a dispatch was on its way to the enlarged force at Gronu Kizh'klaëdhiyu, instructing troops to proceed as planned to the estuary, and there expel the Hrin, using minimum force, if possible without bloodshed. To execute these orders, it was good to have Freighanai there. Kambanal would have been still better, but would have been puzzled how the need for reinforcements at Zelu Bablakhi could have ben foreseen, and his continued belief in the justice and rectitude of Kamin-Tolagh's motives was too valuable a commodity to risk; the young officer had been sent on a tour of inspection in the Froghushei, and would hear all about Huolafidn's perfidy when he returned.

Yet with Kamin-Tolagh drilling tribal troops with a new ruthlessness, ignoring injury and even death in his determination to build a force for a war large and difficult beyond any he had so far fought, the *Hrithust* Iolfrant was slow to respond. What was taken for an early counter-provocation was staged entirely by Lavsila; Kamin-Tolagh gave permission for him to arrange an apparent desecration of his shrine at Kafai Zhaëli, and without comment ordered it when Lavsila asked that the Man-mani squadron under Chamya, among best of all tribal formations, be brought to Larghamit and given patrol-duty there. The thought, obviously, was that Man-mani, beyond any others, had a personal stake in a shrine to their Noh-Sra-Lal-Hin with their Siv'loi. Chamya, who passed through the Abu, was overjoyed at the prospect of important duty outside his home valley, routine as it was. Now seventeen, his skills with sword and lance on a level with most young princelings of the Great Families, he was in everything but height and breadth of shoulder a true *péfrapravádai*, an outstanding squadron-leader.

Lavsila, luxuriating in conspiracy, achieved new levels of self-importance, informing Kamin-Tolagh his imperial standing required he be kept a small distance from these necessary deceptions. "A little mud on my hands, Lord," he said, "will not be noticed." Rather than offended, Kamin-Tolagh decided to be amused by the notion of his purity, but in the event discovered he had not outgrown his capacity to be appalled.

Chamya, suspecting nothing from his instructions to keep special watch on the Hill of Shrines, broke discipline to behave like the tribesman he was, riding back from Larghamit through the night and pestering his way into the morning conference, to present him with the severed head of a man interrupted, he said, in the act of setting fire to the Imperial banner at the shrine to Noh-Sra-Lal-Hin and Siv'loi, having already broken votive bowls and trampled their flowers. Accustomed now to thinking of the youth as almost a young Owani, Kamin-Tolagh was shaken by return of the savage, caked to the elbows with black blood, regretting having "fouled his blade" with this refuse, and begging earnestly to be allowed to carry a fresh Siv'loi Banner back to the shrine without delay. Yet that was, after all, only a subsidiary shock; the trophy he had carried through the night was the head of Dvasslo.

"Very good," Lavsila said when they were alone, after overcoming evident surprise. "Now only young Valubran, beside ourselves, knows the story of the candlestick; Dvasslo could have become a nuisance. Already he had made plain he would like to have had a monopoly over dealing in the *dao* spice, and also with re-export of *Atarlum* goods, *raminat*, in particular, when it became available. Renunciation of his native *onhritha* can now be called a ruse; clearly he intended to go on working covertly for Iolfrant, as both a spy and agent."

None of Kamin-Tolagh's men, true, and none he knew of among the other Hrin, doubted desecration had been at Huolafidn's behest, and the Man-mani fighters, left to themselves, would have been willing to ride unsupplied over high desert and storm their way into Iolfrant's domains for an orgy of revenge. It remained baffling that Dvasslo could ever have been persuaded to attempt defiling the shrine.

"Simple greed. I gave him money, Lord, to find a man who would do this; I specified he should be a Hrin, and he was supposed to scrawl insults in their writing on the rock-face there; evidently he was not given the time. I did not, of course, tell Dvasslo the man would almost certainly be interrupted at his task, but I was sure Chamya and his men would kill before any questions could be asked. Dvasslo, as we see, was too much miser to give up any part of his fee. It could hardly have fallen out better."

Curiously, Dvasslo, though never liked, came to be missed; Kamin-Tolagh decreed his business enterprise was forfeit, and later awarded the shop to Navridn, from the following of Nestos, while the enterprising Heartlander, Tavrotosai, found money to invest. Neither had Dvasslo's keen eye for tribal crafts, nor his unabashed willingness to seek profit in many small transactions; the shop remained moderately profitable, but was less useful to the life of the Abu, not where to go for a piece of ribbon or a rivet.

From this time, also, Kamin-Tolagh found he no longer treated Lavsila as a standing joke, not because his respect had increased, except in a narrow sense of perceiving how dangerously far his airy ruthlessness could go beyond mere posturing. Only immediate consequence of the incident was extension of the ban on Iolfrant's following to include those wishing only to visit the Hill of Shrines, and to have Iolfrant advised his ships and cargoes would be seized if they attempted landing anywhere on coasts controlled by the Empire.

Freighanai returned from Zelu Bablakhi to fill out his terse report of the expulsion there, and again reminded Kamin-Tolagh that in absence of any formal learning, he was still no fool. They rode out to oversee battle exercises, and Freighanai remarked half-apologetically that whether or not "this Iolfrant" was looking for a war, to his mind there was something funny about the candlestick affair.

"How's that?"

Freighanai fiddled with his mount's bit. "Most of anything, *Asai*," he said, and began again. "Well, I can't think what put it into Lavsila's head to have that one piece — assayed, is that it? Fraud's fraud, here or in Harbor Way, but it's Hrin who make a religion out of goldsmithing, so the fraud, so to speak, would have been worse for him, H'olafidn, especially when he was doing such a good business here. Either way, there's not much sense to it, *Asai*."

"In my verdict," levelly, "I allowed the possibility Huolafidn himself had been cheated. One of his crew could have stolen the genuine candlestick."

"Very well, *Asai*, but they're all Hrin, aren't they, with the same rules about true gold? Then the shrine business — I never had much use for that Dvasslo, twisty little rat, couldn't give you a straight look, but why of all people would he try to avenge H'olafidn?"

"He was of that following."

"But I've heard him call H'olafidn a miser, and not half the goldsmith he was made out to be."

"Huolafidn must have paid him well. They are a strange people, too, and can forget differences where religion comes into it."

Freighanai shrugged agreement, but remained unsatisfied. Not much later, by way of an oblique warning, he let drop "one we all know" was very thick with young Valubran at the forge, and it was unsure whether Freighanai made an unconscious connection to the mystery of the candlestick, or was merely adding to the catalogue of his misgivings.

"Lavsila, you mean?"

"I mean, it's not my place, is it, *Asai*."

"You do well to remain alert. Lavsila, as it happens, has been working with Valubran to design and produce new insignia and badges of rank for the army. The examples I have been shown are very handsome."

"It will please the soldiers, I don't doubt, *Asai*." Freighanai placed himself above delight in such trinketry, and was visibly making up his mind to be mollified, so long as Kamin-Tolagh was not being tricked by conspiracy into war, the logical conclusion of his suspicions.

Kambanal, coming back from the south filled with confidence in the improved armies, was by contrast as innocently angry over the shrine as Chamya, whose actions he warmly approved, not questioning the coincidence that had moved Manmani to Larghamit just in time to be discoverers, any more than he wondered how the Empire, since winter, could have been stockpiling arrows and lance-shafts in preparation for a war not yet provoked by the Hrin. He was eager to teach Iolfrant respect for the Siv'loi Banner, certain they could count on no less than indifference from the other *hrithuod*, but hoping for applause and assistance.

Through it all, Iruvakh, as if already making lines of demarcation between the Empire's business and his as representative-designate of the Patriarch, maintained a distance. He was back at the Abu when Chamya brought in his gory trophy, and offered only a mild reminder of how seriously the Hrin would regard his banning Iolfrant's people from Kafai Zhaëli. Ahead of the hot weather, at-Sholidu returned across Landegh, his entourage, which as before, included a *ramidu*, again rapturously received by the Owanil. Having pretended lofty confidence, Kamin-Tolagh was obliged to conceal surprise at the Patriarch's acceptance of Iruvakh as deputy, though He made a condition the man would first have to renew his Greater Oaths with a second pilgrimage to the Island.

Lavsila, the authority on conspiracy, was blind to any danger in permitting Iruvakh's sojourn, and Kamin-Tolagh had to point out the opportunities there would be for secret compacts with the Patriarch.

"But there is no real clash, Lord, between your aims and His — differences of emphasis only, and I know we shall find His Enlightenment a more sympathetic friend than He has been able to appear publicly. The climate of Rodlakh's realm must be constantly irksome to any loyal believer." With at-Sholidu had come the story of Dolvid's strange meeting at the Bronze Residence to deny any dispute with the *Mankh'*, not followed by an invitation from Rodlakh that the Patriarch send His envoys freely through the Colony on their way to the West.

Now Lavsila was at home in his land of deviousness, reminding that Dolvid had now gone to Kamsilat, quite comfortable alternating between incompatible views, either that the move was confirmation of a rumored breach between *rabhsai* and *Bôdhrai*, or that Dolvid's true mission was to prepare the Army of the West for an assault on Kargusai. Neither theory made much headway with Kamin-Tolagh; to build up military forces in the Colony, Rodlakh would have sent Shumat;

preposterous to suggest that, losing confidence in Dolvid, he would have sent him where he could be all-but autonomous.

The opportunity for the man Elamirr to increase his influence was, however, worth noting, and for once Lavsila's identification of an implacable enemy to the interests of the Owanil had independent confirmation. "As Dolvid himself is, of course," Lavsila was quick to add. "But the younger man is much less equivocal in expressing his hatred." It should not have surprised Kamin-Tolagh that in Lavsila's world, Elamirr's rise was seen as desirable: "Dolvid is a cunning man, who can pick the pockets of the Heartland without their feeling it, but Elamirr is a bandit who robs on the highway in broad daylight. In guiding Rodlakh, he can only win support for you, Lord, as the last hope of Owan."

Lavsila's, as Kamin-Tolagh remarked to his sister, was a policy which, however unlikely of success, cost nothing for him to dabble in. For the same reason, though with misgivings, he authorized Iruvakh's second pilgrimage.

The little man, invited for breakfast, gave one of his rare smiles. "If I decide to accept the generous offer of *g'Asalladh'*, Lord."

"Why would you decline? What do you imagine as your future, if you did?" Irritatingly beyond comprehension Iruvakh, or anyone else, could undergo torment over oaths he had already sworn to once, and which obviously did not conflict with any belief he held. Great Hrafi, the man could believe anything.

"As with a bride who is asked to take sash, it is easy to accept being bound to one; the harder choice is to be severed from all others."

"You do not recognize amazing good fortune: you renounced a *Mankh'* whose policies you could not serve, and now are beckoned home by a Patriarch with Whom you have no dispute."

"The wide Mercy of Aëlovoi," Kamin-Tarú murmured, piously touching at the base of her right thumb. Iruvakh, teetering at the brink of being *at-Iruvakh* once again, did not take offense at being instructed in devotion.

But it would be worse than useless to warn him against making secret compacts with the Patriarch. "*G'Asalladh'*, if you decide to go," as if indifferent, "must not mistake my posture; I have not signed the Second Treaty, and there will be no division of my sovereignty here. All *atarlal* who come will be subject to my laws, not His."

"They are said to have developed an entirely new strain of wine-grapes on the Island," Iruvakh reflected.

Delivered by one of Svedion's following, Iolfrant's protest against exclusion from the Empire, more strenuously against expulsion from Zelu Bablakhi, was written in a stilted, not quite correct Owanilú, and in putting forward the *hrithust*'s claims, ill-advisedly used the rather rare word, *kególudughai*. Remarkable enough that Iolfrant, or his advisor, had encountered the term, a legal one which nowadays meant *complete exoneration*, but had formerly signified *redress*; impossible for him to know it had weakened from the meaning of its slightly different form in the Old Owanilú, where it meant *retribution*; taken from its relatively mild context, read in that sense to a roomful of Kargul' officers and men, adequate justification for war. From another Hrin merchant, Kamin-Tolagh had heard Iolfrant, so far unsuccessfully, had been trying to call an assembly of all the *hrithuod*, to discuss their common danger, and he was determined to strike before the idea of alliance could make headway, though it meant crossing high desert at the most unsuitable season.

Ending his duty at Larghamit, again passing through the Abu, Chamya begged to be a part of the forthcoming campaign.

Kamin-Tolagh refused him, with the reason that with large forces absent, good men would be needed in their own lands, for defense against anticipated sea-borne raids by the Hrin, or invasions of other enemies, perhaps with Hrin backing.

"My squadron can stay. Lord, I can ride as another lance, nothing greater."

"You are needed by your people."

"My mother can mother the Man-mani. I cannot be honored among my own, if others always go to big battles."

Kamin-Tolagh played high tile. "My sister is to be in your care." Not strictly true; two dozen of Tau-Suaka's best men with the formidable Hunghi would be spared from the campaign to be personal bodyguard for Kamin-Tarú, she was to be be sequestered in Man-mani country, where frequent patrols from Larghai's Notch would visit. Though he had dismissed Lavsila's theory of Dolvid preparing the Army of the West for an attack, and had decided to face the difficulties of the southern desert at a season when the same conditions made a Landegh crossing in force least likely, it remained true the Abu was not really defensible, and the greatest imaginable disaster would be a sudden assault which made a captive of Kamin-Tarú. If such an attack came, Freighanai's confidential instructions were to break out with as many troops as he could hold together, and strike southward into tribal country, where Kamin-Tolagh would make junction with him on hearing the news. His face darkened at the thought of leaving behind Avedhoi and their daughters with most of the Heartlanders (who would no doubt discover they had come here against their will, and their loyalty to Rodlakh had never wavered), but he knew Shumat would not permit any mistreatment of captives, and recognized a successful retreat could begin a new war, enormously difficult for invaders to win.

Kamin-Tarú, though she would miss her brother, and had implored him not to take needless risks in battle, was not displeased at the prospect of summer in the Man-mani country. She would not be alone; Antiyu would be with her, and Pivrekhan, and so would the dour treasurer, Fretasi, with, less publicly, most of the Empire's gold, again disguised as supplies for the Visitors' Hut, where the Karguli party would be installed. Fretasi's cousin, the stonemason Marsilakh, with his laborers, would be continuing work on the great house at the crest of the hill, and in that connection Lavsila would at least pay a visit, to discuss progress on the most ambitious of his projects, the long stone aqueduct that would ensure a supply of water for the house. She was glad simply to be free for a time from the pretensions of Heartlanders, who, seen daily, had begun to exasperate her.

She and her companions, then, rode out with the forces Kamin-Tolagh had collected at the Abu, strangest army he had yet led. Kambanal was field commander, and there were other officers of Kargul, Antighal, Namakhat, Nuvakh, Dubovai, as well as ordinary troopers who now found themselves as squadron and half-squadron officers. But there was only a bare *kímuko*, a double-squadron of true *péfrapravádal*, to be held in reserve for a decisive blow late in a hard-fought battle. By far the bulk of both bows and lances were men of the tribes, some from west of Flamûrai, and additional such squadrons would be added as they moved south through tribal country, Laughing Owl, Jai, Man-mani, a handful of Hwenala and Chon'la, strong contingents from the Gudi-la and Ntara-Golal.

With the troops went a host of horses, spare mounts and pack-animals for the expedition, but also the virile *pefral* stallions and their brood-mares, together with most of their newer offspring; Neliukh's entire breeding enterprise would also be safer for now in the Man-mani valley, and much of the Abu's stock of feed went with them. Though a strong military force remained under Freighanai, uncertainty showed in the faces of Heartlanders who came out to witness the great riding.

He pushed the pace; word of his departure would come swiftly to Iolfrant by way of Hrin traders. Nevertheless, he endured a three-day delay in the country of the Ntara-Golal, seeing to it every available skin and bottle was filled with water from sluggish streams and grudging wells; as before, they would zigzag across the desert from one waterhole to the next, but he had no assurance there would be enough water at this season for his eighteen hundred men and their animals. His care was requited; when, after passing through the scrublands and starting out on the desert crossing, they approached the first waterhole, forward scouts rode back to report an unwounded but recently-dead leopard, as well as bodies of smaller animals and birds, littered on the mud by the water: obviously the Hrin, known masters of poisoning, had made the wells unusable. Kambanal maintained the water must have been poisoned not once but a number of times; some of the animal corpses were far along in decay, and the pool was constantly fed from below, so even the most powerful poison would soon dissipate. This conjecture Kamin-Tolagh found encouraging, an indication the Hrin had been taking precautions against invasion for some time, not that they'd had advance word of his expedition.

A more direct way across the desert, ignoring waterholes, might have been found, but remembering from his first crossing the tales of great impassable pits of soft, shifting sand, unscalable cliffs, and treacherous foul marshlands, he held their march to the former meandering route, always thinking ahead to narrow, defensible ways between the mountains, and beyond, the converging valley with the water-gap where Yaënsilat's timely charge had saved him from defeat three years ago; his tribal troops were better-trained and more experienced now, but he also expected a stronger and more resolute enemy. Dubovai, with his rudimentary maps, conjectured they might find a way through the borderland mountains farther south and east, to strike what at a distance had seemed less harsh seaward regions of Svedion's domain, bypassing the long valley altogether, and crossing into Iolfrant's lands across a broad and open country, hard to defend.
In sight of hard peaks, unreal in their abrupt thrust from the desert flats, Tau-Suaka's scouts reported sighting mounted observers briefly visible on a ridge parallel with their line of march, but quickly drifting away from any approach. Early next day, after a watchful night, the army began the ascent, a long, slow-moving skein of men and horses climbing in narrow ways,

and before long there were bowmen to dispute their passage. A few only, and they were curiously irresolute, considering they had the higher ground, and were shooting from cover, otherwise inaccessible positions reached by paths invaders could not know. They wounded a couple of men and a horse, but most arrows went astray, and none of the enemy stayed to duel with the mounted archers of Tau-Suaka, who boasted they made hits, though no one clambered the cliffs to confirm the kills. Kambanal, alert for earnest resistance, wondered, "If not here, Lord, where will they fight?" He was one of few permitted to use the discarded *Asai* in address, and unique in preferring the newer, more abject title. Having missed the first expedition, he was constantly pressing forward, avid for a first sight of Hrin lands.

"These would be Svedion's men, not Iolfrant's."

"Allies should stand together, otherwise they lose any strength the alliance gives."

"But Svedion, I would guess, has not fully made up his mind to stand with Iolfrant; he does not want to see his lands ravaged, for the sake of *dveyust-ranga-hrindan*."

At head of the pass, idea of resistance was again unmatched by any will to fight, a mixed force of bows and the heavy Hrin cavalry falling away before they could be engaged, or so much as accurately counted, and Kamin-Tolagh's forces were permitted to reach undisputed a place where they could resume squadron formation, and deploy on a broader front.

Tau-Suaka indicated points in the rocky and broken country ahead where bands of enemy were lurking. He begged to be allowed to take a hundred of his bows in a wide circle to flush out the watchers, and was disappointed when Kamin-Tolagh told him merely to remain alert for any hostile move. "I thought we came to fight, Lord," sulkily.

"We came to win. The more they grant us without a fight, the better." Past experience of the Hrin led him to expect an attempt at a parley, and it was not long coming. As they descended from hard uplands to the fringes of habitable parts, they swung leftward to skirt a high ridge Dubovai believed would be easterly wall of the valley with the hamlet they had destroyed in the first invasion. Ahead, an ample but rough track wound downward through clumps of woods, and where it intersected a finished road that came up from the southwest and bent towards the sea, a substantial settlement stood, mainly small, steep-roofed houses gathered into a shabby village. On the near side, a dense mass of soldiery was assembled, numbers impossible to estimate, since rearward tail of the formation was lost to sight among trees and houses. Most were foot, of the same ill-armed and ragged sort as encountered in the battle won by Yaënsilat, with a vanguard of heavy cavalry, not as gorgeous as Iolfrant's, but with the same brocade saddlecloths, leather-fronted tunics and high-crowned helms, armed with the same unwieldy halberds; Tau-Suaka sounded in his throat a low, contemptuous laugh.

Halting forward progress, Kamin-Tolagh let Kambanal arrange a battle-order, lances straddling pathway, with mounted bows at each flank, but before the command was given to resume the march, there was a hoarse flourish of horns from the opposing side, and a small group came forth, two men holding between them a deep-blue fringed banner with a swooping gull depicted, followed by a half-dozen cavalry as guard for a single unarmed man.

"Hyoldaki — " Kambanal recognized the man as the delegation came nearer. "He has been to the Abu, once or twice. His wife is Svedion's sister."

Fairly tall by Hrin standards, but of a slight build, the typically chinless Hyoldaki was most excitable of his people yet encountered, when, with a small guard and the standard-bearer, Kamin-Tolagh rode out to confront him. Gestures were quick and nervous, voice high-pitched and nasal, and he spoke ordinary language of the realm in rapid, breathless phrases, anxious to emphasize his *hrithust* had no dispute with Kargusai or its lord, yet did not ordinarily permit armed companies to traverse his territory.

Prompted only slightly, fortified, no doubt, by genuine belief in the perfidy of Iolfrant, Kambanal did well in reply, agreeing there was no quarrel with Svedion. "Indeed," he said, "Your *hrithust* would do well to join us in chastising this other, who has dishonored principles you are said to share."

"I do not know what *chastising* is, but this, sir, is between your lord and the *Hrithust* Iolfrant," Hyoldaki, swiftly. "My kinsman and *hrithust* does not defend and does not condemn his friend, not knowing with his eyes the *utveyuodn* which make this difference. But these lands are Svedion's lands."

"We make no claim here — " silencing Kambanal, who was ready to debate Iolfrant's guilt. "Nor do we mean any harm to your Svedion. Only, if he tries to impede us, or deny us passage, he will be considered one with Iolfrant, equally subject to our anger. Once fighting begins," with a glance to the restive Tau-Suaka, "I may find it hard to control the fury of my men."

They were remarkable linguists, these Hrin, but menace was the only language that penetrated the oddness of their thought; protesting still his people had no cause for war with Kamin-Tolagh, Hyoldaki was very soon blandishing with gifts, not treasure, but a lavish quantity of food, chiefly fruit and fish, trundled up in their silent-wheeled wagons. This Kamin-Tolagh accepted, but recalling the twisted corpse of the leopard in the mud beside the waterhole, made sure the leaders of his benefactors, Hyoldaki among them, would share in the feast. Evening came, fires were kindled, and astonishingly the Hrin spokesman made reference to additional supplies that would be available, "for your return," he added. Evidently, acceptance of food meant the end of the campaign.

"We want nothing further from Svedion's domains, except free access to your streams and wells as we advance. To make our passage swifter, we should be provided with guides who speak either of our languages — you yourself might be one."

A long, considering pause, as the certainty he did not mean to turn back sank in. "Lord," with a new hesitancy, "Iolfrant is not only our friend, but our neighbor — "

"Soon, you may have a new neighbor, whose gratitude could be valuable."

"If we aid you, we must not be seen to."   Instantly, Hyoldaki began to retreat from this rash admission.   "I am nothing but a messenger. I must get the word of my *hrithust* before any promise is made."

He left riding in one of the wagons, with his mount tethered to the rear. There was a sense the main army of Hrin had quietly withdrawn, confirmed as much as was possible by a careful reconnaissance under a pale half-moon, but watchfires were kept burning, and a strong watch set.

In early morning Hyoldaki returned escorted, and with the air of granting a favor reported Svedion would not resist a peaceful crossing of his lands. "Aye," Kambanal muttered. "But word of our coming is on its way to his friend, if it has not already arrived."

Two younger men were said to have volunteered to ride as guides and translators; one of them, Istaluodn, his nephew, but on his side, not a near relative of the *hrithust*. The youths were all ingratiation, though in their mournful parting from Hyoldaki was detectable the notion they might consider themselves hostages. With two dozen armed Hrin, Hyoldaki simply rode away, past the village taking the seaward road, which Istaluodn confirmed led to Svedion's capital city and main port, Tvaidath.

The march continued southward, descending by shelving stages, sun from a cloudless sky no warmer than was pleasant, while their faces could feel a sensation by now unfamiliar; moisture in the air. They followed generally the course of an unimproved road, which in turn ran near, crossed and recrossed a small, clear stream; uplands were wooded, and there were many nearer stands of trees, alder and willow by the water, familiar beech, linden, sycamore on higher ground, a few old oaks, as well as some unknown kinds; Istaluodn pointed out the large, straight, heavy-limbed *buoth*, with its flat, rounded leaves, saying it was the shipbuilder's tree, used also for big houses; each *hrithust* maintained a "big planting" of *buodat*, and to damage such a tree, or cut it down without permission, was death . There were, too, vast dense tangles of bush and vine, cream-flowered honeysuckle, white and pink-blossomed bramble and hawthorn interwoven with unfamiliar growths, many with scarlet or orange or large purple blooms.

Birds were everywhere, and flashing through dells, some of a silvery blue color with a rippling call; when the army paused for food Kamin-Tolagh watched four or five of these birds climbing the air in a towering spiral till they diminished to specks and vanished. Istaluodn made a superstitious dip of his head, and said this was the *tvenanga*, a name also signifying "news from afar," and "Man's desire for added life." It launched him into a lengthy, complicated explanation about various birds, for none of which he had any name other than his people's, but gestures and drawing in air conveyed the idea of a heron, and a longer-legged bird, perhaps a sort of crane, both significant in Hrin belief. With a slender, bared arm and squeezed hand he vividly portrayed *swan*, and on learning that name, told that among followers of the *Hrithust* Iolfrant especially, swan was holiest of birds; his great river, the Hflen, was often named "swan-path," and Iolfrant called "Swan-Lord."

"What unguessable people they are, Lord," Kambanal said privately, shaking his head. "No one could be with an Owani an hour without knowing how the palm and fingers of the right hand figure in our religious thought; we have been meeting with Hrin for, what? five years now, and this is the first we have heard about birds."

Far from the only reason for thinking them strange; Kamin-Tolagh had been puzzling over wide tracts of good land left wild, when there were more than enough Hrin to cultivate them. Near villages there were multitudes of tiny growing-patches, and short of noon they had passed through wide swathes of both crop and pasture, overlooked from a broad, low hill by a great house Istaluodn said belonged to his uncle, Hyoldaki, yet this was only a somewhat larger island in oceans of the unkempt, the tangled, the unused; Kambanal had remarked that while in

northern Froghushei land not kept tilled and watered reverted to
the barren, here neglect brought excess, this luxuriant riot of
grasses, weeds, vines and shrubs. Yet while the Hrin grew
excellent fruits, and produced some good meat, they also traded
for much of their common food; some of Lavsila's Heartland kin
and cronies had made large sums selling them wheat. With good
farming added to their craft skills and mastery of the sea, the
Hrin, surely, could enjoy general prosperity, but although there
were wealthy men, life for most was spent, clearly, in a poverty
worse than was found anywhere in Rodlakh's realm, except,
perhaps, in least-fertile backwaters.

    "Maybe it suits their religion, Lord —" Dubovai again
displayed his somewhat alarming gift for understanding rule, "to
keep wealth and power in a few hands, while the rest are too
busy scratching for their livelihood to do any thinking for
themselves."

    Tau-Suaka, seldom still for a minute, had other concerns.
Every step of their march, he complained, was being observed
from a distance by horse-soldiers, and though the forward scouts
were vigilant, there was no assurance the Hrin guides were not
leading them all to a place where they could be ambushed by the
force that had withdrawn last night.

    "Or by that force, joined by the army of Iolfrant,"
cheerfully agreeing. "No. From their timidity, it is easy to guess
Svedion's forces will remain as watchers, and only join battle if
his ally can fight us to a standstill. What would you say," he
turned to Kambanal, and put the question exactly like an abstract
problem for an officer in training. "When we fight Iolfrant,
would you detach a part of our force to guard our rear against
Svedion?"

    "Not if it risked losing, or even prolonging the main
battle," the young man promptly decided. "If we can have a swift
victory over Iolfrant, Svedion means nothing; his men will lay
those choppers of theirs at your feet, Lord."

"Exactly."

In mid-afternoon, they had lost the small stream, and their constant descent was interrupted by the rise of rounded, grassy hills. "Past here," Istaluodn, meaning the crest, "the lands of Iolfrant begin."

Ground was open and level enough for the army to spread each side of the track, and to adopt a battle-formation, squadrons on fronts of eight. Tau-Suaka's scouts went on more cautiously than hitherto, bows unslung, arrows to string, but no challenge came; when Tando, Tau-Suaka's kinsman, attained the skyline he waved to indicate no enemy was present.

But they were visible. From the top, the army was looking down into the wide green bowl of Iolfrant's domains; land fell away gently on this side, and two miles ahead in the clear air a larger river, though not yet the great Hflen, curved from the north and west, and made for the eastward sea. Not far this side, a well-made road began, crossing the river on a wide, low-arching bridge of stone, and passage here would be disputed. On the near side a pair of large Hrin formations of cavalry were in the saddle, with more on the bridge, while the dense mass of foot on the other side could be assumed to contain many bows.

"They would be splendid at Pledging time, on the Avenue of Treaties," Kambanal, drily, meaning the caparisoned enemy cavalry. "Will they stand against a charge, *Asai*?" — the change in address occasioned by his return to battle.

Without hesitation Kamin-Tolagh had squadron after squadron streaming down to the road for a hammer-blow attack on the narrowest of fronts, while mounted archers deployed to guard the flanks. Kambanal, after ensuring the plan was understood, a force detailed to guard the supply-train, spurred swiftly to the forefront, standard-bearer struggling to match his pace. Kamin-Tolagh rode ahead of the fourth squadron, and the outcome was virtually decided before he could use his lance. Thundering on the superb road, Kambanal's leading lances were met by a half-hearted, lumbering counter-charge, and swept it away like so much straw, thick Hrin horses rearing and toppling, their riders trying to answer thrusting lances with clumsy mows of their heavy halberds.

Elbowing through, now with his sword out, Kambanal reached the bridge, where for a moment, without effective fighting, by the weight of their numbers pressed in narrow straits, the Hrin cavalry checked his progress. Now Kamin-Tolagh was among the wreck of the Hrin vanguard, killing, unhorsing, scattering them, those that fled from the road making easy game for Hill Froghul bowmen. Others of Tau-Suaka's men had reached the riverbank, their arrows thinning the ranks opposed to Kambanal. He, with a surge from the rear as fresh squadrons gained the bridge, burst out on the far bank, and was upon the ill-protected infantry. There were losses to arrows shot from far back, but the lead squadron, mainly Gudi-la, was too swiftly in the thick of the enemy, and the rout too sudden for the archers, who, with the fightless men at their front, could soon think of nothing but escaping the fury of the charge.

No one could ever be prepared for how suddenly expectation of hard battling could melt away, a formidable enemy transform into a contemptible, cowed and fleeing mob. Recognizing this would not be the final fight, Kamin-Tolagh wanted word of complete destruction here to help demoralize Iolfrant's main army, so long as it could be accomplished without adding to his present light losses, and was gratified to see Kambanal, on the other side of the bridge, understood the requirements, sending cavalry to cross and recross the field, killing retreating enemy, but quickly preventing any squadron from pursuing too far, so his forces would not become scattered, vulnerable to any unexpected rally or arrival of enemy reinforcements.

On both sides of the bridge, attempts at surrender, throwing down of weapons, were ignored, and Tau-Suaka's men, when they ran short of arrows, were quick to jump from the saddle to use their stabbing blades. Those Hrin on the field who lived after most of an hour of slaughter did so by convincingly feigning death, or because the victors were arm-weary and tiring of killing — and that number was reduced when, at the end, with no sign of new enemy, or of Svedion's army falling on the rear, he released fresh squadrons till now held in reserve, men chafing to be allowed their share in the sport.

"A thousand or so," Kambanal replied, when asked for an estimate of enemy dead. The judicious Dubovai thought not so many, but the officer, Antighal, who had led the reserve squadrons, was sure as many as fifteen hundred. It hardly mattered; any disagreement would concern numbers of negligible foot slain, but the indisputable prize was the loss to Iolfrant of about one hundred and seventy of his cavalry, the only Hrin who had shown any inclination to fight. Losses to Kamin-Tolagh were less than two dozen dead, a larger number with wounds, many of them slight; Kambanal had a grazed cheek and a small cut on his wrist, and was restrainedly exultant at success. Kamin-Tolagh, with fierce derision, wondered if their guides could tell him the place in Hrin belief of the crows who, appearing magically, were already circling and hopping over the battlefield, keeping a respectful distance from their betters, a half dozen glossy ravens with first choice at the unexpected feast.

Left to his own impulses, when those who had ventured to the next rise excitedly reported clear sight of the distant Hflen, gold-roofed buildings under the latening sun, with an excellent road to follow, Kambanal would have ridden headlong for the city, a course he came near as he dared to urging on Kamin-Tolagh. The enemy, he said, should be given no chance to recover from their defeat here, and his men were hot with victory.

"And fatigue. I would drive them on if it were a question of taking Hyolenstr by surprise, but as we see, Iolfrant is aware we are coming; it is ground he knows and we do not. A twilight battle in front of a walled city, where cavalry can be hidden under every clump of trees, and bowmen in every shadow? I want a camping-place a couple of hours nearer our goal.

Tomorrow, by good light and with rested fighters, we shall finish this."

"So we shall, *Asai* — Lord." Far from resenting rebuke, Kambanal's eyes were shining with renewed admiration.

The highway, match and better for the Great Stone Road west of Kadon Dinul, surface kept in constant repair, ran straight and true, at times in a shallow cutting, at others raised on a kind of causeway, always with a downhill tendency. No further enemy was met, and with the help of Istaluodn, who said he had travelled this way to Hyolenstr many times, the place Kamin-Tolagh wanted was found well before dark, a domed hill less than a mile from the road, with room enough on its flanks for the entire army to make camp, maintaining a defensible perimeter. From the top, under its crowning flourish of splendid cedars, they could survey the vale of the Hflen and glinting roofs of the city not five miles distant. Tau-Suaka, who was immune to fatigue, returned from a cautious reconnaissance, to give some idea how the land lay. The city, he said, could not be encircled, since its back was to the broad river. Once past areas of cultivation, ground on all other sides was open and perfectly level, without trees except for those lining the several good roads converging there. The walled city, with some large and impressive buildings, was in area quite small, but a clutter of what Tau-Suaka called village huts spread out from the walls, especially along the line of the main road. Istaluodn agreed, most people of Hyolenstr lived outside the walled city, which housed only notables with their servants and guards, besides a few shops and "big holy places," presumably something like the Paowanu *Mankh'*.

Also spreading to either side of the central road was a very large encampment of soldiery, their cooking fires making a great blue smoke, and busy riding back and forth by detachments of cavalry. The enemy also had scouts out, and the Hill Froghul had exchanged arrows at a distance with one patrol.

"They found out, Lord, how much farther we can shoot," with a wolfish grin.

By dusk, the two young Hrin, their guides, managed to slip away, leaving their mounts behind. They had served their purpose, and Kamin-Tolagh did not regret their departure, except as it heightened conviction the armed forces of their *hrithust* were not far away. Despite his easy victory at what Dubovai had already labelled Battle Bridge, the ineffectuality of Hrin infantry, Svedion's men might still imagine Iolfrant had the forces to stop him tomorrow, and would certainly be at hand to exploit such a reverse.

"Going to be a long night," Kambanal remarked, standing near a watchfire, flickering shadows making his face abruptly older and graver.

"Too short for Iolfrant's rabble," lightly.

On the eve of his first big fight, now over six years ago, he had been surprised by a stealthy fear, not of death or wounding, but of a betrayal by his fear. That battle, against a horde of *jinzal*, enough to frighten any man, had been won, and so had a victory over his unfamiliar self-doubtings: he was not a coward, and for a great enough object could ride forward against any terror; once blades clashed he was seized by a ferocious joy, a shouted song in praise of his own prowess.

This night was otherwise; confident in himself, his only doubts concerned his soldiery, and a cold anxiety grew in his stomach as stars began to appear overhead. Injury or death had no terror, but he did fear failure, the inadequacy of the army he had trained, mortal wounding of the empire he had made. Having hounded his enemy to defense of his capital, he found the one risking everything on draw of a single tile was not Iolfrant, but Kamin-Tolagh.

He had found private comedy in the righteous indignation of Kambanal, against a foreign lord whose kinsman was in fact no counterfeiter, and whose orders had not caused desecration of the shrine to Noh-Sra-Lal-Hin. Yet if Iolfrant had not done those things, there were plenty of reasons, equally good, for despising him, for destroying him, surely likeliest consequence of tomorrow's work. A thought on which Kamin-Tolagh could sleep.

"Lord, there is a man, a Hrin — "

He rolled and stood, dislodging a large, curved flake of cedar-bark from his blanket. "What man?" hearing an oddity in Kambanal's voice, as if he was impressed by this visitor.

"Hridveyuth, Lord. That is not his name, he says, but what he is called by."

It meant something. Kamin-Tolagh tipped ice-cold water from a flask into his hand, and rinsed his eyes. Eastward a riot of pale colors was spreading into the sky, pink, lemon, lilac, with a deeper orange beneath. He remembered; *Hridveyuth*, not a name but a title traditional with the Hrin, meaning Truth-Speaker, as well as other things. The man was a religious nuisance, and was going to make some pathetically impractical proposal for settling his quarrel with Iolfrant by negotiation.

Still, if Iolfrant's power was to be broken, something would have to be put in its place, and a grip on religion was a good start. "What language does he use?"

"Ours, Lord. Well, both, actually, three it would be, with his own; he greeted me in good Owanilú, but went on in ordinary language." He shook his head.

"What is the puzzle, then?"

"Lord, his speech is as plain as anyone's, but he is harder to follow than any *atarlai* I ever heard. An ordinary man, he is."

He was, almost ostentatiously so, when brought, dressed plain in cloak, shirt, breeches, boots, the middle range of the Hrin, men of the ship's companies, neither ornate as in the immediate circle of the *hrithust*, nor hopelessly shabby, like those from whom companies of infantry were drawn. A younger man than expected, taller than most of his people though well below Kambanal in height, he had a scrub of beard, finely-shaped but not pampered hands, a strong neck. His forehead, less protruding than was typically Hrin, was broad and well made. "You will fight today, Lord Kamin-Tolagh," he said, without any preliminary.

"I shall conquer today."

The man considered, and when he looked up it drew attention to the least ordinary of his features, amber-brown eyes of luminous depth, lit with intelligence. "No one makes war with defeat as his goal."

"Men may fight knowing they will lose, because they have no other choice."

"Making men share your desires — " Hridveyuth made a slight gesture to indicate the waking camp, "is a power not easily gained, harder to be free of. I keep you from your food. War, they say, is not fought on empty bellies."

His command of a language not his was indeed excellent, with only slightest accent of the south, as if he had learned from someone who in turn had learned at Thenimala. His lack of deference, as with a seer, a garrulous old woman, a drunk, was licensed by tradition — probably because there might be a greater loss of dignity in punishing such creatures than in tolerating their discourtesy.

"You have not walked into an enemy camp at dawn to remind me to have breakfast."

"An enemy camp, Lord? Neither Iolfrant nor any other *hrithust* claims me; I am, as we say it, *hrindaveyuth*, him who speaks to all."

"Yet it would not displease you if Iolfrant was overthrown, and with him the doctrine of the *dveyust-ranga-hrindan*?"

A long, probing look. "*Dveyust-ranga-hrindan*," conversationally, "*tveyusto-hrid-minyist* — these, with me as with you, are playthings for empty minds. I know nothing about death of gods, and cannot think gods care whether we say they are dead or only sleeping. The Hrin are a people whose ruling pack has been corrupted by complacency and bemused by foolish controversy, but not one in a thousand has any interest in the children's stories which divide us."

This was a new experience, a religious leader who assailed religion; it might be there was an offer lurking. "As you say, we are in agreement here. Have you a proposal?"

"A proposal?"

"You wish to bring new thought to the Hrin, and my swords could help you. We are natural allies." He tried not to be over-eager, but would happily assist or help impose ideas that helped him control the Hrin.

"As I perceive it, Lord, we must be rivals. My desire is to banish fear, not to make present fears smaller by setting a greater fear over them."

These extraordinary words Kamin-Tolagh tried to hear again through the ears of Kambanal, who had remained nearby, with no notion of entering debate. This *Hridveyuth*, if nothing else, had the gift of making it seem churlish to take offence, and his influence, with common people or the *hrithuod* other than Iolfrant, was not yet assessed.

"I think we shall be allies," warmly. "When Iolfrant is overthrown, you must come to Hyolenstr, and teach me about your beliefs."

An answering smile. "Your land's *Mankh'* can teach you as much or more; there are men there, I guess, if only a few, who can make what most have learnt no weightier than the *Song of Tales*."

So. He was not above a little showing-off. "Not everyone has a mind made for pure doctrine; men, as well as women and children, still need trinkets. Nor is the *Song of Tales* to be wholly despised."

For the first time, the man bowed, as if admitting Kamin-Tolagh to his circle of respect. "When we do meet again, Lord, I would wish to learn from you. Much about Him you call Zhôl, in particular, though I hear He has had other names."

"In ancient times, He was Zhaëli," Kamin-Tolagh concurred, making His sign.

"And before that, Yalef, I have been told."

"Jalef," Kambanal corrected, with an apologetic gesture to Kamin-Tolagh. "But that was the name of a Vrobani god."

"Zhôl," Kamin-Tolagh said, "is and always was Son of Raëdhi, the Sender."

"A son can be heart's mirror, *tvenanga*, flight to outfly the sun. But mirrors can cheat those who love them too much."

This, with no apparent bearing on their discussion, though the tone still informal, was just the sort of riddling windbaggery the man had professed to despise, spoken directly to Kamin-Tolagh, ending with what sounded like a translated proverb. Perhaps, for all his astonishing knowledge of the realm's ways, his arresting eyes, he was only a more plausible kind of trickster, passing off sententiousness as a mysterious wisdom. Time, as the man had said, for some breakfast; in the lowlands, Hrin cavalry was already on the move, as yet no threat.

Given abrupt leave, the man nodded and strode away, not seeking a tethered mount; evidently he had indeed come on foot.

"Strange," Kambanal watched him go. "From a reputed holy man, Lord, I would have expected a plea for sparing Hrin lives — or a threat their gods would be angry if we did not go away."

Kamin-Tolagh nodded, but could not be sure the *Hridveyuth*, notwithstanding one lapse into portentous utterance, was not simply too practical to argue against the inevitable. Or else he saw the killing of Hrin as an aid to his implied aim of breaking the hold of goldsmith-priests.

"I do not like his lack of respect — " Kambanal discovered almost simultaneously with Kamin-Tolagh that the spell of the man's manner did not outlive his actual presence, and what had been amusing at the time could, if dwelt on, begin to rankle.

"He may prove useful to us," mildly. "As we did with the Man-mani, and again with the gourd-people of Kufshei, we can make superstition our ally here."

Where, half a mile short of the city, the main central road from the north was met by another from half-west, the enemy had assembled and was still assembling a great mass of infantry, perhaps eight thousand, clumped rather than ordered in groups of about one hundred, armed largely with spears and pikes, though bows could also be discerned, and some had only cudgels.

"Iolfrant wants to use them as a wall — " scanning the field, trying to see where the *hrithust* was hiding his main cavalry; only slight formations of horse were so far visible.

"They will never stand, Lord. We can break them with a dozen squadrons."

Maybe, but it would take time for panic to spread through so large and dense an army; lances would cleave lanes but then check, among men with no room to turn and run. Nothing was so vulnerable to counter-attack as cavalry already engaged, at once out of formation and hardly moving.

Iolfrant could not be hiding his horse in the walled city; its high stone gateway was too narrow to permit quick deployment. Leftward, where skirting the city huddles of hutments stretched all the way to riverbank, was where cavalry must be concealed. Calling Tau-Suaka to him and assembling the Kargul' officers, Kamin-Tolagh outlined a rough battle-plan, beginning with a mock-apology for breaking their habit of simply charging any number of Hrin fighters head-on, and watching them bolt.

Amid laughter, one of the Karguli file-leaders promoted to lead a Gudi-la squadron said, "I have hunted rabbits with more fight to them, Lord."

Another man called out, "But you have to pity the poor fish-heads. We trained on *jinzal*."

Good, Kamin-Tolagh thought, they are like boys; they think they are invulnerable. The battle would begin, he told them, since the Hrin showed no sign of taking the initiative, with feint of a frontal attack on the mass of infantry, using mainly mounted bows, to cow the opposing archers, and perhaps to push them back a short way. Tau-Suaka's men would then disengage, ready to wheel left and join what he expected would be the serious fight, with emergence of the main Hrin cavalry. Against this, as against *jinzal* in that war, not a massed attack, but squadron after squadron of lances would come in a series of blows, staying well left, clear of enemy bows, and choosing their points of impact. "When the cavalry is routed, foot won't matter. We had better keep some of them alive, to work the fields for us when we take possession here."

The gathering was dispersing when word came from watchers on the north side of the hill that formations of what must be cavalry were distantly visible, progressing slowly on one of the lesser roads, undoubtedly Svedion's full army.

"Unless they hurry, they will miss the feast," with a laugh. Sword, he tested, was free in its sheath, and his *pefrai* had been brought. "For a gold piece," he called to Kambanal, also mounting, "*Hrithust* Svedion will offer me his submission, in Iolfrant's house, before sunset."

"His *friendship*, he'll call it," grinning. "No wager, Lord."

The sole concession made to the approaching ally of Iolfrant was to strengthen the force left to guard baggage and animals, giving its command to Dubovai, only officer in the whole Empire who could show no emotion, either way, about being left out of a big fight. He was making observations to add detail to his map of Hyolenstr and its surrounds, and having used a sea-navigator's device like a small sundial with a moving pointer, informed Kamin-Tolagh unnecessarily the city must be just about exactly as far south as Zelu Bablakhi, on the other side of Flamûrai.

Thought or brooding could do no more; nothing left but to fight. The sun was up like blare of a thousand trumpets, but there was a curious serenity in the scene, light stone buildings with their shining roofs, open plain with puffy trees throwing elongated shadows, even the opposing army, scarcely stirring now. *Waiting to be beaten*, he thought, and it applied to this people in general; they lacked some essential spirit to keep what they had.

Not that they lacked courage; fighting here in front of their sacred city they showed a new determination, but that, in the absence of skill, concerted discipline, or intelligent tactics, only made battle bloodier. From the moment the feigned attack against infantry wheeled to help assail the mounted enemy emerging from their concealment among outbuildings of the city, best the Hrin could do was delay defeat. The high-helmed, brocaded heavy cavalry tried to come in unwieldy ranks of twenty, two deep, against lancers in tight squadron formation; much better troops could not have held together, and individually their armament made them ineffectual. A single group of what must be a newer light cavalry, modelled on Kamin-Tolagh's or those Iolfrant had observed in Rodlakh's realm, carried a more practical long lance, but either with this weapon or in formation riding, they were inadequately drilled, and their swords for close-quarter work were of inferior make; Kamin-Tolagh snapped three in moments with his Dakbân blade.

The bulk of the infantry, as before, had little effect, but breaking through beaten cavalry and spurring for the city, Kamin-Tolagh saw little knots of resistance, clusters of men on foot carrying small, round shields and better blades, who stood to fight off cavalry and were hard to scatter or kill. They were, as could be told, in part from their clothes, ships' companies, men who knew and had learned to trust each other, and with a personal stake in the battle. One such, twenty to two dozen men with steel-tipped lances, broke an entire squadron of Gudi-la, and their slow, step-by-step retreat allowed many others to gain refuge within the city, before Tau-Suaka's bows began to fell them.

The walls to the city were decorative rather than defensive, not above the height of a tall man, and without slits for bowmen, or crenellation, while the gate which faced roughly east, a lacework of gilded metal, gave way at the second charge. Within, broad, shallow steps mounted low stone platforms on which principal structures rested, on either side of a flagged avenue broad enough for forty men to ride abreast, and with double rows of large trees. Trees, too, were set about the great stone edifices, and many free-standing pillars and shaped blocks of carved stone, but none seemed to be made in the likeness of men or beasts.

Though entry had been so easy, the defense had saved some from death or capture; the main avenue ended at riverside in pillared quays, and a number of Hrin vessels, crowded with defeated men, were standing out in the wide waters. Farther downstream, at a landing well beyond the city, other craft were aiding a similar rescue. It seemed of small consequence; with masters beaten, the lowly foot, judging by past encounters, would gladly lay down their arms, and not less than half the Hrin cavalry was dead on the field. No one had seen Iolfrant, but after such losses, and a failed defense of their most prized place, he would find it hard to whip up survivors for another trial. Not wishing to have the entire population of the *onhritha* for enemies, Kamin-Tolagh had instructed his officers on this occasion to accept surrenders once the battle was clearly won, and having had their bloodbath yesterday, they were glad to comply, quite properly declining to engage any part of the main infantry still interested in fighting, while the Hill Froghul methodically shot down its mounted officers.

Kambanal, tunic blotched with blood, rode up, his gauntlets tucked under the left arm. He kept touching three fingers of his right hand to the reopened wound on his cheek, and examining the blood he found there. Interrupting this exercise, he redrew his blotched sword to salute Kamin-Tolagh. "*Hyolenstrai-Kindhri*! But there should be someone to offer you the city's submission."

His sense of propriety was soon gratified. Down eight shallow steps from the platform where stood the most ornately-decorated building on the central avenue, there came a brocaded delegation of Hrin, apparent dignity in their stately pace in fact dictated by their following the uncertain steps of aged Oyestri, kinsman to Iolfrant. Behind him came the same banner as had preceded parley on the first invasion, depicting a golden eye.

"Greetings once again, Oyestri," Kamin-Tolagh called as the man shuffled nearer. "This time, we shall not be sent home with trinkets. Where is your *hrithust*?"

"Not here, he is gone, Lord Kamin-Tolagh," the unlovely man replied. "If you were to demand gold, it would be an embarrassment to us. Little of value is left here at Hyolenstr, unless you wish to peel gold from our roofs."

"A pleasant place to stay, however. We may well remain here."

End of the Fourth Part

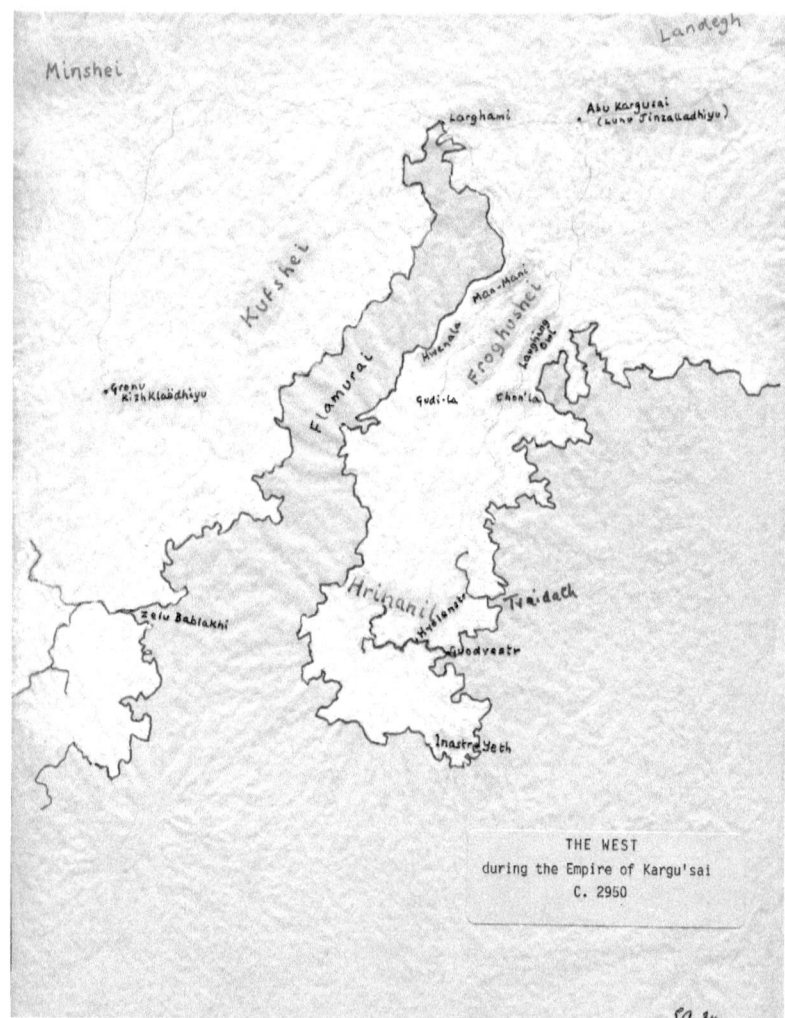

THE WEST
during the Empire of Kargu'sai
C. 2950

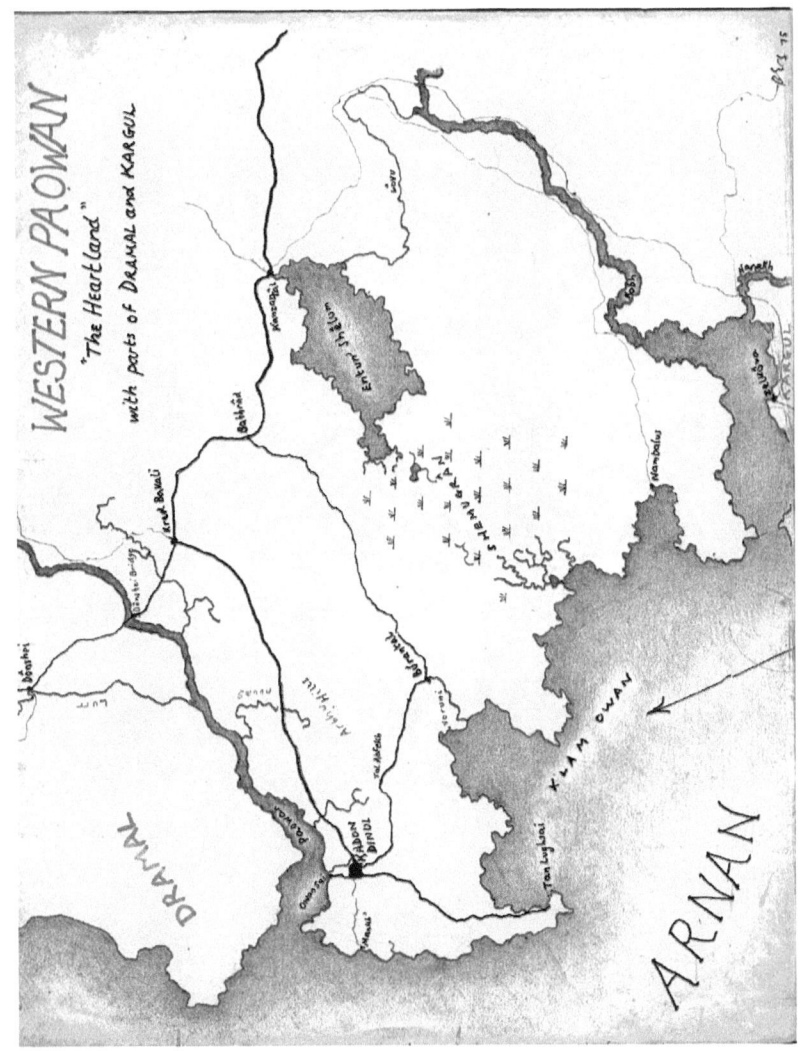

Genealogy
Rabhsayum: Owen Navu

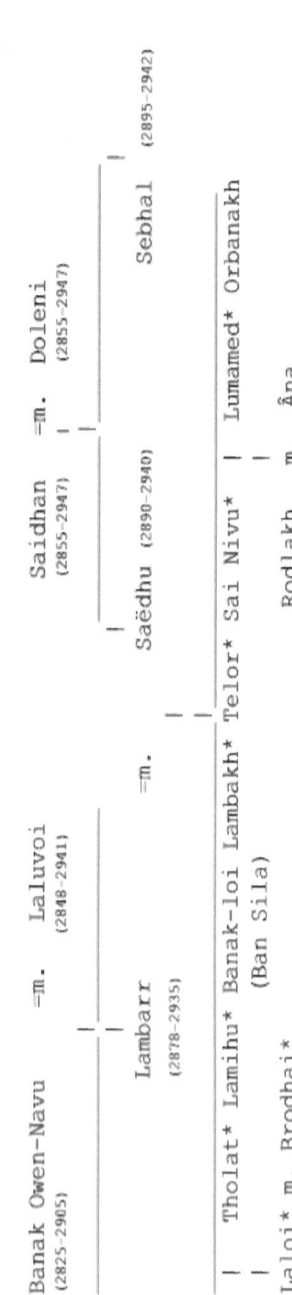

Kargúl

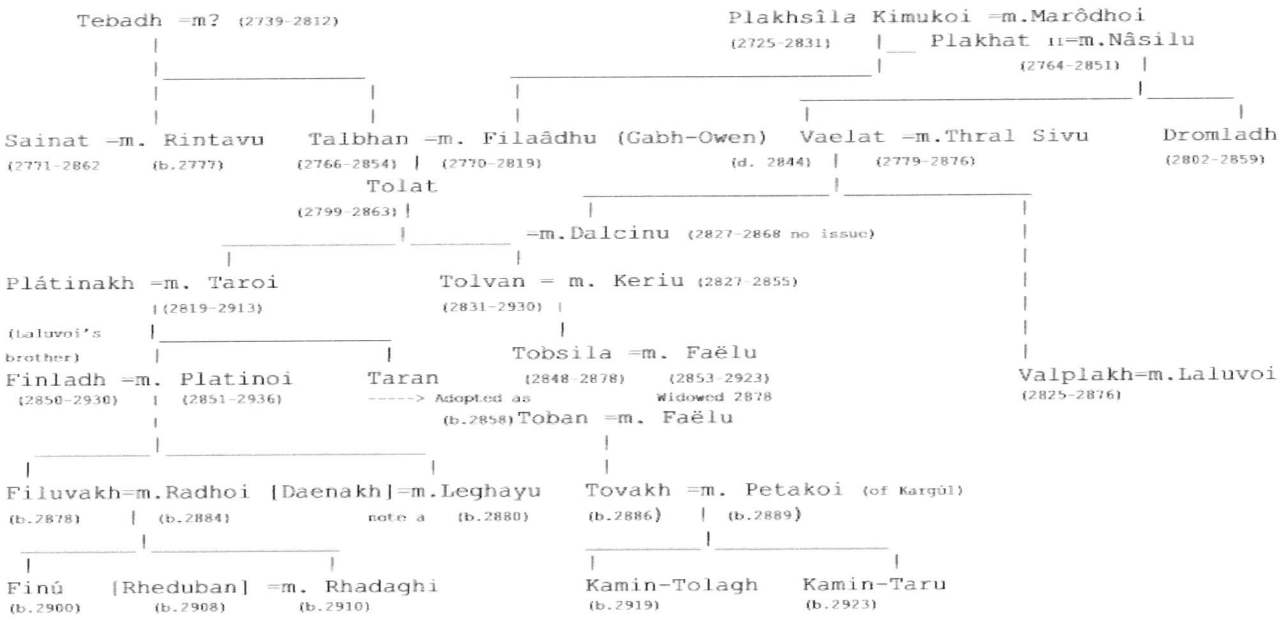

Plakhsíla Kimukoi =m.Marôdhoi (2725-2811)
Plakhat II=m.Nâsilu (2764-2851)
Dromladh (2802-2859)

Tebadh =m? (2739-2812)

Sainat -m. Rintavu (2771-2862) (b.2777)

Talbhan -m. Filaádhu (Gabh-Owen) (2766-2854) (2770-2819)

Tolat (2799-2863)

Vaelat -m.Thral Sivu (d. 2844) (2779-2876)

Valplakh=m.Laluvoi (2825-2876)

-m.Dalcinu (2827-2868 no issue)

Plátinakh =m. Taroi (2819-2913)

(Laluvoi's brother)

Tolvan = m. Keriu (2831-2930) (2827 2855)

Tobsíla =m. Faélu (2853 2923) Widowed 2878

Tovakh =m. Petakoi (of Kargúl) (b.2886) (b.2889)

Kamin-Taru (b.2923)

Finladh =m. Platinoi (2850-2930) (2851-2936)

Taran (2848 2878) ----> Adopted as note a (b.2858)

Toban =m. Faélu

Kamin-Tolagh (b.2919)

Filuvakh=m.Radhoi |Daenakh|=m.Leghayu (b.2878) (b.2884) note a (b.2880)

Finú |Rheduban| =m. Rhadaghi (b.2900) (b.2908) (b.2910)

(a) Biodhai, son of Leghayu and Daenakh m. Laloi bi Arbhi Navu, 2932; both killed at Tan Lugsai in 2935. Brahdíal, their second son (b. 2910), led the Cavalry of Án under the command of Bolan Bakir, Yuvakh Din 2928.

Telnauv ("The Colony")

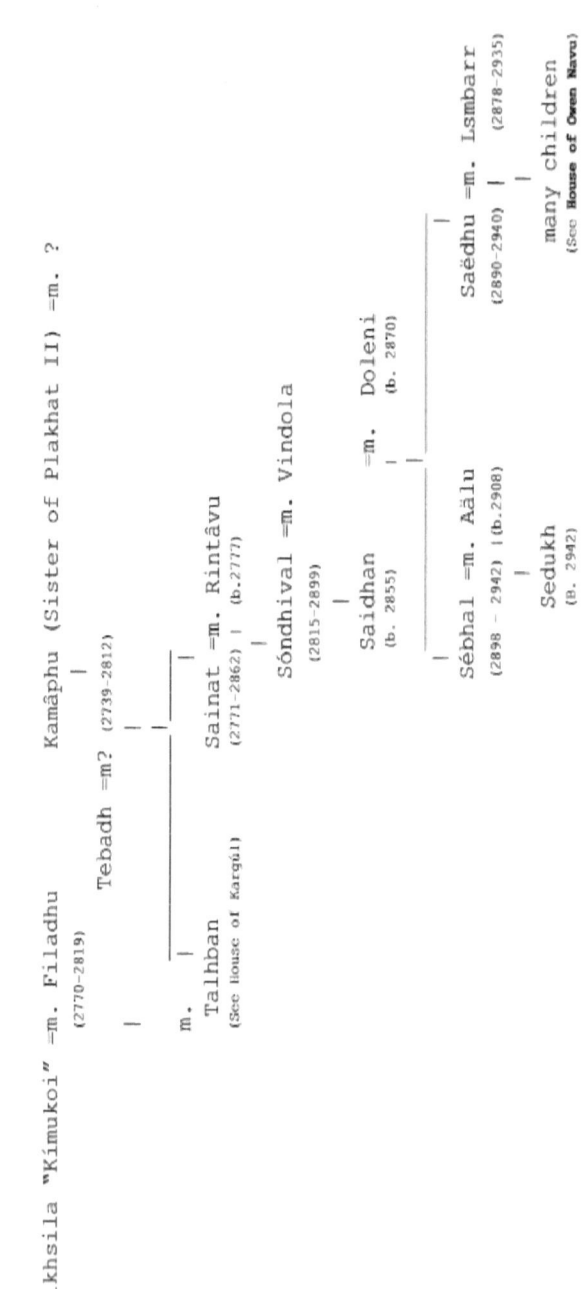

Plkhsila "Kímukoi" =m. Filadhu   Kamâphu (Sister of Plakhat II) =m. ?
                  (2770-2819)

          Tebadh =m? (2739-2812)

   m.
   Talhban   Sainat =m. Rintâvu
   (See House of Kargúl)   (2771-2862) | (b.2777)

                    Sóndhival =m. Vindola
                    (2815-2899)

                        Saidhan   =m. Doleni
                        (b. 2855)   (b. 2870)

                            Sébhal =m. Aälu   Saëdhu =m. Lsmbarr
                            (2898 - 2942) | (b.2908)   (2890-2940) | (2878-2935)

                               Sedukh   many children
                               (B. 2942)   (See House of Owen Navu)

www.ingramcontent.com/pod-product-compliance
Lightning Source LLC
Chambersburg PA
CBHW020729210626
46807CB00016B/535

* 9 7 8 0 9 9 9 8 4 6 0 0 1 7 *